T0328737

One Corner
of the Secret . . .

A heat built within Val. She didn't want to wait. She had forgotten what it was to need him inside her, to feel as if they were one, to long for release as if it were salvation. She slid beneath him, opened to him like a flower, urged him with her hips, her hands. She cried out as he thrust deep within her, then rocked with him to a beat of their own making, a rhythm that grew wilder and wilder until it built to a shattering crescendo.

Brian was silent for so long she thought he had fallen asleep. Then he reached across her to a small table and switched on the lamp.

"Will you marry me, Val?" His face was grave, tender.

She stroked his cheek with the back of her hand. "Aren't you forgetting something?"

"You mean Eva. I'm going to leave her, Val."

FEVER PITCH

BETTY FERM

PUBLISHED BY POCKET BOOKS NEW YORK

Another *Original* publication of POCKET BOOKS

 POCKET BOOKS, a Simon & Schuster division of
GULF & WESTERN CORPORATION
1230 Avenue of the Americas, New York, N.Y. 10020

ISBN: 978-1-4767-9143-2

First Pocket Books printing August, 1980

10 9 8 7 6 5 4 3 2 1

POCKET and colophon are trademarks of Simon & Schuster.

Printed in the U.S.A.

For Max,
who made this possible . . .

FEVER PITCH

Chapter 1

Despite the January snow that iced the highways on Long Island, Brian Anslow drove to Traynor Laboratories with a speed to match the turmoil inside him. If he could have foreseen the tragic results of the events he would set in motion that morning, he might have turned the car around and pointed it toward his home in Marbrough Glen, some twenty minutes away. But Brian Anslow was not clairvoyant. His concerns were very much of the moment and centered on the decision he would have to make in the next hour.

The sudden death of Alexander Traynor, the company's president, had plunged him into a quandary. If he quit Traynor at the board meeting today as he wanted to, he shirked the responsibility Alex had entrusted to him. If he stayed, he watched everything he'd built up disintegrate under the new leadership. The fact that Alex had been his father-in-law only compounded the problem.

Damn Alex for dying, he thought. And damn the sense of loyalty that prevented him from just walking out.

He pulled his Mercedes into the crowded parking lot that could have doubled for a baseball field. He reached to turn the radio off, then paused as the newscaster extolled the death count on the newest epidemic that was sweeping the nation—Blasa Fever, the deadly disease that had come out of Africa with neither a method to prevent it nor a cure to stop it. It had killed or crippled hundreds in the past eight months, the terror of epidemic mounting with every new outbreak.

In the face of that, his problem suddenly seemed minute. If the researchers didn't come up with an answer soon, it wouldn't really matter much who ran the company. They'd all be fighting for their lives.

He cut the ignition and got out. Clutching his attaché case under his arm, he thrust his hands into the pockets of his Aquascutum trench coat and strode across the lot. He was powerfully built, an energetic man of thirty-eight with forthright blue eyes and a determined set to his jaw that had earned him the nickname Bulldog in his football days at Northwestern. The scar above his right lid, also a souvenir of those days, showed raw against the winter pallor of his skin as he bent his head to avoid the cutting wind.

To Brian, the block-long stone and glass pharmaceutical building was as awesome a sight today as when he'd first set eyes on it in 1963. It had seen its beginnings in the late eighteen hundreds housed in two small barns behind a railroad track, fed by the money of Jasper Traynor, pharmacist, and the inventiveness of his doctor son.

Through the next century, what had begun as a backwoods dream became a three-hundred-million-dollar dynasty. The buildings grew as the products multiplied. Insulin financed the huge research facilities, sulfa drugs the animal quarters, and penicillin the warehouses—while the Traynor wives produced the sons to ready themselves for the sceptre that was theirs by right of succession.

And now that sceptre was about to change hands again, Brian thought. But David, Alex's only son, wasn't capable of taking over the company. Like so many other sons nurtured by prominent fathers, David was indecisive, unable to stand up to pressure. For three years he had been head of manufacturing. Instead of showing his strength, it had proved his weakness. And the worst of it was that he had chosen to be guided by Paul Haversham, a member of the Board and Brian's implacable enemy.

Brian scaled the steps to the main entrance two at a time. A black wreath hung on one of the white double doors. It would be removed as soon as David was elected this morning and loyalties would shift like sand in a windstorm. The king was dead. Long live the king!

Inside, the lofty marble-pillared reception floor was colder than usual because Traynor had been closed for two days out of respect. To the right of the doorway, running the full length of the room, was a brilliantly lit "wall of products" behind a glass casing. It was divided by rows into the broad prescription drug categories: analgesics, anti-infectives, psychotherapeutics, heart preparations, hormonals like the oral contraceptives, steroids, gastrointestinal drugs . . . The list was endless; the packaging, whether in capsule form, tablet, liquid, or injectable, always in the same blue and orange, recognizable at a glance by any physician or druggist in the country as the Traynor colors. ·

From behind the circular desk that she manned like a turret fortress, the receptionist, Mildred Benson, was speaking to a friend on the phone. Her nasal voice had an upward inflection and a hysterical edge.

"First the Legionnaire's disease, now this killer fever. Three outbreaks in less than a year. Even with all the big shot government scientists we support with our tax dollars, we'll still end up dying like flies." With a murmured, "hold a minute please," she broke off and greeted Brian with a smile that emphasized the creases in her face.

"Morning, Mr. Anslow. It's a big day for Mr. David, isn't it?"

"It's a big day for all of us," he said grimly, then aware of her puzzlement, smiled back. Mildred was a gossipy mother hen retained by Alex out of sentiment and the fear that her penchant for listening in on telephone calls had armed her with enough ammunition to blackmail half of Traynor. Yet Brian liked her.

"They're waiting for you in the small conference room," she informed him.

"Tell them I'm on my way."

He took the elevator to the carpeted upper level, the sanctuary reserved for Traynor's administrative echelon.

As he strode past the familiar corridor with its clacking typewriters and divided secretarial mazes outside executive offices, Brian realized how much of an emotional wrench leaving the company would be. He had spent the major part of sixteen years on this floor, ever since Alex had guest lectured at a senior Marketing class at Northwestern and singled him out for a job because he felt Brian's challenging questions would "get the marketing boys off their placid asses." From then on his life had been inextricably bound up with Traynors. First with Valerie, twin to David, and Medical Director of the Labs; then with Eva, the youngest and most publicized of the Traynors, whom he'd married.

Outside the conference room he paused, his hand on the knob. He took a deep breath and pushed the door open.

Heads pivoted and he was the target of forty eyes, a few friendly, most antagonistic. But all acknowledged him as a force to be reckoned with. Some said he was a born leader. Others, less charitable, claimed he had the instincts and charisma of a riverboat gambler. For the last five years he had wielded an authority at Traynor superseded only by Alex's and rumors had circulated that he wouldn't accept David's ascendancy without putting up a fight.

Like the portrait of Alex that hung between the windows, the conference room had the elegance of a bygone era. The walls shone with the muted luster of beveled walnut blocks, the deep red carpeting was thick underfoot, and the brocaded drapes were suspended from heavy brass rods.

The Board of Directors was made up of eleven members, among them stockbrokers, accountants, bankers, and two former company execs. The others were vice presidents of the various Traynor departments, as was Brian, in his position as head of marketing.

Brian spotted Ernie Bedlock, the company stockbroker whose asthmatic wheeze sounded like a worn-out bellows, and Burt Findley in personnel whose sudden weight loss emphasized his sagging jowls and somber face. In the far corner was Lester Pryor, in charge of Quality Control, whose gangling body was topped by a shock of bright red hair that framed a thin, freckled face.

Except for Dr. Valerie Traynor, they were all seated at the gleaming walnut table that was a miniature of the one in the adjacent main meeting room. Above the table, the oversized chandelier, kept on a dimmer except for special occasions, burned at its brightest.

Brian's glance gravitated toward Valerie as it always did when she was in a room. The last time he'd seen her was at her father's funeral. She hadn't shed a tear—her grief was a private emotion she chose not to share. But her face had held a stricken look that had made him want to reach out to her.

Dressed in black, she stood near a large silver urn on a sideboard complete with initialed linen napkins and white china cups, helping herself to some coffee. She was a tall, slender woman with blonde hair drawn into a soft chignon at the nape of her neck. Above high cheekbones her hazel eyes were shaped like almonds, giving her face an inquisitive, sensuous look. They were bright with anticipation now as she nodded a greeting to Brian and took her place at the conference table.

David was her blind spot, Brian thought. She excused her brother's incompetence and saw in him the same qualities of leadership that her father had possessed, certain that he needed only the chance to prove it.

Arthur Perrault, the acting Chairman of the Board, rose and shuffled the papers in front of him. "Glad you're here, Brian. If we filled up with any more coffee, we'd be able to float our way out of here." A few polite chuckles greeted his words.

It was out of character for Perrault to be flippant, Brian thought. He was a tall, balding banker with a pallid complexion and a normally ponderous manner. He was perspiring profusely, mopping at his brow with a white handkerchief.

Paul Haversham, white-haired and steely-eyed, waved a forgiving hand. "I'm sure Brian had as much trouble getting here as the rest of us. It's no fit day out there."

Brian inclined his head. Haversham could afford to be generous this morning. Vice President of Manufacturing until he was fifty, he had left Traynor for an unsuccessful career in politics, but had managed to retain a position on the Board and a hold on David

Traynor, whom he had trained. At the end of this meeting he would be firmly entrenched as the power behind the throne.

Brian's eyes moved to David, sitting next to Perrault. At thirty-four, he had the presence of a fledgling actor in his first part. Sandy-haired and pink skinned, he blinked spasmodically, a habit he had when under tension. He spoke up testily. "Now that we've welcomed Brian and heard the weather report, can we please get on with it, Arthur." His diction had a textbook preciseness.

Brian took the empty seat diagonally across from Valerie. Her fine hazel eyes were fixed anxiously on her twin brother, willing him to make a good showing at this, his hour of glory. If only he had had his father's support all these years, what potential he would have realized, she thought. Conscious of Brian's gaze, she turned toward him. In a rare moment her eyes met his, held, acknowledged what had been between them, what was still between them, bowed to the futility of it, and withdrew.

Arthur Perrault cleared his throat. "Ladies and gentlemen. In calling this meeting to order, I'm sure I speak for all of us when I say that the passing of Alexander Traynor will leave an empty space in our hearts." He turned and glanced at the painting behind him for effect. It was a gold framed oil of Alex in his early fifties that had captured the strength and humor in his face, along with the quality of breeding that only generations of wealth could produce.

"Alex was respected not only for his business acumen," he continued, "but for the compassion he was known to extend to his employees at Traynor no matter how high or low their standing." He took a blue-backed paper from the conference table and held it up for all to see. "I have in my possession a statement dictated to me by Alex shortly before his death, which he asked that I read to you now." He blotted the perspiration on his forehead and made a show of unfolding the paper. His voice unconsciously took on the clipped cadence that had been characteristic of Alexander Traynor's.

"My Dear Friends,

"When Arthur reads this to you, I won't be here, but I don't want my passing to be a cause of sadness. I've lived a full life, a good deal of it spent here at Traynor, and I have no regrets to keep me from enjoying what awaits me on the other side. This last is not meant as a jibe at the atheists among you, but rather to convince myself that the future will be as fruitful for me as the past.

"Most of you have worked with me for a long time, some as many as twenty years. I cherish those years and your support. I also value the differences we had. In spite of them, or perhaps because of them, we built up a mutual regard which I call upon now in asking your understanding of what I'm about to say.

"It is my suggestion that Arthur Perrault be named Chairman of this Board. It is also my strong recommendation that my son-in-law Brian Anslow be named president of Traynor Laboratories. This is not a decision I have arrived at lightly. I ask that you respect my judgment and honor my wishes in death as you did in life."

The silence in the room was devastating. Brian looked stunned, Valerie confused. David's eyes resembled those of a whipped dog. But far and away the most affected was Paul Haversham. His face had aged in the few seconds it took Perrault to read those words and his hands shook as if palsied. The room buzzed with exclamations of shock and disbelief.

Perrault used a gavel to restore quiet as Paul Haversham requested the floor. He was a commanding figure, tall and barrel-chested with silvered hair and piercing gray eyes.

"Fellow Board Members . . . a point of order. The selection of a new president is the prerogative of the Board, not of its past leader. Much as we all respected Alexander Traynor as head of this company, I submit that his illness may have affected not only his personality, which we all witnessed, but his faculties as . . ."

"No!" The protest came from Valerie Traynor accompanied by the crash of her fist on the table. She rose to face Haversham and spoke in a trembling voice. "There is no one here who would like more than I to see David succeed Alex as head of Traynor Labs. But I will not have it at the cost of questioning my father's sanity. It's true that after his first heart attack, Alex became impatient and quick to temper, but that was because he felt the pressure of time." She shot Haversham a scathing glance. "It had nothing to do with his 'faculties.' Up to the day he died, Alexander Traynor was as sane as anyone sitting at this table, and you all know it."

Brian silently applauded. He had no doubt that what Alex had done was deliberate. The question was why? Traynor Labs was a predestined heritage. The reason Alex hadn't passed it on to David had to be calamitous—and recent. He had lunched with Alex in the company cafeteria three days before his fatal heart attack to discuss the marketing potential of a new drug for diabetes. Alex had seemed cheerful and engrossed, and there had been no hint of his intent by either word or manner.

"I must agree with Dr. Traynor," Arthur Perrault was saying. "At the time this statement was dictated to me in the hospital, Alex's attorney and another witness were present. After hearing it, I reminded him that he was breaking a tradition of eighty years and questioned his reasons. He said that upon occasion it was healthy to break with tradition and that his reasons were none of my damned business." There were smiles around the room at his recollection of Alex's words.

Essentially, they were a rubber stamp board, Brian thought. Alex had helped each of them achieve financial security. They owed him and despite their shock, unless mightily provoked, they would never go against his wishes. Haversham knew it too. He was whispering into David's ear, gesturing emphatically to forestall the younger man's protests.

They were going to name him president, Brian suddenly realized. A feeling of exultation took the place of the numbing shock he'd first experienced. He'd never doubted that he was capable of running Traynor. He'd tried not to think of it because it had seemed impossible, but there were times, when he and Alex had clashed on policy, that he would have sold his soul to prove he was right.

Though Traynor was one of the best known pharmaceutical companies in the world, it ranked tenth in volume of sales. Alex had been conservative, leery of unproved innovations, bent on maintaining status quo. Brian's scope was larger, his ambition greater, his vision of Traynor's potential unlimited. Through some quirk of fate he was going to be granted the chance to plumb that potential now, and he would fight against any odds to keep it.

After a moment, David rose to address his peers. He seemed to have shrunk within himself, his pink cheeks pale, his fingers restless at his sides.

"I'm not going to pretend that this hasn't been a surprise," he said in a low voice, blinking rapidly, "because it has. But there's something more important at stake here today than who inherits the presidency. And that's Traynor Laboratories itself. What it stands for, what it provides for all of us, what it represents to the outside world. It's important for *that* heritage to go on. I don't know the reasons my father chose to do what he did, because he didn't confide in me, but for the good of the company, I for one am ready to abide by his decision."

He walked to the end of the table and held out his hand to Brian. A spontaneous burst of applause came from the onlookers as Brian reached to clasp it. "Congratulations," David said, lifting his eyes to Brian's. It was only then that Brian saw the fierce resentment in their depths.

It took the Board only minutes to confirm Perrault as chairman and Brian as president, after which Paul Haversham rose and inclined his silver head in a slight bow. "I do not know when I have seen a more magnanimous gesture than that which David Traynor has just made. But I nevertheless feel obliged at this time to remind this Board of the right of review. It is the yearly evaluation of the president's actions instituted by Alexander Traynor himself in a laudable effort at democracy, in which the Board may choose to reconvene to replace the current head of Traynor if his performance has been less than acceptable."

So that was to be the ploy, Brian thought. The right of review had been an annual farce at which Alex was formally given a vote of confidence by the Board for another year. As in most dictatorships, no dissenting voice had ever been raised and its only accomplishment had been to salve Alex's conscience in the knowledge that the opportunity had been given.

Haversham raised a hand to halt the rumble that had risen around the table. "Alexander Traynor was proud of his eighty-year heritage. He told me often that he felt tradition was the very backbone of Traynor's steady growth pattern. I don't know what influence was used to change his mind, but I do know that a blow was struck against that tradition this morning. One that can, however, be rescinded. I move that we close this meeting on the note that—"

"Aren't we going to hear from our new president?" The interruption came from Lester Pryor, Vice President of Quality Control, who was Brian's staunch friend and supporter.

Perrault's thin lips twitched into the semblance of a smile. "You are out of order, Mr. Pryor, but your point is well taken."

Brian took stock of the confused and hostile faces about him. He rose slowly, spread both hands on the table, and leaned forward.

"Gentlemen . . ." he nodded his head toward Valerie, ". . . and Dr. Traynor." Anger lent his deep voice impetus. Their shock at Alex's choice of him as president was understandable. Haversham's implication of duplicity and their ready belief in it was not.

"Alexander Traynor's death affected us all deeply, but obviously in different ways. To some he was a parent, to others an employer, to those willing to listen . . . a guide. For me, he was all three. I came here sixteen years ago, cocky and running off at the mouth, totally unaware of the complexities of a business empire. I learned. And I came to admire Alexander Traynor . . . his patience, his strength, mostly his integrity."

There were tears in Valerie's eyes as he spoke. She hadn't realized before how much her father had meant to him.

Brian glanced around the room contemptuously. "Paul Haversham speaks of influence. Is there one of you here who honestly believes that Alex could have been coerced into anything?" There was silence. Brian nodded, accepting that as an answer. "As most of you know, much as I admired Alex, we didn't think alike. For Alex, Traynor Laboratories was a trust given to him to be kept intact, then passed on. I don't see it the same way. Despite the right of review that you've hung over my head like a sword, I expect to expand Traynor domestically and internationally until it stands as the foremost pharmaceutical company in the world. In that endeavor, I will need, expect, and demand your cooperation," he said, glancing toward Haversham.

Except for Pryor's smiling face, and Val's shaken one, there were no reactions to his speech. Haversham doodled on a paper in front of him and David slumped forward in his chair, eyes downcast.

Perrault adjourned the meeting a few minutes later. Those that were there congratulated Brian before he left, some with good grace, some with none at all.

The first to leave the conference room was David Traynor. Bent on following him, Paul Haversham was stopped by several members of the Board who felt certain that because of his closeness to David he could clarify why Alex had named Brian president. When he insisted there was no reason he knew of, they conjectured about David's marriage. It was common knowledge that Alex had never approved of his son's alliance with the beautiful but socially unacceptable Southern girl he'd married ten years ago. Would that have been enough cause for Alex to cut him off from his heritage in that way?

When they had speculated enough to satisfy themselves that the only ready answer was Brian's manipulation of Alex, they left, vowing to support Haversham in his effort to scrutinize every move that Brian made.

Relieved, Haversham took the service elevator down to the manufacturing level. The doors opened at the packaging division which was closest to David's office. A pang of nostalgia went through Haversham at the familiar clanking and grinding sound. Until he'd decided to try his hand at politics, this floor had been his domain.

His eyes automatically checked the packaging lines as he strode the length of the area. There were thirty women on one line, all in white uniforms with caps to cover their hair. Those who touched open bottles or products wore plastic disposable gloves. A metal placard hung from a thin wire above each line identifying the particular tablet being packaged.

The operation, for the most part, was automatic. The tablets were fed from a hopper chute into a disc-like counting machine with holes in it, then dropped into bottles riding on a belt beneath the hopper. Cotton wadding was forced into the container to keep the pills from bouncing and breaking in transit. Then the caps were screwed on by mechanical hands before the bottles moved on to be labeled.

Overhead, there were service pipes through which flowed hot and cold water, steam, nitrogen, and air. Each was painted a different pastel color. They stemmed from the boiler room and were pressured to feed the various manufacturing operations for which they were needed. A leak in any one of them could cause trouble. Haversham remembered the year there was an overnight break in the nitrogen pipe just before the annual Christmas party. By the time the break was discovered late in the day, enough oxygen had been displaced by nitrogen in the plant for the employees to be acting like clowns at a circus. The need for liquor at the Christmas party that night was almost nil.

Haversham found David in his office. He looked out of place in it. The sophisticated decor was Haversham's, or rather his wife Bernice's, each piece hand-picked from the designer building on Third Avenue in New York, but for once Haversham didn't resent David's presence there. He had bigger things on his mind.

As usual, David resembled a misplaced professor in his tweed suit and knit tie. He stood near a window smoking his pipe in short, agitated puffs, the honeyed tobacco filling the room with a cloying odor. Oblivious to the condensation on the panes and the spiky barren trees and frozen stream beyond, he stared unseeingly at the ten-acre plot on which Traynor was situated. In the distance a train whistle shrieked a raucous warning and nearer, the barking of the dogs could be heard as they took their turn on the snowy exercise run outside the animal quarters.

Haversham locked the door and came to stand near him. He passed a hand over his white hair, striving for a calm he didn't feel. "How the hell did it happen?" he demanded, his florid face mottled with the frustration he'd kept in check for the last hour.

"How?" David's voice sounded strangely unconcerned. "I don't know how. But when you stop to think about it, it's really a stroke of genius on Alex's part." He blinked twice. "All my life Alex put me down." His face twisted into a mockery of his father's. His voice barked at a staccato clip. "An eighty-five's not good enough on that bio test—I had to donate half of Traynor to get you into Yale—You'll work under Haversham until *I* feel you're ready to head manufacturing." He blinked twice more. "But you see they were all private put-downs. I could walk around pretending that he cared. That underneath it all he felt that I really measured up and that he was badgering me so I would do even better. And that wasn't good enough for Alex."

"You're wrong, David."

"No. I'm not wrong. Alex conceived the greatest put-down of all. He announced to the world that I wasn't capable of running Traynor. And the way he did it, I couldn't even confront him with it. Couldn't even demand an explanation."

Haversham put a hand on his shoulder and gripped hard. "David, when I spoke to Alex right after his first heart attack, he had every intention of naming you president. I swear it. Something happened in the last month. Something devastating enough to make him change his mind. What was it?"

"I don't know."

"Is there something he found out about you? About Claire?"

"Dammit, leave my wife out of this!" He shrugged off the older man's hand, went to the bar against the wall, and poured himself a shot of Scotch. Like his father, he was slight of build, but he lacked Alex's bearing.

"All right," Haversham soothed. "What's done is done. It's the future we have to deal with now. As it stands, Brian Anslow doesn't have a chance of keeping the presidency past this year, if he keeps it even that long. The Board is ready to hand it to you if, and this is an important one, if you don't make waves." He fixed David with a penetrating gaze. "I assume everything's running all right on the manufacturing end?''

David hesitated. A chill ran along Haversham's spine. He strode to where David stood. ''What is it you haven't told me?''

''Nothing. Look, I have to get down to the Sampling Room now, Paul. There's a batch of high priority Reysin compound that Quality Control is rejecting because the drum it came in is banged up.'' He put the shot glass on his desk. His skin was pale and his movements uncertain. He turned to Haversham diffidently. ''You know, Paul, when someone makes you feel inadequate long enough, you begin to believe it. I've never confided how I felt to anyone before, but today I've had my guts kicked out.''

''What are you trying to say, David?''

His eyes were wide, their expression vulnerable. ''Even if I get Traynor at the end of the year, how do I know I can run it?''

Haversham breathed a little easier. He could cope with uncertainty, not with foolish mistakes. He flung a reassuring arm around the smaller man's shoulder and walked him to the door. ''That's something I'm not worried about at all. Despite your lack of confidence, you're still Alex's son. All you need is a chance to show what you can do.''

''You really believe that?''

''Of course I do.'' He opened the door. ''What else has kept me at your side all these years?''

Haversham watched him straighten his shoulders, stride down the corridor, then turn toward the stairs. He walked back into David's office. You lie down with dogs, you get up with fleas, he thought. He unbuttoned his collar and slumped into a chair. Even in death, Alex had cheated him. He had come to Alex two years ago, badly in debt from an expensive, mismanaged political campaign, and asked for a fifty-thousand-dollar loan and reinstatement to an active position in the firm. Alex had given him ten thousand and named him Acquisitions Consultant, a job that required him to seek out smaller companies with viable products that could be absorbed into the Traynor complex and make arrangements for their purchase. The job paid forty thousand, half of what he had been earning as V.P. of Manufacturing, and kept him traveling a great deal besides. This, after thirty years of service to Traynor Labs that hadn't even netted him a single share of stock to call his own.

Yet, it was this very consultant's job that had presented Haversham with the opportunity to more than recoup his losses and place him in the position he'd always dreamed about. Three months ago, while negotiating to acquire a liquid compound from Anshul-Bulden, a multi-billion-dollar chemical company based in Western Europe, they had approached him on another matter. They were interested in buying into pharmaceuticals in the United States and, after investigating several companies, were offering to purchase Traynor Laboratories for four hundred million dollars, provided its president was agreeable to the sale. A private finder's fee of roughly one million dollars would go to Haversham if he was able to negotiate the deal.

Haversham had bargained with them. He would give up part of the fee if, when the deal went through, he became president of Traynor Labs. They had balked at first, then after reviewing his qualifications, they had agreed.

Until a month ago, he hadn't even thought of broaching the sale to Alex for fear of incurring his anger, but after Alex's heart attack he had put it to him as a concerned employee seeking a possible way out for his ailing president. Alex had seen right through him. His reaction hadn't been anger. It had been amusement. After assuring Haversham that the Labs were and always would be Traynor-founded and Traynor-run, he had laughed that dry laugh of his and said. "By the way, what would a finder's fee be on a deal like this? Enormous, eh, Paul?"

Haversham reached into his jacket for a Havana cigar, clipped off the end and lit it. Despite Alex's reaction, he hadn't given up. He had known that it was a matter of time before Traynor passed into David's malleable hands. Once there, the deal would be all but consummated. Today was a setback, but not an unalterable one. He was sure that Anshul-Bulden would wait. Within a year the presidency would revert to David and the negotiations could take place then. The problem was that David required a keeper, and with the amount of traveling the acquisitions job demanded, it was impossible to be on hand to watch him.

What he needed. Haversham thought, was an ally. Someone with enough influence over David to give him the daily reassurance he needed, with enough foresight to block any wrong decisions he might make, with enough wiliness to find out what had made him hesitate when asked if his department was running right. Someone, preferably, who could be bought.

He watched the cigar smoke curl toward the ceiling for a long moment, then buttoned his collar, reached for the phone, and dialed Claire Traynor's number.

Chapter 2

On leaving the conference room, Brian went to his own office. His inclination was to spend the day there reviewing the current marketing plans, budget reports, and advertising curriculum with his assistant, who would be promoted to vice president now. Instinct told him not to. A delay in taking over could be construed as weakness and with Haversham sniffing at his heels like a dog tracking prey, the only way to back him down was by a show of strength.

With the reluctant help of Alex's secretary, Dora Watkins, he moved into the president's office by twelve thirty. Dora was a walking file cabinet. Sharp-tongued and graying, she had worked for Alexander Traynor and his father before him and could, at a moment's request, tick off the name of every prescription drug on the market since the nineteen thirties. There was no smile on her face as she presented the morning's mail to the new president.

"Dr. Traynor called earlier," she informed him coldly. "She said that as soon as you're settled she'd like to talk to you about something important."

"Tell her I'll see her now."

"Yes, sir." She turned on the heels of her orthopedic shoes but Brian stopped her. There were two thousand employees at Traynor. If all of them displayed the same kind of hostility he felt from Dora, he was in for a rough time.

"Dora, let's understand each other. I didn't ask for this job, but now that I have it, I intend to keep it. I can fight the battles outside this office, but I can't do it inside as well. I need your help, but if you don't feel you can give it, then tell me now and I'll transfer you elsewhere."

Her craggy face softened as she looked into the intense blue of his eyes. Brian Anslow was six feet one. He dwarfed the chair that Alexander Traynor had sat in and there was that about him that made her wish she was thirty years younger. But she sensed a drive in him, an irreverence for custom that threatened an upheaval she wasn't sure she could sustain.

She took a white handkerchief from her jacket pocket and brushed at a speck on the lapel of her black jacket. "I was just speaking to Mildred Benson. People downstairs are saying you talked Mr. Traynor into this somehow. . . ."

"Do you believe that, Dora?"

"Not for a minute. What Mr. Traynor did was a surprise; yet I've never know him to do anything without good reason." She cleared her throat which had suddenly clogged with emotion. "I respected him in life, Mr. Anslow. So I'll respect his decision afterward too. But it may take a little getting used to." Without waiting for his dismissal, she walked quickly from the office, the handerchief trailing behind her like a wilted flag of truce.

Left alone, Brian glanced about him. It was his office now, but he had no sense of belonging. Paneled in cypress, it was decorated in muted shades of beige and white that Alex had seen as restful and Brian found colorless. He had admired his father-in-law, yet they had differed in many ways. Alex had been formal, conservative, his taste in dress leaning toward pin-striped suits and nondescript ties. "You are what you wear," he'd often said, gazing with disdain at Brian's geometric tie or plaid blazer, the jacket more often than not draped around a chair instead of on Brian. It was a theory Brian had never subscribed to and Alex had finally given up trying to change him.

On the wall behind the desk, a "gallery of Traynors" hung, beginning with a line drawing of the two founders. It included a photo of Gertrude Traynor, Alex's wife who had died when Eva was three, and ended with portraits of the Traynor children taken some ten years ago . . . David, just returned from Vietnam, Valerie holding up her medical degree from Johns Hopkins, and Eva, Brian's wife, schussing down a slope in St. Moritz, flashing her famous smile.

Brian stared at his wife's photo with the dispassion of a critic who has lost the capacity to feel. The press had dubbed her one of the beautiful people. To the imperceptive, her face was more provocative than her sister's. To him it wasn't. Instead of determination, it held worldliness. Where there should have been compassion, there was self-centeredness. Her body lacked Val's heroic proportions. It was smaller, more shapely and agile. It seemed to Brian that she showed even then the restlessness that drove her to seek change and amusement the way an alcoholic seeks drink. It had wedged them further and further apart until all that was left of their marriage was the facade that Eva insisted on, and their son Mark, whom he cherished.

Where had the fault lain? he wondered. With Eva, catered to from birth by a series of housekeepers, cushioned by generations of wealth, bent on collecting people and places the way others collected stamps? It would be easy to shrug blame and say yes, except that he knew that Eva's pleasure seeking was a substitute for the love she'd never had from either a dead mother or a too-busy father. A love he might have replaced if his feelings for her had deepened through the years. But they hadn't.

He crossed to the carved antique bar between the windows and poured himself a Bourbon. He was his own jailer in this marriage, he thought, but it wasn't guilt toward Eva that held him to it. It was his eight-year-old son, Mark. Eva had never openly objected to a divorce, but she had made it very clear that if they separated, she would prefer to live in Europe. It went without saying that she would take Mark with her, and that he could never allow.

Brian reached for the phone and dialed his home number. The rules of his arrangement with Eva were very clear. Image was important to Eva. There were to be no *faux pas* that would mar her status as Mrs. Brian Anslow. She would want to hear the news of his being named president of Traynor directly from him. He had no illusions about her feeling any compassion for her brother, David. Eva had a contempt for weakness that bordered on repugnance.

The phone rang twice then was picked up. "Anslow residence."

"Mrs. Garvey, this is Mr. Anslow. Is my wife there?"

"No, sir. Mrs. Anslow left a while ago. I believe she was on her way to work at the museum."

"Did she say when she'd be back?"

"If you'll wait a minute, I'll check her calendar."

He heard the clunk of the phone being put on the desk, her receding footsteps, then nothing. He wondered idly if his marriage to Eva would have deteriorated more rapidly if Eva's work hadn't given her the constant change she craved. In 1965, Alex had talked the Board into setting up the Traynor Museum on Eighty-fourth Street in New York City, a philanthropic institution to house the medical memorabilia of bygone eras. As scout for the museum, Eva divided her time between Europe and the United States in the hope of tracking down a "find" such as Roentgen's first attempt at the X-ray machine or the outdated hypodermic Ehrlich used to inject his "magic bullet."

Mrs. Garvey's voice came over the wire. "I'm sorry, Mr. Anslow. There's nothing on her calendar."

"That's all right. Did Mark get off to school okay this morning?"

She hesitated. "After a while he did."

"What was wrong?"

"Another one of those bellyaches."

"Did he take his medication?"

"No. He said he was sick of pills and that he could make it without them."

Brian was silent. There was an acrid taste in his mouth. The sins of the father . . . he thought in remorse. How well he remembered those stomach aches from his own childhood. He had grown up in Akron, Ohio, the only child in a loveless match that had somehow held together through twelve years of bitter fighting and cold silences. His father, a poorly paid high school chemistry teacher, had left when Brian was ten years old, after carefully explaining that his leaving had nothing to do with his love for Brian. Six months later he had married a woman with two sons of her own, and Brian had scarcely seen him after that. The rejection he'd felt had stayed with him through the years, and the thought of subjecting Mark to either a prolonged custody battle or the kind of loneliness and self-questioning Brian had gone through was unbearable to him.

"Shall I tell Mrs. Anslow anything if she phones in?" Mrs. Garvey asked.

"Tell her I'll call her later."

He clicked off, moved to the undraped window behind his desk, and looked out. Far enough away to shield the main building from risk and odors lay the animal quarters and nearby, also on ground level, the flat-topped research facilities: microbiology, pharmacology, toxicology, the chemistry and biochemistry labs, all separately housed.

Before a new drug reached the point of marketing, it went through many phases of testing, each carefully researched and documented. Usually, the initial discovery, the tissue culturing, the animal testing and the toxicity studies took place in those labs. The clinical (human) testing, preceding the submission to the Food and Drug Administration for permission to market, did not.

It was Valerie's job as Medical Director to supervise the setting up of a clinical development program which took the drug from the animal studies to the testing in humans. The program normally took place in university affiliated hospitals, and the type of study used was a "double blind" one, where the test drugs were coded so that neither the volunteer patient nor the doctor administering the medication knew which was the test drug. This was done to avoid bias, especially in analgesic studies where tension was of prime importance.

Since twelve studies of a drug at one time were not uncommon and there was always more than a single drug being worked on, the Medical Director's job should have been enough to occupy any doctor's time and interest. Not so for Valerie. Brian had known for a long time that the microbiology lab, where she spent her spare time working on some pet project she didn't choose to reveal, was Valerie's real home. The three-room apartment she slept in at Hicksville was there to assure herself and others that she had a life aside from her work, a fact he knew to be untrue.

How ironic, he thought, that the very work that had kept them apart in those early years should be the only means through which they could be together now without causing comment. And even that was questionable. Traynor was a gossip factory, always alert for any tidbit it could chew on endlessly like a juicy piece of cud. There were those at Traynor who remembered his relationship with Val, before he'd married Eva. He had to be very careful not to feed any rumors that a remnant of it still existed.

For a moment, he had the irrational desire he'd had a dozen times before. To throw it all away. The presidency, the estate in Marbrough Glen, the trust of his son . . . leave it all behind and start anew somewhere with Val. But even if he had the guts to do it he questioned whether Val would go with him now. And if she did, there was no guarantee that it would succeed. When he'd fallen in love with Val ten years ago, he'd wanted a woman whose life would revolve around his (as Eva's had at first), not a dedicated scientist who would leap from her lover's arms at midnight because she'd forgotten to inject a rabbit with an experimental drug. He hadn't been able to accept the fact then that Val's need for achievement was as great as his own. Could he accept it now?

A knock sounded at the door.

"Come in."

She entered wearing a lab coat and low-heeled shoes. Even so, she was tall, standing almost to his chin. She used no makeup; she'd never needed any. Her skin was of a creamy translucence, the cheeks flushed with color of their own. Her hazel eyes, wide and tilted, were outlined by a fringe of dark lashes that contrasted sharply with her pale hair. In one hand she held a folded *New York Times,* while the other tucked back a loosened strand of hair in an unconsciously feminine gesture. It brought her full breasts into sharp relief and caused a reaction in Brian he tried to suppress. She stiffened as she saw him in her father's place.

"I'm sorry it has to be this way," he said gently, motioning her to a chair across the desk from him.

"Why? It's what you always wanted." There was no malice in her voice.

"Yes. But not at this price."

"You don't mean David?"

"No, I mean Alex." Her mouth tightened imperceptibly. He held out a placating hand. "Val, you know I like David. There was a time when Haversham left the company that we got very close. I tried to help him then until he suddenly turned from me with no explanation. But my liking for David has nothing to do with my feeling about his running Traynor."

She was silent for a moment. Then, "Brian, did you know Alex was going to name you president?"

"No, I didn't. Have you seen David?"

"I spoke to him right after the conference."

"How is he?"

"Bitter."

Brian said nothing.

He looked strained, she thought. There were lines around his mouth she hadn't remembered and the scar above his eye seemed raw against the pallor of his face. She should have felt anger that he had usurped her brother's position, but unexpectedly she felt pity. No. Not pity. Pity was a maternal emotion she reserved for children and weaklings. It had no place in what she felt for Brian. But she understood his reactions, sometimes better than her own. Brian's chances of retaining the presidency against a hostile Board past this year were not good. Yet fighter that he was, he would break his neck trying. She couldn't stop him. She wouldn't belittle him by trying. And what she had to ask of him today wasn't going to make his battle any easier.

"What was it you wanted to talk about?" he asked.

"The same thing everyone's talking about. Blasa Fever." She spread the *Times* across the desk and pointed to the front page. Under the heading: THIRD OUTBREAK OF BLASA FEVER IN EIGHT MONTHS, the lead article dealt with the most recent eruption of the fever, this time at a prison in upstate New York, and blasted the government for its budget-cutting research program that was costing the lives of hundreds and courting the fury of an epidemic.

"It's gotten out of hand, Brian."

"I know. Tom Nordsen in shipping told me his little girl came down with it six months ago. She's still feverish and hasn't been able to walk since. But contrary to what the *Times* says, the government is doing everything possible. We can only hope that some bright scientist comes up with something soon."

"That's why I'm here, Brian."

He looked at her sharply. "What do you mean?"

Valerie folded the newspaper carefully. She had to dredge up recollections that would cause them both pain, but there was no other way. "If you remember, when I graduated from Johns Hopkins in 1967, I worked at the National Institutes of Health in Bethesda."

"If I remember?" He looked at her as if she'd taken leave of her senses.

"Brian, don't make it any harder," she whispered.

He nudged at a glass paperweight while his mind

veered back in time. They had been lovers then. He had flown from New York every weekend for two years to be with her in the small apartment she'd taken near the Institutes. He recalled it so clearly. The Murphy bed in the middle of the room they kept open more than closed, the cuckoo clock on the wall that chirped sporadically, the refrigerator crammed with beer and cheese, energy food for peasants she called it. . . .

She read in his eyes what he was thinking. A part of her reveled with him in the memory. A part of her despaired. Brian had never been able to separate Valerie the scientist from Valerie the love object and it was essential that he do that now.

She made her voice as business-like as possible. "At that time, the government put a few of us to work on Blasa Fever because it had caused thirty deaths in three months. We couldn't find the cause of the disease, but in the next two years we cultured the bug, then tried every known antibiotic or anti-infective to kill it. The only thing that worked was an experimental antibiotic called Tetra-2. But it proved too toxic in the animal studies for the government to give its approval for human testing."

Brian nodded. "Then in 1970 the government withdrew its grant because no new cases had shown up in a year and a half."

"Right. The government lost interest, but I didn't."

Brian rubbed at the scar tissue over his eye. "No," he said softly, "you didn't. You talked Alex into supporting it and flew to Africa where the disease had started, with a team of researchers to continue the work." They had parted angrily, he remembered, with Valerie accusing him of trying to dominate her while he retorted that she didn't love him enough to stay.

"As I recall, nothing much came of it," he said. Except the loneliness that had driven him to marry

Eva. He wondered for the hundredth time how he could have been deluded into thinking that Eva could fill the void Val's absence had left. Perhaps it was the resemblance between them or Eva's rapt attention to his work or her insistence that a family was all the career she'd ever wanted. She'd fed him the lies he was hungry to hear and through the haze of his hurt and pain, he'd believed her.

"You're wrong," Val was saying. "Something did. I came up with a theory to nullify the toxic side effects of the antibiotic. I've worked on it for the last few years here at Traynor, mostly in my spare time."

"Is that what you've been doing nights in the microbiology lab with Wally Chandler?"

"You've heard about that?"

He nodded. Dr. Walter Chandler had joined Traynor as head of Microbiology eight months ago. He was young, personable, and talented. He was also very much attracted to Valerie. Brian stared at her intently. He knew he shouldn't say anything but he couldn't stop himself. The thought of anyone touching Val triggered a fury in him over which he had no control. "Is there anything else I should know about?"

Her hazel eyes were cool. "Only that according to the animal studies I've just carried out, I believe I've been successful."

"God, Val, that's great! Have you contacted the government yet?"

"Dad did a few weeks ago."

"What was their response?"

"The same as yours. The Commissioner of the Food and Drug Administration called Alex shortly before he was taken to the hospital."

"To arrange for the clinical testing?"

"That was part of it."

"What else?"

She paused. She had always held in contempt women like her sister-in-law Claire who used guile to achieve their ends when no other means were in sight. Right now, she would have given a lot to know how they did it.

"What else?" he repeated.

She met his unrelenting gaze. "At present, Tetra-2 is unstable. It changes structure rapidly after it's synthesized, so that it has to be administered at once to have any effect. Because of this, it's impossible to do the human testing at the site of the infection." She spoke quickly as Brian's eyes turned incredulous. "Brian, we've got twenty volunteers, begging to be tested."

"What kind of volunteers?"

Valerie's gaze shied from his. "A few army men . . . the rest prisoners. We're one of the few pharmaceutical houses with the facilities to . . ."

He cut across her words. "Look at me, Val. Are you asking me to allow the human testing of a killer disease on our own premises with over two thousand people working here every day?"

"Yes, I am. The newspapers have distorted the facts, Brian. Blasa Fever isn't transmitted by air. It strikes only where people live closely together and sanitary conditions are poor. That just doesn't exist here. The testing can be confined to the laboratory and hospital at the end of the main building that were originally used for that purpose and the raw Blasa Fever cultures which present the greatest danger of transmission can be carefully guarded." The sun streaming from the window behind him turned her eyes an olive green. "Brian, I think you should know that Alex already okayed this—by phone to Washington a few days before he died."

"Then why are you asking my okay?"

"Because it isn't valid now without your signature."

Brian rose, jammed his hands into his pockets, and paced the floor. Damn Alex and his attitude of *noblesse oblige*. It had been their biggest bone of contention. Alex saw himself as a patron, a savior of humanity. He was less interested in seeing the business grow than in serving the community at large. "The trouble with you, Brian," he used to say, "is that you don't see people, you see dollar signs. I hope for your sake you rise above it some day, because until you do, you won't be the man you could be."

For Alex, the Traynor Foundation set up in 1940 as his personal contribution to support research and issue grants to hospitals had never been enough. In 1968 he established the Traynor Museum and in 1974 he talked the Board into issuing scholarships for worthy but underprivileged students to attend medical and graduate schools, and now he had gone even further with this testing program.

"Why couldn't it be done at a nearby hospital?" he asked.

"We tried. The hospitals are either too scared to touch it or they don't have the facilities."

"Alex must have been out of his mind," he muttered. "The risk is staggering."

She swung to face him. "The risk to whom, Brian? Is it really the employees you're thinking of, or could it be that the prospect of the Review Board you have to face at the end of the year is coloring your thinking?"

His glance was scornful. "You know better than that."

Her face flushed. "I'm sorry."

He knew how much this project meant to her. The pressure of her wanting disconcerted him, but it didn't alter the facts. "All right. Let's say we go forward with the testing. There's no way to know if the drug will be effective or sufficiently safe in the end. If it's not, then we've gone to a great deal of expense for nothing."

"Suppose the government funded the research?"

"You know the answer to that. If the government funds the research, Tetra-2 becomes public domain. Any company can market it after that, so we lose the exclusivity."

Valerie hunched forward in her chair. "Tetra-2 will work. I know it will."

"What if it does? The only way we can ever make a profit on it without pricing it way out of line is if the demand is enormous. To put it plainer, Blasa Fever would have to reach epidemic proportions to make it worthwhile."

The effect of his words triggered a response he hadn't foreseen. Outwardly contained up to now, she rose from her chair in a single fluid movement and came to stand beside him. He could smell the perfume of her hair and feel the anger that tensed her body as if it was his own. With an effort he restrained himself from touching her.

"Let me tell you a little about Blasa Fever," she said in a passionate voice, "before you speak so lightly about an epidemic. I won't bore you with ten years of details. I'll stick to just one of the recent outbreaks in the U.S. This summer it hit a children's back-to-nature camp in Maine. That's where Tom Nordsen's daughter got it. I went up to offer my help. I felt that I had seen enough of it not to be horrified. I was wrong. If you could picture this little boy Stephen as I saw him, burning with fever, unable to move his limbs, apathetic to the point of being a zombie, too weak to even cry, you wouldn't talk in terms of profit.''

''What happened to him?''

''He died, Brian. He was one of the lucky ones. Most of the others wound up blind or crippled. The newspapers played it down at the request of the government because they didn't want a riot on their hands.''

Brian reached toward the desk for a pack of Kents. ''All right, I concede that the disease is horrendous. But that only makes it worse. If the employees ever found out that we were testing . . .''

''The F.D.A. has asked that we keep a low profile on the project. I'm not suggesting that we hide what we're doing, but there's no reason we have to advertise it either. The lab I'm thinking of using is perfect. It was built in 1950 for just this type of testing and has a twenty-five-bed hospital next to it that has scarcely been used for years.''

He moved a few feet from her and used the lighter on the credenza for his cigarette. He knew he was weakening and he knew it was a mistake. It would be *his* signature and *his* responsibility that the Blasa Fever project would go through on. If it backfired and harm came to even a single employee, he wouldn't be able to live with himself. But he was caught in a peculiar bind. The Food and Drug Administration had a verbal okay from Alex on the human testing of Tetra-2. It was perfectly legal for Brian, as the incoming president, to veto it, but it wasn't good business policy.

The F.D.A. was the most powerful arm of the government for any pharmaceutical company involved in prescription drugs. When a new drug was researched it was the F.D.A. who approved the animal data and sanctioned the testing of humans. No permission for marketing a drug was ever given without a thorough investigation that sometimes stretched into years. It was the F.D.A. who monitored the accuracy of advertising and promotion. They could force a company who had misled their consumers to spend monies equal to that spent on advertising to correct it. They could, also, insist on the modification or withdrawal of a product from the market that they felt lacked efficacy or deemed harmful for any number of reasons.

"First, I have to confer with our legal department, then check our insurance," he murmured. "And I'll need more details from you. Who you'll be working with, who'll take on your duties as Medical Director, the length of time you'll need, the safety measures you'll employ in the lab . . ."

Her face lit with joy. "You'll have my part of it on your desk by five tonight and I'll show you the lab whenever you're ready." She moved toward him, reached out a hand. "Brian, I don't know how to . . ."

Closing the distance between them, he clutched her shoulders. "Don't thank me," he said. "It's *you* who'll be placed in the greatest danger. If anything were to happen to you—"

"It won't."

The phone rang. His hands reluctantly dropped from her shoulders as he swung around to answer it.

"I'm sorry to interrupt," Dora Watkins said crisply, "but Lester Pryor just called. He's got an emergency situation in Quality Control."

"Is he in his office?"

"No. He's in the number five lab on the second floor."

"Tell him I'll be right there."

"Yes, sir."

When he turned around, Valerie was gone.

Chapter 3

Traynor's main building was divided into four floors. Besides the goods for packaging, the lower warehouse level held the quarantined material (products both raw and finished still undergoing testing to see that approved Food and Drug Administration standards were being met), and released (approved) material. The materials were carefully separated into two vaults according to F.D.A. regulations and those vaults were constantly under surveillance through closed circuit television in different parts of the building.

The first floor, where Manufacturing was located, held the machinery that pulverized the powders and shaped the pills. There were concrete block areas for weighing, blending, screening, and drying before the granulated material was fed into the hopper that compressed it into tablets. For products in liquid form, tublike vats with temperature gauges farther along the floor mixed and dissolved the liquids, using portholes for inserting additional ingredients. Sterile injectable solutions were made in tightly supervised areas and high security divisions were allocated for manufacturing narcotics—all before the last operation was reached, the packaging and labeling of finished goods.

The mid or entry level was split between reception in the front and Quality Control in the rear.

Quality Control was the safety catch on the trigger

that could blow Traynor's reputation for reliability sky-high. It was their job to check the quality of raw and finished drugs and to develop methods to assure the uniformity of every product.

When a new drug came out of research, ready for production, the control group (made up mostly of chemists) was aware of every ingredient used. They purified the drug, analyzed it, then set up standards so that their inspectors could check the manufacturing process from then on to see that the original properties of the drug—taste, odor, stability, appearance, and texture—were kept intact. Whatever the phase of manufacture, whether the distilling of the drug itself, the bottling, capping, labeling, or packaging, quality control inspectors were there checking batches.

Still, mistakes were made.

There were thirty Quality Control laboratories on the second floor for testing drugs. Brian found Lester Pryor in the one marked number 6. He was reprimanding a young chemist who was standing near a counter-current distribution machine made of fragile glass tubing. It was automatically separating the physical and chemical properties of the sedative Norvol, now being manufactured. The separated ingredients then fed into a spectrophotometer which measured the ultraviolet absorption of the drug. The final calculation was done by a computer which converted the spectro data into actual concentration per tablet. This concentration, called the assay, would then be compared with the original assay approved by the Food and Drug Administration as the standards to be met by Norvol, before the drug would be allowed to be shipped.

Above the noise of the machines, Pryor's angry voice carried clear to the door. "You think that ruling on safety glasses is there for the fun of it? I once saw a technician no older than you splash some acid into his eye. He's blind in that eye now. Is that what you're bucking for?''

"No, sir," the red-faced chemist mumbled.

"Then get the hell out of here and don't come back until you've got those glasses on."

Lester Pryor caught sight of Brian at the door. He held up a hand in greeting and crossed the lab to meet him as the chemist slunk by.

Brian nodded at the retreating chemist's back. "Is that your emergency?"

Pryor laughed. "I wish it was."

Papa Pryor, as his associates called him in tribute to the seven children he'd fathered, looked more like a basketball player than the vice president of a pharmaceutical company. He was six feet three with a beanpole physique, and hair the color of rusted iron. Right now, his freckled face held the baffled expression of a veteran detective stumped by a fresh twist, as he pulled a small object from his pocket.

He opened his palm to Brian. In it he held a half-filled vial of clear liquid. "Sorry to do this on your first day, Brian, but I think you should take a look at this."

The ten milliliter vial was marked, "Morphine 10mg/ml" and labeled with the traditional blue and orange seal across the top, which had been broken when the cap was opened and the metal beneath punctured.

"So?" Brian prompted.

"It was sent to us three days ago, special delivery, by a Catholic nun in a hospital in Utah. She had used it on a post-op patient with no results. She felt the morphine lacked potency and thought we ought to have it checked. I got it only this morning because we were closed for two days."

"Have you had it analyzed yet?"

Pryor nodded.

"What was in it?"

"Water. Plain water."

Brian drew a sharp breath. "Is this the first time it's happened?"

"You'd better believe it."

The same thing was in both their minds. Like all pharmaceutical houses engaged in the manufacture of narcotics, Traynor Labs was monitored by the Drug Enforcement Administration. This incident would now have to be reported to them. If it was a single one, the Administration would do nothing about it. If it was of larger scope, they would shut Traynor down like a sealed coffin until they could determine how the substitution was made and who was responsible for it.

"What's the batch date on the morphine?" Brian asked.

"It was made up two months ago, almost to the day."

"Have you checked the preservation samples we have on hand?"

During every phase of manufacture, Quality Control inspectors picked random samples of the drug being made and held them for comparison for a period of at least five years, in case accusations of spoilage, contamination, or substitution arose long after the drug had left Traynor Labs.

"Yes. There's morphine in every one of them." At Brian's open sigh of relief, Pryor shook his head in warning. "I wouldn't write this one off that easily, Brian."

Brian controlled his annoyance. Lester Pryor was the last one he would have called a worrywart, but this time he seemed out of line. "Frankly, Lester, I don't see the significance of this. The incident seems to be an isolated one. I don't even see the point in trying to track it down. You and I both know that when a narcotic with as highly marketable a value as morphine is sent back opened, there's almost no method of checking where along the way it's been tampered with. That vial was handled by a jobber, and there are personnel and technicians in the Utah hospital that had access to it long before the nurse . . .''

"According to the nun, the seal hadn't been broken before she touched it."

Brian frowned. "What are you trying to say, Lester?''

Pryor beckoned with a long bony hand. "Come into my parlor."

In contrast to Pryor's double-windowed administrative office on the third floor, his cubbyhole on the second looked like a fishbowl, glassed in on three sides, with stacks of books piled on top of rows of filing cabinets backed against the only wall in the room. Lester's desk held an assortment of pills, powders, vials, and labels. He pushed them to one side, perched his elongated frame on the edge of the desk and motioned for Brian to seat himself in the director's chair a few feet away.

His freckled face broke into the semblance of a smile. "Brian, in case I didn't say it loud enough this morning, congratulations on the presidency. I know the odds you're bucking. Haversham won't rest until he gets you out. I want you to know that whatever happens, I'm on your side. I've never made a secret of the fact that I think David's a jackass, and if I seem to be making more of this morphine substitution than is warranted, it's only because I want to make sure that you're aware of everything that might cause trouble.''

"I appreciate, but I don't understand."

Pryor nodded. "If this turns out to be a single case

of morphine hijacking done somewhere after the vial left the labs, I'll be overjoyed. What I'm worried about is that the substitution was an inside job managed somewhere right here in manufacturing. In two weeks we start making Trinicitate, the narcotic compound for anesthesia Alex signed those government contracts on six months ago. There'll be a shipment of ten kilos of bulk morphine arriving a few days prior to that, the largest amount we've ever kept on the premises at one time. Properly cut, it's worth at least two million dollars on the open market, and the thought that there might be someone here who's supporting a habit, or pushing the stuff, makes my blood run cold.''

Brian nodded. He knew that the Drug Enforcement Administration did its utmost to prevent the theft of narcotics. Under federal law, no former convicted addict was allowed to hold a job at the plant, and it was mandatory for anyone wishing to work for Traynor to be subjected by a company doctor to blood and urine tests to determine whether or not he was an addict at the time. But no amount of preventive regulations could completely stem the theft of narcotics, and they were both aware of it.

''Have you told David about the water in the morphine vial?''

''I gave him the gist of it on the phone a few minutes ago, but our temperamental prodigy said he had no time to discuss it now. He was on his way to have lunch with the beauteous Claire, and would send Dennie Redmond up here to get all the facts.''

The contempt in his voice was obvious. It was common knowledge among the executives that David lunched at home with his wife every day at twelve thirty, come what may. Most of the jokes about it were good-natured and ribald. "A quickie a day keeps the traffic away."—"Biff, bam, thanks for lunch, ma'am." But personally, Brian shared Pryor's view—that it wasn't lust, but distrust that prompted David to drive the twenty minutes back and forth to Randolph Harbor every day.

There were rumors that Claire Traynor had flown the coop more than once to nest with a rooster closer to her size than the heir apparent to Traynor. Pryor, whose boastful advice about wives, "keep 'em pregnant and barefoot" jokingly belied a secure, loving marriage, was convinced that David wasn't fit to lead a Scout Troop through Central Park, let alone head a company the size of Traynor Labs.

As if aware that he'd been mentioned, Dennie Redmond rapped sharply at the window, then at sight of Brian, withdrew his knuckles hastily, uncertain as to whether he'd chosen the best method of announcing himself.

Dennie was the lesser of David's two assistants. What he lacked in forcefulness and leadership, he made up for in perseverance. At thirty-one, he was short, stocky, and moved at a slow pace. As Lester Pryor beckoned, he tugged at the vest of his brown suit and entered the room like a cautious turtle.

"Mr. Traynor said you wanted to see me." He spoke to Lester Pryor but kept his eyes on Brian's face. What had happened in that conference room this morning was phenomenal to Dennie Redmond. He was a person who believed in the order of things and the inability of man to change them. Until today, Brian had also been a second echelon man, on a higher level to be sure, but still assistant to Alexander Traynor as Dennie was to David. Though Dennie lacked the stature and ambition to climb above what he thought of as his "station at Traynor," he saw Brian's ascension to the presidency as a coup for all of them and his glance was filled with awe.

Brian held the vial out to him. "Dennie, take a look at this. Water's been substituted for the morphine in this vial. The substitution could have happened on the outside, or it could have happened right here in the plant. What we'd like to know from you is if anything suspicious has happened in manufacturing in the last month or two that Quality Control hasn't been informed about."

Dennie's brown saucer eyes bulged. "Oh, no. There's been nothing like that."

"What about breakage of vials or ampules?" Pryor asked.

"Well, there's always some of that. But it's been reported and we saved the pieces of glass to pass on to the Drug Enforcement Administration. If we didn't, you know they'd close us down faster than I could make it upstairs." He grinned feebly at the allusion to his slowness, then looked uncertain when there were no answering smiles.

"Can you think of any way that substitution could have taken place here?" Pryor persisted.

Dennie shook his head. "I don't see how. We've got Quality Control inspectors checking every step of the way. But I'll talk it over with Mr. Traynor and see if he has any ideas on it."

Brian took a cigarette, accepted Pryor's offer of a light, and inhaled deeply. Anxious to get back, Dennie Redmond was fidgeting on his seat. In a way Brian felt sorry for him. Dennie was a conscientious worker with a good mind, but he was destined to remain the butt of David's unpredictable moods and never rise beyond his current level. With the aggressiveness that drove Brian, it never occurred to him that there were people like Dennie Redmond who were quite content to remain in a secondary position of responsibility. They lived not with the hope of promotion, but with the fear that something would alter the present order of things, and indeed, Dennie Redmond had scarcely slept for a week, wondering who would become V.P. of Manufacturing when David became president. It had never occurred to him for an instant that he himself might aspire to the job.

Pryor ran a hand through his red hair. "Dennie, you know about the morphine on its way here in the next few weeks for the manufacture of the Trinicitate compound, don't you?"

"Yes, sir. Ten or twelve kilos, I think."

"It'll be taken to one of the vaults, right?" The vaults were large concrete rooms with massive steel doors on the warehouse level where narcotics, raw and finished, were kept.

"Well, not until it's checked in the sampling room."

The sampling room was on the manufacturing level next to the loading dock. When any raw material was received it was sampled by Quality Control for potency and impurities. The physical container that held the ingredients was also checked to see that there was no breakage or denting and that the labeling was correctly designated by the right code number and supplier.

"Will those ten or twelve kilos be coming in a drum?" Brian asked.

"Yes."

"A drum small enough for one man to carry?"

"Yes, but as you know, no one person is ever left alone with any amount of narcotics. We always designate two people . . ." He caught the look that passed between them and drew in his breath sharply. "Why? You don't think for a minute that someone might try to . . ."

"Calm down, Dennie. We're just asking," Brian soothed. "Since Mr. Traynor is out to lunch, I think it would be a good idea if you got back to manufacturing now. Talk over what we've said with him and if he has any ideas on it, have him get in touch with Mr. Pryor. Okay?"

"Okay. I hope I was some help." He slurred the words together so quickly the sentence came out garbled, but Brian caught the meaning of it.

"You were fine, Dennie, just fine."

They waited until he left.

"Well, what do you think?" Pryor asked.

Brian kept a straight face when he answered. He was feeling light-headed, almost giddy, and his stomach was growling. It was nearly two o'clock and he hadn't had a damned thing to eat since coffee that morning. "I think when we look into it, we'll find that the ward at the hospital in Utah is being run by a clever, drug-addicted lady of the cloth."

Chapter 4

At eleven thirty that morning, in the marble bathroom adjoining her bedroom that had cost ten thousand dollars to install, Claire Traynor was taking a bath in her sunken tub. She thought of everything in the house as hers, because, in truth, mentally she shared nothing with David, not her thoughts or her body, or her nine-year-old daughter Melody, who was, thank God, a miniature of herself.

The bathroom was white, as was the rest of the house. White towels, white walls, white Karastan rugs, white furniture. "The place is a goddam hospital," David had protested, but Claire had overridden him. White was the antithesis of dirt and as long as she immersed herself in this sanitary cocoon, dirt would never touch her again.

When asked where she got that "charming Southern accent," Claire always recounted her middle-class Virginia upbringing, making sure that the "li'l ol house" she described left the impression of a demi-plantation at the very least. It couldn't have been further from the truth.

Claire had grown up poor, the eldest of seven children. Her father had eked out a living on a small chicken farm in Tennessee, while her mother worked from dawn to dusk trying to stretch the few dollars the farm brought in. She died at thirty-five, looking more like fifty, and staring down at the worn face in the chapel, Claire vowed she wouldn't come to the same end.

A week later she hitched a ride to New York. Her assets were a high school diploma, a superbly proportioned body, auburn hair, green eyes, and the advice of a teacher that "she ought to go in for acting."

During the next year, she attended drama school by day and worked as a waitress at night, sure that fame would be hers "if she could get the right break." After three years with as many agents and no success, she managed, by sleeping with the casting director, to land a bit part in *Oklahoma* at the Westbury Music Festival. Her performances were enthusiastic, in bed and out. When the show closed, the grateful casting director, a semi-impotent former actor of fifty-five, found an off-Broadway part for her in a remake of *Picnic* and it looked like she was on her way. Her notices were good, she got a small mention in *Variety* and she started a scrap book.

Then she fell in love.

Chris Androtti was the handsome curly-headed young drifter with the sensuality of a stallion in perpetual heat who played the lead in the William Inge vehicle. He was aptly suited to the part. In the afternoons, when he wasn't dancing attendance on the producer's wife (the lady who had secured the part for him), he was making passionate, innovative love to Claire, popping pills and thinking up positions that she had never known existed.

For three months she wallowed in a sensual morass, scarcely sleeping, waiting in between performances for Chris to unpeel himself from the "Dragon Lady" so that he could come to her in the one-room Village apartment that had become a haven of sexual fantasy, "a place to scourge the flesh-pots of human decadence'' as Chris put it in his booming John Barrymore voice. At the beginning of the fourth month, the bubble burst. The Dragon Lady found out.

Within a week Claire was out of a job, and worse. She was pregnant. She had refused to stay on the birth control pills because they kept her overweight and, although the clinic had warned her, she'd never found the time to have a diaphragm fitted. Remorseful, Chris gave her whatever money he had, but sent her to the abortionist alone. He explained that although his love for her had in no way changed, in order to stay in the show he had to stop seeing her for a while. There was no point in both of them losing their jobs, now was there?

Claire never remembered whether she agreed. It didn't really matter anyway. When the doctor refused to perform the abortion because he found that she was anemic, she remembered a valuable lesson she had forgotten. A man and a woman shared the ecstasy of love, but not necessarily its consequences. The next man she went to bed with would pay dearly for the privilege.

She met David three days later when she performed gratis at a rally for returning Vietnam soldiers. He was drunk, morose about something that had happened in ''Nam'' that he wouldn't talk about, and obviously very rich. He took her to bed that night in an orgiastic semi-stupor, declared his intentions by early morning and dogged her footsteps like a love-sick puppy for a whole week before she consented to marry him. Melody was born seven months afterward, a full-sized premature infant with her mother's green eyes and Chris Androtti's curly black mane.

Claire rose from the tub, pulled a fluffy white towel from a gold ring, and patted herself dry. She never rubbed, because rubbing caused red spots and she couldn't bear to see her skin marred even for a second. It had been impressed upon Claire, ever since she traded her virginity at fifteen to a neighboring farmer for two Thanksgiving turkeys and a tub of butter, that her body was more than a vessel for pleasure. It was an asset that could be bartered and, as such, it deserved infinite care.

Holding the towel behind her for a backdrop, she shook her long auburn hair until it toppled loose from the pins that held it and pivoted in front of the floor-length mirror. She looked more twenty than thirty she decided. Her skin had the taut suppleness of youth, her breasts were high and pointed, the nipples small and pink. She had refused to breast feed Melody because she had feared that she would sag afterward and wind up with those crinkled brown nipples that she associated with used-up hags. Her long shapely legs tapered down to slender ankles and delicate little feet with carefully pedicured nails.

Still nude, she moved into her pale velvet bedroom with the oriental rugs and antiqued white furniture. She ran a hand across her flat belly and thought of her first night with David. He'd been a lousy lover then and he was a lousy lover now, she mused. She wondered how she'd stood it those first few years, caged in during the day with Melody and during the night with David, putting on an act for Alexander Traynor that he saw right through, no matter how hard she tried. She may have fooled David with her Virginia plantation routine, but her father-in-law's eyes read ''white trash'' every time he looked at her. The only thing in her favor was that she had David so mesmerized that his transition from Vietnam back to Traynor Labs, rocky at first, was going better since he'd married her.

At the end of five years, the boredom became stagnation, and Chris Androtti came back into her life. He was "between plays" and thought he'd give her a call. She met him at his apartment in New York the next day and it was as if the lapse of time had never existed. It was as good as it had ever been—better, because this time she wasn't in a position to become dependent on him for anything.

She was wrong. At first sex with Chris was a craving, then it became a need, then an obsession. The days she couldn't get into New York to see him, she became irritable, upbraiding Melody for unimportant transgressions, curt with David to the point of contempt.

Lately, the situation had become acute. The parts Chris got were few and further between. He had begun talking of going West and starting a theater group of his own if he could find a backer. The thought of losing him was unbearable to Claire. She would have divorced David in a second, but what would her gain have been? She had no money of her own. Appalled by what he called her "reckless spending" on clothes, furniture, and jewels, David kept a tight rein on the pursestrings. If she left, he would cut her off without a dime. And even if Chris was willing to marry her, he could scarcely support himself let alone a wife and child. She felt hopeless, trapped. . . .

Until Paul Haversham called this morning.

She glanced at the clock. Almost twelve thirty. David would be here any second. She zipped into a turquoise nylon jumpsuit that molded to her like a second skin, then slipped into a pair of matching velvet scuffs. She heard the key turn in the lock.

"Is that you, David?" she called from the upper landing.

There was no answer. She swept down the curved stairway, barely touching the gleaming mahogany bannister the maid had finished polishing less than an hour ago. The house had been built for her. It was a thirty-room Georgian with a huge center hall and the carved ceiling moldings that gave it the authenticity of a "true" Virginia plantation.

She found David in the downstairs bathroom, screwing the cap back on the Valium bottle. His sandy hair was askew, his boyish face looked haggard. She wondered as she had in the past whether the professor-like suits he chose, the first editions he collected, and the operatic arias he was always listening to with that pipe in his mouth were really the mark of an intellectual, or if it was all a put-on to bolster his sagging ego. Either way, it left them with as much in common as a drunk and a teetotaler, a gap she would somehow have to close if she was going to be effective for Haversham.

She leaned over and loosened his knit tie. "Essie prepared lunch before she left," she murmured in a soft Southern drawl. "That's about all she's capable of doing lately. She comes in so stoned in the mornings, she trips over herself half the time. I've a good mind to fire her." She looked at his face. He was barely listening to her. She tugged at his tie. "Did you hear what I said? There's shrimp salad in the refrigerator, honeydew . . ."

"I'm not hungry." There was a petulant note in the precisely spoken words.

He wasn't communicating. But what had she expected? For years she had discouraged anything but a sexual relationship between them. The daily exchange of intimacies she thrived on had taken place with Chris, not David. Somehow she would have to change that. The fifty-thousand-dollar deal she'd made with Haversham was dependent on David's being close enough to her to reveal anything that could jeopardize his becoming president at the end of the year. She would have to work some to achieve that. But she wasn't worried. Her years on stage hadn't made her a star, but neither had they been in vain.

She followed him into the den and waited until he'd poured himself a Scotch from the crystal decanter on the bar. "I know what happened this morning," she said. "I spoke to Paul. I want you to understand that your not being president doesn't matter to me."

He slammed the shot glass on the bar with such force that the Scotch slopped over the side. "It matters to *me!*" he said with a fierceness that she had seen in him only once before. It was the night she'd first met him when he'd told her drunkenly that a man had to live up to his own convictions, abide by his own decisions, otherwise he was like a poor imprint of a negative, with no definition of self. He'd babbled morosely that the last few years in Vietnam had been a mistake. That he never should have gone. He should have stolen away to Canada and taken his chances with the rest of the draft evaders.

"If you felt that way, why did you go?" she had asked.

"Because my father made me, dammit!"

His face had been filled with the same kind of fury it held now.

She put her hand on his arm as he started to move away from her. "David, you didn't let me finish," she said huskily. "It doesn't matter to me as far as the prestige is concerned. I don't give a damn about being the first lady of Traynor Labs. What does matter to me is what Alex did to your pride by naming Brian instead of you in front of all those people this morning. So help me, if I could find a way to get back at him I would."

He blinked twice. "Do you really mean that?" Uncertainty battled with hope in his voice. Lately, he had despaired of ever getting close to Claire again. She had become so brittle and distant, nothing like what she'd been when he married her. At first, he attributed it to her isolation out here. She hated suburbia. She'd made no friends and his sisters took their cue from Alex. Valerie and Eva barely tolerated her. When she started going to New York to meet some of her old friends she seemed happier, but recently even that didn't seem to suffice. If he tried to probe her unhappiness she retreated further from him. For the past few months their going to bed together had resembled the coupling of a prostitute and her john. It had left him physically satisfied and emotionally bereft. And now this unexpected solace.

She moved nearer to him. A faint odor of lilac clung to her and he knew she'd just come out of the tub. "Of course I mean it. But why did I have to find out about it from Paul? Why not from you? That's part of the problem between us, David. You shut me out as if I was an acquaintance instead of your wife, then expect me to feel a closeness you haven't given me a right to feel."

He gaped at her in complete bewilderment. "*I* shut *you* out?"

She unbuttoned his jacket and probed between the buttons of his shirt with her fingers. "Don't you? Here, I'll show you. What happened to you ten years ago when you were in Vietnam, David?"

He pulled her hands away from his shirt. "Leave it alone, Claire." His voice was as taut as a bowstring.

"There, you see." It had been a predictable triumph. Except for his drunken revelation prior to their marriage, if the subject of Vietnam came up, David retreated into himself and his face took on the haunted, almost terrified look it held now. She wondered idly how formidable these ghosts of his past really were and whether it paid to relay this information to Haversham.

His face sagged. He was tired of coping. The morning had left him drained and now Claire was acting in a way he didn't understand. "What do you want of me, Claire?"

She put her arms around his neck and let her body press against his. "I'm lonely, David," she whispered. "I want to be close to you again. Not only in bed. But the way we used to be when we were first married. Talking and telling each other things that mattered. You remember." She lowered her eyes to hide her triumph as she felt him harden against her. David had the control of a seventeen-year-old.

He held her off, his eyes narrowing in momentary suspicion. "Why the sudden change, Claire? Yesterday you couldn't have cared less."

"Melody is growing up, David. She doesn't need me the way she used to. I feel useless . . ." Her voice dropped to a whisper, ". . . old."

He pulled her to him fiercely, protectively. It was incredible that she should seek reassurance. Up to now he had thought of her as self-contained, somehow invincible. It had made him feel the weaker of the two. "You haven't aged one iota in ten years. You're still the most beautiful woman I've ever met and I want you now more than I ever have before."

Her eyes were tear-filled, incredulous. "Really?" He nodded. She ran her tongue over her lips. "Essie won't be back for two hours," she murmured.

"Then what are we waiting for?"

She smiled a slow sure smile and unzipped the jumpsuit to her navel, letting her breasts spring free.

"Christ," he groaned.

She ran from the room, the top of the suit flopping

about her hips, and took the steps two at a time. She could hear him pounding up the stairway close behind her. She leaped face downward onto the satin covered bed and flipped over just as he reached it, panting, his pink-toned skin blotchy and sweating, his small piggy eyes intent on the perfection of her breasts and the blue-veined line that trailed from between them down to where the zipper of the jumpsuit still held.

"Take your clothes off," she whispered. She glanced at the clock as he did. Seven minutes, she said to herself. He'd never hold out for more. She sighed ecstatically as she stripped off her jumpsuit. Chris could make it for ten times that. She closed her eyes and thought of Chris, whom she would see in less than an hour and a half.

David's mouth came down on hers hard, his teeth battering her lip. She opened her eyes. The shades had been pulled and the room dimmed out. He had the inhibitions of a priest, she thought in disdain. He was straddling her, his pudgy hands kneading her breasts, making small growling noises in his throat like a hungry dog. She ran her fingers down his back, letting her nails bite into his wet skin, knowing the pain would heighten the sensation for him. David was a masochist. If he wasn't so repressed he would have craved whips and pincers to get his kicks, like the casting director had. As it was, he contented himself with milder forms of self-punishment. She bit his ear until she tasted the saltiness of blood. She heard him moan in ecstasy and felt his fingers touching her body, awkward as always, probing, uncertain. She encouraged him, held him beween her hands, blanked her mind out and used her mouth as she did on Chris.

He was making mewling sounds now, begging her with his hands to let up. He put his palms beneath her hips as she lay back and hurriedly entered her. She clawed his thighs until a long shudder shook his body. She locked her legs around him, crying out to him, simulating a passion she could never feel, urging him on with her hips, her hands, waiting for the final "Oh God . . ." that broke from him with the downward surge, the last victorious thrust that accompanied the outpouring of the seed that renewed his manliness and left him as she wanted him, content, pliable, trusting. . . .

They lay against the satin headboard, he smoking, she with her head pillowed on his hairless chest.

"Was it good?" he murmured.

"You get better all the time."

He chuckled, smoked on. "I've got to get back to the office," he said finally.

"Must you? I thought we could go again."

He pinched her soft buttocks. "Glutton. There'll be other times."

She curled into him, rubbed at the nape of his neck. "David, don't feel badly about what happened at the meeting this morning. Paul told me about the right of review the Board has. At the end of the year he feels you have a good chance of being named president."

There was a long pause. "If everything goes right." He spoke so low she scarcely heard it.

"Why shouldn't everything go right?"

There was no answer.

"You're shutting me out again." Her voice was hurt, plaintive. She made a move to leave him.

He grasped her arm, switched on the lamp, turned to face her. "All right. I'll tell you. I made a stupid mistake last month and I don't know what to do about it." He blinked several times and reached to pull up the covers.

"What kind of mistake?"

He relit his pipe and puffed rapidly. "When I first

started at Traynor, my father wanted me to learn the business from the ground up. He made a big show of a 'no favoritism' policy, which everyone laughed at behind his back, and put me on a detailing route peddling pills to hospitals and physicians in the New Mexico territory with a more experienced salesman named Clarence Robling. Of course, I didn't stay there, but Clary did. Last month he sent me a vial of morphine that a surgeon at a hospital had complained to him lacked potency. The surgeon had the remains of the vial analyzed, found it contained water and suspected there might have been a substitution at the hospital. By rights he surgeon should have informed the hospital, but he didn't want to make waves, so he told Clary, who sent it on to me. I wrote back, thanked Clary, and told him I'd give it to Quality Control."

"And did you?"

"No."

"Why not?"

A long pause again. "I don't know why not." His tone forbade her from pressing it further. David could be oddly secretive at times. Probing enraged him and she had learned to back off.

"Well, why can't you give it to them now? Claim it was an oversight."

"Because another morphine vial filled with water has just turned up in Utah."

"I don't understand."

He nodded and shifted positions. "It's like this, Claire. If a thing like that happens once, chances are it took place on the outside. If it happens more than once in two different locations, then it probably took place at Traynor in my department. If I show up with Clary Robling's complaint now, it'll look as if I was trying to cover something up."

"Who else knows about this Robling thing?"

"No one."

"Then leave it alone."

"It's not as easy as that. There's a large shipment of morphine coming into the plant in about two weeks. I have to alert someone as to what's going on or stand the chance of jeopardizing . . ."

"You don't *have to* do anything," she stated flatly. "Your duty is to yourself, not Traynor. Didn't Alex prove that to you by what he did this morning?"

"It . . . it isn't fair to Brian," he murmured.

"Has Brian been fair to you?" she shot back. "He's had Alex twisted around his finger since he married little Eva. Everybody knows it but you."

A feeling akin to pain passed through David. He remembered how close he'd been to Brian in the years Haversham was off campaigning. Brian was the brother David had never had and the man he longed to be. Physically powerful, with the grace and know-how that attracted women like a magnet, Brian had a natural authority that drew respect from his peers. Always wary of his father's contempt, David had been grateful to bring his problems to Brian, until he realized that Alex was doing the same. It was on Brian, not his own son, that Alex had bestowed the coveted role of confidant, and the friendship had ended abruptly.

Claire pressed her point. "Do you honestly think Brian went into that meeting not knowing he would be named president?" She didn't wait for his response. "Face it, David. Only one of you is going to wind up in the top spot at the end of this year. The in-fighting isn't going to be pretty. Do you think you can stand up to it?" Her dark eyes challenged him.

"I can stand up to it." He spoke with more bravado

than he felt and was rewarded when she pulled his body down to hers.

In his office, a thirteen-foot-square windowless cubicle that was a constant reminder of his demotion at Traynor, Paul Haversham was preparing to leave for Mexico. An attorney friend of his in Washington had called to tell him that Laboratorios Ramirez in Mexico City was interested in licensing a product they had developed which they called a "Rejuvenator." The product was a vasodilator, which improved the flow of blood to the extremities—the brain, the hands, the feet—relieving numbness, pain, and cold, especially in the aged. Exciting as the product seemed, Haversham was wary of it. It might very well be that the "rejuvenator" was capable of performing as stated, but Mexico had one of the poorest techniques in the world for documenting animal research to show efficacy.

Traynor's advantage in licensing a product from another company was twofold. First, the discovery itself. If it was exciting enough or filled a current need in the market, then the desire to be leader with it was a spur. The second advantage was that Traynor could avoid doing some of the research.

The Food and Drug Administration refused to accept most data on the human testing from a foreign country as authentic enough to be used in submission for marketing in the United States; therefore, the only research that could be avoided was the animal testing. But, if the believability of that research was questionable, as Haversham was afraid it might be, coming from Mexico, then all that was left was the discovery aspect of the product, which wasn't always worth buying.

Funny, Haversham thought, as he checked his attaché case for his plane tickets, how you could almost relate the quality of the research to the standard of medicine in the country. The physicians were the key to the Health Ministries, which were similar to our Food and Drug Administration here. The better trained the doctors were, the more they asked for. Great Britain was almost as stringent in its requirements as the United States. Next came Japan, then France, Germany, and Switzerland. The Latin American countries were on the lowest rung of the ladder.

He put the plane tickets inside his jacket pocket, snapped the attaché case shut, and was almost out of the office when his private phone rang. It was Claire Traynor.

He listened intently while she related what David had told her. What concerned him more than anything was the reason David hadn't reported the substitution Clary Robling had told him about to begin with, but he didn't tell Claire that.

"You did well," he complimented in his strident voice. "I'll handle the loose end from here."

"What loose end?"

"Clary Robling, of course. If he checks with Quality Control to see what they made of that morphine substitution he reported, we're all dead."

Her voice filled with admiration. "You have a mind like a steel trap, Paul."

"Thanks." Privately he thought her body functioned the same way. He didn't like Claire Traynor. He conceded that she was beautiful, but she lacked the kind of class that an Eva Traynor had and Haversham was a snob about women. He was married to a former senator's daughter, who had come to him impoverished but impeccable in taste, manner, and sexual habits. She was a terrible bore in bed, a fact which Haversham remedied from time to time, but always with a woman he considered up to his standards. Claire Traynor was not.

"You have the number where I'll be in Mexico?" he asked her.

"Yes."

"Use it if you need me." He clicked off.

Chapter 5

Brian left for the day at five thirty. Coming out of the snowy parking lot he was almost sideswiped by a '73 Chevy whose driver checked neither right nor left but careened forward like a horse hampered by blinders. To Brian's astonishment, he caught sight of the usually mild Dennie Redmond behind the wheel, looking as if he was about to explode. Brian made a mental note to question him about it in the morning, if Dennie survived the icy roads that lay before him.

Traffic was bumper to bumper on the Southern State Parkway and Brian chafed at the delay. As predicted, it had been a long day. For two hours after lunch at a staff meeting, he had debated the feasibility of using only white for the manufacture of all pills in the future. The Food and Drug Administration had banned the use of so many color dyes—red number two, number six, number forty, and was now starting on the yellows—that it was suggested that in the coming years no color would be proven safe. The wise alternative, therefore, would be to institute the use of white pills immediately to stave off the need for change, should the F.D.A. suddenly rule out one or more of the colors now being produced.

Brian disagreed. No matter how precise the machinery for manufacturing and how carefully Quality Control checked and balanced, cases of mislabeling had been known to happen. If the druggist or doctor didn't catch it, the only factor that might alert an unsuspecting patient from taking a tranquilizer instead of a life-saving heart stimulant could be its color. It was argued that numbers were used on labels and on the pill itself to designate a drug. Brian argued back that most people didn't read or weren't aware of the numbers. And so it went. In the end the subject was tabled for future re-examination and colored pills would continue to be produced until then.

Brian braked and allowed the Rambler that had been signaling from the right lane for five minutes to get in front of him. Once Valerie had told him that he drove a car the way she plunged a hypodermic—with no quarter given. He'd rebutted that if there were fewer Sunday drivers on the road during the week, he wouldn't have to take such a hardnosed line. She'd looked at him scornfully and made some remark about "poor justification." Since then, when he remembered, he made a conscious effort at being less of a roadhog.

He glanced at the mirror and rubbed a hand across the stubble of beard that darkened his jawline. The one new convenience that Alex's office afforded was the bathroom adjoining it. He'd had it in mind to shave before heading home, then gave it up in favor of meeting with Val to go over the hazards of the Blasa Fever testing setup that had been on his mind since early that morning. What he'd seen hadn't reassured him in the least.

The clinic that would be used as the laboratory for the culturing of the Tetra-2 antibiotic was on the first floor of the main building at the end of the manufacturing facilities. It sat between the plant on one side and the small, now empty, hospital on the other and was separated from each by heavy oak doors, that were visible, and steel doors that were not. The only change Valerie intended to make before the volunteers arrived was the removal of the existing garbage disposal in favor of a crematorium. She had seen too much disease passed on in laboratories due to poor waste disposal.

Valerie explained that the clinic had originally been built as a testing lab and the steel doors were an emergency precaution. Should any of the deadly bacteria being cultured accidentally escape from their glass prisons, the steel doors and the vents would be triggered shut immediately, sealing off the lab from the hospital and the plant like a self-enclosed capsule until the danger was past. When Brian had asked what would happen to the doctors and other personnel in the lab under those conditions, Valerie's hazel eyes had censured him. "A football player doesn't ask about the possibilities of leg injuries on the field, does he?" she'd countered.

It was an old thing between them, he thought. His love for her could take many forms: physical, emotional, intellectual. But the moment it took the guise of the natural male toward female protectiveness that cropped up in him when he sensed danger for her, she balked. Val insisted on an equality that he understood, even admired, but found hard to contend with.

Brian turned off the parkway at exit 22 and in the gathering darkness maneuvered the twisting frozen mile to the snowy cone-shaped yews that heralded Marbrough Glen. The attaché case on the seat beside him was stuffed with letters, budget proposals, and marketing data that would occupy him for half the night. But he had no choice. The backlog that had accumulated since Alex's death was tremendous.

With a muttered "damn," he suddenly realized that he had forgotten to call back Eva to give her the news of his being named president. She would be angry, and he wasn't up to coping with her anger tonight.

He rounded the corner and the small estate came into view. In the foreground, shielded by high hedges, were the tennis courts and swimming pool, buried now under mounds of snow. The house itself was an eighteen-room stone-faced Tudor with leaded windows and oversized chimneys, set far enough back from the road to accommodate a poplar lined driveway. Its inner decor would have done credit to a museum. Despite Brian's protests, Alex had partially furnished it with antiques as a wedding gift. Brian, with his untaught middle-class upbringing, hadn't realized their value until years later.

"Let it be a beginning," Alex had said in a voice that made hope sound like fact. "You can add to it together as the years go on."

It hadn't been a beginning, Brian thought. It had been an end, a dead end from which he saw no way of turning back. In retrospect he realized that Alex had been aware of Eva's shortcomings. He'd spoken of her as "restless" and "fun-loving" in comparison to Val, but the worry had been there in his eyes and the guilt that he'd allowed her to be reared by circumstances without a mother, and by default without a father.

In the belief that it would have a settling influence on Eva, Alex hadn't hesitated to give their hasty marriage his blessing, though he knew of the love that had existed between Brian and Val for the two years prior. Yet he couldn't be blamed for that, Brian reasoned. Brian's relationship with Val had been stormy, unpredictable, openly broken at the time with Val on one continent and he on the other. There was nothing to indicate that it wasn't a closed issue, and his feelings for Eva had seemed genuine and intense.

Brian laid the thoughts aside. From past experience, he knew that they, also, led to a dead end. He left his car in the driveway, unsure of the slickness at the garages in the rear. He used his key to open the door, wondering at the dimness in the hallway and the quiet of the house.

"Eva?" he called. "Mark?"

There was no answer.

Frowning, he crossed toward the library. Slits of light came from beneath the closed doors and he could hear muffled whispers from within. He reached to press his palms against the mahogany double doors. They were flung open before he could touch them. He blinked rapidly against the brilliant light that came from inside and the people that crowded around him, pounding him on the back and shouting congratulations. He felt himself tighten with dislike. They were Eva's friends, all of them. International jetsetters who traveled in packs seeking the constant amusement they needed for sustenance. There were the titled few who harped on their family tree like an endlessly played record. They hopped from one place to another, eschewing *la dolce vita* and making a practice of looking bored. He spotted the tennis player who hadn't won a match in five years, the Iranian couple who were reputed to be bi-sexual, the aging actor who turned up at each party with a younger girl. This one looked to be about sixteen with a Barbra Streisand curly cut and an embroidered peasant blouse.

In their midst stood Eva, cool and beautiful in a long white dress with a diamond clasp between her magnificent breasts that did more to call attention to the cleavage than to hide it. She moved toward him with an unhurried elegance that spoke of finishing schools for deportment and fencing lessons for body control. Her silken black hair, cared for by a hair-

dresser who swished into the house each morning as
Brian left, was worn in a shoulder-length page boy.
The only facet of Eva's personality Brian had ever
envied was her ability to dissemble with ease. Right
now her mouth was smiling, but her dark eyes were
cold.

She kissed him dryly on the lips. "Surprise, darling.
You didn't think I'd let something as big as this go by
without celebrating, did you?"

He was too angry to wonder how she'd found out.
He stood unshaven among them with his trench coat
slung over his shoulder and his attaché case jammed
under one arm, trying to smile, because protocol demanded it, unable to communicate by word or movement because of the furor inside him. Had the party
been a genuine gesture, he could have forgiven her.
As his punishment for slighting her, he couldn't.

Covering for his cool response, Eva turned gaily to
the crowd. "Take a lesson, friends. How to turn your
husband speechless in one quick take." There was a
sprinkling of laughter. She pointed toward the paneled
den on the other side of the hallway. "Come on,
everybody. Drinks and hors d'oeuvres are being
served at the bar."

He clasped her wrist in a tight grip as she moved
with the others. "I want to talk to you."

"We have guests." She spoke in a clipped undertone.

His grip became steel. *"I want to talk to you."*

"You *are* a boor." She appealed to the crowd with
a fluttery wave of her slender white hand. "Listen,
everybody. The host and the hostess are going upstairs for a short tete à tete."

"Bravo!" the tennis player called out. "Can we
take turns after that?" There was more laughter as
they filed across the hall.

He followed her up the stairs, aware of the bareness of her back and the shapeliness of her hips beneath the white gown. He felt no desire. That had disappeared along with his respect for her. They slept in the same room because Eva insisted that servants gossiped, but there had been nothing between them for over a year. Their marriage was a sham in every way, and in the destructive atmosphere that existed, Mark was being buffeted between them like a pawn in a chess game.

It wasn't that he hadn't tried, Brian thought. At the beginning of their marriage, there was the newness and the challenge and the willingness to compromise. Eva was like a sponge, drawing him out about his unhappy childhood and his aspirations at Traynor. She never once talked of Valerie, but she made it clear that she felt a woman belonged at her man's side. She was an inventive lover, amusing him by insisting he go on an oyster diet to increase his virility, then begging him to come off it because he was too much for her. Her attentiveness ended abruptly when she became pregnant.

No matter what assurances he gave her, she couldn't stand her ungainliness. She became moody and restless. She wanted gaiety and distraction. At night he accompanied her to parties where he drank and smiled and tried to fit into the inane conversations, hoping that after the baby was born their relationship would revert to what it had been.

The only thing that reverted was Eva's figure. The confinement that accompanied motherhood bored her, and contrary to sharing the baby in any way with Brian, she saw her son at first as a rival for Brian's attention. The relationship went steadily downhill after that. With Mrs. Garvey firmly entrenched in the household, Eva's jaunts to Europe "on business" became more prolonged, and when she was home, more often than not she would show up at parties without him. Knowing his wife's appetites, Brian suspected there were other men, but with Eva, discretion was a byword, and there was never anything definite.

One way or the other, the marriage would surely have ended in divorce if Valerie hadn't come back from Africa two years ago. Her sister's return effected a change in Eva that Brian didn't understand. Whereas before she had acknowledged that the marriage was a failure and they had begun to discuss separating, Eva now became adamant about staying married and retaining the "in name only" title that gave her nothing but a status she didn't need.

Brian closed the bedroom door behind him. It was pale yellow with gray oak furniture and led to a large sitting room off to the right that served as Eva's salon when she chose to have guests for brunch. He flung his case and coat onto the quilted spread of one of the twin beds and turned to face Eva where she stood in the center of the room.

"How could you do this, Eva? I know you don't give a damn about me, but Alex has been dead exactly six days. Even if you're not broken up in mourning, I wouldn't call it good taste to . . ."

The coolness she wore for her admiring public dropped from her features like a mask. Her voice was low and concise, her eyes narrowed. "Good taste," she said bitterly. "Don't *you* talk to *me* of good taste. Do you know how I found out you'd been named president today? Roberta Cleary of *New Frontiers* magazine called me. She'd just been speaking to Paul Haversham's wife and phoned to congratulate me. She was waiting for me to say 'about what?' but I wouldn't give her the satisfaction. I thanked her and bluffed my way through until I found out what this was all about.

It was then I decided to give the party, not only to save face, but because I needed some friends around me. People who cared what I thought and felt, because you sure as hell don't.''

"Friends," he scoffed. "You call those people downstairs 'friends.' I saw those same faces six days ago at Alex's funeral and except for the fact that they weren't smiling, they looked the same as they do now. Empty. They're not capable of feeling or giving. Only of taking. They're parasites, Eva. If they work at all, it's only for idle amusement."

"Like I do at the Traynor Museum?"

"I didn't say that."

"But it's what you think, isn't it, Brian? I know you don't respect what I do. I've known it for a long time. Because it isn't only work you mean when you use the word. It's dedication, self-sacrifice. The giving over of one's self to a cause, like what my precious sister Val does."

"Let's not bring Val into this."

"Why not? Are you afraid I'll sully something by bringing out in the open what's on your mind half the time anyway?"

He turned from her and lit a cigarette with shaking fingers. He inhaled deeply, winced as the smoke burned his nostrils passing through and felt steadier. He turned back to her. She had moved to the dresser mirror opposite the bed. Her expression was dispassionate as she examined her makeup with the critical eye of a connoisseur.

"Eva, we can't go on like this," he said quietly.

She reapplied her lipstick and raised a plucked brow with studied nonchalance. "What do you propose we do about it?"

A faint knock sounded at the door. A second later

it opened and Mark appeared in the doorway. His face brightened at sight of his father, then grew cautious as he sensed the turmoil.

"I heard voices," he said, uncertain of his welcome.

"It's okay, Mark," Brian reassured him. "Come on in."

He was too solemn for an eight-year-old kid, Brian thought, yet he had an unexpected sense of humor at times. He was small and slender with Eva's dark hair and Brian's blue eyes. Mark didn't make friends easily and when he did, he gave too much of himself and got hurt when the response wasn't the same. How do you teach a kid emotional self-defense, Brian wondered, when you're not sure you ever really learned it yourself?

He ruffled his son's curly hair and elicited a shy smile. "How's that stomach ache you had this morning?"

The smile became broader. "What stomach ache?"

He hugged the slender body closer. "Atta boy!"

With a final glance of approbation, Eva tore herself from the mirror. "Never mind the macho heroics. Have you been studying for that French test tomorrow?"

He winked at his father. *"Oui, maman."*

She leaned down to kiss him, her expression softening, her dark eyes, larger and less tilted than Val's, intent on the mischievous face that awaited her approval. Mark had learned early that the key to Eva's "love" was achievement. There was reflected glory for her in being able to boast to her friends that Mark spoke French almost like a native.

"Your accent is getting better, *mon cher,*" she said. "How would you like to come to Paris for a while soon?"

The small face became animated. "And see the Eiffel Tower and the Bateau-Mouche?"

"And the Champs Elysées and the Louvre Museum and the Jardin de Tuilleries. It would be great fun, *mon petit chou*."

The boy became aware of Brian standing beside them motionless, his hands hanging limply at his sides. A look of apprehension crossed Mark's face. "Would Papa be coming too?"

"Would it matter so much if he didn't? After all, I leave you for weeks, sometimes months at a time and you don't seem to mind."

The blue eyes, huge in the diminutive face, pondered for a minute. "It's different." Aware that the explanation was insufficient, he tried to elaborate, floundered, then stopped. "It's just different," he muttered. The break in his voice betrayed the panic he was feeling.

Anger flooded Brian. Eva had started traveling when Mark was less than six months old. The boy had grown up looking to his father for the stability his mother couldn't give. If he allowed Eva to take Mark to live in Europe, he didn't know if his son could handle the transition. And he was certain that sooner or later Eva would turn Mark against him.

He thought of his own mother, something he rarely did. She had never remarried. Bitter and lonely, she had taken pleasure in fueling Brian's hurt and disappointment in his father. It wasn't until many years later that Brian had learned how many times she'd blocked his father's efforts to reach him. And by then it didn't matter. His hatred of his father was firmly entrenched.

He knelt beside Mark and put an arm around his shoulders. "You're not going anywhere without me."

"Promise?"

"Promise." He felt the rigid body relax. Above the curly black hair, Brian met Eva's triumphant gaze.

"Come on, Mark," she said, guiding the boy toward the door. "Time to get back to those French lessons. Besides, your father has to shave and dress because our guests will be going in to dinner in twenty minutes." She paused with her hand on the carved silver doorknob and looked back at him with the fatuous expression she reserved for their public appearances. "You won't be late, will you, dear?" Her tone made it a statement rather than a question.

"I won't be late," he said evenly. Her nod of satisfaction galled him. He turned his back to blot out the sight of her even before the door swung shut behind her.

Chapter 6

By six o'clock at Traynor Labs, even the stragglers were gone—Dora Watkins who had lingered to get out her overload of mail and Mildred Benson who had waited to extract the last bit of gossip to spice her empty life. In the early January darkness, Traynor rested, a sleeping stone and steel giant, disturbed only by the icicled branches that cracked against each other as the wind whipped the trees, and the occasional baying of a dog whose ears had picked up a stray sound outside the animal quarters.

Only the microbiology lab in the complex of research buildings nearby was wide awake, its lighted windows shining like beacons into the blackness around it. Inside, Valerie Traynor stood with Dr. Walter Chandler in front of the hutches that held the mice that were being used in the testing of the Tetra-2 antibiotic for Blasa Fever. The day had taken its toll on Valerie. She stood stoop-shouldered from an afternoon of bending over a microscope checking the potency of the Blasa Fever cultures that were being transferred to the clinic-turned-laboratory. Her hair had loosened from its coil and several blonde strands were straggling toward her face. There were hollows under her hazel eyes that hadn't been there in the morning, and her skin had the pale lackluster look of a shut-in.

Valerie was intent on watching Arby, one of the mice, struggle to break the hold she had on him. He squirmed in her clutch, his tiny feet pedaling the air furiously. She injected the Tetra-2 into his pink and white abdomen, then put him back into his cage and slid the door into place. The mouse ran round and round, his body temperature up, his spindly tail whipping the bars of his prison, his beady eyes wild with the need to keep moving.

"It's that damned hyperactivity," she said to Wally Chandler. "It cuts out as a side effect only when the Tetra-2 dosage is too low to do any good."

He shook his head in disagreement. "Look, we've tested for months on mice, rats, rabbits, dogs, and monkeys. The hyperactivity has only cropped up in mice and with continued use of the drug, it abates. Besides, as you know, it isn't uncommon for a side effect that has shown up in animal testing to be minimized in humans."

"Or maximized," she murmured, watching the mouse's fruitless rampage.

His warm gray eyes regarded her with infinite patience. "There you go with that pessimism again. I'll bet as a little girl you were a real downer."

There were times Valerie had to remind herself that they were the same age. There was a maturity, a certainty of outcome that never wavered in Wally. She wished she could say the same for herself. "I guess the urgency of this thing is getting to me, Wally. I just heard from the doctor I worked with in the children's camp in Maine. One of the kids who didn't show symptoms of the fever up there just came down with it now. That's six months later, Wally. Do you know what that can mean?"

"Everything and nothing. You know that as well as

I do. Come on, Val, settle down. We've got enough to handle without your getting skittish."

Wally Chandler was tall and lean with brown hair graying prematurely at the temples. His face was sensitive, his voice low and serious, his fingers slender as an artist's. Valerie had known for close to six months that he was in love with her. She hadn't encouraged him. But she hadn't discouraged him either, she thought, angry with herself for her ambivalent motives. She needed Wally, but she didn't want to confuse need with love and she wasn't about to make a commitment she might regret.

She poked at the bars of Arby's cage and tried to keep the concern from her voice. "Wally, starting Monday, we've got twenty volunteers coming into the hospital with Blasa Fever. A good percentage of those are convicts with a proven record of violence who'll be accompanied by armed guards. I don't expect them to be very lively coming in, but if a Tetra-2 injection creates a hyperactive, supercharged effect in one or all of them that the guards can't control, what do we do?"

He pursed his lips in careful thought. "Sedate, if possible. Run like hell if not."

Valerie laughed despite herself. It was at moments like this that she valued Wally most. His sense of humor had kept her buoyed through months of futile testing that had turned out to be not so futile after all. Wally never anticipated disaster but he was a rock beside her if it occurred. At thirty-three his record in scientific research, especially in hypertension, was an impressive one, with scores of papers in medical journals that had earned him the respect of doctors twice his age.

He charted the last dosage of Tetra-2 in the research

notebook that never left his side. "I guess it takes the threat of an epidemic like Blasa Fever to get the F.D.A. off their butts," he said resentfully. "We never would have gotten approval of the clinical testing otherwise."

"You're thinking of Beytril, aren't you?"

He nodded, the frustration evident in his dark eyes. Beytril was a "breakthrough" drug in hypertension that Wally had developed on his own, several years before he came to Traynor. It worked rapidly and dramatically to reduce elevated blood pressure with the added safety factor of not producing hypotension (below normal pressure). When Wally had applied for marketing sanction through Traynor Labs, the Food and Drug Administration had demanded that voluminous research data be included with it, which he had painstakingly done. To date, the F.D.A. had still not approved Beytril for marketing.

"In a way you can't blame the F.D.A., Wally."

"You mean because of what happened with Thalidomide?"

"No. Because of what the Thalidomide scandal led to."

Originally marketed in Europe, the sleeping pill Thalidomide had been pending approval before the F.D.A. in 1962, when evidence was made public that pregnant women who had been taking the pill were giving birth to deformed babies. Unfortunately, the Kefauver-Harris bill to require prolonged testing of new drugs was being considered in Congress at the same time, and public indignation at the Thalidomide scandal helped push it through.

"Think about it," Valerie said. "When's the last time you heard of a Congressional hearing to investigate the failure of the Food and Drug Administration to sanction a new drug? But there've been plenty in the last ten years to criticize approval of innovative breakthroughs. What you've got is Congressional pressure for negative action, and the F.D.A. has gotten the message."

"It's too bad the public hasn't."

Valerie nodded glumly. In the past few years, life-saving drugs had been developed in Europe and Asia that were being widely used throughout the world. They were unavailable to American patients because the massive research now demanded by the Food and Drug Administration before sanctioning a new product had caused a serious drug lag.

"The government is talking about a drug reform act," Wally said, "but I've got no faith in it." He stretched his arms upward and stifled a yawn.

Valerie put a sympathetic hand on his arm. "Wally, you've been here four nights in a row now and your eyes look like an advanced case of conjunctivitis. Why don't you go home and go to bed?"

He grinned. "I will if you come with me."

"Is that a dishonorable suggestion?"

"Would you listen to an honorable one?"

She was silent.

"It's still Brian Anslow, isn't it?"

"Not as much as it used to be," she murmured.

He didn't pursue it. He stripped off his lab coat and hung it on a wooden peg. "What about you?"

"I'll stay for a little while."

"All work and no play . . ." he chanted.

She laughed. "Look who's talking."

A few minutes later she heard the door close behind him. She sobered as she continued to watch the mouse, her thoughts returning to the twenty incoming volunteers. The patients would have to be monitored carefully following each injection of the Tetra-2, but especially after the first. Aside from the hyperactivity that had shown up in Arby, the dangers in the initial reaction could range from internal bleeding to convulsions to respiratory obstruction to death.

But then no drug was "safe," she consoled herself. She remembered her pharmacology professor who shocked his class by stating, "There is a drug on the market that when administered in low doses may cause indigestion and bleeding and in higher doses can result in changed blood chemistry, stupor, seizures, even death. The name of this scarce-used medication? *Aspirin*, my soon-to-be-colleagues. You see, despite its detrimental side effects, the benefits of aspirin far outweigh its risks. And that balance, or imbalance, if you will, of benefit to risk is one that the researcher must strive for over and over again in his search for new medications."

She crossed to the desk in the corner, gathered up some of the notes she'd made on Arby, and put them in the drawer. If you wanted to be philosophical, she thought, you could say that life itself was a balance of benefit to risk. No one had known that better than her father when he chose to stay at Traynor against his doctor's orders for the last month of his life. But Alex had his own set of rules when it came to making decisions. She remembered the day, eight years ago, when she'd had to decide whether to stay at the Labs and marry Brian or go to Africa to pursue her work on Blasa Fever. She'd come to Alex then, as she'd come to him so many times before. "Choices are hard to make," he'd told her, holding both her hands in his. "You have to look deep inside yourself, weigh all the possibilities, and come up with what is most important to you. The trick is in knowing yourself well."

There had been no coercion on Alex's part, yet she'd always felt he'd known what her decision would be. Why not, she thought with an edge of bitterness. It's what he'd raised her for.

"You're the son I always wanted," he'd told her when she graduated from medical school *cum laude*. The subtle slap at David had hurt her for him, but the pride she felt was enormous. Alex's rewards for success had been generous. Ample funds for whatever research project she chose. Recognition in medical journals for advances where the name Traynor carried as much weight as the achievement. Appointment as Medical Director of Traynor Labs immediately upon her return from overseas two years ago. But she had often thought that Alex viewed her as something of a neuter gender. Certainly, he never allowed for her as a woman.

She took her coat from the closet and stared at her face in the mirror on the door. "The trick is in knowing yourself," Alex had said. She thought she had known herself eight years ago. She knew herself a lot better now. If she had to make the choice all over again, she would have stayed here and married Brian, fought for her independence within the marriage, instead of running off to do her "thing" as he had accused. It would have meant compromise, something neither of them was good at then, and maybe it wouldn't have worked out. But at least they would have tried.

She remembered the day she'd received the letter from her father telling her of Brian's marriage to Eva. She had been working on Blasa Fever in a field hospital in Tanganyika with a handsome young chemist who tested blood samples with her by day and urged her to go to bed with him at night. The letter had come as a terrible shock. Despite all they'd said to each other, she had believed that Brian's love for her was strong enough to withstand their separation and that he'd be waiting for her when she got home. The belief had been a lifeline for her. Sometimes, lying lonely in her tent at night, she had relived the moments they had been together in Bethesda so vividly that she was able to recall every nuance of their lovemaking as if it were flashing on a screen before her.

The night she got the letter, she took the young chemist to her cot with its gray slab of mattress under the tightly woven mosquito netting and allowed him to make love to her. So great was his elation that he scarcely noticed her passivity, but he did ask afterward if she always cried when she made love, or if it was only this time with him.

She had stayed on in Africa after that, much longer than she had intended. When she received word that Eva had borne Brian a son, a part of her was torn with jealousy; the greater part rejoiced for them. Time, distance, and her absorption in her work helped to heal the wound Brian had dealt her. In the four years she lived in Africa, there was nothing ever in her father's communications to suggest that Brian and Eva weren't the ideal married couple. She came home totally unprepared for what she found.

She remembered that it was evening and close to Christmas. The living room with its heavy drapes, overstuffed furniture, and priceless antiques hadn't changed. Most of the family were gathered near the star-topped tree that had come to life every year in the same corner for as long as she could recall.

Her father was the first to greet her. Even in his own home he was perfectly turned out in a shirt and tie, dark trousers and a velvet collared smoking jacket. "The house hasn't been the same without you," he said, enfolding her in his arms.

"Speak for yourself, Dad," David said at his elbow,

jealousy warring with pleasure at seeing her. "Good to see you, Val," he added quickly. "Claire and Melody couldn't make it, but they send regards."

Alex's look said plainer than words what he thought of his son's wife. Over his shoulder, Val saw Eva appraising her weary face and travel-rumpled clothes and knew she hadn't come off well. More beautiful than ever in a beige silk pants suit that showed off her shapely curves, Eva stood near the mahogany baby grand where a small boy plunked discordantly on the keys. Brian was nowhere to be seen.

Eva put her fingers over the child's. "Come and meet your Aunt Val."

"I don't want to." The boy's jaw set in a stubborn mold reminiscent of his father's.

Pain knifed through Val. He should have been mine, she thought, then was appalled at her treachery.

Angry at being challenged, Eva yanked the boy from the piano stool.

"I don't want to!" he screamed. He pulled from her grasp and ran to Brian who had just walked into the room. He clasped his father's thigh and buried his curly head against it.

Brian knelt beside him. "Leave him alone, Eva."

She shot him a furious glance, but he wasn't aware of it. Over the child's head, he was staring at Val as if there were no one else in the room.

A jumble of emotions assaulted Val. They were as fierce and primitive as the bush country she'd just left. He was unhappy. It was written all over him. And she was glad. He didn't belong with Eva. He never had. His eyes met hers and she knew he felt the same. Nothing had changed between them. Nothing!

Eva came to stand beside him. One slender hand curled possessively inside the crook of his elbow as he straightened up. The other came to rest on her son's head. She smiled in malicious enjoyment. "Welcome home, Val," she said.

In the years that followed, Val often wondered why Brian had chosen Eva. Her sister was bright and attractive, irresistible when she wanted to be, but her values were contrary to everything Brian believed in. Then it had come to her. Brian hadn't chosen Eva. It was the other way around.

Once, when she and Eva were children, a cousin from Paris had sent them gifts—a chemistry set for Valerie and a beautiful doll for Eva. Eva had cried for half a day, insisting that she had no interest in the doll. It was a chemistry set she had wanted all along, but the better gifts always went to Valerie because she was older and considered smarter. Tired of the tears and feeling guilty without understanding why, Valerie had finally exchanged gifts with her. A week later, Valerie had accidentally found the chemistry set in the garbage can, unused, smashed beyond repair. When questioned, Eva claimed the set had disappeared and she knew nothing about it, but Valerie had known she was lying.

A surge of hatred washed over her. Nothing had really changed since then, Valerie thought. Eva had to have what her sister wanted. And when she got it, she sought to destroy it.

Only Brian wasn't an inanimate object with no defenses. Because of Mark, he was doing nothing to remedy the situation, but it couldn't go on forever. Sooner or later he would battle Eva for the right to a better life for himself. The question was, would Valerie be there waiting?

When she'd first come home the only thing that had kept her from having an affair with Brian was the knowledge that it would have been too tawdry and painful for her to sneak a few hours with him, then send him back to her sister for the rest of the time. But each day she had seen him her desire had grown and her resistance had weakened until she was sure she would end up doing just that.

In the eight months since Wally Chandler had joined the firm, a subtle change had taken place in her feelings. Valerie had never been willing to settle for anything less than what she had had with Brian. It had filled every part of her being and made her feel more of a woman than she'd ever felt in her life. But lately she'd begun to wonder if there wasn't another kind of fulfillment besides the one she sought with Brian.

Wally's lifestyle more closely paralleled her own. Unlike Brian, he didn't worship the power structure and the almighty dollar. Wally understood the desire she and her father had to better humanity. Brian tolerated it. She knew he had agreed to the Blasa Fever project only because it was good business policy and it galled her. And though now he accepted that her work was important to her, he could never share it with her in the way Wally could.

Was it that her desire for Brian was lessening? she wondered. Or her feelings for Wally growing? Or both?

She pulled off her lab coat, walked to Arby's cage and took a long last look at the mouse. He was still on his hyperactive treadmill, the sound of his claws beating a fierce tattoo on the bottom of the cage.

"If it's any comfort to you," she whispered to him softly, "you're not the only one going round in circles."

Chapter 7

After almost sideswiping Brian Anslow's car, Dennie Redmond reached Manhattan safely that evening only because the heavy traffic and icy roads forced him to slow the Chevy down to a crawl. His mind was in a turmoil. His boss, David Traynor, had returned from lunch that afternoon like a crusader on a religious mission.

"Dennie, I have to talk to you," he'd said in that schoolteacher's voice that always put Dennie on the defensive.

He'd drawn Dennie into his office, a spacious double-windowed room, lavishly furnished. It had dark red carpeting, a carved walnut desk, and a glass bar adjoining the large steel safe against the far wall.

"Would you like a drink?" Traynor asked, waving him to a chair. Dennie had felt himself warm with pleasure. His immediate superior, who was on vacation, had been offered a drink many times from this bar, but this was the first time for him.

"Scotch," he said. "On the rocks," he added with a flourish. He sat down. From past experience he knew that David Traynor liked to have an employee sit while he remained standing. Dennie supposed it made David feel superior in some way he didn't understand, like his wanting to be called "Mr. Traynor" even though they were only a few years apart. But his was not to question why. His boss was a Traynor, and as such entitled to whatever fetishes he chose to have.

David Traynor handed him the drink, waited until he took a sip, then put a hand on his shoulder. "Dennie, it seems we have a narcotics thief on the premises. I've been sure of it for a while." He jammed his hands into the pockets of his tweed trousers and began to pace the floor. "Now, I'm not about to call in the Drug Enforcement Administration and face a manufacturing shutdown when I know it's something we can handle ourselves."

"We can?" Dennie echoed faintly.

"You're damned right we can. You see we have an edge now. Whoever is stealing that morphine doesn't know we've found out about it. He or she is bound to try it again and this time we'll be prepared. All we have to do is keep alert and be in the right place at the right time."

He paused in his pacing and his boyish face took on an earnest cast. "I'm counting on you, Dennie. So much so, that I'm making that five thousand dollar raise you asked for contingent on our flushing the son-of-a-bitch out. That ought to give you the incentive you need."

"But, Mr. Traynor . . ."

The telephone had rung then and Traynor had signaled that the discussion was at an end.

Dennie raced the motor of the Chevy now in frustration. It wasn't fair, he seethed. He had more than earned that increase. It was his job to see that the machines and vats were kept in working order and that the proper flow of raw materials into the plant coincided with the production schedule of the particular drug for which they were intended. Not once in the past six months had a single piece of machinery idled in disrepair, nor had he ever neglected to have the apparatus checked when a run was finished to see that no residue was left over that could contaminate the next batch of pills or powders. The man who had been in charge of that before him hadn't been half as diligent, he knew. Maybe David Traynor had forgotten about the contamination scandal that had rocked the industry in 1965, but Dennie hadn't.

In August of '65, Traynor Laboratories had manufactured a diuretic named Thiazone in tablet form which reduced high blood pressure by removing salt (and water) from the body. Before that, the drug that had been made on the same machines was a digitalis-like substance taken by heart patients to stabilize irregular heart beats. Through improper cleaning, a residue of the digitalis-like substance remained in the chemical processing equipment and was carried over into the diuretic.

For people with high blood pressure having some heart disorders, digitalis in the diuretic they are taking may cause heart irregularity, or even death. By November of 1965, doctors who had prescribed Thiazone to their patients were shocked to find that many of them who did not have heart fibrillations were suddenly developing them. An investigation by the Food and Drug Administration disclosed the contamination at Traynor and an immediate recall of Thiazone was put into effect.

The cost of the recall was half a million dollars. But as Dennie knew, no recall could ever be measured in money alone. The damage to Traynor's reputation, the fear of patients to use the drug again, the lawsuits that followed, and the deaths that occurred were nightmare enough to make Dennie check those machines after each run as if his life was at stake.

But David Traynor didn't realize his worth. He treated Dennie like a lackey, sending him to pick up visitors at the train station and using him as a chauffeur to drive him around when his Caddy broke down. It had been different when Paul Haversham was head of manufacturing. *There* was a man who knew how to delegate responsibility and reward those who could carry it out.

He braked at the corner of Second Avenue and waited for the light to change. He'd never make it without that raise, he thought. His mother's doctor bills had doubled in the last few months. She was seventy-six years old. It wasn't unnatural for her "condition" to deteriorate, but Dennie knew that wasn't the reason for the extra bills.

Dennie had been a change-of-life baby. His mother had doted on him from the minute he was born, yet lacked the patience at forty-five to bring up her first child. Dennie never remembered doing anything right for her. His father, a misplaced insurance salesman who couldn't coerce a prospective client into putting a signature to a premium, had died when Dennie was five, leaving the two of them with little more than an insurance policy to take care of Dennie's tuition at New York University. His mother had managed all the rest as a dressmaker, "taking her eyes out at night working over a broken-down sewing machine that had ruined her back for life." She had exacted her pound of flesh for that ten times over.

Through the years, Dennie had resigned himself to the fact that he would never live as other men did. His mother's need for him dominated every facet of his existence. From the time he was able to make a living, she had become "ill." She went to the doctor at least twice a week now. Between the visits and the medication and the diathermy treatments, the bills mounted steadily. Her list of complaints was varied. High blood pressure, "touch of" phlebitis, hardening of the arteries . . . It took Dennie a while to realize that the intensity of her complaining rose in direct ratio to the amount of time he spent with her, and as his social life, never great at best, dwindled to nothing, his feeling of obligation toward her became laced with a resentment that bordered on hatred.

Lately, that resentment was tempered with guilt, because Dennie had taken to staying away nights. He had found a secret life for himself, one his mother would never approve of, and despite the sudden astronomical rise in her doctor bills, he intended to hold onto it.

It had started several months back, when he'd made friends with a twenty-year-old mailboy named Sid Draper at Traynor Labs. Sid was an orphan, completely ambitionless, a high school drop-out whose reading matter consisted, almost solely, of comic books. What drew Dennie to him was the freedom he boasted and his tremendous capacity for enjoyment.

On a Saturday night in June, Sid had taken him to the Helicopter Club, a discothèque on East Fiftieth Street, where he knew the performer. Dennie had never seen anything like it. The dimly lit room was lined in purple suede and filled with satin-clad couples dancing to the accompaniment of flashing lights and blasting music. A large silver hoop was suspended from the ceiling by invisible wires. It crackled and shot sparks as a girl in a white sequined bra and bikini jerked backward and forward, her pelvis rotating in practiced gyrations for maximal effect.

To Dennie, whose main contact with girls had been church dances and blind dates with eligible candidates for marriage, Angela Borden was the most exciting thing he'd ever seen. She was dark-haired and long-legged with thighs a shade too heavy for perfection, but magnificent breasts. Her expression was detached, her glossy red mouth slightly open, her huge eyes fixed on the spinning ball of light that bathed her moving body in the changing hues of the spectrum. For just a second as he sat down, she took her heavily mascaraed glance from the light and smiled at him, a knowing, inviting smile. Dennie's eyes bulged. A part of him felt like leaving. A part of him was fascinated. He had walked into Hell and found sin a headier brew than respectability. He smiled back shyly. During the break when Sid asked him if he wanted to meet Angela, he accepted willingly.

That had been six months ago, Dennie thought, and his life hadn't been the same since. He flicked his windshield wipers on. A light snow had begun to fall and visibility was poor. It was funny about Sid Draper, he mused. He'd joined the Army in September without a hint in advance to anyone. The last Dennie had heard, he was stationed at a base in South Carolina, hoping to go overseas any minute.

Dennie squinted up at the street signs and turned right on Fiftieth Street. He checked his watch. Almost six thirty. The timing was perfect. He'd meet Angie at the Club and take her for dinner at Beefsteak Charlie's before she went on. He never watched Angie perform. Despite the fact that she'd told him a dozen times that she wasn't even aware of the men who looked at her, he couldn't stand to see it. Angie was special. And she belonged to him. When he had her in his arms in the small apartment he kept for her in Soho he could believe that. And it was necessary that he did.

He pulled his car into a lot around the corner from the Helicopter Club. He pushed the door open and kept his eyes off the semi-nude photo of a coy-looking Angie on the billboard in the entryway. The club was hushed and dim with a few diehard early birds hunched over their stools drinking and staring into space.

The bartender greeted him just inside. "Angie ain't here," he said. "She called in sick."

"What's wrong with her?"

The bartender glanced at him contemptuously. "You know what's wrong with Angie same as I do."

He ran from the Club and hurried around the corner, unmindful of the snow that wet his face and trickled down the back of his neck. Despite the traffic, he drove down to Soho in record time.

The four-story building was one of two residential dwellings on the block with a fire escape scaling the front. It was sandwiched between a modern apartment complex and an industrial plant, and had a faint light burning in the musty entryway. Dennie pelted up the steps.

Angie's apartment was on the top floor. Dennie used his key at the door. The one room the landlord insisted on calling an efficiency was dark.

"Angie," he called, the fright apparent in his voice.

There was only silence.

"Angie, answer me."

"Here," she said faintly. "On the couch."

He turned on a lamp and she flinched. She was huddled on the couch in a thin flowered robe, her shapely body shaking as if fevered, her long dark hair half covering her face, her ashen skin slicked over with sweat.

He crouched near her and took her in his arms. His voice was anguished. "Angie, you promised."

She pressed her body close to his. "I know. I tried, Dennie." She sought comfort, not passion, but Dennie's reaction was immediate. It had been that way from the first time he'd held her.

He pulled a handkerchief from his pocket and dabbed at the droplets of perspiration beading her hairline. "Maybe if I would have been with you last night. But I couldn't, Angie. My mother was sick."

"It's not your fault." A spasm shook her. She sensed his withdrawal and hid her head against his chest. "Just this time," she whispered. "Help me, Dennie . . . like I helped you."

Her words took him back to the first time he'd made love to her. Only it had really been the other way around. He had never slept with a girl before he met Angie. It was something he hadn't confided to anyone, not even Sid Draper. At thirty-one it had made him laughable. Worse. It had made him afraid. What should have come naturally became a self-conscious effort that could end only in ridicule and rejection. It was easier not to try. In one ecstatic night, Angie had dispelled all that. She'd made light of his awkwardness and congratulated him on his prowess. For the first time in his life, Dennie had felt like a man. But he'd paid for that privilege. God how he'd paid!

She moaned and doubled over. He drew the half-empty vial of morphine from his jacket pocket, but held it from her clutching fingers. "Angie, you have to understand. I can't bring you any more of it. They found out at the plant and all hell broke loose." He waited for the words to sink in. From past experience he knew she comprehended very little when her need was this great.

"Over a couple of bottles of morphine?" She was breathing hard and the words came out choppy.

"It isn't only that. There's a big shipment coming in a few weeks. It's worth millions and they're worried someone will try to steal it."

She licked her chapped lips. Even now Dennie

thought her beautiful, her eyes huge and black, her mouth puckered like a doll's with small white teeth that pushed forward slightly and a smooth olive skin that was a reflection of her Italian heritage. "I only need it for this time, Dennie. I'll kick it after today for sure."

A few months ago he might have believed her. Now he knew better. "What if you can't?"

"Then my brother will take care of me."

"I didn't even know you had a brother."

She nodded. "Niko's been in South America. On business." She gasped and reached for the vial. "Dennie, *please* . . ."

He handed her the morphine, helped her up, and turned away. He couldn't stand to watch her shoot up and she knew it. Seconds later he heard the bathroom door close. He hung his coat in the closet and went about straightening the room. It was small, with a stove, sink, and refrigerator against one wall, a convertible couch against the other and a table flanked by two chairs in the middle. When the couch was opened into a bed, there was scarcely room to move around.

He pulled the shades down at the window, stepping gingerly to avoid Angie's plants. There were too many of them for so small a space, but they were Angie's "pets" and she cared for them as if they were children. He crossed to a near-empty refrigerator. Angie's horoscope was taped to the door. He opened it and helped himself to some milk. He was feeling light-headed. But it wasn't from hunger. It was from relief.

For months now he'd walked in fear at Traynor Labs, knowing that what he'd done would be discovered at any instant. The moments he'd spent in David Traynor's office today, where he'd been given the responsibility for finding the thief, would have been laughable if they hadn't been so hellish for him.

The three morphine substitutions had been absurdly simple. He'd replaced a vial of liquid morphine with an exact replica filled with water on the packaging line in the split second between the time the vial was filled and sealed, and the instant it was labeled. Each time, he had slunk away, sure it would be found out by Quality Control inspectors before it ever reached the shipping department, waiting to hear the shout that would proclaim him a thief, knowing that exposure would mean not only the loss of his job, but a black-listing of his name throughout the drug industry so he could never work within it again. He didn't allow his mind to dwell on what it would do to his mother.

That the substitutions hadn't been brought to light until today had been a miracle. That his employers still had no idea who'd done it and might never find out was a reprieve he had prayed for, but never expected to get. He drank his milk with gusto. It was all over for him now. The anticipation of discovery, the awful shame of exposure, the dreaded need for repetition . . . All over. And he hadn't lost Angie as he'd feared. He made a silent vow never to allow himself to be caught in that sort of bind again.

Chapter 8

On Monday at two fifteen, Brian mapped out the final questions he would raise at the meeting which had been called to discuss the feasibility of acquiring a pre-clinically tested foreign drug for relief of daytime tension.

If the new tranquilizer bore out those claims in the clinical testing, it would be a real moneymaker, Brian thought. He checked his watch. The meeting would start in five minutes. He gathered up his folders and was about to leave, when Dora Watkins buzzed through on the telephone.

He picked it up. "Yes?"

"The Chief of Police just stopped by at Mildred Benson's desk. He wanted to know if you had a few minutes to see him. I explained that you were leaving to . . ."

"Never mind that. Tell him to come up."

"But, Mr. Anslow, the staff meeting."

"Delay it, Dora. Tell them I'm not back from lunch yet or that I'm on a long distance call from Washington. You'll think of something." He hung up.

It was at times like this he knew he disconcerted Dora most. She preferred everything regimented and predictable as it had been under Alex, but he couldn't always keep it that way for her. A warm feeling of anticipation came over him as he thought of Roy Pen-

zinger, the town's burly, crew-cut Chief of Police.
They had been friends for over nine years now, ever
since Brian had helped him foil a hold-up by a fifteen-
year-old in the town's only liquor store on a rainy
night in July of '69.

Brian remembered it as if it had happened yesterday. Roy hadn't been Chief then. He was thirty-five
years old and had spent most of his life in the Midwest.
He had requested duty in New York after his wife
died of leukemia.

The night had been a steamy one—hot and humid
and drizzling with a fog rolling in that was causing
uncertain visibility. Eva was pregnant. Faced with another of her interminable parties, Brian used the excuse of working late with the promise to join her later.
After leaving the office at eight, he stopped off at the
local drugstore to buy a pack of cigarettes before heading home.

Traynor Labs was in the town of Clayville, halfway
between Huntington and Wantagh. Many of its inhab-
itants were employed by the Labs. It was a trim,
sleepy town, seemingly unaware of its access to one
of the greatest cities in the world. Its main street was
quiet. The Clayville Cinema had broken half an hour
before and all but a few stragglers were already inside
for the new showing. Only a handful of shoppers
combed the aisles of the glass-faced A&P next to the
liquor store up the block. The acne-pimpled clerk in
the drugstore, already counting the bills to balance the
register for the following day, smiled gratefully when
Brian produced the exact change for the cigarettes,
then locked the door behind him as he left.

Outside, the air had the clammy feeling of a tepid
sauna bath. Brian opened his collar and yanked his tie
downward. He started across the street to where his
car was parked, then halted as a police car, sirens

screaming, careened around the corner up the block and lurched to a halt in front of the liquor store. Before the policeman could get out, the door of the liquor store burst open and a thin boy in blue jeans and torn tee shirt backed out. He clutched a white paper bag in one hand and waved a gun wildly at the few startled onlookers who had just come from the nearby A&P.

At sight of the police car, the boy began to run down the block toward the drugstore. He ran with a curious loping gait, as if he'd sustained an injury to one leg. His face was knotted in desperation, his eyes darted back and forth seeking some side street he could duck into, but there was none.

Brian instinctively moved back onto the curb as the officer gave chase. The teenager was no more than ten feet from him when the policeman's command of "Stop or I'll shoot!" echoed through the nearly silent street.

The boy stiffened at the command and turned halfway around. The drugstore's neon sign accentuated the pallor of his face, the new-grown fuzz on his cheeks. Uncertainty flickered across his immature features. For a moment they were suspended in time like the image on a photo. Then the boy's gun hand moved a fraction.

"Don't try it, son," the policeman grated. The voice was firm, but there was a pleading quality in it. He was broad shouldered and stocky, his blue eyes narrowed to slits.

The boy's body was tense as a coiled spring. Brian could almost read his thoughts. He was scared to shoot, but he wouldn't give up. He was going to run. And he would die for it. Reluctant as the cop was, he would have no choice.

Crouching low, Brian circled behind the youngster then dropped to a hand and knee position. The boy turned to run, let out a yell, and jackknifed face forward over Brian's bent back. He fell with a thud, the gun sliding from his hand to land a few feet away. The policeman was on top of him before he could make a move to get it.

It took a few minutes for the boy to be read his rights. He was led away to a second police car that had arrived on the scene. The small crowd that had gathered quickly dispersed, and Brian was left alone with the arresting officer.

"Damn fool kid," the policeman muttered to himself, wiping the sweatband of his cap with a red bandana handkerchief. "You die soon enough in this world. No sense pushing it." He spoke in a flat drawl that took Brian back a lot of years. His thick hair was cropped and lemon-colored. His broad face held the sunburn and early furrows of a dedicated outdoorsman.

He clapped the cap back on his head and eyed Brian as if taking his measure. "That was a fancy hijink you pulled off out there, bucko." He pointed to the scar over Brian's eye. "Learn it in the war?"

Brian shook his head. "I played football at Northwestern."

He squinted up at Brian. "In Evanston?" Brian nodded. "I used to fish not far from there."

Brian grinned. "For bass on the south side of Lowery Lake."

A slow smile lit the weatherbeaten face. He put out a hand. "Name's Roy Penzinger. How'd you like to go fishin' with me some Sunday out at Montauk Point?"

"I'd like that fine." He clasped the outstretched palm. "I'm Brian Anslow."

The smile was withdrawn with the hand. "You the

same Anslow that's married to old man . . . to Alex Traynor's daughter?''

Brian nodded. Thre was silence for a moment. ''Want to take that invitation back?'' Brian challenged.

Penzinger stuffed the bandana into his pocket and fixed Brian with a clear blue glance. ''I never take anything back. Like I said, I'll call you some Sunday.''

And he had.

Through the years, Brian and his son had spent many a summer day at the small waterfront cottage Roy rented in Montauk, where the fish were plentiful and the option in dress was bathing trunks or shorts. The friendship was one Eva had never approved of. ''Befriending a policeman is like being intimate with a servant,'' she warned. ''It undermines their usefulness when you need them.'' But for Brian, and especially for Mark, who was surrounded daily by Eva's jaded, hothouse friends, Roy Penzinger was like a gust of fresh wind after the staleness of a torpor.

A knock sounded at the door.

''Come in.'' Brian came around the desk to greet Roy as he strode in.

The police chief's wide face was wreathed in smiles. He had grown heavier in six years and had taken to wearing suspenders. The bulge above his waistline testified to his love of Heinekens, and there were sprinklings of gray in the cropped blond hair. He clapped an arm around Brian's shoulders and thumped him soundly on the back. ''Son of a gun, if Alex didn't finally use his noggin and name you president. How's David taking it?''

''How would you expect?''

Penzinger nodded. He had always been sympathetic

toward David. Penzinger believed that Alexander Traynor had never let his son grow up. "You have to let a kid make his own decisions, even if he falls on his face," Roy contended. "Otherwise he comes up like a weak-kneed pansy, never sure whether he can fend for himself or not." Though the chief had no children of his own he was good with them. The P.A.L. in Clayville was the best on the Island, thanks to the enthusiasm of its leader.

The police chief looked around the office now, pursing his lips approvingly. "I was in Chicago visiting my mother for a few days. Otherwise I would have been here sooner."

"I know. I called your office."

His eyes lit on the bar then swung questioningly toward Brian. "The finest there is," Brian informed him. "Including a six-pack of Heineken's on ice. What'll it be?"

He shook his head reluctantly. "Not when I'm on duty."

"I thought this was a social visit."

"Not exactly." He unbuttoned the stiff collar of his blue shirt and grimaced. Clothes were a necessary evil to Roy and he found the uniform of his office particularly constricting. He sat down in a wing chair opposite Brian's desk and spread his palms on his brawny thighs. "I got a call this morning from the warden at Arbor Prison in upstate New York. He told me that sixteen sick prisoners were on their way to Traynor Labs in two ambulances and he thought I would want to know about it. They should be here around six tonight and they'll be under armed guard. What the hell is going on here, Brian?"

Brian hesitated. In the last few days Traynor's clinic had been moved to the second floor to make room for the lab in its former quarters. Under Val's supervision, the small hospital attached to it had been cleaned and painted, new mattresses supplied and its equipment brought up to date. Brian knew there was speculation among the employees. The rumor going around was that some kind of pollen vaccine was going to be tested. It was a rumor Brian hadn't bothered to deny.

"Those prisoners are coming in for an important testing program," he told the police chief. "They'll be isolated in the old Traynor hospital at the far end of the first floor. I'm sorry, Roy, but that's all I can tell you about it."

Penzinger's concern was written on his face. "Look, Brian, if you want to keep this under wraps, I respect your reasons for it. But the warden gave me a rundown on some of those birds. That's not a petty larceny crew you're bringing in. Those sons-of-bitches are guilty of murder and manslaughter with a few rape and felony raps to round out the bunch. Now you may be confident that the guards can handle them, but I'm not. I'd like to send over a few of my men to . . ."

"I can't let you do that, Roy."

"Why not?"

"Because the less fanfare on this the better. If the police chief or some of his men are seen near the hospital, anyone looking in would suspect that something dangerous was going on and that's the last thing we want them to think."

"You sound as if I don't have any choice on this?"

"You do if you want to tangle with the government."

"It's that way?"

Brian nodded. "It's that way."

He took a long moment before answering. "I'm not happy with it, bucko."

"I know."

Penzinger rose and Brian walked him to the door.
"You'll call if you need me?" the chief asked.

Brian held up two fingers. "Scout's honor."

Brian waited until after the budget meeting to phone
Eva and tell her he would be late. He didn't relish the
call. Since the party there had been an uneasy truce
between them, punctuated by cold silences and sarcastic backbiting.

Eva answered the phone herself. "Hello." Her
voice held the breathless quality he remembered from
their first meeting.

Taken aback, Brian didn't answer for a moment.
Then, "You sound as if your entry in the Derby just
placed first."

"What do you want, Brian?" she asked coolly.

"I'm going to be late tonight. I know you planned
to be out, but I hate to see Mark eat alone."

"I changed my mind about going out, so you
needn't worry."

"Well . . . thanks." He felt the moment called for
something more. Some small talk or attempt at civility,
but he had gotten out of the habit. "I shouldn't be
long," he managed.

"Be as long as you like," she said.

He hung up hoping nothing would puncture the balloon that was buoying her up. He hadn't heard her
sound this amenable in years.

Eva had good reason to be amenable. She was about
to pull off a "coup" in both her work and her personal
life that would give her a great deal of satisfaction.
Her triumph was the result of persistence in the face
of what had seemed insurmountable odds.

The day had begun like any other Monday, with
two hours of tennis at the Murray Hill Racquet Club,

followed by a massage to loosen the kinks, then a cold lobster platter at Lutèce. Eva believed that the time and expense required for a beauty regimen of rigorous exercise and selective dieting were negligible compared to the results.

Feeling refreshed and wearing one of the custom tailored suits she reserved for business hours, she took a taxi to the Traynor Museum. She had a two o'clock appointment with a publicist to decide which artifacts to highlight in an article that would appear in the July issue of *Medical Magazine*. The magazine had asked for a photo of her to run alongside the story. She made a mental note to ask her secretary to find the one she'd taken in the off-the-shoulder gown Halston had created for her.

Located in a small brownstone on East 84th Street, the Traynor Museum was three stories high with beamed ceilings, leaded windows, and plushy carpeted floors. Aside from Eva's office on the second floor, the museum was filled with memorabilia that was either mounted to a wall, displayed on velvet clad round tables, or, as in the case of the massive French copper alembic (vat) used in the extraction of quinine at the turn of the century, bolted to the floor and roped off.

The variety and extent of the memorabilia were a source of satisfaction to Eva. Some had been particularly hard to come by, she thought as she strode toward the broad spiral stairway that led to her office. She stopped for a second at a display of a yellowed bill issued by Dr. Crawford W. Long in the nineteenth century.

Long, a country physician in Georgia, was the first to use ether for surgery. He had given it by inhalation before excising a neck tumor in 1842. Assuming that the urban physicians already knew the technique, he hadn't bothered to have it published. The only record of the procedure was the bill that Eva had found in his granddaughter's musty attic. Sneezing and covered with cobwebs, she had managed, after three days of grubbing, to extricate the bill from an ancient bunch of office files and hold it up to the single light bulb that hung from the ceiling by a wire. It had read: "Operation $2.00; ether 25 cents."

Mounted on the wall next to Long's bill was another successful conquest: a letter from Sigmund Freud to a doctor friend, endorsing the use of cocaine. Cocaine, originally isolated from the South American coca plant in 1858, had seen only limited medical use until the 1880s. Freud took cocaine for three years, described it as "a magical drug" and recommended it, particularly as an antidote to fatigue. He turned against the drug when a friend became addicted after taking it for chronic pain.

Eva's secretary, a broad-shouldered woman in her mid-forties, met her at the top of the stairs. Her face was wreathed in smiles.

"The publicist will be late," she announced.

"Is that a reason to smile?" Eva snapped. She hated people who weren't punctual.

"I'm not smiling about that. Dr. Semmel just called."

Eva felt her heart leap. "Dr. Kirby Semmel?"

She nodded. "He wants you to call him right back."

Eva raced for her office and placed the call. The line was busy. She hung the phone up and chafed at the delas. If Semmel's call meant what she thought it did, Eva would be able to include a piece of memorabilia in *Medical Magazine* that would startle the world. Of equal value was the fact that it would give her closer access to Dr. Kirby Semmel himself. At the moment she would have been hard put to say which was more important to her.

In her search for the medical memorabilia to supply the Traynor Museum, Eva had only one noteworthy competitor—the Eli Lilly Company in Indianapolis. Lilly's museum was larger and better known, its funding seemingly inexhaustible. For years, Eva had vied with them for the most interesting artifacts, using her influence and contacts, especially in Europe, to circumvent Lilly's vast buying power. One rare plum had eluded them both.

In the late eighteen hundreds, a Hungarian doctor named Ignaz Phillip Semmelweiss discovered that childbed fever in hospitals was contagious. The fever was killing eighteen mothers out of every hundred and Semmelweiss contended that the doctors themselves were spreading the disease by not properly cleaning their hands or instruments. He was called a fool. But he maintained his stand and in 1860 published his classic work, "The Etiology, Concept and Prophylaxis of Childbirth Fever."

Opponents of his ideas attacked him fiercely. Emotionally battered and sunk in depression, Semmelweiss scourged the medical hierarchy of his time in a blistering thirty-page condemnation that came to be known as the Semmelweiss Indictment. After his death in 1865, fearing recriminations, his family advised that Semmelweiss had destroyed the document, then later refuted it. Through the years, all efforts to locate the Indictment had proved fruitless.

A month ago, Eva had received a call from a friend in Vienna—the Countess Maria Von Ellstein. The Countess had just come from visiting her elderly mother in a posh nursing home at the foot of the Austrian Alps. Her mother's new roommate, a talkative crone in her mid-eighties, confided to the Countess that she was in reality the great-granddaughter of Ignaz Semmelweiss. The Indictment was alive and well, safeguarded, she hoped, by her grandson, Kirby, an intern at some hospital in New York City who hadn't sent her even a postcard in over two years.

After eight phone calls, Eva had finally located Dr. Kirby Semmel, as he called himself. He was an intern at Bellevue Hospital who intended to specialize in research.

Kirby Semmel had been curt on the phone when he learned of her goal. He had the Indictment, but he had no intention of parting with it. However, he had lost track of his grandmother and wanted her address. It had taken much ingenuity and the withholding of his grandmother's whereabouts to coax the good doctor into a meeting at the Traynor Museum.

When he had entered her office three weeks ago, Eva had all to do to retain her composure. Dr. Kirby Semmel was the handsomest man she had ever seen. He couldn't have been more than twenty-eight. He had a lean chiseled face, a cap of curly black hair and the innocent, stubborn eyes of the confirmed idealist. He wore gray slacks, a pepper and salt tweed jacket with worn suede elbow patches, and carried his five foot eleven frame with the casualness of the intellectual whose physical attributes have little meaning for him.

Eva hastily removed her horn-rimmed glasses. The whole setting was against her, she thought. In keeping with the reverence accorded the rare artifacts in its possession, the Traynor Museum exuded a sense of austerity. Her office was no exception. The paneled walls, the lofty arched windows, the floor to ceiling glass bookcases and herself, in a pin-striped business suit seated behind a carved desk in a high-backed chair. The feeling given off was one of solidity—and age—the last thing with which she wanted to impress this young god.

Kirby Semmel perched on the edge of a chair. His back was rigid. His thick dark brows met in a vee of resentment. "I might as well tell you right off. I've never had any use for this kind of thing, Mrs. Anslow."

"I don't understand."

He drummed his fingers on one strongly curved kneecap. "I'm talking of blackmail, Mrs. Anslow. I made it perfectly clear that I have no intention of parting with the Semmelweiss Indictment, yet you forced me to come here to get my grandmother's address. It's a waste of time for both of us. If my grandmother didn't hop from one nursing home to another, my mail would have reached her and you wouldn't have been able to play this little game today."

There was a formality, a primness to his speech that made him seem older. It comforted Eva somehow. She lowered her eyelids and allowed a silence to fall between them.

"Don't you have anything to say?" His tone was less certain, the offensive stance wavering.

"Only that you're perfectly right." She pulled a piece of notepaper from the leather corner of her desk blotter and handed it to him. It held his grandmother's address in the nursing home. "I do thank you for coming up," she said softly.

He folded the paper carefully and slipped it into his jacket pocket. His eyes, chips of ice when he came in, had lost their frosty look. He saw her as a woman now, one who had capitulated at his onslaught and could, therefore, be forgiven her transgression. He held out a hand in a gesture of contrition. "Look, I understood what you were trying to tell me on the phone. About owing something to posterity and giving

the world a chance to see the injustice done Ignaz
Semmelweiss by his peers. It's a situation that's paralleled in medical history all the time. Believe me, I'd
give you the document if I could.''

"You mean you don't have it?"

"No, I don't mean that." He sat back in the chair
and raked a hand through the thick dark curls. "How
can I explain this to you?" he murmured with a boyish
naiveté she found charming. "You see, unlike a lot of
men my age, my heritage means a great deal to me.
When my mother died, I spent a lot of time in Europe
with my grandmother. She taught me a respect, almost
a reverence for Ignaz Semmelweiss—*grandpère* as
she called him. I read everything I could about him.
He became my invisible mentor, my ideal. I've patterned my life after him. I feel that he wrote the Indictment in a time of despair. He never meant for
other eyes to see it or he would have released it himself. In a sense, to expose it would be to break a trust.
I would do it only if I had to."

Eva discounted everything but the last sentence. It
implied a possibility, but she felt it wise not to press
the issue.

"You do understand, don't you, Mrs. Anslow?"

She wished he would stop stressing the *Mrs*. "Of
course I do. But I also know that things have a way
of changing. Would you mind if I called you from time
to time?"

He shrugged. "If you want to."

After he left, Eva sat a long time in the high-backed
chair. Except for Brian she couldn't remember when
she had last been so attracted to a man. There was a
breathless feeling inside her like a runner gearing up
for a race. Contrary to what her friends thought, Eva
indulged in very few affairs. They never lasted long.
For Eva the enjoyment was in the conquest, not the

act. The more reluctant the quarry, the more exciting the game. Her desire for Kirby Semmel at this moment was exquisite. She saw in him a dual challenge. He held a document she had sworn to possess and for all the attention he had shown her, she could have been one of her inanimate museum pieces.

She took out a compact mirror and examined her face carefully. The bi-weekly facials at the Red Door had been worth the time and effort. There wasn't a wrinkle, not even a line to mar the perfection of her skin. It was as young and dewy as it had been when she was nineteen. She unpinned her hair, shook her head and watched it swirl around her cheeks like a waterfall. She smiled in satisfaction. Whoever said never to mix business with pleasure was shortsighted. In this case, it was the only way to go.

For three weeks after that she had called Kirby Semmel. He was polite but adamant. The Semmelweiss Indictment was not for sale and his schedule left him no time for socializing. The last two times she had tried to reach him, she had left a message, but he hadn't even called back . . . until now.

She picked up the phone and dialed his number again. This time it rang through.

"Dr. Semmel, this is Eva Anslow," she said softly. "You called me?"

"Yes. I've got to see you."

She controlled her elation. "Can you make it Friday at two?"

"I'll manage." His voice sounded strained. "What about my apartment? It isn't much, but it's close to the hospital and it's private."

"Why don't you give me the address," she purred.

Chapter 9

Hands jammed into the pockets of his coat for warmth, Brian paced impatiently outside the small hospital attached to Traynor Labs. Where the hell were those volunteers? he chafed. The four soldiers from South Carolina weren't due until later, but the prisoners from Arbor State had been expected by six. It was already seven and the snow that had started in flurries two hours ago was coming down hard now.

He re-checked the Traynor buildings. As far as the eye could see, except for the lab and hospital, there wasn't a light on anywhere. During the week, Brian had sent a memo to all departments prohibiting employees from working late that evening due to an after hours check of the heating system. He knew he was kidding himself. That even if he could keep the arrival of the prisoners under cover for now, it was only a matter of time before the employees found out about the Blasa Fever testing. But it was that time he was counting on. If Valerie could confirm the effectiveness of the Tetra-2 antibiotic his people might see themselves as heroes instead of potential victims.

The door of the hospital opened and Valerie stepped outside. Her blonde hair was hidden beneath the hood of her tweed cape. Her face in shadow showed lines of fatigue. She had driven herself this past week, working twelve to fifteen hours a day to ready the lab and hospital for tonight.

Brian realized how much he'd missed seeing her. Always before there'd been a moment for coffee, a conversation snatched in a hallway, a meeting of the eyes across a conference table. Crumbs for a man who was starving. But it had eased him. Given him the hope that their being together again wasn't as far-fetched as it seemed when he spent those intolerably long nights in the emptiness of his home.

She squinted into the blackness. "Any sign of them?"

"No."

"Damn. I was counting on getting the prisoners settled before that army truck arrives from South Carolina. It'll be bedlam if they all get here at once."

"Where's Wally?"

"Inside, giving it a final check."

His reaction to her choice of Wally as assistant was mixed. A gut feeling had urged him to say no when she told him. The hospital would be a proving ground for them, with all the heightened sensations and rawness of emotion that a battlefield evoked. The thought of Wally Chandler with her every minute of the day and night seared him with a jealousy he found hard to bear. Yet he couldn't have picked a better protector for her if he'd tried.

It was Wally who had cleared the testing plan with him. Besides Val and the technician who would assist Wally in the lab, there would be male nurses attending the volunteers, two by day, one by night. The lab and hospital would be governed by isolation techniques. Semi-cooked food was to be brought in on trays then heated in the microwave oven that had been purchased for the hospital.

There were two entrances to the lab and hospital areas. The one that harbored the hidden steel door led through the plant to the lab. A Traynor security guard would be stationed in the small hallway outside the lab to see that no one from the plant entered. The only other entrance was from outside the hospital. One of the prison guards arriving with the ambulances from upstate would be stationed at that door.

At Brian's insistence (despite Valerie's protests), a third guard would be retained inside the hospital itself so that the prisoners would be watched at all times. The guards, who would alternate shifts, would be quartered in Clayville for the duration of the testing.

In the sterile area of the lab itself, where the danger of transmission was at its greatest, every precaution would be taken to protect the highly contagious Blasa Fever cultures that were being processed for the Tetra-2 antibiotic.

It was a good plan. Like all plans its drawbacks lay in the unforeseen. Even as he okayed it, Brian kept thinking of his football coach at Northwestern. He was a shrewd-faced hard-drinking son-of-a-bitch who qualified every football play he mapped out for his team with the words, "Barring accident . . ."

Valerie's voice brought him back to the present. Her tension was evident in the curtness of her tone. "Brian, when the prisoners get here, I'd rather you left. I want no one exposed to the disease that isn't a part of the program."

"You keep your contagion to yourself, don't you?" he said lightly.

"Don't be sarcastic." His eyes showed surprise, then concern. She moved closer to him. "I'm sorry. I'm uptight."

"We all are."

A snowflake caught on her eyelash. She blinked to shake it loose. It held, melted, and ran down her face like a lone tear.

Brian wiped her cheek with his palm, then let his fingers linger. He pulled her hood closer round her face and shielded her from the snow with his body. "Remember the night it stormed in Bethesda and the roof of your apartment sprang two leaks over the bed?"

She nodded. "We couldn't plug the leaks and we couldn't find the landlord."

"You forgot something."

"What?"

"We couldn't move the bed either."

A smile tipped the corner of her mouth. "So we slept in a sleeping bag underneath it."

"And a loose coil from the flea-bitten box spring kept jabbing me in the ass all night long."

Her face grew still. "That was a long time ago, Brian."

"I love you, Val. I always will."

She turned her head and the overhanging floodlight caught the sparkle of tears in her eyes. "Do you, Brian?"

"How can you ask that?"

"Because I wonder sometimes if that love would still be there if we put it to the test of daily living. Even if Eva wasn't blocking it, could we make it, Brian? We're not at all alike, except that we both want to achieve. But our reasons for achieving are different. I want to help people. You want to help Brian Anslow. It isn't something you can change. It's part of you, like that chauvinistic streak that prefers my work to come second to your needs. It scares me. I couldn't stand to be chained and I don't know if you could give me the freedom I require to move ahead. Forgive me for hypothesizing, Brian, but I'm a scientist.''

He gripped her shoulders. ''You're also a woman, and all the hypothesizing in the world isn't going to help you when you lie in that cold bed of yours in Hicksville and dream of . . .'' He broke off as a rumble sounded in the near distance.

The prison ambulances were upon them in minutes. They were military double deckers devoid of insignia, with huge wheels that smashed the snow into powder and ground to a halt a few feet from the hospital. A muscular guard in uniform and cap leaped from the passenger seat of one of the ambulances and ran the few feet to where they were standing.

''Didn't mean to be late,'' he said, addressing Brian, ''but the snow upstate is piled high to Jesus and we had to plow our way through till we hit the open road.''

Brian pointed to Valerie. ''This is Doctor Traynor.''

The guard's eyes widened. He was broad-faced and swarthy skinned with a nose that looked as if it had been broken in a fight. Yet, there was something gentlemanly about him. He tipped his cap. ''Beg pardon, ma'am. Nobody told me you were a woman . . . not that I have anything against women doctors, but . . .''

''Brian, would you please tell Wally the ambulances are here,'' she interrupted. She raced toward the truck and the guard followed. ''Look, Mr. . . .''

''Santos. Charley Santos.'' He was having a hard time keeping up with her.

''There are sick men in those ambulances, Mr. Santos. Let's get them inside.''

''Yes, ma'am . . . uh, doctor.''

Wally Chandler and the attendants came running from the hospital. Each ambulance was manned by a prison infirmary orderly and a guard. Charley Santos unbuckled his gun holster as the orderlies unlocked the back doors. The prisoners were stacked eight to an ambulance on canvas stretcher beds. They were unshaven and exhausted. A few spoke, a few moaned incoherently as they were jarred from their moorings by the orderlies. For the most part, they were quiet.

The snow hampered their progress. It took half an hour to move the sixteen prisoners into the reception area of the hospital. Brian watched until the last one was inside then signaled to Valerie that he was leaving. She stood near the hospital door looking like a Madonna at a Christmas play. Her hood had slipped off and her blonde hair was a halo of snow. She waved to him briefly, her face preoccupied, her tilted hazel eyes alive with the challenge that lay before her. She disappeared inside.

Brian felt an emptiness inside him. It was her world in there, he thought. One he had signed for and delivered to her. One he could never enter. He'd had the same feeling when he'd seen her off on the plane to Africa eight years ago. He pulled up his coat collar, thrust his hands deep into his pockets, and walked slowly toward the parking lot.

In the reception room of the hospital, Valerie gave orders to prepare the prisoners for entrance into the quarantined ward. With the help of the male attendants and prison orderlies, specimens for the lab were collected and the patients were changed into hospital pajamas. In preparation for the first test dose of Tetra-2, which would be given after the army men arrived, an intravenous solution of D5W (Dextrose 5% in sterile water for injection) was initiated before the prisoners were transported into the quarantined ward. The prison orderlies left shortly afterward.

Accompanied by Charley Santos, who had reluctantly donned the sterile cap, mask, and gown required, Valerie walked beside a handsome young black being carried on a stretcher to his bed. A sudden tug at her skirt caused her to look down at him. His head was tossing; his eyes were feverish, red-rimmed. They pleaded wordlessly with her. He tried to say something, but his voice failed. With an effort, he clutched a handful of her uniform and pulled her closer to him.

Charley Santos was upon him immediately. He seemed to have styled himself her protector, something she would have to talk to him about in the future.

"Leave him alone, Mr. Santos," she said sharply.

She knelt beside the young black. "What is it you're trying to tell me?"

His skin was cocoa-colored, his features aquiline, delicate. "Please," he whispered hoarsely. "Please . . ."

"Please what?"

"Put me near Doc . . ." His voice trailed off and he closed his eyes.

"I'm the doctor, and I'll never be far from you."

"Begging your pardon, ma'am, I don't think that's what he means," Charley Santos said.

"Suppose you tell me what he means."

"He's saying that he wants to be near 'Doc' Golden."

He pointed to a prisoner just being carried into the ward. He was about fifty-five with short gray hair and sunken yellowed cheeks. His eyes were pale blue and slightly unfocused. They were fixed on an attendant setting up an I.V. for a prisoner who showed signs of dehydration. He winced as the attendant tried for the patient's vein and missed twice.

"Is he a doctor?" She saw with relief that the attendant had located the vein.

Santos's face hardened. "He's a con. Manslaughter. Fifteen years. What's the difference what he is?"

"I don't go for that kind of talk in here, Mr. Santos. I ask you again, is he a doctor?"

He shrugged. "I'm not sure. He's got some kind of medical training. If the cons don't trust the prison doctors, and some of them don't, they go to him. That's how Freddie got to know him."

"Freddie?"

He jerked his head toward the cocoa-colored boy on the stretcher by her side. "Freddie Bishop. He's nineteen. Not a bad kid. Convicted of felony theft. He's only got a couple of years to go."

"What was his ailment?"

"Beg pardon?"

"What did he go to 'Doc' Golden for?"

"I wouldn't know."

He was lying, she thought. The prison brotherhood was clannish and she was an outsider.

The boy plucked her skirt again. She took his limp hand and squeezed reassuringly. "All right, Freddie. I'll see to it you're placed near your friend."

She looked up as a commotion started across the room. A powerfully built black shoved Wally and an attendant aside and staggered off the stretcher onto his bed. He resisted their efforts to get him into it and sat on its edge flexing his huge fists and shaking his head to clear it. His face had a pushed-in flat look and the lobe of his ear was missing.

"He's hallucinating," Valerie murmured. "Who is he, Mr. Santos?"

"A bad one, ma'am. Name's Jefferson Montgomery. He was one of the top heavyweight contenders in the U.S. until he wasted his manager for bettin' against him on a fight then gettin' him to take a dive. He's a troublemaker on the inside too." He moved from her side and edged toward the prisoner.

"Goin' six rounds on this one," Montgomery muttered. "Ain't gonna let no punchy white boy whip mah ass." Wally Chandler tried to calm him. He shook the doctor off. Shadowboxed the air. "Got a jaw lak iron. Aim for the kidneys, that's where." Sweat glistened on his forehead, trickled down his temple. His eyes, bloodshot and feverish, focused on the guard, recognized him. His voice grew shrill. "Gotta win this one, Charley."

"Sure you do."

Valerie started toward the boxer, but Santos motioned for her to stop.

"Sure you got to win," he said to Montgomery. "But you gotta rest before the fight. Keep your energy up. You know that." He didn't try to touch the prisoner. He moved his hospital gown aside and unbuttoned his holster.

Montgomery blinked. He was breathing hard. "You're right, Charley. Gotta rest. Don't feel too good, Charley." He allowed Wally Chandler to help him into bed, then lay there staring at the ceiling.

Charley Santos was a mixed blessing, Val decided. He was overprotective of her and unforgiving of his charges, but the prisoners trusted him and that was invaluable.

In the next few hours, wearing a green cap and gown, a mask and disposable gloves, Valerie examined the patients. In order to prevent cross-contamination between prisoners, when she finished with a patient, she removed the gown, then hung it on a hook next to the bed and discarded the gloves she wore. With her cap and mask still on, she washed her hands at the nearby sink thoroughly before going to the next prisoner. Then she donned the new gown on the hook at his bedside and a fresh pair of disposable gloves, before proceeding.

The prisoners were all in the early stages of the disease (a prerequisite for the testing) but their symptoms weren't totally alike. Most were weak and feverish. Some had the gastrointestinal cramping that set in after the fourth day. Only one was ambulatory. A few had the jaundiced look Valerie had seen on the children at the camp in Maine. Until now the doctors had treated symptomatically, with emphasis on dehydration and sufficient nutrition. It had been a holding action, at best, with little hope held out for recovery.

Charley Santos introduced her to the patients. He had a cheering word for each man followed by a biting indictment in an aside to Valerie that always urged the same thing. Caution. In exasperation, Valerie finally pulled him into a corner of the room.

"Mr. Santos. I know you're trying to be helpful, but I think you should understand that I'm a grown woman, and a doctor, fully capable of taking care of myself and these patients."

Santos's swarthy face broke into a sheepish smile. He was a big man, broad in the shoulders but flabby in the waist. He used his hands to illustrate. They were powerful with reddened knuckles and chapped skin through which purple veins protruded. "Look . . . Dr. Traynor. I wasn't trying to put you down. Honest. I think you're great. But there's a kind of savvy you ain't got 'cause you ain't lived with these cons on the inside like I have. You look at 'em and you bleed for 'em and you say to yourself they're just like you or me. But they're not. They're animals, Doc. You got to humor them on the one hand and watch they don't bite on the other."

Valerie flushed in anger. "Mr. Santos, I don't agree with your philosophy. I can't ask that you change it, but I do insist that these men be treated with dignity while they are here. They're patients and they're volunteers and as such they deserve every consideration. Do I make myself clear?"

He nodded, eyes downcast.

She could see by his expression that her words had made no impression, but her anger had. Whatever their differences, Charley Santos wanted to help her.

She relented somewhat. "Mr. Santos, I can finish these rounds alone. Freddie Bishop is asking for something. Why don't you go see what it is."

He nodded eagerly and crossed the room.

"My hat's off to you, doc," a booming voice said in the bed behind her. "You bloody well did Charley Santos in without lifting even a pinky finger. If I had my strength back, I'd be pleased to shake your hand, I would."

She turned around. By the hulk of him under the covers, the man attached to the cockney accent was at least six foot and well over two hundred pounds. His curly hair was dark and straggly. A heavy stubble of beard covered his yellowed cheeks, but his gray eyes were clear and alert.

"You sound as if you don't like Charley Santos."

"Begging your pardon, ma'am, I hate the bastard's guts."

Valerie donned the gown and gloves at his bedside. "Let's see, your name is . . ."

"Alfie Brockwell. 'Brock' to my friends."

Valerie nodded. She remembered his name from the prison charts that had been left at the nurse's station. His was one of the few cases she had come across with no indication of fever. The others she'd seen at the camp in Maine had shown signs of subnormal temperatures due to hemorrhage in the heat regulatory center of the midbrain. They had never recovered.

You know, doc," he said, "we ain't all animals like Charley says. There are those among us that are sorry for what we did and are glad to be paying our dues." His lips twisted wryly. "Of course some dues take a long time to pay. I myself was partial to servicing banks. Helping them to rid themselves of an over-abundance of funds you might say . . ."

"Mr. Brockwell, I'm not here to judge. I'm here to treat. But I'm sure those dues you talk about are being paid in part by your volunteering for this project. There are a lot of people depending on what the outcome will be. Are you in pain, Mr. Brockwell?"

His face had grown taut. He was breathing hard. "It's in my belly," he gasped. "It comes on something fierce."

She checked his pulse. "Did you have diarrhea in the prison hospital?"

He shook his head. "Just this bloody cramping."

His pulse was normal. She squeezed the hand clutching the blanket. "We can give you something for that."

He nodded gratefully. She gave instructions to an attendant and moved on to the next patient.

Meticulously scrubbed, the hospital gave off a sharp odor of disinfectant. It was flanked on one side by the reception dock, on the other by the laboratory. A narrow door at the rear of the ward led to the attendant's station, a supply room, a small kitchen, and a make-shift bedroom. The bedroom was equipped with two cots on which sheets and pillows had been uncere-moniously dumped when time ran short. Thanks to modern sterilization techniques, Val and Wally could come and go as they chose. It wasn't mandatory for either of them to sleep at the hospital, but from past experience, Val knew it would be preferable.

Along with Wally, she worked against the clock, bent on getting the patients comfortable before the army truck arrived with the soldiers from South Carolina.

At nine thirty, Wally pulled her into the kitchen. A fresh pot of coffee perked on the burner and the aroma filled the room.

She yanked off her mask and cap. "Wally, this is no time for a break."

He poured the coffee. "It may be the only time you get."

She sighed. "You're probably right. Did you get over to Microbiology today?"

"I was there this morning. Everything is status quo."

Valerie knew that it was crucial to follow up on the animal studies. Any change in the condition or behavior of the animals due to the cumulative effects of the Tetra-2 could be an indication of what might follow in the human patients once the drug was administered.

"Is Arby still showing signs of hyperactivity?"

"I'm afraid so." He gestured toward the coffee she cradled between her hands. "That's for drinking, not holding."

The liquid scalded her tongue. "God, this tastes good."

A strand of blonde hair fell forward and lapped at the cup. He tucked it back. "You need a keeper, lady."

"I've got one, or hadn't you noticed?"

He grinned. "Charley Santos."

She nodded. "I'll never forgive Brian for hat one."

He leaned over and kissed her lightly.

"What was that for?"

"I haven't figured it out yet. But I like the taste of it."

She smiled up at him. Wally was good for her. She felt safe with him. Unthreatened. With Wally the pattern of her life would be shaped to her measure. And she *was* attracted to him. Not in the same breathless reach-out-and-touch way she felt toward Brian. It was quieter. Bound up with respect and sharing and mutual goals. Damn! Why did she always get the feeling she was trying to talk herself into something when she contemplated marriage to Wally?

And why contemplate marriage at all? She wasn't unhappy the way she lived. And she wasn't sexually starved as Brian chose to believe. She had taken lovers before and she could again, if she chose to.

She sipped her coffee, aware that Wally's gaze probed her features like sensitive fingertips seeking nuances of response. The answer was simple. Almost absurd for a "liberated" woman. She had old-fashioned ideals. She believed in marriage, the family structure, and dual parenthood. And she wanted a child before it was too late.

"You okay?" he asked, caught by the brooding look on her face.

"Fine. I saw you checking the Bishop boy out there. You took a long time with him."

He nodded. "He's one I wanted to talk to you about. Bishop is showing signs of a rash."

She frowned. The clinical features of Blasa Fever included an incubation period of from four to sixteen days. The patient's first symptoms were fever, weakness, apathy, and pain in the gastrointestinal area, sometimes accompanied by jaundice and diarrhea. The rash usually appeared in the secondary stage.

"I wanted to know if you've seen an early onset of it before."

She shook her head. "Never that I know of, but this disease has taken so many twists and turns that nothing surprises me anymore."

The attendant, Tod Preston, popped his head into the doorway. He was about thirty years old, short and heavyset with the muscular build of a wrestler. "The army truck is here. Thought you'd like to know."

The four patients in the truck seemed in better shape than the prisoners had been. Special dispensation had been received from army authorities to mingle them with the convicts inside. One, a colonel named Langsley Darwin, issued orders as if he was mounting a military campaign. Despite his weakness, he sat upright on the stretcher, knuckles showing white where he gripped its edge for support. He was a tall man in his forties with sparse red hair and the rigid code of the "regular army" man stamped all over him. Unlike the others, his uniform was buttoned to the collar. It sported silver eagles on the shoulders and was covered with an impressive array of ribbons across the chest.

"Come on, boy," he admonished a soldier being carried into the reception dock beside him. "Straighten up there. You want these Yankees to think we got no backbone?" He spoke with a heavy Southern accent.

The boy's hands clutched at his stomach. He eyes mirrored his pain. Valerie pushed him back on the stretcher as he attempted to obey. "There's no need for a show here, colonel," she said. "These men are sick and entitled to act like it."

His face froze. "Listen, Miss . . .".

"Doctor."

"All right, doctor. I don't appreciate your interfering. I'm in charge of these men and I . . ."

"Not here, colonel. In this hospital I'm in charge and everyone in it will be treated the same way."

He clamped his thin lips together and looked away

from her. His face ashen with the effort, he held his upright stance until he reached the door of the hospital, then collapsed as he was carried across the threshold.

The last soldier to be taken from the truck looked oddly familiar to Valerie. He was about twenty-one with tight sandy curls, a snub nose, and a weak but engaging grin. "Don't you know me, Dr. Traynor?" He was short of breath and the words came out in choppy phrases.

"Should I?"

"You sure should. I brought your mail to you twice a day for two years before I enlisted in this man's army. I'm Sid Draper." He held up his dog tags as if the statement needed corroboration.

"Of course. I'm sorry you're back here under these circumstances, Sid."

"So am I. I was supposed to take off for Hawaii in two weeks." He stared at the snow and the bleak terrain around him in disgust. "Jeez, Hawaii . . . the sun, the girls . . . I had it all planned." He clutched her arm as a spasm hit him. "Dr. Traynor, do me a favor, will you. Tell Dennie Redmond I'm here."

"First chance I get."

"Thanks." He settled back and closed his eyes.

By midnight the army men had been processed, given the intravenous solution of D5W, assigned beds, and checked over. The ward was quiet. Wally had gone into the lab to prepare the dosage of Tetra-2 that would be administered shortly. Charley Santos was nodding in a chair, waiting for the other guard to replace him on the next shift. Worn out by the fever and the long day, most of the patients slept. A few like Doc Golden and Alfie Brockwell, who couldn't, were content to lie in their beds watching the others.

Valerie was just returning from the nurses' station

where she had checked on the updated hospital charts, paying special attention to the urine output on Freddie Bishop. In some of the cases she'd seen at the camp, uremic poisoning had followed shortly after the onset of the rash, and she wanted to be alert for any signs of it.

A noise from one of the beds caught her attention. Colonel Darwin had awakened suddenly and was sitting up in bed, sniffing the air like a bird dog after prey. He clutched his pajama front tightly together and looked around in an attempt to get his bearings. To facilitate nursing care, while he slept, his bed had been moved to a different part of the room. Freddie Bishop was now on one side of him, Jefferson Montgomery on the other.

"It stinks in here," Darwin said clearly. He plastered the few strands of his red hair to his wet scalp with a sweep of his hand. His eyes were bloodshot, feverish.

Tod Preston bent to hush him, but the colonel pushed him aside. "It's the kind of stink we don't tolerate in the South." His accent was deliberately broad.

Freddie Bishop slept on, but Jefferson Montgomery came awake. He turned his head toward Langsley Darwin, not sure of what he'd heard. He lay very still, fists clenched, liquid black eyes trained on the army man, waiting.

The attendant looked uncertain. Near her Valerie heard the scrape of Charley Santos's chair.

Darwin pulled fretfully at the neckline of his pajamas. His temperature had climbed to 104 degrees. The freckles on his pale scalp glistened like new minted pennies. His head swung back and forth between the prisoners on either side of him. He pinched his nose between thumb and forefinger in exaggerated disdain.

The attendant whispered something to him, then retreated as Darwin took a swipe at him.

Montgomery moved before Santos could. He slid from his bed and, crouching low, put his face close to the army colonel's. "What you sayin', man?" he whispered softly. His feet against the tiles were bare and cold. His oversize pajamas flapped loosely at his sides.

The colonel's feverish eyes gleamed recklessly. "I'm saying you're a . . ."

The word never crossed his lips. Montgomery's hand moved and Darwin's head jerked suddenly backward. A glint of silver caught Valerie's eye. She drew in her breath sharply. From somewhere, Jefferson Montgomery had produced a knife. He pressed its edge against the colonel's throat. There were stirrings in the room. Men sat up in their beds, excited, anticipating.

Darwin's reddened eyes were wild with fear. "Say it now," the boxer taunted.

Charley Santos came up behind the convict. He placed the cold muzzle of his gun against the boxer's right temple. "Give me the knife, Montgomery. Or I'll blow you to hell."

"Thought you was my friend, Charley?"

Santos's face could have been carved in granite. "The knife, Montgomery!" His fingers tightened on the trigger.

Valerie never remembered moving. She did recall the "No!" that burst from her lips like an explosion. She found herself on the other side of the bed facing Jefferson Montgomery and Charley Santos. She ignored the guard.

"Listen to me, Mr. Montgomery." Her voice was tight, pleading. "Colonel Darwin here is a stupid man. It doesn't matter that he's an officer in the United

States Army. He's a prejudiced, stupid man. But I'm not interested in the colonel. I'm concerned with you. And with this testing project. Mr. Montgomery, you've done a brave and wonderful thing in volunteering to be tested for Blasa Fever. A lot of people, a lot of kids, are depending on you. If you don't surrender that knife to Charley Santos, you let them down. And you let me down. Because if Mr. Santos is forced to harm you, this whole program will probably fold because it will be judged too dangerous to go on with. Is that what you want?''

He was silent for a long moment. The hand that held the knife shook in an agony of indecision.

The colonel's eyes were closed. He was mouthing words in prayer. Beads of sweat bordered his upper lip. He gasped as he felt the knife withdrawn, clutched at his throat defensively.

Montgomery gave the knife to Santos and climbed into bed without a word.

Valerie pulled the covers up around him with shaking fingers. "Thank you, Mr. Montgomery."

Across the bed her gaze met that of Charley Santos. "Animals!" his eyes said. "You got to humor them on the one hand and watch they don't bite on the other."

Chapter 10

Paul Haversham returned from Mexico City late Wednesday night, feeling disgruntled. His concern about the "rejuvenator" offered by Laboratorios Ramirez for licensing had been proven correct. The product itself had possibilities, but the documentation was too poor to be of much value.

Sancho Ramirez, the owner, had tried to talk him into buying the drug at a lower price and researching it from scratch.

"Look at Gerovital H3," he had argued, "the prescription drug that's been legalized in your country now. Thousands have been running to Bucharest for it every year because it claims to slow down the aging process, improve memory, and revitalize sex. All it is, is a mixture of procaine and some other chemicals . . ."

"Procaine, that's similar to novocaine, isn't it?" Haversham had asked.

"Essentially. The Romanian government is making a fortune on it. They've put it out as an injection, a pill, a face cream, and a hair lotion. How can they go wrong? And what about the youth spas that are springing up all over the world to administer these concoctions? Take *La Prairie* in Switzerland that caters to the rich and famous like your Kirk Douglas, Marlene Dietrich, Gloria Swanson, and Greta Garbo. They claim that by taking the fresh cells from a fetal lamb a month before its estimated birth and injecting them immediately into a patient, they can revitalize those organs or glands that have run down.''

"Isn't there a place in Nassau . . .''

Ramirez nodded. "The Renaissance Revitalization Center. It specializes in the 'rejuvenation cocktail' that's supposed to improve memory, skin tone, and hair texture. It's made by placing a live chick embryo in a glass of carrot juice and swallowing it whole. If people are willing to go to those lengths to look and feel younger, think what my drug could bring in your market.''

He was missing the point, Haversham had thought. With the documentation so flimsy, the question was whether Ramirez's discovery would ever get to market under the current strict F.D.A. regulations and delays. Haversham decided to return immediately. The trip had been taken at a time when he felt it was imperative that he stay close to what was happening at Traynor Labs.

Before he had left for Mexico, he had succeeded in reaching Anshul-Bulden in West Germany. They had not taken the news of Brian Anslow's being named president lightly. They wanted to buy into a pharmaceutical company in the United States. They preferred Traynor Laboratories. But if they couldn't be given some reassurance that the sale would go through within the next year, they would seek elsewhere. Haversham had pleaded for enough time to bring them the proof that Traynor would be theirs. In the end, they had reluctantly agreed to give him two months.

Haversham spent most of Wednesday night pacing in his den. It was a custom-built den paneled in beveled walnut blocks. Gilt-framed oil paintings hung on three walls and seventeen feet of mirrored bar and bookcases covered the other. A Sarouk rug bordered all but one foot of the parqueted flooring. If nothing else, his wife had taste, he thought. Expensive taste. When he married the senator's daughter, an unspoken bargain had been sealed between them. She supplied the name, the "class" he sought. He supplied the money. Never a beauty, she aimed for style. Their house, on two and a half acres in Kings Point, had been photographed in *Town and Country* and right now she was a runner-up for the "ten best dressed" list.

He wondered what she would do if she knew how precarious her position was. A few months ago, on the strength of a "reliable" tip, he had bought $250,000 worth of Sayco Electronic stock, putting up a small percentage on margin. In the last two weeks the stock had dropped by twenty percent and the broker had called him for an additional fifty thousand dollars. Necessity had forced him to take a second mortgage on the house and even keeping up with the payments on her Mercedes was becoming a strain. There was one compensation, he thought cynically. Bernice's name was associated with half the charities in New York. It might prove a boon when she was forced to hold her own hand out.

He cursed Alexander Traynor for placing him in this position and knew it was a waste of emotion. His only hope for solvency and the control of Traynor Labs lay in that sale to Anshul-Bulden.

He came into the office Thursday morning looking haggard. His eyelids were reddened, his florid face puffy. The first thing he did was call Claire Traynor.

"Paul . . . you're back," she murmured in a sleepy voice. The Southern drawl distorted the words to "Pole . . . youah back."

"Sorry if I woke you. I'll speak to David later, but

I wanted to know if you had anything to tell me before I did.''

The whole time he'd been in Mexico, Haversham had thought of nothing but David's deliberate withholding of information on the morphine substitution. When David had been under his wing in manufacturing, the first thing he'd taught him was never to court the distrust of the Drug Enforcement Administration. If anything, the opposite. Go overboard to convince them of complete openness. For David to involve himself and the company in this kind of duplicity, the reason had to be a powerful one. Haversham would have given a lot to know what it was.

"Not much," Claire said. "David mentioned the morphine problem, but said he was taking care of it."

"What does he mean?"

She sounded irritated. "I don't know, Paul. That's all he would tell me for now. You have to understand there's only so much I can ask him each time." She paused. "There's something else I think you should know about. While you were gone, Brian had the clinic at the company moved to another floor. The old clinic has become a laboratory and there's some kind of testing going on in the hospital attached to it."

Haversham was skeptical. "That hospital hasn't been used in years."

"Well, it's being used now."

"Who's in charge of the testing?"

"Valerie. She's turned over all her work to her assistant and can't be reached except for emergencies."

"Do you know what's being tested?"

"Some kind of vaccine for hay fever."

"It doesn't make sense."

"That's what David said."

After he hung up, Haversham took the elevator to the manufacturing floor. Some of the employees were still straggling in. By a recent four to one vote, they had decided to start work at eight thirty and stop at four thirty, instead of the usual nine to five. For the local employees this was no hardship, but for those who traveled a distance, it was proving difficult. Haversham greeted those who called to him and strode toward the doorway that separated the lab and hospital from the plant. He stepped into the small hallway that led to the laboratory.

A security guard stood just inside. He wore the traditional navy trousers, light blue shirt and cap with the Traynor insignia on it. Haversham recognized most of the guards who had been with the company a number of years. This one was new.

"Sorry, sir," he said. "But you can't go any further." He was about forty, powerfully built, with a cleft in his broad jaw.

"Why not?"

"This area is in isolation."

"By whose orders?"

"Mr. Anslow's."

"Because of the pollen testing?"

"I wouldn't know, sir."

Haversham glanced beyond him. The guard's bulk blocked most of his view, but he was able to catch a glimpse of the lab through the glass cutout in the door. On shelves along the gleaming white tile walls, he could see small incubators, racks of test tubes and petri dishes, and in front of the workbench, the lab technician himself. He wore the sterile coat and mask normally used in experimentation with contagious disease, and there was something familiar about him.

Haversham left without another word. By the time he reached his office, he had come to several conclusions. One, that Valerie would never have taken a leave of absence from her job as Medical Director unless what was going on in that lab was of vital importance. Two, that there was no pollen vaccine he had ever heard of that required scrub gowns and isolation techniques in its testing procedures.

What intrigued him more than anything was the elaborate smokescreen that had been thrown up as camouflage. If there were people in that hospital being tested, where had they come from . . . and when? Nobody seemed to know anything about it. And why the phony story about the pollen testing?

He buzzed his secretary. "Thelma, could you come in here a minute?"

"Yes, Mr. Haversham."

She came in with a steno book in her hand, a thin, flat-chested "girl" in her early forties. She had a sallow complexion, straight brown hair, and the amber eyes of a faithful basset hound. She had been with Paul Haversham for nineteen years and felt certain that her star would rise with his when David became president.

She seated herself in the chair opposite his desk. Haversham came around the desk and perched on its edge near her chair. "Tell me, Thelma, is your brother Jimmy still working as a lab technician at the plant?"

"Yes, he is. He's in the new lab that's just been fixed up next to the hospital."

"What's he working on?"

"He didn't say."

He covered her hand with his. His voice held a solemn timbre that brought a flush to her colorless cheeks. "I want to know what's really going on in that lab, Thelma. Not the pollen vaccine story that's circulating. The truth. Do you think you can get it for me?"

"Is it important?"

"Very." He squeezed her hand.

The stain on her cheeks deepened. Paul Haversham had been her idol for almost twenty years. Masculine, glib-tongued, assertive, above all, self-sufficient. Thelma had known there were women in his life, besides his wife. She had also known she could never compete with them. She had wanted only to get closer to him, prove her value, make herself indispensable somehow. The opportunity had finally been afforded her.

"I'll get the information," she said.

By eleven o'clock, Haversham had all the facts he needed. It was even better than he had thought. That Brian could have knowingly placed himself in this vulnerable a position was hard to believe, but Haversham wasn't one to look a gift horse in the mouth.

He called the Chairman of the Board, Arthur Perrault, in his office at Bankers Trust and caught him just as he was leaving for lunch.

"I'm sorry to disturb you, Arthur, but I think there's something you should know."

"It sounds serious."

"It is. Anslow has authorized the testing of Blasa Fever in the old hospital attached to the plant. He's set up a lab not ten feet from the manufacturing area to culture the bug for use in making the antibiotic they're experimenting with. Now I don't have to tell you how contagious the disease is. Just pick up any newspaper and read it."

"I believe the newspapers have exaggerated the contagion, Paul."

"Arthur, I don't think you understand. Anslow has brought in a bunch of convicts under armed guard to serve as guinea pigs. He's keeping it all hush-hush, but when the employees find out what's going on . . ."

"Let's hope they don't."

Haversham was flabbergasted. "Is that all you have to say?"

"I'm afraid so. You see, I knew the Food and Drug Administration had approved the clinical testing of Tetra-2. Before he died, Alex told me about it. For Brian it was a question of reneging on a commitment with the government or going ahead and hoping Valerie came up with some answers before word got out of what is going on." His tone became somewhat cautious. As in his banking practices, Arthur Perrault was never one to go too far out on a limb for anyone. "Now, I'm not saying Brian made the right choice. I'm only setting forth the reason he did it."

"It isn't good enough, Arthur. It certainly doesn't justify exposing two thousand people to a killer disease without their being aware of the chances they're taking. I think the rest of the Board would agree with me."

"You may be right, Paul. At any rate, it's your privilege to poll the others. Naturally, I'll go along with whatever the majority wants."

"Naturally." He didn't bother to keep the sarcasm from his voice.

Haversham hung up and leaned back in his chair. His full lips curled in contempt as he thought of Arthur Perrault. He might have expected this kind of response from him. Perrault was a fence straddler, always careful to wind up on the winning side. Right now he was leaning toward Brian, because Alex's influence was still in effect. Yet a strong uproar could push Perrault the other way. Haversham was sure of it. The principle was the same as it was in politics. Line up enough power behind you and you could topple any administration.

He picked up the list of Board members and dialed

the next number down. It belonged to Ernie Bedlock, the company stockbroker.

"Ernie, I'm sorry to disturb you, but I think there's something you should know . . ."

At two o'clock that same afternoon, Claire Traynor tugged her brown suede boots on and belted her Swakara coat tight about her. If there was no traffic on the expressway, she could drive it to Chris Androtti's apartment in less than thirty minutes. He'd be mad as he always was when she was late, but he'd try to control it. Normally short-tempered, Chris had been very careful of her lately. He knew about her deal with Haversham. His attempts to find a backer for his theater group had failed and he wasn't about to threaten the goose who could lay the golden egg for him.

Claire never really minded his anger. It was the only time Chris allowed her to be aggressive in their lovemaking, a role she relished and he felt emasculated by, unless he could justify it by allowing her to "make up" with him.

What a pity Chris's sexual image of himself was tied up with who thrust and who parried, she thought. It would be so much more enjoyable if she could do what came naturally.

She checked herself in the full-length hall mirror, flipped her auburn hair back over her shoulders and crossed to the front door. The bell rang before she could open it.

"Never mind, Essie," she called as the maid's footsteps sounded from the kitchen. "I'll get it."

She opened the door. The man who stood outside was huge. He wore a gray gabardine raincoat, frayed at the lapels, with the middle button stretching to make it across the girth of his waistline. His face was round and fleshy. His eyes, intelligent but calculating, were half hidden beneath the folds of his lids. He doffed a battered brown felt hat and asked, "Is this the Traynor residence?" The voice was cultured, the tone high pitched. He must have seen the withdrawal in her glance. "I'm a friend of David Traynor's," he added.

"If it's my husband you want to see, he left here twenty minutes ago. You can reach him at Traynor Laboratories in about . . ."

He held up a hand with surprisingly slender fingers. "On the contrary, it's you I want to see, Mrs. Traynor. It *is* Mrs. Traynor, isn't it?"

"Yes, it is." His diction was good. He was obviously educated. Yet there was something repellent about the man, almost evil. "I'm on my way out now, Mr. . . ."

"Rankin. Asa Rankin."

The name rang a bell, but she couldn't place it.

"I won't take up too much of your time, Mrs. Traynor. I've got something to tell you I think you should hear."

She closed the door a trifle as he took a step forward. "I'm sorry, Mr. Rankin. This happens to be a very inconvenient time."

He twirled the felt hat in his hand, not in the least disconcerted. His cupid's bow lips were smiling; his eyes had grown cold. "Funny, those were almost the same words Alexander Traynor used when I first came to see him."

"You knew Alexander Traynor?"

"Knew is an all-encompassing word, Mrs. Traynor. Let's say we did business together."

Claire Traynor weighed the odds. Chris would be mad as hell if she didn't show, but there was something in the way this fat man had stressed the word *business* that convinced her it would be a mistake to turn him away. She opened the door wide. "Come in, Mr. Rankin."

He waddled into the front hallway then preceded her into the living room. "Would you excuse me a moment?" she murmured, then left to call Chris Androtti.

Rankin scarcely heard her go. His glance took in the pale antiqued furniture, the white Karastan rugs, the mirrored walls, the Mandarin ivory statuettes. A low whistle escaped him. He sank into the softness of the white velvet couch and fingered the crystal decanter on the glass table in front of him.

When Claire returned, she noticed that he had taken off the raincoat and helped himself to a drink from the bar. She seated herself in a chair opposite him then drew upright as she saw his eyes go over her in appreciation. She wore a blue knitted dress that clung to every line of her body.

"All right, Mr. Rankin," she said tersely. "What was it you wanted to see me about?"

"Well, I'm a newspaperman, Mrs. Traynor." He smiled ruefully, gesturing toward his rumpled suit. "A little down and out at the moment as you can see, but nevertheless . . ."

"Mr. Rankin, is this a trick to get an interview of some kind with me?"

He flung up a pudgy palm in protest. "No need to get huffy, Mrs. Traynor. I come here as a friend. Believe me I do."

"You said you knew my husband," she countered. He nodded.

"Through Traynor Labs?"

"No, ma'am. We go back a long time before that." He took a long sip of his drink. "You see, David and I were in Vietnam together and there's a story attached to it I'm sure you'll want to hear."

Twenty minutes later, Claire called Paul Haver-sham in his office. "Paul, I think you should come out here right away."

"Why?"

Her voice was guarded. "I can't explain over the phone. There's someone here with a lot to say about David. It would be better if you heard it first hand."

"I'll be right there."

When Haversham arrived, the maid took his coat. After a whispered conference in the hallway with Claire, she led him into the living room and introduced the two men.

Haversham's nostrils flared in distaste as he shook hands with the slovenly newspaperman. Always fastidious, the silver-haired executive was impeccably dressed in a worsted charcoal suit, a shirt of lighter gray hue and a maroon patterned tie. He seated himself in a white wing chair and regarded Asa Rankin with a cool stare.

"Mrs. Traynor says you have something to tell me."

He nodded. "As I was explaining to Mrs. Traynor, I'm from Ohio. I'm a newspaperman out there. A damned good newspaperman," he repeated, staring from one to the other belligerently. "When I have a paper to work on. Trouble is, the *Banbury Tribune* closed a year ago, and I've had a hell of a time locating since."

"Why is that, Mr. Rankin?"

He shrugged. "Lousy economy. There aren't that many jobs around." He lifted his empty glass toward Claire and gestured for a refill. Haversham's stare was beginning to disconcert him. "All right, Mr. Haversham. I have a failing. One that I'm afraid has earned me a reputation by now. I'm a gambler. A compulsive one. I'm not very selective about it either. Cards,

racetrack, crap tables. As long as the element of risk
is there, I gravitate toward it like a bee after honey.''

"And you lose?''

He nodded glumly. "And I lose. Right now, I'm
not only broke, I'm in debt. But I'm not a bad sort
really. I'm a family man, Mr. Haversham." He
reached into his jacket pocket and pulled out a flat
wallet. "I've a wife and two children back in Ohio,
sweetest kids you've ever . . .''

Haversham waved the pictures aside. "Tell me
about your friendship with David, Mr. Rankin."

He sank back on the couch and stretched his stubby
legs out in front of him. "I got to know David when
we were both in Vietnam. I had taken a pre-med
course in college before I chose journalism, so the
army trained me as a rehabilitation instructor. I was
in a hospital in Da Nang when they brought David in
with a smashed kneecap. A sniper's bullet had caught
him just below the patella and he was out of his mind
with pain.''

"David didn't tell me he was wounded," Haversham interrupted.

"I've seen the scar," Claire said. "But he would
never talk about it."

"If you let me go on, I'll explain why," Rankin
said. "David was operated on almost immediately.
The doctors were able to put the knee back in one
piece, but it took months for him to recuperate. The
pain during that time was so severe that he had to be
given high doses of morphine or Demerol to bear it.
Unfortunately, when the pain disappeared, David still
kept insisting on the shots."

"Did the doctors know that?" Claire asked.

"They knew. It's down on David's record out
there. They tried to wean him off the drugs, but it was
no go. At about that time, Johnson escalated the war

in 'Nam and the casualties started coming in thicker than flies on sticky paper. There was no more time for David. The doctors figured he was ready for rehabilitation anyway, so they took away most of the narcotics, handed him over to me and told me to 'get him on his feet.'" The trouble was that by then David was a confirmed junkie. Without the stuff, he would go into immediate withdrawal."

"So you supplied it to him," Haversham said.

Rankin gestured angrily. "Don't sound so God Almighty accusing. I've had my bellyful of civilians who played judge after 'Nam. You weren't there. You never saw this kid doubled over heaving his guts out, begging for one shot so he could straighten up and learn to walk again. Yes, I supplied it to him, and I'd do it again if I had to."

"At a price, no doubt."

Rankin half rose from his seat. Claire put a soothing hand on his arm. She poured some Scotch into his highball glass. He grunted his thanks. "Go on with your story, Mr. Rankin," she murmured.

He took a sip of the drink then continued. "David didn't remain a junkie. But he didn't kick it easy either. David and I were discharged on the same day. By then we had gotten real close. He told me he couldn't go back to New York the way he was. It would kill his father. He offered me money. Begged me to take him to some hotel room and stick with him while he went cold turkey. I told him he'd never make it."

"And he did?" Haversham asked.

"Not the first time," the fat man said grimly. "It took him two months, and I stuck with him in some hole of a hotel room in Vietnam with the stink of his sweat and vomit all around us and him clawing at me for relief till I could hardly stand the sound of his whining voice anymore. 'Asa,' he said afterward. 'No amount of money could pay for what you've done. I couldn't have licked it without you. If you ever need anything, come to me. I'll be there for you. I swear it.' We parted after that. I went to Ohio and he left for New York.''

He stared down into his glass and his face sagged into lines of discontent. ''I didn't see my *good friend* David for ten years after that. Things had gone well for me. I'd married, bought a house, gotten a good job. Then a year ago, I ran into a streak of bad luck. My paper folded and I lost heavily at the track. I managed for a while on freelance stuff, but unfortunately, one assignment took me to Vegas.'' He looked sheepish, then shrugged as if his failing were something that was out of his hands.

''And you gambled again,'' Haversham prompted.

He nodded. ''This time I tangled with the Syndicate, and that's not the outfit you hold out on. I owed them seven thousand and they wanted it right away. I didn't know what to do. I couldn't find a job. My savings were gone. I had already re-financed my house. And then I thought of David. 'If you ever need anything . . .' he'd said. So I came. I used my last fifty bucks and took a bus to New York.''

''I don't remember meeting you before this,'' Claire said.

''You didn't. For some reason, your husband wasn't too happy to see his old buddy. We conducted our 'business' in a bar in Clayville. David gave me the money but he made it pretty clear that he never wanted to see me again. 'This wipes the slate clean, Asa,' he said. 'Goodbye and good luck.' I walked away hurt and puzzled.''

Had he wanted to, Haversham could have clarified the situation for Rankin. David was undoubtedly scared that Rankin would reveal his addiction in Vietnam. It would have meant a confrontation with his father and the end of his future at Traynor or any other pharmaceutical house in the United States. For the first time Haversham understood why David hadn't reported the morphine substitution that Clary Robling had told him about. If Quality Control had called in the Drug Enforcement Administration, their probing might have uncovered David's addiction in Vietnam, and David himself might have been suspected of the theft. For a fleeting moment, it occurred to Haversham that David might still be on drugs, that he could indeed be the thief, then he discarded the thought. If it were so, David would never have been that open about the substitutions to Claire. Also, in David's position as head of manufacturing, he had the kind of access to narcotics that precluded petty theft of that sort. It was more the pattern of an underling with less resources.

Haversham became aware that Asa Rankin had begun talking again. Complaining of the heat, the fat man had undone the bulky red knit tie crowding his adam's apple, and opened his checkered shirt.

"When I left New York," he was saying in his high pitched voice, "I never expected to see David again. I paid off the seven thousand, vowed never to look at a crap table again, and took a temporary job as an advertising copywriter." He grimaced. "The job didn't last long and neither did the vow. Within seven months, I was back in the same fix."

"So you came East again," Haversham stated.

He nodded.

"What made you think David would give you more money?"

Rankin's smile was triumphant. "Because I had done my homework this time. I'd come across an article in a magazine concerning Drug Enforcement Administration rules for employment that explained why it was so necessary for David to keep his addiction a deep dark secret." His moon face sobered rapidly. "The trouble was David didn't seem to understand what was at stake. When I called, his secretary gave me a run-around and refused to put me through. I finally reached him on the phone one night at his home."

So that's why Rankin's name had sounded familiar, Claire thought. She remembered the call, only because David had snatched the phone out of her hand with a violent expression on his face totally uncharacteristic of him. He had taken the mouthpiece as far from her as the wire would stretch and spoken in a clipped undertone. All she could catch were the phrases "finished business" and "monkey on my back." When she had questioned him later, he had refused to talk about it.

"In essence," Rankin said, "David told me to get lost. At first I was furious. I swore I'd break him if it was the last thing I did. Then I realized it was really the money I wanted, not David's hide. I began to zero in on who besides David might be willing to pay to keep this information quiet."

"That's when you went to Alexander Traynor," Haversham guessed.

Rankin smiled. "You have remarkable powers of deduction, Mr. Haversham. David's father paid. Handsomely, I might add."

Haversham didn't comment. He was deep in thought. So the iron man had been broken, he mused. Alexander Traynor, whose integrity was a by-word in the industry, had stooped low enough to deal with a blackmailer in order to save his son. In keeping with his pattern, he hadn't discussed it with David, hadn't even asked if it were true. He had taken it for granted that David had fouled up again and had gone about covering for him as he had for years. Haversham suspected that Alex had decided to suggest Brian for president after that not so much to safeguard the future of Traynor Labs as to protect David from further repercussions should his past be exposed again.

Instinct told Haversham that it would be better for now if David didn't know that Asa Rankin had blackmailed his father. David's push for the presidency was based on a revenge motive. To learn that his father's decision to deny him his heritage was motivated by love for him instead of malice would destroy that motive. And that was something Haversham couldn't afford.

He thought with bitterness of this afternoon's poll of the Board members to call an emergency meeting. Without Arthur Perrault's sanction, they had been like a flock of sheep with no direction. The consensus had been a "wait and see" policy, a stall for time that could mean the loss to Haversham of the Anshul-Bulden sale. If he could only light a bomb under their tails how he'd watch with pleasure when the wool began to fly.

Rankin coughed discreetly.

Haversham focused once again on the blackmailer before him. He was a repulsive tub of lard, but he had to be dealt with.

"Mr. Rankin, why have you come here?"

"I need money."

Haversham laughed shortly. "Rankin, you may be holding a keg of dynamite, but your fuse is defunct. In case you're not aware of it, Brian Anslow was named president of Traynor Labs when Alexander Traynor died. All you could do if you expose David now is cause some embarrassment. It won't net you a dime."

The fat man wasn't perturbed. "Don't underestimate me, Mr. Haversham. I told you I'm a newspaperman. I have connections here. I was informed that Brian Anslow was named president instead of David. As a matter of fact, I was thinking of going to see him if you and I couldn't get together."

Claire paled but Haversham seemed not to have heard. An idea had just occurred to him. There might be a way he could use this conscienceless slob and light that bomb under the Board members at the same time.

He rose from his chair and strode purposefully toward the couch. "Mr. Rankin, those newspaper connections you talk about here. Are they valid?"

"They are."

"Which ones are they?"

"The *Post*. The *Enquirer*. Why?"

"Because you and I are about to do business together. Understand this, Mr. Rankin. Before Mrs. Traynor or I pay you a cent for the information you're peddling, we'll see you behind bars. Blackmail is a federal offense in this state."

With a roar of anger, the fat man heaved his bulk upward. Haversham rammed a hand flat against his chest and pushed him back on the couch. "Sit down, Mr. Rankin. I'm not through talking. You tell me you're in need of money?"

Some of the anger went out of the moon face. He nodded cautiously.

"All right. What would you say to writing a series of newspaper articles for me and getting paid for it?"

He squinted speculatively at the executive. "How much?"

"Two thousand apiece."

He thought about it a minute, then put out a hand. "It's a pleasure to do business with you, Mr. Haversham."

Haversham clasped the flabby hand. It would be like killing two birds with one stone, he thought triumphantly. His gray eyes narrowed in thought. But why not try for three?

"Rankin," he asked, "how good are you at playing detective?"

Chapter 11

Dennie Redmond managed to get to the laboratory area at the end of the manufacturing floor just before the plant closed on Thursday evening. He was carrying a shopping bag filled with the comic books that Sid Draper liked to read.

He pushed open the oak door that separated the plant from the lab and hospital area, and confronted the security guard that stood before it. He was a husky six footer who topped Dennie by half a head and by his glance made Dennie feel smaller than he was.

The guard hooked his thumbs in his broad belt and regarded Dennie dispassionately. He was new to the company, but he prided himself on judging the level of a man's corporate status, and this uncertain fellow with the slight paunch was no executive.

"Is there something I can do for you?"

Dennie hesitated. Dr. Traynor had been very specific about not visiting. Dennie had been surprised and puzzled when he'd received her note. The last he'd heard of Sid, he was on an army base in South Carolina waiting to go overseas. What was he doing in a pollen testing program at Traynor Labs?

On impulse, Dennie had called the hospital and asked for Sid. He'd been turned over to Dr. Traynor, who was polite, but firm. None of the volunteers were receiving calls, but she would be glad to take a message to Sid.

It was then that Dennie had decided to go see for himself.

He cleared his throat. "I'm here to see a friend of mine. Sid Draper. He's in the pollen testing program. In the hospital."

"Sorry, this area is in isolation."

"Well, can I leave a package for him?"

"I'll have to check that." He picked up the wall phone, buzzed through to the laboratory, and spoke in an undertone for a few seconds. Then he turned to Dennie. "It'll be all right, Mr. . . ."

"Redmond. Dennis Redmond."

Instead of stopping off at his house as he'd planned, Dennie decided to go straight to Angie's apartment. He was worried about her. She seemed restless. Strained. Always after she left the Helicopter Club she'd been content to have dinner out and relax at the apartment. Or take in a good movie. Angie enjoyed old Westerns like *High Noon* and Dennie would scout to find one that pleased her. But in the last few days nothing seemed to please her. She couldn't stand to be inactive for a minute. She told him it was because she was trying to kick the habit, but he didn't know whether to believe her. Last night she insisted they stay at the disco, knowing he would be more spectator than performer. She "hustled" through three dances with some bearded stranger, guzzled four gin and tonics, then turned morose and pleaded with him to take her home immediately.

In the apartment she began to weep uncontrollably. He held her until the tears subsided. "I love you," she said. She opened her mouth, kissed him deeply, and sought his tongue with hers. He could taste the salt of her tears on his lips. He reached to pull her to him, but she broke away.

She spoke like a tired child. "I'm no great shakes, Dennie. But I didn't mean to harm you." She wore a silky black dress with a fake red rose at the shoulder.

He dried her eyes with his handkerchief. There were shadowed pouches above her cheekbones he hadn't noticed before. "Is that what's been bothering you all along? The morphine I took? I told you. Forget it. That's all over now. There's just you and me, Angie. Starting fresh again."

Her lips quivered. "Like it was all new?" He nodded. Her eyes were huge black olives, moist, glistening. Her little-girl mouth puckered with hope. "Wouldn't it be something if we could start over again. Just you and me . . ."

She pressed herself into him and ground her body against his and Dennie forgot the tears and the desperation in her voice. They made love until they were exhausted. Dennie crept home at four in the morning, his legs weak, his mouth acrid and bitter tasting. He fell asleep with Angie's name on his lips and the feel of her body still beneath his.

This morning she'd called him at work. It was the first time she'd ever done that.

"Dennie?" She sounded tense.

He tried to keep the worry from his voice. "Are you okay?"

"A little tired." She laughed, but it was forced. "How would you like to come to my place for supper tonight?"

"Aren't you working?"

"I quit."

"How come?"

The words came in a rush. "I'll tell you when I see you. Be here at six." She hung up.

He patted his jacket pocket now as he sped toward Soho, checking to see if the Rolaids were there. The last time Angie had tried to make him breakfast, she had curdled the eggs and charred the toast. He had made light of it, but his stomach had rebelled for three days afterward.

He pulled up before the small gray building on Prince Street. The night was clear and cold, and the stench of the plastic-bagged garbage piled high for collection in the gutter offended his nostrils. He ran the four flights to Angie's apartment. The odor of scorched meat permeated the hallway. His keys jingled as he turned the lock of her door. He pushed it open, crossed the threshold and halted.

Angie was at the stove with her back to him. But she wasn't alone. There were two men with her, both in their mid-thirties. One was short, no more than five foot four. He was dark haired and muscular with a sallow pointed face. He wore dungarees and a flannel shirt and his eyes were never still. They darted from person to person and place to place with the crafty expression of a hunted fox.

It was the other who held Dennie's attention. He was tall, with close-cropped curly black hair that framed a sensual face. He was dressed in a denim suit and Frye boots with a white linen shirt open wide at the collarline. A silver medallion nestled in the coarse hair on his chest. There were only two chairs in the room. He sat on one and propped a booted foot on the other. He looked to Dennie like an actor and there was something familiar about his dark eyes and olive skin.

"Close the door." His voice was deceptively soft. "Introduce us," he demanded of Angie.

She turned from the stove. Dennie could see that

she'd been crying, but her eyes refused to meet his.

"Dennie, this is my brother, Niko Bordini." Her voice faltered.

Bordini held out a hand. His grip was powerful, hurting.

"Pleased to meet you, Dennie." He gestured toward the shorter man. "This is Finch, a friend of mine." Dennie nodded.

Bordini took his foot off the seat, used it to push the chair toward Dennie. "Make yourself at home." He looked around the room contemptuously. "I understand you're paying for this place."

Finch grinned, revealing uneven discolored teeth.

"Leave him alone," Angie said.

"Shut up." Her brother's voice was harsh.

Dennie felt himself shrink inside. Once, a year ago, he'd been mugged outside his building. There had been one man, short and squat with wild eyes and big hands he kept flexing spasmodically. He hadn't touched Dennie and he hadn't flashed any weapon. But Dennie had sensed an uncontrollable violence in him that had made him want to run as fast and as far as he could. He felt the same way now.

Bordini put out a placating hand. He wore a large gold ring on his finger in the shape of a serpent's head with emerald eyes. "Relax, Dennie. You act as if someone's going to hurt you. I wouldn't let anything happen to you. I always protect the people I owe. Don't I, Finch?"

The fox-face nodded.

"You don't owe me anything, Mr. Bordini."

"But I do. You looked out for my sister all the time I was away and that's a thing that has to be squared away. We're a close family, my sister and me. We swore after our parents died to look after each other.

Take care of one another's debts. Didn't we, Angie?''

There was no answer from the direction of the stove.

He threw her a black look. "We have to put up with my sister, Dennie. She's got bad manners."

"I understand you just returned from South America," Dennie said.

Finch laughed dryly. His shifty eyes shuttled around the room, settled covertly on Angie's breasts.

Bordini shook his head in mock despair. "I'm afraid Angie's been lying again, Dennie. You see my sister's ashamed that I've been in prison on and off. So she tells people I'm in South America on business. And that makes for bad relations. You can see that, can't you, Dennie? Only this time I've got nothing against her. Because this time Angie's made up for everything. Hasn't she, Finch?"

"She sure has."

Bordini pulled a white handkerchief from his pocket and bent to wipe a smudge from his boots. "Dennie, I'm going to level with you. This last time I was in stir, I did a lot of thinking. Twice I've pulled heists that wouldn't have added up to more than a hundred grand apiece. Even if I got away with them, how long would the money have lasted? Six months? A year? The Feds were right when they said crime doesn't pay." His eyes, a cunning version of Angie's, laughed up at Dennie. "Unless it pays big, eh, Dennie?"

He scraped his chair along the floor until he was almost upon Dennie. He put his face close to Dennie's and lowered his voice to a confidential tone. "You know, Dennie, once in a while, a guy like you gets a chance at a pot of gold. But he doesn't always know it. Sometimes it takes a friend to point it out to him. A friend who owes him, maybe." He put an arm around Dennie's shoulders. Dennie huddled under the weight of it. "Tell me about the shipment of morphine coming to Traynor," he murmured.

Dennie shook the arm off and stood up. His eyes swung accusingly toward Angie. Her lips trembled and she looked away.

"Sit down," Bordini commanded.

Finch had been riffling through a copy of *Hustler*. He rolled it into a tight tube now and came to stand beside Dennie. His eyes were cold, unpredictable.

Dennie sat down. His hands were shaking, his mouth dry.

"Tell me," Bordini repeated.

"There is no shipment, Mr. Bordini."

He smiled. "Call me Niko. You and me, we're going to be friends, Dennie. More than friends. Business partners. Now try again, Dennie. How many kilos of morphine in that shipment?"

"I told you, Mr. . . . Niko . . ."

His face twisted angrily. "How can we be friends when you make me show my worst side?" Dennie shook his head uncomprehendingly. Bordini sighed. "Dennie, your mother . . . Angie tells me she's sick. I wouldn't want to see her get worse. Because a woman that age has a right to live out her years until God sees fit to take her."

Kneeling over her plants, Angie began to cry.

A numbness came over Dennie. *This couldn't be happening.* "You wouldn't hurt my mother," he whispered. Never in his life had he felt this kind of fear.

"How many kilos, Dennie?"

"Ten. Maybe twelve," he mumbled.

"What does it come in?"

"A drum."

"Small enough to be carried?"

"Yes."

"When's it coming?"

"A week, maybe two. I don't know yet. But you'll never get it out of there."

"With your help we will." He put out a hand as Dennie half rose from the seat. "Relax, Dennie. You got nothing to worry about. The way we'll set it up, nobody'll ever know you had anything to do with it. And then it'll be two million split four ways."

"Four . . ." He didn't want to ask it, but he had to know. "Is Angie a part of this?"

"No."

"Then who?"

Finch poked his shoulder with the rolled tube. "You don't ask them questions, unnerstand?"

Bordini pulled Dennie up from the chair and guided him toward the kitchen table. He pushed the napkins and silverware to one side and spread a large sheet of white paper across the top. He handed Dennie a pencil.

"All right, now, draw the inside of Traynor Labs for us. It doesn't have to be exact. Just close enough so me and Finch can make out what's where. Start with the place where the morphine comes in and go from there."

Dennie drew painstakingly. He began with the loading dock at the end of the manufacturing floor where all the materials were received. He sketched the sampling room, the manufacturing areas, the sterile injectable division and the high security narcotics operation, before heading down to the warehouse level. With each stroke he felt himself committed further and further to the treachery being contemplated.

He stopped when Bordini tapped the paper with his finger. "Why are there two vaults in the warehouse?"

"The Food and Drug Administration requires that finished goods and raw material be kept separately.

They also insist that quarantined material be segregated from released material."

"What's quarantined material?" Finch asked. "Diseased stuff?"

"Quarantined material is raw goods that's still undergoing testing. When the ten kilos of morphine comes in it will be considered quarantined until it's sampled and measures up to specifications. Then it will be labeled 'released.'"

"In other words that morphine can be in two different vaults on two different days," Bordini murmured. Dennie nodded. "And when is it brought up to manufacturing?"

"When the Trinicitate is ready to be made."

"What's Trinicitate?" Finch asked.

"It's a narcotic compound for anesthesia."

"Who gives the order to bring the stuff up?"

"My boss, David Traynor." He held the drawing up to Niko Bordini. "It's finished."

Bordini studied it for a few minutes, then tossed it back on the table. "You left something out."

Dennie stared at the drawing in front of him. It was by no means professional but it was certainly complete. Yet even if it wasn't, how could Bordini know that?

"What have I left out?"

"The lab and hospital."

"How did you . . ." Finch's hands tightened spasmodically on the rolled tube and the words died unspoken. "The lab and hospital aren't really a part of the plant. I'm not that familiar with them."

"You will be," Bordini said. "Draw them."

Even as he complied, a spark of rebellion flared in Dennie. The prospect of allying himself with these two turned his stomach. What if he stood up to them, he thought suddenly, as he couldn't bring himself to do with the mugger last year. He remembered the contempt in the policeman's eyes when he'd told him afterward that his "assailant" had neither attacked nor shown a weapon. Dennie had sworn then that nobody would ever look at him like that again. His pencil slowed. The spurt of bravado made his blood run quicker. What if he stopped drawing now? Told them he wasn't going to fall in with them, mother or no mother. What if he demanded Angie's release? Threatened them with police action? He put his pencil down.

The rolled magazine whistled past his ear as it slammed across the tabletop. Dennie's insides turned to putty.

"Move it!" Finch grated.

Dennie picked up the pencil and bent over the table.

Chapter 12

For a whole week Valerie and Wally had rehearsed the exact dosages of the Tetra-2 to be given in the Blasa Fever testing program. Because of the strong possibility of endotoxin shock, which could produce internal bleeding, respiratory obstruction or convulsions, they had decided to keep the maintenance dose of the antibiotic small, no more than 175 mg. to be given every six hours. An initial dose of 50 mg. would be injected, after which they would monitor the volunteers for an hour. If the reaction was mild, or absent (pray God), the dose would be increased at the second hour by 75 mg. and at the third by another 50 mg.

At midnight she and Wally injected the patients with the 50 mg. test dose. The actual administration should have been as anticlimactic for her as it seemed to be for him. But it wasn't. Valerie had the awful sensation of a ski jumper taking off on her first run with a great "whoosh" of air hitting her at gut level.

The last volunteer she injected was a huge prisoner called Tiny Anderson. Lying prone, he resembled an inflated balloon topped by silken blond hair and very blue eyes in a baby-smooth face. Valerie remembered that he had caused a commotion at the reception dock. He had allowed the prison orderlies to take his clothing docilely enough. But when they insisted on removing the wallet that he clutched in his hand, he had let out a roar of protest. In the ensuing battle, the wallet had been wrenched from his fingers and photos of his young daughters had scattered across the floor. It had taken both orderlies and Charley Santos to subdue the cherubic-looking giant and they had accomplished it only because his sudden spurt of strength had ebbed as quickly as it came.

The attendant, Tod Preston, held Tiny Anderson's arm firmly now. Anderson scarcely flinched when the needle pierced his skin.

"When am I going to get my wallet back?" he asked. His voice was soft and wispy—ludicrous in so big a man. His fever was low but the weakness and apathy were more pronounced in him than in some of the others.

"It's being kept under lock and key at the reception dock," Valerie told him. "You'll get it back when you leave here."

"*If* I leave here." His pink cheeks were splotchy, his expression morose.

"We don't hold with that kind of talk, Mr. Anderson."

Tears of self-pity welled his eyes. His lashes were pale and sparse, outlining his lids with the colorless fringe of an albino. He put a limp hand on her arm. "I miss my girls, doc. I miss them bad. It helped for me to see their pictures once in a while. I could remember the times we had together. Live them over and over in my mind. It made the days go by."

His hand was a dead weight. Valerie lifted it, tucked it under the blankets. "Why don't you try to get some sleep now. It'll make you feel better." Only a slight tremor in her voice betrayed the revulsion she was feeling.

He nodded then turned his face to the wall to hide the tears that slid down his cheeks.

Valerie stripped her gloves off and gave them to Preston to discard. Someday, she promised herself, when this was all over, she would do a study on the criminal mind. In rebutting Charley Santos's contention that, given the chance, all the inmates would attack without mercy, she had brought up Tiny Anderson's love for his daughters, based on the scene she had witnessed in the reception dock.

"If he has animal instincts as you accuse, Mr. Santos, then they're the natural ones of a father for his offspring. And there's nothing wrong in that."

Santos's craggy face had furrowed in concern. He had rubbed his roughened hands together in a dry agitated motion, the knuckles glistening white where the skin spread thin above them. "Listen, Doctor Traynor. I'm going off shift soon. I'm not gonna be here for the next eight hours. Do me a favor and don't go near Tiny Anderson without having someone with you. Okay?"

Her sigh of exasperation must have been audible to half the ward.

"Mr. Santos, will you never change?"

"You don't understand, doc. Tiny Anderson is a lifer. He's got no kids. Those pictures he carries around are of girls he's raped. Little girls."

Valerie had fought the nausea that rose up in her. Not for anything would she show Charley Santos how revolted she was. "Thank you for telling me, Mr. Santos. But there's still no cause for you to concern yourself."

She had put a brave face on it, Valerie thought, but she had been more shaken than she cared to admit. She blotted it out of her mind now as she watched Wally administer the Tetra-2 to Ansel Golden.

At fifty-five, Golden was one of the oldest prisoners in the ward. He talked little and smiled less, but he was accorded a respect among the prisoners that was evidenced by the deferential way they spoke of him. If some of the patients became uncertain of their symptoms or previous medical history, they would instruct her to "ask Doc Golden. He'll know." Several times, in tending to him, Valerie was on the verge of asking if the title "Doc" was an honorary one or if he'd actually had medical training. For some reason, she'd held back.

Golden was Wally's last patient. Wally stripped his gloves off and crossed the ward toward her. He slouched as he walked, a habit he had when tired. There were lines at the corners of his eyes and the gray at his temples looked less premature than it had before the program started.

He managed a smile. "So now we wait."

"And watch," she added, checking the clock above the nurses' station.

The time crept by slowly. They took turns monitoring the volunteers. Their faces became engraved in Valerie's mind as she honed in on the slightest change that could herald an endotoxemic reaction to the Tetra-2.

The boxer, Jefferson Montgomery, complained of a tingling of the skin. It could mean nothing. Or it could signify internal bleeding. Valerie checked his urine for blood cells, but found none. She and Wally decided to go further before ruling it out as a reaction. They did a spinal tap, seeking blood in the cerebro-spinal fluid, a sure sign of internal bleeding. There was none. They breathed a sigh of relief. The hour was almost up.

They administered another 75 mg. of Tetra-2.

Twenty minutes went by. Alfie Brockwell began to twitch, a possible sign of hemorrhaging around the nerves of muscle function, until he assured them he'd had the twitch since he was "a small babe in me mother's arms."

Freddie Bishop cried out in his sleep. He awakened and cringed when Wally tried to touch him. His pulse was irregular and the rash had spread from his body to his face. He refused to let them minister to him until "Doc" Golden in the bed next to him assured him it was all right. They checked him every ten minutes. His pulse steadied down. Their luck held. The second hour drew to a close.

They injected the final 50 mg. of Tetra-2.

Wally was called into the lab by the technician. Valerie continued to monitor the patients. Colonel Darwin's fever climbed to 105 degrees. His bed had been moved next to Sid Draper's, but his disposition hadn't improved. He railed at Valerie for the lack of discipline in the ward, claiming she had less sense than a private in boot camp. He began to retch and demanded water. It was refused, because Valerie had seen a spot of bright red blood in the mucus and felt it best to discontinue oral fluids.

Another ten minutes went by. Ansel Golden signaled to her from his bed. Though slight of build, he had a wiry constitution that had withstood the onslaught of Blasa Fever well. Oddly enough, there was something about him that reminded Valerie of her father. She knew the comparison was ridiculous, even demeaning, yet she couldn't help making it. So far the injections of the Tetra-2 had caused him no ill effects that Valerie had noticed. But that could change in a split second. Her gaze focused on his jaundiced cheeks and watery blue eyes as she approached the bed.

He shook his head. "It's not me," he said. "It's Freddie. I don't like the way he looks. Would you check him?"

"I just did."

"Check him again." His eyes met hers and Valerie's indignation faded. She didn't need the "please" he tacked on as an afterthought. Ansel Golden was not given to idle requests.

She turned toward the young black boy in the next bed. Once again she was struck by his dark good looks. His eyes were closed, the fringe of his lashes an inky smudge against his rash blotched cheeks. The only change in the picture of five minutes ago was the shallowness of his breathing. She frowned, reached for his wrist and mentally counted.

Ansel Golden's voice was grim. "It's rapid, isn't it?"

She nodded.

"Dangerously so?"

"No." His pulse had climbed past 108, but there was no need for alarm yet. "Mr. Golden, are you a doctor?"

He smiled, a slow engaging smile that minimized the hollows in his cheeks and afforded Valerie a glimpse of the man that once was. "I'm a surgeon. I took my training at Bradley Medical in Boston and was Chief of Surgery there for ten years."

"I'm impressed. I've noticed that the men come to you for help. With conditions in the prisons what they are, the doctors there must have appreciated that."

Valerie had read recently that a study of prisons on a par with Arbor State revealed an average of two doctors to sixteen hundred inmates, with hepatitis, TB, and urinary infections rampant among them. Psychiatric and dental services were also at a premium and the caliber of help was not always up to professional standards.

A flicker of humor lit Golden's rheumy blue eyes.

"The doctors shuttled between gratitude and exasperation. You'd have to know the prison mentality to understand why." He looked around the room at his fellow inmates. "Some of these cons are smart enough to understand that a prison doctor is a 'neutral.' He doesn't take sides, he doesn't ferret out secrets, he just tries to heal. But a lot of them don't see it that way. To those cons, the cops, the warden, the trustees, and the prison doctors are all symbols of authority. All lined up against him. They won't go to any one of them unless they're forced."

"So you give out with in-house remedies."

"Something like that."

"What did you treat Freddie Bishop for?"

The smile disappeared from his face. "Charley Santos talks too much."

From the corner of her eye, Valerie saw that Wally was walking toward her. She stepped away from Golden's bed to meet him.

"How's it going?" he asked.

"Okay. Wally, do me a favor. I'd like to keep tabs on Freddie Bishop for a while. Would you check on the others?"

He glanced at the sleeping boy. "Trouble?"

"Borderline." She knew that Ansel Golden was watching her face.

"Call if you need me."

She nodded.

Back at Freddie Bishop's bedside she saw that the boy had opened his eyes. His pupils were dilated, the sclera yellowed. A light sweat had broken out on his forehead. He turned his head toward Ansel Golden. "I can't breathe," he croaked.

"It'll pass, Freddie."

He moved his head from side to side. "No it won't. It's my answer from God."

"I told you, Freddie. You have nothing to blame yourself for."

The boy licked his lips. "It's okay, Doc. You gotta understand that. I told the Lord that if the only way he could deliver me from that hell-hole was to take me to him, it was okay. 'Cause I'm not goin' back there." His breathing became rapid, labored. Valerie reached for his pulse. "Tell me I'm not goin' back there, Doc."

There was a pleading note in Golden's voice. "Listen, Freddie. You've got to try. You've got to put up a fight. The doctors can't help you if you won't help yourself."

The boy closed his eyes. "It's my answer, Doc."

Valerie tightened with alarm. His pulse was over 140. Ansel Golden must have sensed it. He edged his feet over the side of the bed. "Stay where you are!" Valerie ordered. She signaled to Wally. "Set up an EKG. Stat!"

The boy began to gag. His eyes rolled upward in his head, his legs thrashed beneath the blankets. He gasped like a beached fish. Within seconds his airway passage closed down: his face turned ashen. Valerie tilted his head back to maximum extension. It lifted his jaw and drew his tongue away from the pharyngeal wall. Wally set up the electrocardiograph and moved to her side. She waited for spontaneous breathing to occur. It didn't.

The boy lapsed into unconsciousness. The blips on the electrocardiogram slowed down. The pulse rate was erratic . . . 30 . . . 40 . . . She pinched Freddie's nostrils shut, opened his mouth wide and prepared to give mouth-to-mouth resuscitation. Wally's hand clamped down on her arm. "Val, you can't. He's got the Fever." She looked at Freddie. It was too late anyway. The dreaded blue of cyanosis tinged his face a ghastly hue.

"Wally!" she cried sharply. "Get me a trach tube." She heard his running footsteps. She didn't take her eyes off Freddie. The tube and scalpel were in her hands in seconds. Wally held the unconscious boy's head firm, extended the neck. Her hands were steady. She palpated the trachea with her fingers, felt for the thyroid cartilage, then made a single incision. She used the handle of the scalpel to spread the edges of the tracheal incision and inserted the tube. She waited for the rush of air, the gasp that would signify life.

There was nothing.

The blipping of the EKG became a continuous hum. The wavering line flattened ominously. She *had* to save him!

"Adrenalin," she whispered in a tight voice. The hypodermic was in her hand almost instantly. She injected directly between the fourth and fifth ribs, grateful for the show of blood in the syringe that told her she was in the heart. She waited, hunched over Freddie Bishop like a guardian angel, eyes fixed on the flattened EKG, praying for the miracle that had to come.

The EKG stayed flat. Wally's face mirrored her shock and disbelief. She put her stethoscope to the boy's chest, willing the beat to be there, however faint. She rose from the bed and pulled the stethoscope from her ears. Her eyes met Ansel Golden's. He was crying. Wally raised the sheet to cover Freddie Bishop's face.

He put an arm around her shoulders. "I'll take care of things here. Why don't you go back to the kitchen for some coffee."

She nodded. A whisper went through the ward as

she walked through it, head held high. The words were grim, unemotional. "Freddie's bought it." It wasn't commiseration for Freddie they felt. It was fear for themselves. Speculation at who would be next. She wished she could reassure them. Tell them it was a fluke. Convince them that the Tetra-2 was the elixir of life she had hoped it would be. But she couldn't do that anymore.

She sat on a kitchen chair, staring unseeingly at the cold stale coffee on the burner. No staler than her dreams, she thought. Tetra-2, the wonder drug. She, *Valerie Traynor*, was going to do what no other scientist had been able to do. Find a cure for Blasa Fever. It had been an ego trip for her. One that had cost the life of Freddie Bishop. It was easy to say that he might have died anyway. Or been crippled. But that would have been an act of God. And she wouldn't have felt responsible for it.

She knew she should get back to the ward. There were the other volunteers to contend with and it wasn't fair to Wally. But she couldn't bring herself to it. Always, before, she had found some reservoir of strength within herself to combat reversals. Brian had called her the "rah-rah girl" with a mixture of pride and chagrin. But something had gone out of her this time. And it was her own fault. She had allowed the fear of an epidemic to create a need for success instead of a calculated hope. And this, for any researcher, meant disaster.

Wally appeared in the doorway. He leaned against the frame, his eyes sunken.

"Ansel Golden wants to see you."

"What for?"

"He won't say."

"How are the others?"

He shrugged. "Holding. No signs of internal bleeding. No further cases of respiratory obstruction." He smacked his palm against the door. If it was Brian, he would have put his fist through it, she thought.

"What could have caused it, Val? And so fast. There shouldn't have been that much concentration of endotoxin in the respiratory tract tissue at this early stage. There was only a slight indication of it in the animal studies."

"Wally, you know as well as I do . . ."

"I know, I know. Animal testing and clinical testing are two different things." He tore the green cap from his hair, wiped his sweating forehead with it. "Is that coffee ready yet?"

"It will be in a couple of minutes. Why don't you get some rest now? I'll take over the ward for a few hours." He started to protest, but she stopped him. "I'll feel better if I work. Really."

He nodded, then called to her as she reached the door. "Val . . . I'm sorry I blew up."

She smiled ruefully. "You know what's wrong with us scientists? We apologize too much for being human."

Inside, a pall had fallen over the ward. Even the querulous Langsley Darwin lay mute and brooding. Freddie Bishop's bed was gone. The empty space between Ansel Golden and Jefferson Montgomery was a conspicuous reminder of his death. Valerie knew that his mattress, bedclothes, and the gown and gloves used to tend him would be burned or sterilized immediately to prevent contamination.

Ansel Golden was waiting for her. The recrimination she expected to see in his face wasn't there.

"You wanted to talk to me?"

He nodded. "You asked me earlier what I treated

Freddie Bishop for. I felt then it would have been breaking a trust to tell you. I feel now it would be breaking one if I didn't."

She shook her head wearily. "It doesn't really matter anymore, Mr. Golden."

"You're wrong. It does." His pale eyes held hers.

She pulled up a chair. "All right. I'm listening."

He tilted his head toward the empty space as if the boy was still there. "Freddie was eighteen when he came to prison a year ago. He was more a mixed-up kid than a bad one. He was the oldest of six. His father, an odd jobs man, deserted his mother when Freddie was fourteen, and Freddie took his place as 'provider.' He didn't know how to earn, so he took. After four years of petty thievery and juvenile detention, he graduated from Boys Town to Arbor State. You saw what he looked like. Young. Pretty." He grimaced. "An untried virgin thrown to a pack of lechers."

He sighed and continued. "Freddie did what a lot of 'chickens' do to survive. He took on a protector. A bully named Big Ed who had influence in the prison. In exchange for easy work and extra yard time he let Ed use him. At first it revolted him, but after a while Freddie accepted it, even gloried in it. He began to boast like the head prostitute in a whorehouse. Then, being young, Freddie got carried away. He made the mistake of trying to ape his protector, down to badmouthing some of Big Ed's rivals who made advances to him. He offended some powerful cons. It might have been all right if Big Ed had stayed on at Arbor, but he didn't. His lawyer won an appeal for him and pending further action on it, the warden thought it best to transfer him downstate."

He shifted position as a cramp caught him in the lower right side. He winced, breathed deeply, then went on. "It took four days for the wolves to close in on Freddie. Seven of them caught him in a laundry room with the guards either looking on or looking away. It didn't matter much. When he came to me he was so beaten and ripped up inside, he could hardly walk. He wouldn't go to the prison doctor. For days he hardly ate. He cried when he slept and kept talking about God. He saw what happened to him as some kind of punishment for the perversion he'd allowed. I did what I could for him. It wasn't much, but it eased him. Afterward, Freddie took to following me around a lot. His dependence on me increased every day. By the time Blasa Fever spread through the prison, I was the only one there that Freddie trusted."

His expression turned reflective. "I suppose, in a way, I encouraged it. I should have broken that dependence the minute Freddie got back on his feet. But there was something that touched me about this boy looking at me like some kind of father figure." He cleared his throat. "A prison is a lonely place, you know."

Valerie tried to curb her impatience. There were others there she should be checking on. She didn't begrudge Golden the need to voice his grief, but now was not the time.

"Mr. Golden, I don't see what this is leading up to. If you're trying to tell me that Freddie's poor physical condition predetermined his reaction to the Tetra-2 injection . . ."

"I'm trying to tell you just that, but not for the reasons you're thinking. You see Freddie came down with Blasa Fever three weeks before the rest of us did."

Her eyes widened in disbelief. "Are you saying Freddie was in the secondary stages of Blasa Fever?"

"I'm saying just that."

"But I specifically told the prison doctors . . ."

"I know. They owed me a couple of favors and they felt as I did. That if Freddie stayed on there without me, he didn't have a prayer. I know it was wrong, but I thought with luck—" He blinked rapidly to hold back the tears. "I did you and Dr. Chandler a disservice and I'm sorry."

She took his hand in hers and wrung it gratefully. "Thank you for telling me, Mr. Golden. Thank you very much."

She sped through the ward, keenly aware of the despondency of the men. She felt as if she'd been through an emotional wringer—raw, battered. But it wasn't solace she craved. Freddie's death had been a blow, but it had ended for her in triumph. She wanted to give vent to that triumph. Purge herself and be renewed, like a soldier with a woman after battle. A longing filled her. It was Wally she was running to, Wally she wanted to share the news with—but Brian she wanted to be held by.

She walked quickly to the small resting room behind the ward and eased the door open. Except for a night light on the floor in the corner, the room was dark. Wally hadn't even bothered to put the sheets on the cot. He slept in an undershirt and green hospital trousers. His forehead was pressed into the coarse ticking on one pillow and his body was curled fetus-like around another. Sleep had rendered his lean face defenseless, but denied it peace. His eyes were tightly shut, the lashes scarcely visible.

She closed the door behind her, debating whether to wake him or not. He was exhausted. What difference if she told him about Freddie Bishop now or three hours from now? Her eyes became accustomed to the dimness. He shivered and she saw there were goose pimples on his arms. She pulled a blanket from a chair in the corner, draped it loosely over him and tucked the edge around his shoulders. His eyes flew open. He grasped her arms as she tried to straighten up.

"Val?" His voice was sleep-fogged, uncertain.

"Yes." His hair was tousled, his eyes bemused, his expression vulnerable as a small boy unsure of a prize he's been presented with. On impulse she leaned down and kissed him. His arms started to fold about her, but she shook her head. "Wally, listen. We've been granted a reprieve."

He pulled her down to the edge of the cot. "I don't understand."

"Freddie Bishop was in the secondary stages of Blasa Fever. He had it for over three weeks before he got here."

He squinted up at her. "How do you know?"

"Ansel Golden told me. He's responsible for getting Freddie in here on false documentation. He thought we might be able to save him anyway."

"I forgive him." His voice was husky. His sensitive fingers stroked her forearms in rhythmic circular motions. "Do that again."

"What?"

"This."

He pulled her down beside him and kissed her deeply. His body was lean and hard, his urgency obvious. Instinctively she began to back away. If she allowed Wally to make love to her it was tantamount to a commitment. A commitment she wasn't sure she wanted to make. "Wally, no," she murmured. He kissed her again, stifling her protests. "Don't stop me, Val," he whispered. "I need you. I love you." His hands groped beneath the buttons of her uniform until he cupped the fullness of her breasts. A moan escaped her as he buried his head between them then swelled their peaks with the flicking of his tongue. It had been too long, she thought. She couldn't control herself anymore. She didn't want to.

She lay pliant as Wally undid the final buttons of her uniform. She was strangely passive. Perhaps it was the newness. She stopped thinking as his hands slid past her stomach, then rebelled as they hastily probed her thighs. She put up a hand to block him. "Wally, wait." she murmured. "It's too fast." If he heard her, he gave no sign. His eyes were closed, his face slack with desire. He tore his undershirt off, reached for his trousers . . .

A knock sounded at the door.

They lay like a pair of statues. Immobile. Waiting.

"Dr. Chandler?" It was Tod Preston.

"Yes?"

"I didn't mean to wake you, but Colonel Darwin is vomiting again, and I can't find Dr. Traynor anywhere."

"I'll be right there."

They dressed hastily, avoiding each other's eyes. It wasn't until they were at the door that Wally stopped her. He brushed a strand of her blonde hair back into the loose coil she had rearranged at the nape of her neck. His gaze warmed her face. "Val, what there was of it was beautiful. I'm sorry it had to end so soon."

"So am I," she answered, kissing him lightly on the lips. But deep within her, she was confused. What she'd felt for Wally had been very different from her reactions with Brian and it would take some getting used to.

Chapter 13

Kirby Semmel's apartment building was located near Bellevue Hospital at Twenty-seventh Street and First Avenue and was one of the few brownstones that hadn't been torn down to make way for high rises.

Its absentee owner had ordered it converted into as many units as possible at the cheapest price. Still bearing its original rococo facade, it now held twelve apartments on five floors. Eva discovered, as she climbed the five drab flights to the young doctor's apartment, that all the units led from a winding stairway that narrowed and grew more rickety as it spiraled upward.

Outside Semmel's door, she hesitated. She was breathing so hard she was almost panting. It wasn't from the climb. Her daily ski exercises kept her in the kind of shape that would allow her to race up those stairs in stride had she wanted to. It was her anticipation of seeing Kirby Semmel again. In the four days since he'd telephoned, he hadn't been out of her mind. Her only fear was that she had exaggerated the memory of him and the living image would be a disappointment.

She braced herself and rang the bell.

He opened the door so quickly, he must have been behind it waiting for her. "Come in, Mrs. Anslow."

She exhaled on a long breath, smiled, and stepped inside. He was even more attractive than she remembered. His face, capped by curly black hair, had the sculpted perfection of the young David in Florence. His nose was prominent, but aquiline. His lips were full and sensual. He wore a black turtleneck sweater, jeans, and soft beige moccasins. It was hard to believe from the taut muscles of his body that his profession was a sedentary one.

He fumbled with her coat as he helped her take it off. He was less in command of himself than he'd been in her office, she thought. She felt a twinge of disappointment. It was his certainty, his indifference that held the greatest drawing power for her. She wanted it to vanish only if she overcame it. Otherwise, the prize wasn't worth the game.

She remembered she'd felt the same way about Brian the first time she'd met him. It had been in her father's office, shortly after Val had gone to Africa. The magnetism had been there for her, but not for him. He'd looked at her with the disinterested glance of a eunuch in a harem. His gaze had lingered, deepened to a haunted, puzzled stare. She knew he was seeing Val in her and it infuriated her. She determined then that she would have Brian Anslow. She would wipe her sister's image from his mind and wind herself so tight around him he would think of her every time he breathed. She had succeeded, but the game had palled. She would have rid herself of Brian a long time ago if Val hadn't returned and shown that she still cared for him.

There was a perverse pleasure in denying Val that which only she could withhold. She recalled a short stint in a psychiatrist's office when she was nineteen. They had probed this very point.

He was a fat Park Avenue doctor who smelled of spicy after-shave lotion and charged eighty dollars an hour.

"You're vindictive toward Val, but you don't feel the same way about David," he stated.

"I despise my brother for being a weakling. But I feel sorry for him too. I don't feel sorry for Val."

"Did it ever occur to you that you're trying to get back at Val because she was your father's favorite?"

She had struck his desk in fury. "That's not true. Alex was more affectionate to me than he ever was to her. I never even saw him kiss Val."

His eyes had regarded her gently. "Was it only his affection you craved?"

She hadn't answered because he was causing her pain. She stopped going to him two weeks later for the same reason. Besides, he was wrong. Alex had always loved her. He had proved it a million times over. Hadn't he always sent her gifts when he was away? And he was away much of the time when she was small. In adolescence he never ceased to tell her how pretty she was and what a heartbreaker she was turning out to be. He took her to restaurants with him and wore her as proudly as the Phi Beta Kappa key on his watchchain.

Years later she stopped lying to herself. The trouble was, she admitted, that he never *talked* to her the way he did to Val. There was no common ground for them to meet on. She hadn't achieved in the sense that he understood achievement. She was a sex symbol to her own father. When he talked to Val, he addressed an equal. When he spoke to her, he indulged a female.

The only time it changed was when she bore him a grandchild. She had hated carrying Mark. She saw no beauty in the pendulous ovals of her body, and Brian's "consideration" of her deprived her of the one thing that had made the marriage palatable: the sexual bouts in bed where she sought victory and settled for a draw. Brian had been a marvelous lover with the staying power of a stallion. Approaching fatherhood changed that. In the final months he tempered his drives and silently reproached her for not doing the same. She realized then what the pattern for the future would be. The needs of the child would come before hers.

It was Alex who made motherhood bearable. She had given her father the one thing Val's strivings had denied him. A grandson. For the first time, through her son, she had the status and attention from her father she craved. Instead of going to his own home for dinner, Alex came to theirs. On Mark's third birthday, Alex gave him a real microscope and crowed with elation when it fascinated the boy. On his fourth, he talked to them of Mark's future at Traynor. On his sixth, Valerie came home from Africa and Alex's visits slackened.

She looked up now as Kirby Semmel touched her arm. He guided her to a brown couch in the living room that had "furnished" written all over it. Small and dark, it was papered in a faded print, with a nondescript rug and drapes meant to soften the "decor." Backing the couch was a magnificent carved desk, the only piece in the room she suspected belonged to Semmel. It was heaped with fat textbooks carrying markers stuck in between the pages, reminders of passages consigned to memory, and an open binder unlined, with scrawlings in a large childish handwriting.

Semmel gestured ruefully. "You know, I'm so involved in my work, I never realize how bad this place is until I have someone up here."

He used his hands a lot, she noticed. They didn't belong to the rest of him. They were wide and blunted, the skin chapped and reddened. Coarse hands. Common, like those of an outdoor construction worker's. They looked insensitive, and they excited her.

"Do you have many people up?" she asked.

"No, I don't."

He turned away from her. He was annoyed with himself. Something had gone awry. In his mind this meeting was to have led to nothing but a business discussion. Yet from the moment Eva Anslow had walked in everything had shifted out of kilter.

For one thing, she didn't appear the same. The woman he had met nearly a month ago had looked like the head of Traynor Museum. She had sat behind a big desk wearing horn-rimmed glasses, with her dark hair pulled back from her face and her pencil tapping an impatient tattoo on the blotter. This "girl" he faced now wore a fleecy white sweater, a gray wool skirt and suede boots to match. Her hair was long and shiny, she wore almost no makeup and there was a softness in her expression he found disconcerting. He squared his shoulders. The thing to do was march this back on the right track before it got out of hand.

He cleared his throat. "Mrs. Anslow . . ."

Eva rejoiced at the forcefulness of his tone. "Why don't you call me Eva. Mrs. Anslow sounds so . . ." she wrinkled her nose at him, ". . . old."

"Well, you certainly aren't . . ." He stood up, dug his hands into his pockets and began to pace without looking at her. "All right, Eva. I called your office a few days ago because something's happened to change my life. My grandmother died in that Viennese nursing home two weeks ago."

"I'm terribly sorry."

The sinews of his thighs were clearly outlined as he trod the floor like a restless panther. His eyes were fixed on the frayed carpet beneath him. He reversed himself every few seconds to avoid hitting the walls.

"Thank you. What hurts most is that she died still angry with me. My letter to her didn't arrive until almost a week later. Her solicitor called to tell me that in a fit of rage she changed her will at the last minute to exclude me. Which presents me with a big problem. You see it's my grandmother who's been financing me through med school and was to help me open an office when I'm finished at Bellevue. That office is a pipe-dream now. To put it simply, I'm broke.''

Eva decorously pleated the folds of her skirt. He was going to come all the way by himself, she thought. He owed her that much for the hard time he'd given her in her office.

"How can I help you, Kirby?"

He stopped pacing. The words came to his lips with difficulty. "How much will you pay for the Semmelweiss Indictment?"

"I'd like to see the condition it's in before I say."

"Of course. Follow me."

He led her through a connecting door to a small bedroom. Aside from the double bed in the middle of it, the room was a shrine. There were piles of scrapbooks on the dresser and pictures of Semmelweiss all over the walls. Booted and bearded, he was a stocky balding practitioner with a piercing glance and a heavy-handed manner. In most of the photos he wore the dark frock coat with the narrow lapels so popular in Vienna in the eighteen hundreds.

On top of a bureau covered with a linen scarf were various memorabilia, all neatly labeled. One was an outdated stethoscope. Eva picked up the small card that nestled against it. "To Ignaz with great affection," it read. "Perhaps this will serve you better than the gavel and the bench." It was signed, "Karl."

Kirby Semmel came up behind her. He touched the card reverently. "It was sent to Semmelweiss by a friend who'd studied law with him."

Eva could feel his warm breath on her neck. She

turned so her face was very close to his. "I thought Semmelweiss studied medicine?"

He shook his head. "His father sent him from Budapest to Vienna in 1837 to become a lawyer. A chance visit to an anatomy demonstration changed his mind." His expressive eyes softened reminiscently. "My grandmother told me he was quite a blade in those days. He danced a lot and studied a little. His friends changed his comical first name and nicknamed him Nazi instead. They swore he'd come to nothing professionally. He confounded them when he graduated by choosing obstetrics—at that time the most tragic medical specialty of all."

Her perfume filled his nostrils. Her eyes were downcast, the long black lashes resting on the satin of her cheeks. Her expression was unreadable. "I'm not boring you with these details, am I?" he asked anxiously.

"Of course not."

She was tempted to laugh. In every campaign she'd broached to win a man, there had always been a tenuous thread to draw him to her before a relationship could be formed. In Brian's case it had been her reminder to him of Val. With Kirby Semmel it would be, of all things, her "genuine" interest in the foibles of his Hungarian ancestor.

She sat on the bed and crossed her booted legs. "You told me in my office that you've patterned your life after Semmelweiss. Tell me about him . . . and about you."

The gratitude in his face was her reward. He smiled for the first time since she'd met him. It was a boyish, trusting smile and the difference in their ages was brought sharply home to her. He sat down beside her.

"Semmelweiss and I aren't alike, except maybe in

the stubbornness of our convictions. Do you know that when he went to work in 1846 at the First Maternity Division of Vienna General, he saw 451 women die that year of childbed fever?"

"My God!"

"The irony of it was that even after he proved that the doctors doing the deliveries were also doing autopsies, and that the contagion was being carried from the cadavers to the women by these very doctors, the fat-bellied bigwigs of his time refused to believe it."

Eva marveled at the intensity in his face. His fists were clenched and there was outrage written in every line of his body. "They broke him, Eva. He struggled for close to twenty years to make them see. And in the end they broke him. He was taken to a public insane asylum in August of 1865. He died two weeks later, but not before he'd written this." He rose from the bed, lifted a black-bound manuscript carefully from the bureau drawer and handed it to her.

"The Semmelweiss Indictment," she crowed.

He nodded. "It's all there. His accusations against Klein, the idiot professor who ran the Maternity Division of Vienna General, against Braun, the doctor who replaced Semmelweiss as first assistant there, against Professor Scanzoni of Warzburg, whom he denounces 'before God and the world as a murderer.' It's wild, it's repetitious, at times the raving of a half-crazed madman. It's also the most heart-rending documentary of medical obtuseness you'll ever see."

She opened the binder. There was no title page. The thin book was written on parchment with a fine steel pen. The pages had yellowed and the black ink faded a bit, but the script was legible. She flipped the pages quickly and breathed a sigh of relief. It was clearly signed on the last page. "Ignaz Phillip Semmelweiss."

It was worth a blurb in *The Times*, she was sure.

And that was important. Publicity was half the battle in attracting the owners of medical memorabilia. They were a reluctant lot at best. Most of them held to their corroding treasures for what they called "sentimental reasons," when in reality the crumbling relic they clutched so tightly was the closest brush with fame they would ever have in their humdrum lives and they knew it. Sometimes their willingness to part with the item hinged more on the promise that they would see their names in print than it did on the amount of money she offered.

She doubted that this would be the case with Semmel. He was standing over her, waiting for her verdict, rubbing the sides of his jeans with flat sweaty palms. It had been difficult enough to bring himself to part with the heirloom. Talking about money for it would be harder. He really was a poor bargainer, she thought indulgently. No one in his right mind admitted to a buyer that he was badly in need of money. But it was this very naiveté she found so attractive.

"Well, what do you think?" he asked.

"It's in very good condition."

He passed a hand over his curly hair and fidgeted with the neckline of his sweater. "Look . . . I'm a better doctor than I am a businessman so you'll have to help me."

"All right. How much was your grandmother going to give you to open that office?"

"A hundred thousand dollars."

"I think we can give you a quarter of that."

His jaw dropped and his black brows drew together in an incredulous vee. "My God, you're being generous."

"Not really," she said truthfully. "It's quite a find." She knew that Lilly would have offered him much more.

He plopped down on the bed beside her. "You know, I always owed my inspiration to Semmelweiss. I never thought I'd owe my future to him also."

She looked at the stolid, balding researcher in the photo above the bed and wondered idly how any woman could have been attracted to him. "Did Semmelweiss have a wife?"

He nodded. "Marie. He didn't marry until he was thirty-eight and she was much younger than he was. But she was an inspiration to him."

Her face turned wistful. "I envy her."

"Why?"

"It must be wonderful to be really needed by a man. I'd like to know what that feels like some day."

"But surely, in your marriage . . . I mean, your husband must . . ." He floundered, awkward in his probing, uncertain of his ground. Her face had closed like a lily at sunset. He touched the fleecy sleeve of her sweater, reacted to her softness and withdrew. He was by nature passionate, but controlled. He felt himself getting in beyond his depth now. He would have liked to extricate himself with a clever phrase, a turn of words that would alter the sexual overtones that had somehow crept in. But all he could think of was that her dark eyes had filled with tears and her rounded breasts were heaving with the turmoil of her emotions.

"My husband needs only himself," she murmured, not looking at him. "He's an executive, a robot who's lost the capacity to feel. Our marriage has been an arrangement for years. The trouble is," she whispered, "I'm lonely in it." She dabbed at her eyes with the back of her sleeve and smiled bravely at him. "But why am I burdening you with my problems? You have your own to think about, and I'm sure there's some girl who's as close to you as Marie was to her 'Nazi.'"

A brooding look crossed his face. His blunted fingers smoothed the binder she held in her lap with long, loving strokes. "There is no girl, Eva. Oh, there has been. I'm no celibate monk. But I'm too serious for most of them. I'm a throwback, I guess. To *grandpère* Semmelweiss. I get my kicks out of working and achieving and I think that kind of thing has gone out of style."

"You belittle yourself," she said. "And there's no need."

He covered her hand with his coarse one. She could feel its roughness against her tender palm. She had all to do to keep from reaching out to him.

He spoke in a low voice. "Do you know when I first met you in your office I didn't like you. But after I left, I kept thinking about you. Seeing you at the oddest times. In the eyes of a patient, or the quick turn of a nurse's walk. I felt you could only be trouble for me, so I deliberately tried to kill the attraction. I went to the library and looked up everything I could find on Eva Anslow in the newspapers. And there was plenty. 'Traynor heiress opens season in Monaco,' 'St. Moritz welcomes Eva Anslow,' 'Cannes Festival wines the jet set.'"

"I ran because I was unhappy."

"I know that now. I didn't then. It gave me the strength to turn you off when you phoned all those times." He kissed her lightly, as if in apology.

She smiled tremulously. "I can be persistent."

"So can I."

He kissed her again, less hurriedly this time. His breathing quickened, his hands slid beneath her sweater, groped awkwardly for her breasts. His love-making was that of a boy's, enthusiastic and untutored, with all the rawness of emotion that her last jaded lover had forfeited with practice. How she would enjoy teaching him, Eva exulted, her senses reeling at the prospect.

Her arms slipped about his neck, her fingertips teased the lobes of his ears, her lips parted beneath his. His kiss deepened, exploded quickly into exploring hands and whispered caresses. "I need you, Eva." A wave of heat washed over her as his coarse hands slid beneath her skirt and roughed the silken flesh of her thighs. She worked her fingers beneath his sweater, caressed his back in wide, circular motions, letting her nails flick the smooth skin at intervals. The momentary pain roused him uncontrollably.

He urged her back on the bed. "Eva, please," he whispered. He had kicked his moccasins off. His face was slicked with sweat, his dark eyes vulnerable, his upper lip puffy where she had drawn it between her teeth.

He tore at her skirt, pulled the sweater over her head. There was time to teach him, she thought, shivering as those workman's hands kneaded the bare flesh of her buttocks. She moved to accommodate him, lifted her hips.

From the walls, the specter of Semmelweiss glowered in disapproval as the priceless Indictment slid from between them to lie abandoned on the floor.

Chapter 14

The first inkling Brian had that something was wrong that Monday morning came from Mildred Benson. Surrounded by her circular desk in the reception area of the marble-pillared lobby, she was hunched over the switchboard at nine o'clock like a soldier under attack. The board was brightly lit and Mildred's mouth was working at gunfire speed.

"I'm sorry. I don't know about that. No, I can't put you through to his secretary. She's tied up now. You'll have to call back." She flicked to the next call. "No. The lab is busy now." She bridled noticeably. "You want *me* to authenticate?" she shrilled. "What do I know? I'm only the receptionist." Her wrinkled face was creased as tightly as her gray sausage curls.

Striding toward her, Brian was already unbuttoning his coat. The prediction of rain had been superseded by a wet snow. Clumps of it slipped from his shoes and melted into muddy zig-zags on the white terrazzo floor. "Good morning, Mildred. What's going on? You look as if you're under siege."

Her expression was as sour as her voice. "What did you expect, Mr. Anslow?" Her owl-like eyes focused on his face, turned incredulous. "You don't know, do you?"

"Know what?"

"Haven't you read the paper yet?"

"I didn't get a chance to."

She reached into the bottom drawer and slapped a folded copy of *The Post* on her desk. "Here. Be my guest." She turned back to the clamor of the board.

Brian didn't have to look far. The lower half of the front page was given over to Blasa Fever. To the left the caption read: FOURTH ATTACK OF BLASA FEVER SPURS NATION'S FEAR OF EPIDEMIC. The article stated that an overnight beach party held to herald a rock star's performance in Fort Lauderdale, Florida, had become the scene of yet another fever episode. Twenty-seven teenagers were now isolated in a Lauderdale hospital with the dreaded symptoms of fever, jaundice, and gastrointestinal cramping rampant among them. The rest were in quarantine, pending further developments.

To the right, the caption was labeled: "BLASA FEVER TESTING REPORTED AT DRUG LAB." Brian felt a sinking sensation in the pit of his stomach as he read:

At the request of the Food and Drug Administration, a possible cure for Blasa Fever in the form of an antibiotic is being tested at a small hospital attached to Traynor Laboratories in Clayville, Long Island. The patients are volunteers from an upstate prison who are in the early stages of the disease. It is too soon to ascertain the results of the testing at this time.

"Jesus!" Brian muttered.

Mildred covered the phone. "Likewise, I'm sure."

Brian strode toward an open elevator. The only occupant in it was a sixty-two-year-old vat operator named Morgan Effram. Usually verbose, he nodded curtly to Brian, then looked away.

Brian wished he could ignore the slight. It had hurt

him that co-workers and employees he had thought of as friends had turned from him in distrust after he'd been named president. He had hoped in time to regain that trust. This morning's publicity on the Fever testing was going to make that impossible.

Up on the third floor, a harried Dora Watkins was waiting for him at her desk. Her coat was still slung over her arm. Never had he appreciated her professionalism more. She was trying to extricate herself from a phone conversation with a pushy reporter. Only her eyes showed the frantic pressure she'd been under since she arrived. Her voice was as matter of fact as the dark print dress and orthopedic shoes that accented her plump figure.

"No. Mr. Anslow isn't available now. I'm sure we'll have a statement for the press later. I'm sorry, I can't tell you if the *Post* account is true."

She hung up the phone. Her myopic eyes regarded him without expression. "It is true, isn't it?"

"Yes."

"I'm glad. It's something Mr. Traynor wanted very much to implement before he died. But I think you should know the rest of the employees don't feel the way I do. They're scared, Mr. Anslow." She handed him the morning's mail. "Dr. Traynor is waiting for you in your office. I thought it would be all right."

He nodded. "Dora, while I'm with Dr. Traynor I want you to contact our public relations man. Ask him if he can use his pull at the *Post* to find out who the reporter was who turned that story in, and where he obtained his material."

Inside his office, Valerie was staring out the window at the puddles of slush clogging the parking lot. A copy of the *Post* was rolled between her hands. She whirled at the click of the door and hurried to meet him. He was shocked at how haggard she looked. Her eyes had pouches beneath them that spoke of many nights of aborted sleep.

"My God, Brian, how did it get out this fast?" she demanded.

"I'm trying to find that out now." He slung his coat over a chair. "Val, how far along are you and Wally with the proof on this Tetra-2?"

"You too?" she accused.

He frowned. "I don't understand." Temperament had never been one of her failings.

"It's not hard to understand. The first call I got this morning was from the Food and Drug Administration. Why the publicity they wanted to know? Hadn't we spoken about keeping this quiet? However, now that the cat was out of the bag, they didn't want to pressure, *but* how close was I to an answer? Because you see, that would get everyone off the hook. If I could prove that Tetra-2 was the cure for Blasa Fever, it would justify it all. The unorthodox government permission for human testing, the outlay of monies for the program, the risk to the employees. All of it wiped out like magic."

She groped backward for the edge of the desk and slumped tiredly against it. "Well, we're not magicians. We're just your common variety scientists trying to do the best we can. As of now you'll have to look elsewhere for your justification. The nineteen volunteers are on a maintenance dose of 175 mg. of Tetra-2 per day. They're sustaining it well. None of them have worsened. But none have shown significant signs of improvement either. And that's where it stands."

He put his hands on her shoulders. "Val, I wasn't blaming."

She looked at him with despairing eyes. "Why shouldn't you blame? If it wasn't for my insistence with Alex, you wouldn't be in this mess. In a little

while I'm going back into my quarantined cocoon
where nobody can get at me. But you'll be right out
here. A prime whipping boy for whoever wants to take
pot shots."

He put his arms around her and kissed her lightly.
"It's nice to know you're hurting for me."

She stirred under his touch. "A lot of good it will
do you."

The phone rang. He reached for it with one hand.
He listened to Dora's explanation, muttered "hold
on," then muffled the mouthpiece against his jacket.
"There's a mob trying to get past reception," he said
to Val. "Lester Pryor and the security guards are
trying to control it, but they're having a tough time."

She grimaced. "You'd better get down there." She
ducked under his arm. "Kiss Mark for me. I'll be in
touch from the lab." She crossed to the door and let
herself out.

He lifted the phone to his ear. "Dora, call Joe Barbetta and tell him to meet me down at reception in a
few minutes. Then get hold of Roy Penzinger and tell
him to get out here as fast as he can."

She was still on the phone when he strode past her
and headed for the elevator.

Joe Barbetta was head of security. Middle-aged but
still brawny, he was a former police lieutenant who
had retired into the job at Traynor Laboratories after
twenty years of service on the force. For years, Alexander Traynor had turned a deaf ear to Barbetta's
complaint that security at Traynor was too lax. Alex
had claimed that Barbetta's gripes were the frustrated
bleatings of an ex-cop craving for action. But Brian
had never agreed.

In an emergency, except for the steel doors between
the plant and the laboratory-hospital area, which could
be triggered shut from inside the lab, there was no

way to automatically seal off any door in the plant. During the day, the guards stationed at the entrance doors identified the employees by the plastic blue and orange cards they were issued each year, *if* they bothered to wear them. More often it was a question of recognition or a guard's "good judgment" that gained a person entry. The fact was, it was as easy to get in and out of Traynor Labs as pushing a revolving door. Except in the divisions where maximum security was enforced.

The two maximum security divisions were the narcotic manufacturing areas where the doors were locked and only authorized personnel were allowed to enter, and the vaults on the warehouse level which operated under a separate security system of their own.

As the elevator doors slid open, Brian saw that the lobby was overflowing with people. It took him a second to realize that there were two distinct groups to contend with. One surrounded Mildred Benson who could no longer be seen. Her desk was engulfed by newspapermen and women clamoring for attention. The other was closer to the entrance where Lester Pryor and a security guard were trying to keep order.

Joe Barbetta met him as he stepped off the elevator. He swaggered a bit in his uniform, aware of the women in the lobby. White haired, with a bulbous nose and a caustic tongue, he was a big fish in a little pond, who, because of Alex, had never had the chance to throw his weight around. His leathery face held a cynical expression.

He gestured toward the bedlam in front of them. "Hell of a way to prove a point," he said in a gruff voice. "Too bad old man Traynor isn't here to see it."

Brian was annoyed by his vindictiveness. "Never mind that now. Let's try to handle it."

"How?"

"Shift to weekend security for a few hours. Close off the front doors and station a guard at every other entrance. Anyone who doesn't have a card or can't be definitely identified isn't to be allowed in."

"That won't hold at lunch break. I can't keep all the employees in and once those doors are opened . . ."

"I've sent for the Chief of Police. He should be able to reinforce your staff by then so it can be handled. After that, we'll see."

"What about the people in the lobby now?"

"I'll take care of that."

Brian watched him stride off then waded into the melee. Mildred's tired face sagged with relief as she caught a glimpse of him. "Here's Mr. Anslow now," she said. Within seconds Brian was surrounded by a bevy of reporters. Some held notebooks. Some held cameras. All of them seemed to be talking at once.

"What's the name of the antibiotic?"

"Does it work?"

"Why was *The Post* the only newspaper to be given the story?"

A flashbulb went off in Brian's face. He blinked, held up a hand for silence. "Ladies and gentlemen. I can understand how anxious you are to get this story, since the *Post* seems to have scooped the rest of you on it . . . how, I don't know. But I can't answer your questions now." There were protests and groans.

"Can you tell us how close you are to a cure?" one pretty dark-haired girl called out.

Brian ignored her. "At three o'clock this afternoon, I will hold a newspaper conference in the small Board room on the third floor. At that time I'll answer your questions to the best of my ability. Now the front door has been closed off for security reasons. So if you'll all please follow the blue-uniformed officer at the rear of the lobby . . ."

They moved grudgingly, talking among themselves, and jotting notes as they left.

The second group was larger and by far the harder to control. They stretched four deep in an uneven line from the front door past the glass wall of products. They were belligerent and compliant in turn, hooting at Pryor and the security guards, some of the younger ones threatening a sit-in. They were from every walk of life; a tearful teenager in blue jeans and peacoat, a well-dressed elderly gentleman with white hair and proud mien, a swarthy woman in somber black.

"What do they want, Lester?" Brian shouted above the din.

Pryor's arms were outstretched like the savior on the cross. He twisted his red head at an impossible angle to talk to Brian. "That antibiotic or your hide," he panted. "Most of these people are relatives of Blasa Fever victims."

The babble of the crowd rose to a crescendo.

"Let them go," Brian ordered.

"Are you mad?"

"Let them go."

Pryor and the security guards stepped back. The crowd surged forward. For a moment they threatened to swamp Brian, then from the chaos came a haphazard kind of order. They pushed and jostled each other to form a tight circle around him, those in the back craning their necks for a better view.

The sea of faces swam in front of Brian, all different, all alike. Hope was the common denominator, and he was about to take it away from them. "You don't see people," Alex had said. Well, he was seeing them now . . . with a vengeance. There but for the Grace of God, he thought. If it was Mark who was stricken with the Fever he would be out there pleading with them.

A lump formed in his throat. He lifted his hands to them for understanding. "Look, everybody, I know that you all have loved ones who are afflicted with Blasa Fever in varying stages. I realize that after what you read in the *Post* this morning that you're looking to us for answers. I wish we could give them to you. It's true that we're testing an antibiotic for Blasa Fever but there's no way yet to tell if it will succeed or fail."

"When will you be able to tell?" the elderly gentleman asked.

"I'm sorry, the hospital hasn't been able to name any time span. I wish we could give you more promising news."

They were silent. Tears coursed down the swarthy woman's cheeks. She made no move to check them. Brian had an urge to comfort her, but there was nothing to say. They parted ranks for him. He turned on his heel and strode toward the elevator. He had no desire to see their faces as they filed toward the exit.

Outside the office, Dora Watkins was just getting off the phone. Usually poker-faced, her expression was indignant, her back stiff with outrage. She slammed the phone into its cradle. "Freedom of the press . . ." she muttered.

Brian's eyes questioned her.

"It's the *Post*," she burst out. "Our P.R. man couldn't get to first base with them. He finally got some rude flunky who informed him of what he already knew. The *Post* is in no way bound to reveal the source of their information on this morning's story. Of course, if it's inaccurate or we want to refute it, that's another matter."

Brian nodded. It wasn't inaccurate and he couldn't

refute the truth. At the newspaper conference this afternoon he intended to ask that in the interest of science, the reporters play down the testing program in the future. He could only hope they would comply.

He turned toward his office but she halted him with a gesture. "Mr. Anslow . . ." Her voice was apologetic. "Tom Nordsen from shipping is on his way up here to see you . . ."

Brian shook his head. "Dora, how could you . . ."

"I tried to stop him. Honestly, I did."

Brian felt emotionally wrung out. The last one he wanted to see now was Tom Nordsen. Refusing help to a crowd of pleading strangers had been hard enough. But he had known Tom for sixteen years.

The sound of heavy footsteps coming down the corridor told Brian there was no longer any choice. Nordsen bore down on them like a racer on his last lap. He was of medium height, in his fifties, a muscular, once amiable man whose Swedish heritage was reflected in the blond hair and ruddy complexion of his broad face.

Shy and untalkative, "the Swede," as he was fondly called, was head of shipping. He was a hard taskmaster with a loyal following that kept the cartons rolling out of Traynor with assembly-like regularity.

He stopped in front of Brian, started to put out a hand, then awkwardly drew it back and wiped it on a handkerchief before stretching it out again. Born in Sweden, Tom had migrated to Norway ten years before the Germans invaded it. His fierce resistance to their domination led to his capture and arrest. The nightmares he suffered from and the tattoo on his arm bore proof of the horrors he'd witnessed in Auschwitz. In 1943 he managed to tunnel his way free of the concentration camp and escape with his wife to the United States.

Like most Europeans, Tom had a strong sense of

class distinction. He saw Brian as part of "ownership" and himself as a workman. Though Brian had urged him to drop the formal "Mr. Anslow" many times, he had refused to do so.

"I appreciate your seeing me," he said. They shook hands. He didn't smile. Brian hadn't seen him smile since his eight-year-old daughter had come home from camp in August with Blasa Fever.

Brian put an arm around his shoulders. "Come into my office, Tom."

Inside the office, Nordsen sat in a wood backed chair next to Brian's. His face was haggard, his eyes pouched from lack of sleep. He wore a red and black checked wool shirt and chino trousers cinched tight at the waist with a braided brown leather belt.

"Would you like a drink, Tom?"

Rumor had it that since his little girl had become ill, Tom had been hitting the bottle too often. There were criss-crossed patches of purple on his cheeks to bear it out.

He shook his head. He had difficulty with the language and he was worried about putting his thoughts into words that would persuade. "Mr. Anslow . . . you know about my daughter?"

"Yes. I'm sorry, Tom."

"We didn't have Wendy until very late and we cannot have more children. My wife . . . she isn't a well woman." His throat clogged. "I think I'll take that drink now."

Brian rose to the sideboard, glad to be away from that pain-filled stare if only for a few seconds.

"Scotch?"

"Fine."

The drink seemed to give the Swede courage. His voice, uncertain at first, grew deeper, more natural.

"My wife sits in the house all the time now with

Wendy. Looking at her twisted legs. Listening to her cry in pain. She doesn't cry loud. She has no strength." He lowered his voice as if there were someone else in the room. "Mr. Anslow, I worry for my wife. If something happens to Wendy, she will never be the same."

"Tom, you have to understand . . ."

He didn't hear. "This morning my wife reads the newspaper about the Blasa Fever. She leaves the house and goes to St. Catherine's on the corner of our block. It is the first time she has gone from the house in six months." His lips quivered. "Do you know what it is to be given hope when there is no hope?"

"Tom, listen to me," Brian said. "I feel for you and your wife. Believe me I do. But I couldn't give you that antibiotic if I wanted to. There has been no proof that it works."

He nodded acceptingly. "We talked of this. We are willing to have Wendy be a volunteer in the program. There is nothing to lose."

"There's a life to lose. A prerequisite for the program is that the volunteers be in the early stages of Blasa Fever. One of the volunteers wasn't. He died because of it. You wouldn't want that to happen to Wendy, would you?"

The Swede's mottled cheeks flushed a deep red. "Let that be up to God. Let him cure her or take her. She is not alive the way she is now. Nor is my wife." He took out his handkerchief, blew his nose and strove for calm. "Mr. Anslow," he said in a quieter voice. "My wife and I do not ask that you be responsible. We ask only that you give us the way."

"I can't do it, Tom."

"Why not?"

"The Government would never allow it."

"Who is boss here? You or the Government?"

Brian rose and went to the credenza for his cigarettes. "You don't understand."

The blue eyes turned suddenly furious. "Oh yes. I understand. The others, they told me not to come to you. 'Brian Anslow looks out for himself' they said. I say 'That is not true. Brian Anslow is my friend. He will help me.'"

There was desperation in Brian's voice. "Tom, I have no choice here."

His broad face clamped shut. His blue eyes regarded Brian contemptuously. "There is always choice. When you are made president the others say you force Alexander Traynor to make you boss. I choose then. I say no. Brian Anslow is a good man."

Brian made a helpless gesture then shook his head in resignation.

Nordsen's mouth became a spare line. "I choose again. The others make plans to hurt you. I listen now. Brian Anslow is no longer my friend."

He rose from his chair. Sick at heart, Brian made no move to stop him. He stalked from the room with his heavy stride and slammed the door behind him.

Chapter 15

Valerie's statement to Brian about retreating to her quarantined cocoon to avoid the repercussions of the *Post* article proved a wish rather than a fact. In the next few days, she and Wally Chandler were bombarded by phone calls from the Food and Drug Administration, the National Institutes of Health, and the Center for Disease Control.

Aside from the four outbreaks, which had been mostly contained in the areas where the infection had struck, Blasa Fever was now spreading throughout the country at an alarming rate.

The news didn't surprise Val or Wally. It was their theory that Blasa Fever, like typhoid, was being transmitted by carriers who had survived the disease and become immune to the organisms in the intestinal tract. Any poor sanitary practices on the part of these survivors, such as inadequate washing or hand scrubbing after toilet use, could be transmitting the organisms to food or drink for others. This would be especially true in the case of recovered food handlers such as cooks, waitresses, supermarket personnel, and butchers, whose touch could infect half the country within a short time.

But theories weren't important now. Facts were what the Government needed. And above all, a cure.

Val chafed under the pressure. It was impossible

for her to give any reassurances of being near a solution. Only two of the patients had shown improvement since the administration of the antibiotic, but the change was too slight for judgment.

The first had been Sid Draper. Upon entering the ward, Draper's temperature had been 102 degrees. He was jaundiced with intermittent stomach cramping and severe headaches. After the second dose of Tetra-2, his temperature climbed to 104 degrees, then the headaches subsided.

Early on Tuesday morning Draper sat up in bed and looked around him. The ward was quiet with most of the men asleep. In the bed to the left of him, Colonel Darwin snored with rhythmic abandon.

To Draper's right lay Tiny Anderson. Big blubber, Sid had dubbed him. He was all flab with those washed out features and whiny references to "his little girls." It turned Sid's stomach after a while.

Draper couldn't judge the time, but he knew it had to be before seven o'clock because Charley Santos wasn't there yet.

Across the room, Dr. Traynor was attending to the boxer, Jefferson Montgomery. Montgomery seemed to have been hit hardest of all. He'd been up half the night moaning and flexing those huge black fists as if he could punch his way out of the misery that engulfed him. His inky face was slick with sweat and under the blankets his body was jackknifed in an effort to ease the intestinal cramping.

Draper licked his chapped lips and called to Val in a voice crusty with disuse. "Dr. Traynor, can I brush my teeth?"

She put a finger to her lips, bidding him to be silent, and crossed the room to his bedside. The yellow had faded from his skin and his eyes had lost their sunken look.

"You can in a little while," she said. "The nurse will be making the rounds and most of the men will be up by then. How do you feel?"

He grinned. "Like I could make it to the Helicopter Club without keeling over." His strong white teeth were coated with a glutinous film.

She checked his temperature. It was down to 100 degrees. A seed of hope took root inside her. It meant nothing, she schooled herself. She knew enough not to raise her hopes on the fluctuation of a few degrees. Still, he *looked* better.

She remembered the cardiologist at Johns Hopkins who had cursed the interns out on rounds when they diagnosed strictly by the book. "Dammit," he'd shouted. "*Look* at the patient. His eyes, fingernails, the color of his skin, the way he's breathing. These are as important as the textbook symptoms you're spouting at me like programmed robots."

Draper shifted his legs under the blanket as if testing their mobility. "How about it, Doc?" he asked.

"How about what?"

He shook his head at her obtuseness. "The Helicopter Club. I could use a little rest and relaxation."

So could they all, she thought. After giving the first injection of Tetra-2 she and Wally had taken turns sleeping in the cramped little room the small hospital provided. They averaged about five hours sleep a night and the pace was beginning to tell on her. In the mirror this morning, she had been startled by her appearance. Her eyes were bloodshot, the hollows under them so indented she looked more like a patient than a doctor. Her blonde hair was in need of a washing and her skin had a dry, flaky look. But it wasn't her physical appearance that bothered her. It was her emotional state. And that wasn't due to a lack of sleep.

Since the aborted love-making in the "rest room,"

there had been a possessive look in Wally's eyes as if something had been settled between them, when in fact it hadn't.

Last night he had come up behind her in the kitchen as she was cleaning the dinner tray from the table.

He slid his arms around her waist and nuzzled the back of her neck. "Marry me," he said.

She turned to face him. "Just like that?" She kept her voice light, but her heart was pounding like a trip-hammer.

"I'd get down on my knees, but I'm so beat I'm afraid I'd never get up again." He kissed the corner of her mouth. "What do you say?"

"I . . . I'm not sure."

"Because of Anslow?"

She was silent.

He stroked her cheek with the back of his palm. "Darling, you're such a masochist. You're holding to an outdated dream as if it were a reality. Anslow doesn't care about you. If he did he'd get rid of his wife no matter what the consequences."

"He'd lose his son. He loves him very much."

"More than he loves you? Val, don't you see what you're doing? You're allowing Anslow to dangle you like a puppet. He won't have you and he won't release you." He took her hands in his and held them tightly. "Darling, don't waste your life dealing in unrealities. I love you. I want to marry you. I'm not afraid of what you feel for Anslow because I know he's not right for you. And you know it too."

He kissed her long and deeply. She pressed close to him, savoring the warmth of his body. When he released her, she felt shaken, confused.

Her eyes pleaded with him for understanding. "Wally, everything you've said is true. I don't know what's holding me back. Maybe it's the Tetra-2 program. Maybe I'm so wrapped up in what's going on, I can't think straight. I don't know the answer. I only know that I need more time."

"How long?"

"The end of the week."

"What will you know then that you don't know now?"

She didn't reply.

He sighed. "All right. I'll wait."

That had been three days ago, Valerie thought miserably. On Friday she would have to say yes or face losing Wally. And she wasn't prepared to do either.

Sid Draper tugged at her arm. "What about that 'R & R'?" he reminded her.

"What you could use is a little more bedrest," she told him. "Why don't you read those comics Dennie sent you?"

From the bed near the corner, the cockney, Alfie Brockwell, rolled over. He had refused to let the nurses shave his beard, claiming that, like Samson, his hair was his strength. By far the most tractable of the patients, the lack of delineation between his unkempt locks and the dark fuzz on his cheeks gave him the appearance of a hulking bear.

His case was a puzzle to Val and Wally. Brockwell had entered the hospital with a normal temperature and his recent stool cultures showed no signs of the Blasa Fever organisms. Yet he continued to cramp intermittently, the pains so severe at times that sedation was required.

"Listen, chum," he whispered to Draper. "Mind if I share those comics with you? All I've got to read is my mail," he grinned, "or what's left of it after the censors chop the best parts. I'm a bit balmy in here what with the colonel snoring and that bloody bastard Santos on my tail." He caught Valerie's eye. "Begging your pardon, doctor."

She ignored his apology. "Has Charley Santos been bothering you?"

"In a manner of speaking."

"What manner of speaking?"

He looked uncomfortable. His black brows drew together in a shaggy vee as he sought to explain. "Well, you see, Charley hates cons. But he hates foreign cons worse. If it was up to him, Charley'd have my hide on a platter and ship it back to London for a main course." He scratched the side of his nose. It was broad with deep indentations and widened pores edging the nostrils. "No need to bother your head about it, ma'am. Alfie Brockwell can take care of himself."

She didn't doubt that for a second. When she had examined him the first time, she had been astounded by the bulging muscles on his hairy arms and torso. Brockwell had explained that before going into his more lucrative "bank ventures," he had been a weight lifter in Manchester, "picking up tuppence for balancing dumbbells over my head."

Valerie's eyes went over the men in the ward. Though some were beginning to stir, she was glad to see that Ansel Golden slept on. Since Freddie Bishop's death, he had been morose, wakeful. She had sat with him the first night, hoping to ease his grief by drawing him out. But he had talked little of himself. Instead, he had done the questioning. She had found herself telling him about her research on Blasa Fever and her uncertain hopes for Tetra-2. His questions were pointed, his grasp of the difficulties as astute as any man of science she had encountered yet. She had come away with a feeling of sadness. Behind bars,

Ansel Golden was a waste of a human being. She couldn't help wondering what had put him there.

At two A.M. this morning she had found out.

Past midnight, the ward was hushed, the lights dimmed. The smell of antiseptic permeated the room. Except for Jefferson Montgomery, who moaned and tossed fitfully, the men were sleeping quietly. Dressed in isolation garb, the guard kept vigil from his chair in the middle of the ward. From time to time his eyes drooped and his head fell forward before he caught himself and jerked upward like a dog on a choke leash.

On her final rounds, Valerie halted at Ansel Golden's bedside. She could barely make out his features in the shadow of the night light. His thin face was a mixture of angles and planes. His short gray hair stood away from his head like the quills of a porcupine. She bent closer. His pale blue eyes were wide open.

"Why aren't you sleeping, Ansel?" she whispered.

He smiled. The smile softened the rigid line of his jaw. "To sleep . . . to sleep. Perchance to dream."

"Are your dreams that bad?"

"Bad enough. Sit beside me for a few minutes."

"If you like." She pulled a chair close to him. She felt his eyes examining her features with an intensity that puzzled her. It wasn't the first time he'd done it. There had been moments in the ward when she'd looked up from a patient to find him staring at her with that penetrating yet impersonal gaze. It disconcerted her.

"Why do you look at me like that?"

"Like what?"

She pondered. It was hard to put feelings into words. "As if you're not really seeing me at all."

"You're very astute." He was quiet so long she thought that was all he was going to say. Then, "Would it offend you if I told you that you remind me

of my wife?" She shook her head. "Oh, not in looks,"
he qualified. "The only thing you have in common
that way is your hair. She was blonde too." He
reached up and touched her hair softly, reverently.
When he spoke again his voice was low, lonely. "My
wife worked with recently blinded people, teaching
them to compensate for their loss by using their other
senses. It's a pity she never taught me the same
thing." He cleared his throat. "It's her strength of
spirit I see in you. She was a remarkable woman."

"Was?"

He nodded. "She's dead." There was a short
pause, then, "I killed her."

A wave of shock passed through Valerie. The absence of emotion in his voice was more frightening to
her than if he'd said it menacingly.

He pleated the sheet between his thumb and forefinger and creased it to a thin line with his fingernails.
"She had cancer. Inoperable. I loved her very much."
The words were tight, choppy. His face was ashen
against the pillow. She reached for his pulse, but he
pushed her hand away. "It was cancer of the colon.
She suffered a long time. Trying to spare me until she
couldn't anymore. She didn't ask to die. She wouldn't
do that to me. It was I who made the decision. But
she knew. She said 'goodbye' instead of 'goodnight'
when I gave her the pills that evening."

"Are you sorry?"

"No. I would do it again."

He released the sheet and smoothed it absentmind-
edly over the blanket with long sensitive fingers. "You
know, we live in a strange world. If a horse breaks a
leg, we shoot it because we don't want it to suffer.
Yet a human being is condemned to live on in an agony
of pain until 'nature takes its course' or 'God has his
will.' Those were the clichés that self-righteous pros-

ecutor used in court to sway any of the jurors who might have been on my side. I think it offended him that I was a doctor and might be setting a precedent for others if any leniency was shown."

Val was silent. Who was she to cast a stone? As an intern she had done her stint with terminal patients and had been tempted to do the same thing Ansel Golden had done. And she hadn't been related to any of them.

"I don't know much about legalities, Ansel, but it seems to me that euthanasia isn't regarded the same way now as it was years ago. I read of a case in New Jersey where a man was acquitted for killing his brother who would have lived his life out as a vegetable. And there have been others. Couldn't you appeal on that basis today?"

"My lawyer has been after me to do just that."

"Why haven't you?"

"What for? I have no children. What would be waiting for me on the outside?"

"But you're a surgeon. You have a talent. A means to give to others."

He held up his hands. They trembled as he stared at them. "These?" He laughed dryly. "It's been fifteen years since I touched a scalpel."

"You could start again."

He shook his head. "No. It's over for me. I stopped kidding myself about that a long time ago."

She left him then because Wally came to relieve her. But the look of resignation on his thin face stayed with her for a long time afterward.

At three o'clock the following afternoon, Wally was called down to the microbiology lab while they were mid-way through administering the antibiotic to the volunteers. At three thirty, when Val finished with the injections, Wally still hadn't returned. Surprisingly, Charley Santos was still there. Normally, he left at three, and today she knew was especially important because he was driving upstate to see his family.

She stripped off her gloves and walked to where he stood near the window. Unlike the other guards, Santos rarely sat. He was by nature restless and prowled the ward like a hunter seeking game. He smiled as she came toward him and his broken nose spread across his swarthy features.

"Mr. Santos, why are you still here?"

"Because the other guard isn't. I told him to get here early, but he's takin' his own sweet time."

"You'll never make it upstate at this rate. The roads are still icy from that sleet last night. Why don't you go on ahead?"

"And leave you alone with these cons? No way."

Charley was a throwback to a "damsel in distress" era and there was nothing she could do about it. She swept the room with a broad gesture. "Mr. Santos, *look* at 'these cons.' If one of them had the strength to get up and do any harm, I'd cheer. Besides, Tod Preston is with me and I'm sure your replacement will be here any second."

He delayed for ten minutes more then reluctantly left.

Val continued to monitor the ward. She speculated about the call Wally had received from microbiology. She had been down there yesterday. The monkeys and rabbits that were continuing to be tested on the Tetra-2 were all doing well and Arby's hyperactivity was subsiding.

A sudden movement from one of the beds caught her eye. Tiny Anderson had thrown the blankets aside and was sitting up in bed. He dangled his feet over the edge and wiggled his toes.

Anderson was the other patient who had shown improvement. When she'd last checked him his fever had still been up, but he was less weak and the apathy had abated. She hurried to his side. He was a mountain of a man with a broad flaccid face and baby fine platinum hair. He stood up and flinched as his bare feet touched the icy tiles. Tall as she was, the top of Val's head reached only to his shoulders.

Smiling, she put a hand on his arm. "I'm glad to see you're feeling better, Mr. Anderson, but you're not ready to get up yet."

From the bed next to her, Colonel Darwin made a sound of disgust. "Does *better* mean that tub of lard is going to toss and turn the way he has been for the last half hour? Because if it does, I'd appreciate being moved."

Valerie ignored him. She increased the pressure of her hand. "Come on, Mr. Anderson. Back in bed now."

Her words fell on deaf ears. He didn't budge. His glance darted about the room as if he'd never seen it before. His fingers tugged incessantly at the hem of his pajama top. He mumbled something she couldn't understand. She looked into his eyes. They were dilated with a rapid uncontrollable movement she had seen somewhere before. For a moment she couldn't think. Then it came to her.

Arby! My God, he was hyperactive!

"Preston!" she called to the attendant, trying to conceal her panic. There was no way to know what form a hyperactive reaction would take in a human being.

Preston was at her side in seconds. He was broad rather than tall, with muscular arms and legs. "Help me get Mr. Anderson back in bed," she said. They held his arms, coaxed and pleaded, to no avail. Tiny

Anderson was in a world of his own. His head was shuttling to and fro with nervous jerky movements. His mumbling, incoherent until now, became suddenly clearer. "Gotta get out a' here," he said.

His glance focused on the door leading to the reception dock. In the bed next to him Sid Draper made an effort to distract him. "Hey, Tiny . . ." he called. Anderson didn't hear him. He moved toward the door with great lumbering strides. Preston tried to block him. Anderson grabbed the attendant by the arms, lifted him high in the air and tossed him effortlessly at the food cart in the middle of the room. He went down with a crash. His head struck the iron leg of the cart and he lay still.

Valerie didn't stop to tend him. Her mind was racing ahead. Tiny Anderson was bound for the reception dock then the front door of the hospital. If he made it out that front door, the guard there would order him to halt. When he didn't he would be shot as a prisoner trying to escape.

Unless she headed him off.

She caught up with Tiny just as he opened the door. He stared into the reception room, momentarily confused. She darted ahead of him and halted a few feet away. The room was dim and drafty. The desk in front of the railing was deserted. The only light came from the few windows on either side and the cutouts in the front door. From where she stood she could see the back of the guard's head out there. She prayed he would look in and understand, but she couldn't count on that.

She waved her fingers in front of Tiny, wishing she could have known what went on in Arby's head. *There had to be a way to reach Anderson. There had to.*

"Mr. Anderson, it's Dr. Traynor. Do you hear me? Doc . . . tor Tray . . . nor!"

He blinked rapidly, spasmodically.. His hands rotated aimlessly at his sides. He gave no sign that he'd heard her. His face was blank, rigid. He advanced a few steps until he was almost on top of her. She stood her ground. Her heart beat fiercely, her breath came in gasps. She pounded her fists against his chest. "Tiny," she shouted. "Turn back!"

He stopped. His shifting gaze focused on her. His cupid's bow lips curved into a loose, vapid smile. He touched her cheek, her hair. His pale brows met in a frown as if trying to remember. "It's Dr. Traynor," she repeated.

His hands cupped her shoulders. His pink and white face sagged into amorous lines. "Little girl," he murmured. His nostrils flared. His hands moved to caress her back. He pulled her close. "Don't be afraid, little girl," he simpered. "Tiny won't hurt you."

He backed her into the railing. She pleaded with him in incoherent phrases. He didn't hear her. His eyes were wild, his lips wet with spittle. His hands roamed over her body. Ecstatic grunting noises issued from his throat. He bent his legs and rotated his body against hers, panting, the sweat running down the sides of his face.

"Hold me, little girl," he whispered fiercely, guiding her fingers. "Tiny's gonna show you a good time."

She was suffocated by tons of rolling flesh pressing against her legs, her breasts, her face. She groped backward for the iron railing and using the spokes for leverage, wrenched herself to one side. On hands and knees she began to crawl away from him. He laughed in enjoyment. "Fight me, little girl," he whispered hoarsely. "Fight me!"

He flipped her over and fell to the floor on top of her. His fingers ripped at her uniform, tore it halfway down the front. She felt his hands on her naked breasts. Revulsion swept through her. She stopped thinking like a doctor. Her nails reached for his face, tore at his eyes, his cheeks. A roar escaped him. He lifted a clenched fist. Her lids closed in terror. She anticipated the feel of those huge knuckles smashing into her face.

Miraculously, nothing happened.

She heard a commotion. A cool rush of air washed over her body as Anderson was pulled from atop her. She opened her eyes.

Alfie Brockwell's face came into focus. He was wrestling with Anderson, holding him at bay. Anderson bellowed his anger. The hyperactivity gave him abnormal strength. He hammerlocked Brockwell's head in the crook of his arm. The cockney elbowed him in the ribs, broke the lock. They grappled like dinosaurs, circling each other, intent on a kill.

Brockwell ducked a punch, closed in, rammed a knee into his opponent's groin. Anderson screamed in pain, collapsed to one knee. "You stinking bastard." Brockwell yelled, "Here's one in the kidneys for you." He punched Anderson low in the back and angled a karate chop to the side of his head. The blond giant went down like a felled tree.

Breathing hard, Brockwell staggered a few feet then clutched at his stomach and doubled over in pain. "It's my bloody insides," he grated. "They're on fire."

Valerie tried to reach him, but her legs were putty. She heard footsteps from the doorway. Seconds later Wally was bending over her, helping her up. The replacement guard was with him.

"Can you walk?" Wally asked anxiously.

She nodded. "I . . . I need your lab coat." Her breath was coming in gasps. Her uniform gaped open to the waist. Her hair was tangled about her face.

She gestured toward Brockwell and Anderson. "Help them, Wally. And . . . and see to the attendant . . . inside. He's hurt." He hesitated. "I can make it alone. Please, Wally." He nodded and handed her the lab coat.

She made her way slowly to the rest room behind the ward. She sat down hard on the cot. Her mind was a blank. She shivered and pulled the blankets around her.

Ten minutes later, Wally joined her. He sat on the side of the cot, took her hands in his and rubbed them. Her face was white and drawn and she was still cold.

"How are they?" she asked.

He frowned. Her voice was a monotone. "Better than we expected. Preston was more stunned than harmed. Brockwell's cramping has eased and Anderson came to even before we got him into bed. Except for a couple of bruises, he seems to be okay."

She hadn't bothered to re-coil her hair. He'd always marveled at her neatness, even under stress. This was the first time he'd ever seen her disheveled. "Did he hurt you?"

"No!"

Anger roughened her tone. How do you define hurt, she thought, when there are no outward bruises? How do you explain that there are assaults on the mind like fear and shame and being forced to descend to animal level that are more corrosive than physical harm? She relived the sensation of Tiny's hot, moist hands crawling over her body and a shudder escaped her.

"He's hyperactive, Wally. Like Arby."

"I know. I had him sedated and the attendant has orders to call me if he wakes up." He pulled the blanket closer around her. "Are you sure you're all right?" There was a detached quality about her like that of an amnesiac.

She nodded.

He put his arms around her to brace her. "I have to tell you something, Val. Arby's dead. The hyperactivity affected his capillary system. He bled to death."

"My God." She closed her eyes. A picture of Tiny Anderson floated in front of her, huge and flabby and white-skinned. He reached to grab her with his pudgy hands and his skin began to dissolve. It became opaque, then transparent, baring a criss-crossed network of arteries and veins and capillaries. The capillaries began to ooze, then drip, then gush, the blood running red on the tiled floor until the life had drained from his body.

"Val, it doesn't have to affect Anderson." Wally's voice was urgent.

"But it already has. Can't you see? It's a pattern . . ." She trembled uncontrollably. Her face crumpled. "Be thankful, Wally. It's over. All the watching and waiting. The sleeplessness. The anguish. We don't have to think about how it will end, because we know now." She began to cry, harsh wracking sobs that bent her like a sapling in a storm. She used the blanket to muffle them. When she was spent, she put her head on his shoulder and whispered, "But who's going to tell them, Wally? Who's going to tell those poor slobs in there that they're going to die?"

He gripped her shoulders. Forced her upright. "No one. Because we don't know that yet." His voice was firm. "Val, you've been through a hell of a day. I want you to go home tonight and get some sleep. We'll talk again in the morning."

"But I'm needed here."

"Not like this you aren't."

She smiled tiredly. "Physician, heal thyself. That's what you're telling me."

He pushed her hair back from around her face. "There's hope for you yet." He kissed her lightly and helped her to her feet.

Chapter 16

The first thing Val did when she reached her apartment was draw a bath and strip bare. She wanted to rid herself of the stench of the fever and the ward and the feel of Tiny Anderson's hands pawing her like some degenerate animal.

The tub was hot and steamy, with the pungent fumes of the bath oil she'd thrown in rising like incense from its depths. She soaked in it for an hour. For the first time in years she felt no desire to do anything, least of all to go back into that ward. There was an emptiness inside her, a feeling of loss akin to what she'd experienced when her father died. She didn't try to probe it. She only knew that she wanted to lie where she was, watching her hair float to the surface and her toes shrivel to half their size.

There were going to be more hours like this, she decided. The hell with working twenty-four hours a day, seven days a week. It wasn't worth it.

She got out of the tub, pulled a fluffy towel from the rack and rubbed at her skin until spots of pink rose to the surface in protest. She looked down at her body. When she was still sorting out who she was, it had bothered her that she was tall and big-boned. In high school boys didn't find her attractive. They associated big with aggressive and small with feminine. For years she'd told herself it didn't matter, then just as it all began to change, it didn't.

At thirty-four her body was still shapely, the breasts firm, the legs long and tapered. Brian had always thought her the least vain woman he knew. He was wrong. It was simply that the needs of her mind were more important than the desirability of her body. But that didn't mean she wasn't aware of herself as a woman.

She went into the kitchen and made herself a cup of coffee. Her eyes strayed toward the clock. Five twenty. By six o'clock the lab would have a report on the daily stool cultures. A decrease in the count of the organisms could mean a breakthrough in the testing. On the other hand, should there be a rise in the count . . . What difference, she thought. Wally could handle whatever came up. She took her cup into the living room. The coffee had suddenly become tasteless.

After the clutter of the ward, the apartment seemed enormous. Actually it wasn't. The living room, kitchen, and bedroom were adequate, but so sparsely furnished that they gave the appearance of being larger. Brian had always teased her about being a rich bitch with a miser's soul. It wasn't so. The apartment was unfinished because she didn't get around to it. But that was going to change now also.

She would add a few things, she thought, looking around, but she would keep the simplicity. She had grown up in a thirty-room colonial with a decorator's personality stamped on it. It had so many outstanding "things" in it that the house never merged into a whole to become a home, but kept the faceless grandeur of a museum. As a little girl she had never been comfortable in it, always afraid she would break some priceless object that couldn't be replaced.

She put her coffee cup on the desk in the living room. There was hardly any space for it. To the left was a sheaf of papers condensing the animal studies on Blasa Fever over the last ten years. To the right was the microscope her father had given her when she left Johns Hopkins. Strewn across the rest of it were discarded slides, a treatise on the fallacy of using mice in animal testing because they were cancer prone, and two copies of the "pink sheet" which carried the pharmaceutical industry news.

For a fleeting moment, she wondered whether Wally would remember to do a urine analysis and culture on Jefferson Montgomery. The last one had contained bacteria that pointed to a kidney infection. She stretched her hand out to the phone then drew it back. Habit dies hard, she thought. But given enough time, it does die.

The emptiness inside her persisted.

At seven o'clock the doorbell rang. She roused herself from the couch. She had been dozing in a corner of it, her bare feet curled beneath her terry robe. The bell rang again in short sharp spurts. She frowned. Who could it be? No one but Wally knew she was there.

She opened the door. Brian loomed inside the frame. His straight black hair fell across his forehead where the wind had blown it every which way. His face was narrowed, his square jaw rigid. The scar on his lid was rubbed raw. His brows were contracted in fierce lines of worry.

"You forgot your coat," she said inanely. His gray suit was rumpled; the print tie hung like a noose about his neck.

He stepped inside, took her in his arms. "I know what happened. Are you all right?"

A rush of feeling swept over her. His hands were

moving to her shoulders, her back, her face. Wherever he touched, pinpoints of heat rose to the surface then diffused.

"Are you all right?" he repeated.

She nodded. Unexpected tears sprang to her eyes. She hadn't realized how much she'd wanted to see him.

"I could kill the son-of-a-bitch," he muttered. The door swung shut behind him.

"Brian, he was sick. He didn't know what he was doing."

He raked a hand through his hair. "Then where was Chandler or the guard or the attendant? We purposely worked it out so you couldn't be set up like this."

She shook her head. "It just happened. It's hard to explain. Wally should never have told you."

"He didn't. Wally was too busy to answer the phone when I called. I got it from some attendant on duty there."

He pulled his jacket off, tossed it on a chair. It was the act of a man who'd come home, she thought. Yet he'd never been there. She remembered the first night in Bethesda when she'd apologized for the cramped surroundings and he'd told her it didn't matter, that home for him was wherever she was. He was looking at her now in the same way he had then.

She moved a few feet away from him. Within the confines of Traynor Labs she could cope with her attraction for Brian. Here, in the state she was in, she wasn't sure she could cope with anything.

She touched a hand to her hair, acutely conscious of his gaze on her body. She wore nothing beneath the robe.

"You look like hell," he said. "Do you want a few days off?"

"No." She cinched the belt tighter on her robe. "I

want you to replace me on the Blasa Fever project."

"With who?" His voice was incredulous.

"Wally."

"Why?"

"Because I'm tired, Brian. Does that surprise you? I don't want to put so much of myself into this thing anymore. For ten years I've been plodding like a horse with blinders on. It's time I took them off. Did something else with my life."

He closed the distance between them. She turned her face away, but he cupped her chin in his palm and forced her eyes to meet his. "Is it because of what happened today?"

"That only brought it to a head."

"You're hiding something from me, Val. Or worse yet, you're hiding it from yourself."

She pushed his hand away and walked to the window. Why couldn't he take what she'd said at face value? Why did he have to cross-examine her?

She moved the drapes aside and looked out. The night was cold and starless, the street deserted. Across the way, the lamplight illuminated the parked cars lined up bumper to bumper like immobilized tin soldiers. Her eye was caught by a piece of cellophane fluttering from the open window of a tan Plymouth. A heavyset man was hunched in the driver's seat devouring a sandwich. She sympathized with him, remembering the many times she'd either skipped dinner or grabbed a bite between chores. But that was all over now.

She clutched the collar of her robe and turned to Brian. Anger lent her voice a sharp edge. "Why do I have to prove what I've said? Why can't you take it for what it's worth? I've had it. It's as simple as that. I'm thirty-four and I have nothing to show for it. I live in a laboratory, not a home. I've substituted medical degrees for a husband and patients for children. I've scoffed at other women who weren't goal oriented but secretly envied them. I want to stop giving and take for myself now. Is that so hard to understand?''

"It wouldn't be if it were the truth." He went to her, gripped her shoulders and shook her lightly. "This is Brian you're talking to, remember? Don't make speeches to me about how much of yourself you've sacrificed because I was there. You've been 'taking' every minute of those ten years, because that's really what you've wanted to do. There was a time I would have given anything to hear what you just said and believe you meant it. I know better now. Your work is your life, Val, and anything else you take on will revolve around it. Now what's the real reason you want to quit?''

She resented his probing, hated him for being so perceptive. She lowered her lids. Her voice was tight, tortured. "I came apart in there today," she whispered. "Things went wrong and I came apart."

"And Chandler didn't."

"Wally would be better for the project. He's more stable."

"But you're more knowledgeable."

She was silent.

"Did you think you were infallible?" he asked gently. "What you went through today would be enough to break anyone down. What has that got to do with your running the Tetra-2 project? There's no one better qualified to do that than you."

"Do you really believe that?"

He grinned. "Do you want me to pull rank to prove it? As president of Traynor Labs I can order you back, you know."

"You wouldn't do that."

"Sure I would. I need you there to go on with the

testing. But more important, it's where you belong."

She felt as if a weight had been lifted from her. One she hadn't known she was carrying. How incongruous that it should have been Brian who sought to restore her faith in herself. For years she had thought that her love for him was seducing her into a cage that would bar her from her work. She had stigmatized their relationship. Labeled it a meeting of the body, not the mind. But just as she had grown in ten years, so had he. She felt closer to him now than she ever had. Her hazel eyes shone with gratitude. She looked for words to express it and came up empty.

He took her in his arms and kissed her. A warning bell sounded in her head. Only some things had changed. Brian still belonged to Eva. And Wally was waiting for her answer.

She brought her hands up to his chest and tried to break free. "Brian, let me go."

He captured her hands in his. "Is it because of Chandler?" he demanded. "He called me back and told me what had happened. He made it clear that it was my place to know about you, but not to care."

"He asked me to marry him, Brian."

"What did you tell him?"

"Nothing yet."

"You can't marry him, Val."

"Why not?"

"Because you don't love him." He kissed her eyes, the bridge of her nose. His lips moved to her earlobe, bit lightly on the tip. "You love me," he whispered. His rugged face held the intent, passionate expression that had always preceded their lovemaking.

"Brian, no . . ." She didn't remember whether she said the words or if they echoed in her head, because everything blurred into sensation after that.

He treated her with the tenderness reserved for a

virgin. He seduced her with his lips, his body. He waited until her resistance melted into acceptance then became a desire to match his own. She felt his hands at the tie of her robe. Usually sure, he fumbled with it. She undid the tie, let the robe fall to the floor. His eyes feasted on her body as if at a banquet. "I'd forgotten how beautiful you are," he murmured.

She went willingly into the bedroom with him. She knew it solved nothing, but she didn't really care. There would be time for introspection later. Right now she didn't want to think. She wanted to feel.

She lay on the bed and watched him undress. The years had been kind to him. Except for a thickening around the middle he was the same as when she'd first known him. His powerful shoulders tapered to full fleshed hips, his legs were corded and muscular, the calves rock-like and bulging. Only the hair on his chest confessed to the passage of time. It was tinged with gray where it had once been all black, and it gave her a feeling of sadness.

He slid in beside her. He caressed her breasts, her hips. The blankets became a barrier between them and he threw them off. "I'll freeze," she murmured. He covered her body with his and stilled her lips with a kiss. She opened her mouth to him, moaned as he probed it with his tongue. His fingers caressed her thighs, eased between her legs. The sensation was exquisite, painful. She pushed his hands away. His body rolled from hers. She felt his mouth pucker her skin as it inched from her breasts to her navel and teased its way downward. A heat built within her. She didn't want to wait. She had forgotten what it was to need him inside her, to feel as if they were one, to long for release as if it were salvation.

She slid beneath him, opened to him like a flower, urged him with her hips, her hands. She cried out as he thrust deep within her, then rocked with him to a beat of their own making, a rhythm that grew wilder and wilder until it built to a shattering crescendo.

She lay on her right hip, one leg entwined with his, her head buried in his chest. The blanket made a cozy mound above them.

"I love you," he said, toying with a strand of her hair.

"Mmm . . ." she murmured in muffled content-ment.

"No. Say the words." His vehemence surprised her.

She rubbed her cheek against his chest. "Why the need for statements?"

He was silent for so long she thought he had fallen asleep. Then he reached across her to a small table and switched on the lamp.

She blinked, waited for her eyes to become accus-tomed to the light. "What did you do that for?"

She raised herself on an elbow as he slid back against the brass headboard. The hair on his chest was matted. A thin coat of sweat covered his shoulders. His jaw was shadowed with a dark stubble of beard.

"Will you marry me, Val?" His face was grave, tender.

She stroked his cheek with the back of her hand. "Aren't you forgetting something?"

"You mean Eva. I'm going to leave her, Val."

"What about Mark?"

The tenderness left his face. It became rigid, hard. The expression of a man deliberately tying knots in his emotions. "Mark will have to fend for himself. He's getting to be a big boy now."

Looking into his eyes, she knew that nothing had really changed. They were a barren desert. Wally had been right, she thought. She was clinging to unreality. Other men left their sons, but Brian couldn't. He saw it as a parallel of what his father had done to him and the memory was too bitter.

"It wouldn't work," she said.

He pulled her to him and kissed her passionately. "It *has* to work. I can't go on living without you. The days I don't see you I go through the motions like a robot, waiting for four thirty so I can call you at the lab and at least hear the sound of your voice. I want more than that, Val. I want us to be together, to be able to meet openly without worrying about what everyone thinks, to have you wake up in my arms in the morning instead of wanting you half the night."

"The marriage wouldn't be worth a damn with you torn up inside like this and you know it."

"Then what do I do? Wait until Eva goofs to give me grounds? Or hope she meets someone she cares for and wants out as badly as I do? She's walking around like she's on Cloud Nine lately. It could be happening right now, for all I know."

"I wouldn't count on it," Val said grimly. Eva had no intention of divorcing Brian while she thought her sister wanted him.

"Then what's left for us?"

"This. Now."

His lids became hooded. He bent to kiss the hollow of her neck. "What about the future?" The words were muffled, slurred.

There was none for them, she thought bleakly as his arms closed about her.

Across the street in the tan Plymouth, Asa Rankin watched the light go out again in the bedroom and charted the time in a small green book. He took a last swig from the bottle of Budweiser propped at his side and shook his head in reluctant admiration. Son-of-a-bitch, if that Haversham wasn't a sharp one.

Until now Rankin had scoffed at this vigil of Brian that had yielded nothing that couldn't be printed in *Good Housekeeping*. But tonight had really paid off. Exactly what Haversham intended to do with this information was a mystery to him, but he had no doubt that it would be put to good use. By now he had learned that the politician's brain had more twists and turns in it than a spiral staircase.

He rolled the window up as a cold blast of wind sent a chill down his neck. Hell of a night for a stake-out. He shifted his heavy legs in the cramped space and reached to pull the blanket up to his chin. It looked like it was going to be a long night.

Chapter 17

Paul Haversham spent the early part of the week in Washington following up the availability of a small round "band-aid" touted as a new method for treating motion sickness. The "band-aid," impregnated with medication, was pasted behind the ear and the medication was slowly absorbed through the skin for several days. The advantage over other prescriptions for motion sickness was that the slow absorption process eliminated side effects such as drowsiness and dryness of the mouth.

After taking a ninety-day option to license the sale, Haversham returned to his office on Friday morning. Usually, he spent as little time there as possible. The square, windowless box depressed him and though his secretary Thelma sprayed it with air freshener twice daily, he found the stuffiness intolerable. But today, he had no choice. There were phone calls to be returned and letters to be answered that cquldn't wait.

Haversham spent most of the morning dictating to Thelma until a call on his private line interrupted them.

It was Claire Traynor. He dismissed Thelma with a nod, surprised a look of resentment on her face, and turned his attention to the conversation.

"Yes, Claire. What is it?"

"Paul, I don't know how long I can keep David in line."

What she said bothered him less than the way she said it. Her voice, usually modulated for maximal audience effect, was fraught with panic.

Claire was going through a crisis of sorts. In the last few weeks, Chris Androtti had been "unavailable" on some afternoons. Claire was well aware of Chris's sexual appetites. They ranged from aging producer's wives to innocent ingenues with an occasional young boy thrown in for a change of pace. Unable to locate a part, bored with the sameness of his routine, Claire was sure he was seeking elsewhere for distraction. The only hold she had on him now was her promise of the fifty thousand dollars to back the theater group he talked of opening out West. But that money was contingent on her maneuvering of David, which was becoming more difficult with each passing day.

Haversham tried to calm her. "What's the trouble, Claire?"

"The morphine substitution. It's all David talks about. He feels it's his fault in some way and he thinks it's his duty to tell Brian about it. Up until yesterday, I was able to convince him to hold off, but last night he was shaky again, probably because of that visit from the D.E.A."

"What visit?"

"You don't know?"

"No. I was in Washington all day."

"Well, it seems the Drug Enforcement Administration dropped in for a surprise investigation yesterday afternoon. Brian was out and David had to handle it himself. Are they allowed to do that, Paul?"

"Unfortunately, yes."

Spot checking was a situation the pharmaceutical houses were riled about but still could not control.

The Food and Drug Administration and the Drug Enforcement Administration had the right to enter the premises with scant notice (if any at all). It was tantamount to an invasion of privacy as far as Haversham was concerned. The D.E.A. rigorously checked the inventory, the records of narcotics received and dispersed to see if the balance was proper, and noted whether appropriate usage of the drug was being maintained. If there were any discrepancies, no matter the size, an explanation had to be forthcoming immediately.

With the secret of his former drug addiction pressing on him like a weight, the effect of having to lie outright to the D.E.A. must have devastated David.

The tension in Claire's voice accentuated her drawl. "Look, Paul. When I agreed to this deal between us, it was with the understanding that it would be for only a short while. But I don't see anything happening."

"That's because you're on the outside, looking in. A great deal is happening. Since that Blasa Fever story broke in the *Post,* the Board has been very unhappy with Brian. One more push in the right direction and they'll move for a meeting to oust him. I'm sure of it."

"Then for God's sake, push! This Delilah role is wearing thin. I have more influence with David than anyone I know, but he's so loaded with guilt, I'm hardly coming across."

Her other phone rang then and she clicked off.

Bitch! Haversham thought. He was handing her the easiest money she'd ever made and all she could do was carp. He reached into his bottom drawer and took out a bottle of Chivas Regal. His eyes flicked toward the clock. Eleven twenty-two. He was breaking the never-before-lunch rule he'd set for himself a year ago when his doctor had questioned the state of his liver.

He downed the drink in one gulp. The hell with it. He had cause.

His wife, Bernice, had come at him with a vengeance this morning. Breakfast had been served by the maid in the "garden room," a brick, glass, and flagstone addition to his house that had set him back thirty thousand dollars last year. In the whining voice that had prompted him to accede to her demands more than once from sheer irritation, Bernice had informed him that their son Evan had called from California during his absence. Evan *needed* (it was never *wanted*) a hundred thousand dollars to open a dental office in Beverly Hills where the "right people" congregated.

Born to her after a long siege of infertility, Bernice had made their only son into an impractical, snobbish copy of herself by catering to his every whim since infancy. She had agreed to this current request without hesitation. Her response to Haversham's statement that they didn't have the money was a cool "that's ridiculous" and the announcement that she would be lunching at "21" if he wanted to reach her.

There was no point in reproaching Bernice. He had seen what she was when he married her. A trivial, horse-faced debutante whose ideas and tastes were dictated by the latest *Vogue* or *Harper's Bazaar*. She hadn't grown in thirty-five years, he thought, merely aged, her glossy surface reflecting the shallowness beneath.

But the pressure from Bernice had been only the beginning. His broker had called. Sayco Electronics was down another ten percent and he needed the money to cover. And one of the letters on his desk this morning was from Anshul-Bulden. Like Claire Traynor, the European based company was getting impatient. They had succeeded in locating another pharmaceutical company that would not meet their needs as well as Traynor Laboratories, but could be bought immediately. Unless Haversham was prepared to give them full assurance within a month that Traynor would be available for purchase, they would move ahead on the alternate acquisition.

Haversham clenched the shot glass in a crushing grip. The sale of Traynor *had* to go through.

He rose, circled the desk and opened the door, hoping some cross current of air would find its way into the room to relieve the stuffiness. He saw himself in the long mirror his secretary had tacked to the wall, and his spirits rallied. He had spent a few hours in Washington yesterday at the Latham Health Club. His skin glowed with a healthy tan, his gray eyes sparkled with the *joie de vivre* of a man twenty years his junior.

He pulled in his stomach. He wasn't beaten, he thought. Merely stymied. What he had told Claire Traynor was true. The Board needed one more push to oust Brian. But where was it to come from?

The information Asa Rankin had given him last night about Brian and Valerie would be stored away for future use. It might be a gambit to incur the Board's disapproval, but hardly enough in this era of sexual freedom to precipitate Brian's dismissal as president. Only an upheaval that directly affected the company would suffice for that.

Brian's plea to the newspapers to play down Traynor's role in the Blasa Fever testing had been effective. They would print another article only if the slant would titillate their readers enough to overcome their conscience. So far, nothing he or Asa Rankin had come up with had been acceptable, and most of the sources in the plant he had relied on for information seemed to have dried up. His steely eyes narrowed thoughtfully. Including Thelma. She surely must have known about the D.E.A. visit to Traynor yesterday, yet she had told him nothing about it.

He reached for the intercom. "Thelma, would you come in a minute?"

"Yes sir."

He slid the phone into its cradle and thought of Thelma, something he rarely did. Through her brother Jimmy, the technician in the Blasa Fever testing lab, she was a pipeline of information about the hospital. And Thelma had recently become the spokesman for the company union, which kept her abreast of employee gripes and allowed her to add fuel to the fire, if necessary. Yet he had done nothing to acknowledge her newly acquired status—partially in self-defense.

Thelma was a sexually starved old maid, too timid to do more than glance at him fervently, her attraction sublimated in the zeal she brought to her work. The thought of bedding that flat-chested scarecrow produced a sharp pain in Haversham's groin, and he had heretofore studiously avoided even a show of affection for her at Christmas parties that could be misinterpreted.

Up to now there had been no problem. But unless he had misjudged her coldness of the last few weeks and her resentment of today, Thelma was feeling unappreciated. More than that, he was sure she was keeping information from him.

A hesitant knock sounded at the open door.

He straightened his silk tie and smoothed the lapels of the navy Petrocelli suit the salesman had assured him made his silver hair appear darker.

"Come in."

She entered wearing a plaid skirt and a white blouse, ruffled high at the neck to hide the crepey folds of her skin. She wore flat shoes to minimize her five foot seven height and carried her thin unused body as if she was ashamed of it.

"You wanted to talk to me?" No amount of makeup could hide the sprinkling of pimples on her chin or the sallowness of her complexion.

He took her hand in his. "Thelma, how would you like to have lunch with me?"

A flush tinged her cheek and the palm beneath his turned moist. "At the company cafeteria?"

God forbid, he thought.

"No," he said. "Somewhere more private than that."

The flush deepened. Everything she had hoped for was beginning to come true. And he wouldn't be sorry. His reward at lunch would be the information her brother had given her about Valerie Traynor's near rape in the hospital a few days ago.

"Why don't you get your coat," he said.

Another luncheon of equal importance took place a few days later at the company cafeteria between Brian and Lester Pryor.

Because the nearest restaurants were in Clayville where the food was less than average, most of Traynor's personnel ate at the company cafeteria on the second floor. In 1970 the cafeteria had been remodeled by Alex in a spurt of democratic zeal. It was Alex's contention that segregating the executives from the factory personnel for eating as well as working purposes was bad for morale.

Before 1970, the cafeteria had been housed in one large area with chairs and tables placed at random for the plant personnel and a separate room set aside for executives. Alex abolished that. He created an enormous glass and chrome "traynoria" where personnel of all echelons were expected to meet and eat in joyful camaraderie. It didn't work. A natural segregation took place in which people who felt most comfortable together ate together. The division became more pronounced than ever, and the lack of privacy was felt by all.

At one o'clock the lines were long and the noise resembled the babble of hens in a coop. Brian and Lester Pryor took their trays to the "executive corner" and sat down at a small round table.

Pryor jacknifed his six-foot-three frame into a narrow captain's chair then cursed as his bony knees hit the underrim of the table.

"Damn thing is made for midgets," he muttered, rubbing his chafed kneecap. His freckled face lit with a smile. Pryor could be relied upon as much for his sunny disposition as his steady competence.

He looked down at his plate and shook his head. "You know, it hurts my chemist's soul that everybody today is concerned with 'natural foods' as against synthetic ingredients, when the truth is that the amount of risk is relative." He used his knife to point. "You take this shrimp. It's well known that shrimp has some arsenic in it, as well as unacceptably high levels of copper and iodine. And look at these potatoes. Most people don't realize that potatoes contain solanine and that in times of food shortages, when potatoes were the major item in the diet, potato poisoning wasn't an uncommon thing."

Brian watched with envy as "the beanpole" smeared three pats of butter onto his baked potato then brought a forkful to his mouth. Despite a jogging regime that would put an athlete to shame, Brian had to watch his diet to maintain his weight.

"And let's not forget this lemon juice on my salad," the quality control man continued. "It's loaded with citral, which in animal tests has damaged the lining of the circulatory system and the optic nerve. All I can say is that it's a good thing the F.D.A. regulations don't apply to Mother Nature.''

"Lester, you didn't ask me to meet you for lunch just to update me on nutritional trivia.''

"No, I didn't.''

"What's on your mind?''

Pryor lowered his voice. "Two things. The first is the bulk morphine needed to make the Trinicitate. It's on its way here in a few days.''

"And despite the fact that nothing more has happened on the vial substitution, you're still leery about it.''

"Yes, I am. I tried to talk to David about it, but he's as touchy as a virgin in a whorehouse. He's more concerned with pinpointing the blame for the substitution than protecting the incoming shipment. Look, Brian, I admit it's nothing more than a gut feeling at this time, but it's a strong one.''

"And I respect it,'' Brian appeased. "But narcotics security is the one area we're not lax in. Even Joe Barbetta agrees with that, and you know how he is. The only thing I can do is issue a memo reinforcing strictest regulations in sample room and vault supervision so that no unauthorized personnel can get near the stuff. How's that?''

"Better than nothing.''

"Okay. What else is on your mind?''

Pryor took a sip of his coffee. "In the last few days too many of my people have been calling in sick.''

Brian shrugged. "There's a lot of flu around. Maybe . . .''

"No!'' The word was explosive. Pryor modulated his voice. "Sorry, Brian, but I'm riled about it. You should hear the excuses they're making. They must take me for a moron. I've called around to some of the other V.P.'s. The same thing is happening in marketing, manufacturing, and shipping. The only department it isn't affecting is research, which tells the story in itself.''

'You think it's a 'sick-in'?''

''I know it is.'' He hunched forward and brought his face closer to Brian's. His long legs stretched beneath the table until they almost touched the tips of Brian's shoes. ''I don't have to tell you what the mood of the employees has been since they found out about the Blasa Fever testing. I've heard rumbles about company union meetings and job actions and threatened shut-downs, all with Haversham's fine hand behind them in the form of his pimple-faced secretary, Thelma. It wouldn't surprise me at all if this is their first move.''

''Suppose I went to them, called an employees' meeting . . .''

''And told them what? That you're not to blame? That it was Alex who made the decision on the Blasa Fever program? They'd never believe you. They don't trust you. Haversham has seen to that. He's got them convinced that you used some kind of hocus pocus on Alex to get the presidency away from David. You also didn't do yourself any good when you turned Tom Nordsen down after he requested the Tetra-2 for his little girl.''

''Do you think I wanted to?'' Brian said fiercely. ''I've known Tom Nordsen since I came to Traynor. But even if I could have released the drug, the disease has progressed too far in his daughter to do any good.''

Pryor shook his head at the other man's obtuseness. ''Brian, *I* believe that. But *they* don't.''

Brian was silent a moment. ''I'm up against a stacked deck. Is that what you're trying to tell me?''

''In a nutshell. Haversham is using the employees'

discontent as a lever to nudge the Board into ousting you. The only way you might save your skin is to call off the testing program.''

''I can't do that.''

''I didn't think you could.''

''Then what do I do?'' he muttered, almost to himself.

Pryor's voice was compassionate. ''Wait it out. Deal with each move as it comes and hope the presses at the *Post* break down before they print another one of those articles. Because, if anything else happens to rile those employees, the consequences may be more than even Haversham bargained for.''

Chapter 18

At eight o'clock that evening, Dennie Redmond pulled up to the curb in front of Angie's building, braked the Chevy, then slumped down in the seat. His life had turned into a nightmare from which there was no waking. By day, David Traynor badgered him to find the thief who had stolen the vials of morphine . . . a physical impossibility unless he gave himself up. At night when he visited Angie, even if Niko wasn't there, his shadow loomed over them both like a harbinger of evil.

In the confines of Angie's dark little room they had taken to talking in whispers and listening for sounds in the hallway. It had made Angie nervous. It had reduced Dennie to impotency. Huddled in one another's arms, unable to cope with the present, they consulted her horoscope and concocted fanciful plans to run away. Mexico . . . Europe . . . the Orient . . . Camouflage to distract them from the reality of being bound to Niko—Angie by her habit, Dennie through his fear.

At first, he had tried staying away from Angie, until his mother told him that a strange man had called insisting that she check to see if her burial plot was in order. After that, he went every night, because his fear for his mother was rooted in a guilt that outstripped his terror for himself.

He glanced up at Angie's window now. They had devised a signal between them. When she knew her brother was coming, she hung a plant from a hook on the fire escape outside her window. He took heart. It wasn't there.

He got out of the car and walked slowly toward the gray tenement. Bordini had taken all the joy out of seeing Angie. Sometimes when he lay in her arms seeking forgetfulness, willingly roused by her practiced ardor, then unmanned by his inability to complete the act, he was sorry he'd ever met her. Other times, when she fondled him and comforted him and cried out her remorse, he saw her as much a victim as himself, and he forgave her.

He held on to the bannister going up. The wail of a baby followed him to the top floor.

The door to Angie's apartment was flung open before he reached it. A sixth sense told him to run, but it was too late.

Niko Bordini stepped out to greet him. He was dressed in impeccably tailored black trousers and a V-necked linen shirt with a St. Christopher medal on a silver chain nestled in the hollow of his throat. He stood with his feet apart balancing gracefully on black leather boots with one inch heels that made him look taller than his five feet eleven inches.

"Dennie, my friend. You look pale." His voice was hearty, his teeth bared in a broad smile. He slung an arm about the smaller man's shoulders and guided him through the doorway. "Finch, say hello to Dennie. We haven't seen him in a few days."

Finch nodded. His small malevolent eyes jumped nervously back and forth across Dennie's face as if memorizing it. He wore dungarees and a workshirt. His sleeves were rolled up and the tattoo of a nude girl with bowed legs was inked into his right forearm.

"Hello, Dennie." Angie stood with her back against the sink, shoulders hunched, hands twisting at her sides. Her face held the wary expression he'd come to expect in front of her brother. Her huge black eyes were bright—too bright. He knew she was high most of the time now. It was the only way she could cope.

"Hi." The word was almost a croak. Dennie's mouth was parched, his mind in retreat. For the past few weeks, Bordini had been questioning him about the arrival of the bulk morphine. Each time his answer had been, "I don't know," and he had been grateful that it was the truth. But tonight was different. Tonight he did know.

Dennie sat on the edge of the chair Bordini pushed toward him and waited for the inquisition he knew would come.

Bordini fitted a cigarette into a white porcelain holder, lit it, and inhaled deeply. The serpent ring on his finger glittered under the lamplight. He latched a boot onto the rung of Dennie's chair and blew smoke circles past his ear.

"Angie tells me you been coming here every night, Dennie. That's nice. That's very nice. You know, every time I see you and Angie together I think to myself that my sister picked herself a real winner this time." He clapped Dennie on the back in approval. "So what's new at Traynor?" he asked in an even tone.

"Nothing."

Bordini's stare stripped away his defenses. Dennie had the terrible feeling that this man could see inside his head.

He kept his expression bland. *They can't know what you don't tell.* The refrain kept pounding in his head. He'd been using it to bolster his courage since yesterday morning. The only time Bordini and Finch could have access to that bulk morphine was *before*

it was processed into the Trinicitate. If he could withhold the information on the morphine's arrival until it
was too late, he could beat them at their own game.

Finch closed in on the other side of him. His eyes
narrowed in his pointed face. They bored into Dennie's like a laser beam. "He's lyin'," he said flatly.
His fingertips beat an uneven tattoo against his sides.

"You're wrong, Finch. Dennie's too smart for
that." He flicked an ash from his cigarette and
watched it burn a hole in the frayed carpet. "How's
your mother, Dennie?"

His voice was soft, insidious. A chill ran up Dennie's spine. "Fine."

Bordini shifted his aim and smoke billowed into
Dennie's face. He coughed and the tears started to his
eyes. He tried to move out of range, but Bordini put
a hand to his cheek.

"You'd like to keep her that way, wouldn't you,
Dennie?"

He nodded. There was no pressure on his cheek,
yet he felt held in a vise.

Finch fixed Dennie with a baleful glare. "Niko
asked you if there was sumpin' new."

Dennie began to sweat profusely. The smoke stung
his lids and the tears ran down his cheeks.

They can't know what you don't tell.

From the other side of the room, Angie mewed in
terror.

"The bill of lading came in on the morphine," Dennie heard himself saying.

"Meaning what?" Bordini demanded.

"The drum will be arriving in a few days."

Finch punched a fist into his palm in satisfaction.

Bordini held up a cautioning hand. He took from his
pocket the map of Traynor Labs that Dennie had
drawn and spread it across the table.

"Okay. Now I want you to tell us where this morphine will be from the time it gets to Traynor 'til it winds up in the hands of the guys who make this Trinicitate. And don't leave anything out." He reversed his cigarette holder and used it as a pointer. "Now from what you told us, the morphine should arrive at the loading dock . . . here. Right?"

Dennie nodded.

"What happens to it then?"

"It goes into the vault for quarantined material." He indicated a vault on the warehouse level.

"Why quarantined?"

"Because it hasn't been checked out yet. The morphine has to be brought to the Raw Material Sampling Room . . . here, where it's tested by a Quality Assurance group to see that the container and the material are up to standard. That sometimes happens the same day, more likely on the following one."

Bordini nodded. "Where does it go after that?"

"If it's okay, to the warehouse, but in a different vault. You see the F.D.A. specifies that we have to separate quarantined from released material . . ."

Bordini cut across his words. "Tell me about these vaults."

Dennie looked bewildered. "What would you like to know?"

"What are they made of?"

"Steel and concrete." The treachery of what he was revealing bore in on him. There was an unwritten law at Traynor that the vaults were a taboo subject. Even among themselves, the executives never discussed them.

Dennie's hands shook as he used them to describe. "They have walls that are one foot thick and they're electronically controlled so that any vibrations or movements trigger off an alarm system that's hooked up to the police . . ." His voice dropped to a whisper. "Please, Mr. Bordini. Give the idea up. There's no way you can get that morphine out of those . . ."

"Can it," Finch snapped. "Who's keepin' an eye on the vaults?"

"There's a closed circuit TV in a room in the building and someone's always in there watching what goes on at the vaults. Mr. Barbetta, the head of security, keeps changing the room so nobody knows exactly where it is." He pulled out a handkerchief and blotted the perspiration on his upper lip. "It's very hard to get into any of the vaults. No one person can do it. The alarm company set it up so that two people with separate keys for different locks have to be there at the same time to open it. There are special pairs of executives who hold these keys."

Bordini exhaled on a long breath and watched the smoke curl toward the ceiling. "Do you have a key?"

"I . . . no."

His hesitancy gave him away. Finch's hand flicked out and Dennie's head exploded into a thousand pieces.

"Leave him alone!" Angie screamed from across the room.

Bordini pulled Dennie's hands from his face. His right eye was half closed and the red blotch on his temple was beginning to swell. Bordini shook his head ruefully. "I should have told you. Finch can't stand a liar. It does funny things to him. He spent ten years in a prison loony bin because he wasted a trustee who took his money then turned him in when he tried to make a break. Isn't that so, Finch?"

Finch didn't answer. His face held an impenetrable, brooding look.

There was a ringing in Dennie's right ear and he

was having trouble seeing. He had an uncontrollable urge to pray, which was ridiculous, because he hadn't gone near a church in years except for socials.

"I wasn't lying," he whispered, surprised that he was having trouble with his voice. "The key belongs to my superior, but he's on vacation, so it's been given to me."

Bordini crossed to the refrigerator and took an orange from the shelf. His fingers dug through the rind and a stream of juice spurted across the floor. He wiped his hands on a towel and turned back to Dennie. "And who holds the key that pairs off with yours?"

"Burt Findley."

"Who's he?" Finch asked.

"Vice-President of Personnel."

Bordini nodded. "Now when the morphine is ready to be brought up to manufacturing to make this Trinicitate, who sends for it?"

"My boss, David Traynor. He tells two of the keyholders to go down to the vault and sign the morphine out. Then one of the keyholders accompanies an employee from manufacturing who's gone down there to meet him, and they bring the material back."

"To David Traynor's office?"

"Sometimes."

Finch started to say something, but Bordini silenced him with a gesture. He stuffed an orange section into his mouth and pulverized it with his jaws. His swarthy face grew thoughtful. "Tell me about Burt Findley and David Traynor," he said finally.

"What do you want to know?"

Bordini shrugged. "Everything. Anything."

Dennie talked. Under Bordini's seemingly offhand questioning, he revealed that Burt Findley was a workaholic, that he brown-bagged it for lunch because he had a bleeding ulcer and hated restaurant food. He specified what time David and his secretary came in every morning, when David Traynor and Burt Findley left for the day, the precise moment they went out for lunch and returned, and the complete layout of David Traynor's office.

When he finished, Bordini said nothing. His forehead was furrowed in deep lines, his gypsy face hollowed in concentration.

"All right," he said finally. "From now on we meet at Angie's every night. When the morphine gets to Traynor, I'll lay out the plan. Not before. In the meantime, everything goes on like it was . . . except for one thing." He dropped the cigarette butt and ground it into the carpet with the heel of his boot. His expressive black eyes, so much like his sister's, fixed on Dennie's. "You've been bringing packages to an army friend of yours at the hospital."

Dennie's jaw sagged. "How did you . . . "

"Never mind how I know. I want you to keep on bringing them. Understand?"

Dennie nodded, his mind in retreat. No one had known about those packages to Sid Draper. Not Angie, not anyone at the plant.

The answer was as obvious as it was incredible. The fourth accomplice had to be someone in that lab or hospital. His mind fixed on Sid Draper. *It couldn't be*, he thought. *It couldn't!*

Yet it was Sid who had introduced him to Angie and Sid who was receiving the packages.

Dennie reviewed what he knew of his friend.

Draper was an orphan with responsibility to no one but himself. He had a small room on Eighth Street in the Village decorated with bits and pieces he had picked up in thrift shops and at the Salvation Army. Sid didn't stick to one thing for long and he wasn't above getting drunk on a Saturday night. But he'd never been in trouble in his life and there was an honesty about Sid and a lack of interest in material things that made Dennie doubt his involvement. The only thing Sid had ever really wanted was to have fun.

But if it wasn't Sid, then who could it be?

Chapter 19

When Brian returned from lunch with Pryor, he substantiated the "sick-in" with Burt Findley in Personnel. The absenteeism was more prevalent than even Pryor had realized. It was a protest, yet instinct told Brian the employees hadn't solidified into a single viewpoint, or they would have come to him in a body with their demands. It was a fight against time, he thought grimly, and right now the outcome was anybody's guess.

Brian knew that if he could report even partial success on the Tetra-2 antibiotic, he stood a chance of staving off further employee action and removing the weapon Haversham was using against him with the Board. But for the past week the news at the hospital had been "status quo."

According to Valerie, there had been no recurrence of the hyperactivity in any of the patients. Though still weak a few of the volunteers were becoming more alert. One or two were beginning to eat better (Sid Draper was insisting on steak and settling for omelet), but the majority of the men were still showing signs of the organisms in their stool specimens and suffering from the fever and cramping symptomatic of the disease.

Brian suspected that the reason Haversham hadn't succeeded in getting the Board to accede to his demands for an emergency review meeting until now was that Traynor was doing well financially.

Like all pharmaceutical houses, Traynor depended on *ill*-gotten gains. A heavy influx of flu in January had boosted the sales of their preventive drug, Orthofrax, to a record high and though Brian wasn't directly responsible, he was reaping the benefit of the Board's satisfaction. But that, he knew, would be short-lived.

His prediction was correct. On the following day, Dora Watkins handed him a copy of *The Enquirer* and Brian knew that time had run out for him

In an editorial captioned COURAGE ABOVE AND BEYOND, it read:

> No front line battleground could be any more hazardous than the twenty-bed hospital attached to Traynor Laboratories in Clayville, Long Island. Currently the site of a testing project for an antibiotic to cure Blasa Fever, it is a tribute to the times that the Medical Director in charge is a woman. But this fact does not stand her in good stead. Not only must she contend with the killer disease that continues to strike and maim at an awesome rate, but she has been forced to fight off an assault by one of the patients, the majority of whom are convicts. Like Marie Curie before her, this doctor's dedication is unbounded. Let us hope for the sake of Traynor's two thousand employees, who have placed themselves at risk beside her, that her courage is not in vain.

As Lester Pryor had warned, reaction from the employees was swift. The company union met that night in a closed session. On Wednesday morning, Haversham's secretary, Thelma, the union president, called

Brian and arranged for a delegation to meet with him in his office at three that afternoon.

The only good thing about the meeting was that Valerie had insisted on being there when Brian had told her about it. Brian had been out of his mind with worry about her. He hadn't seen her since the night in her apartment but he'd spoken with her every day. Her voice had been distant and cool, and she'd side-stepped his anxious probing like a dancer in a pirouette.

She entered his office a few minutes before the others. Her stance was as rigid as her freshly starched lab coat. He moved to take her in his arms then halted as her eyes rebuffed him.

"What's wrong, Val?"

"Nothing." Her hair was loose, framing her oval face in soft blonde waves that make her look like a young girl.

"Are you sorry about what happened between us?" His voice was a warm embrace.

Her face filled with pain. "Sorry?" She shook her head. "No."

Brian had spent the last six nights alone in his bed reliving those hours. She might delude herself about the importance of them, he thought, but she could never deny their beauty.

"It didn't change anything, Brian. I meant what I said about building a life of my own outside of my work. And what's between us, the way things are . . . it isn't enough."

He felt as if he'd been punched in the stomach. "You're trying to tell me you're going to marry Wally."

"Yes."

"Without loving him?"

"But I do love him," she said vehemently. "It's

different from what you and I had. Less violent, less physical . . . more an intellectual kind of . . .''

He closed the distance between them and gripped her shoulders hard. "You're kidding yourself. There is no different kind of love. That life you're so eager to start will be built around a lie."

She wrenched herself free. "You're wrong about that." She put up a hand to cover her eyes. "Oh God, don't make this any harder, Brian."

He was silent for a moment. "Have you told him yet?"

She took her hand from her eyes and strove for composure. "I haven't had a chance to. We've been very busy."

"You shouldn't have come today. I can handle this myself."

"No, you can't. The union is out for your hide. I'm part of the Fever program, but they don't see me in the same way. As Alex Traynor's daughter, I may have enough influence to dissuade them from any rash moves." She pulled nervously at a button on her lab coat. "Besides, I left the hospital out of self-preservation. Since that story broke in the *Enquirer* the phones have been ringing incessantly." She exhaled on a long breath.

"That bad?"

"Awful. The F.D.A. phoned. They asked if my recent 'experience' had damaged me too much to go on with the testing. I've had a crank call from someone wanting to know if I get my kicks that way, and an offer from a writer to collaborate on a book." She shook her head in bewilderment. "What Wally and I can't understand is who's feeding information to the press. There were only a handful of people who knew what happened and we swore them to secrecy. Why would anyone there deliberately try to sabotage the program?"

"It's not the program they're after," Brian said grimly. "It's me."

"You think Haversham's at the bottom of it?"

"I'm sure of it."

The intercom buzzed. Brian picked up the phone. "Yes?"

"The union delegates are here," Dora announced.

"Send them in."

The company union had been organized during World War II when the employees had insisted on a pay raise based on inflation. Alex had refused to grant it. To compensate for their demands, he would have been forced to raise the price of drugs, which under normal conditions would not have been a problem. But due to the war, a price freeze was in effect, prohibiting him from doing so.

The matter had been settled shortly thereafter when a wage freeze had been instituted along with pricing regulations, but the union had never disbanded. Its membership varied throughout the years, depending on how important the issues were that arose. At last count, less than half of Traynor's employees belonged.

Led by Thelma, three of them filed in now. Brian's heart sank as he saw that Tom Nordsen was among them. The Swede looked as if he'd gotten his courage out of a bottle. The criss-crossed patches of purple on his cheeks were livid and his face held a stolid, uncompromising look. The third man was the former union president, a blow-hard named Zack Cottrell who had relinquished the reins to Thelma only because the women in the union had outnumbered the men at the time of the vote.

"Would you like to sit down?" Brian asked.

"No. We won't be here that long." As expected, Thelma was the speaker for the group. If power corrupted, it also lent stature. She had marched in as if on a religious crusade. Her spindly body was held erect, her amber eyes were fired with zeal. Brian suspected that much of the righteous fervor had been put there by Haversham, but it didn't matter. The outcome would be the same.

She turned toward Valerie. "I'm so glad to see you're all right. We were all very worried."

Valerie jammed her hands into the pockets of her lab coat. Her hazel eyes sparked with anger. "If you're referring to that editorial in the *Enquirer*, the story was exaggerated."

"You mean you're not working with convicts?" Cottrell asked snidely. He was stocky and dark-haired with a harelip and a speech impediment that caused him to slur his r's. Cottrell handled the mixing of the vat machines on the manufacturing floor. He wore a loose khaki jumpsuit issued by the company that minimized the bow in his legs.

"I'm working with very sick men whose reactions to the antibiotic vary," Valerie said. "What the *Enquirer* alluded to was a single incident blown up to appear as if it was the norm."

"Can you promise it will not happen again?" Nordsen asked.

Brian and Val exchanged a quick glance. There was no way she could guarantee the behavior of the volunteers at this time. "I'm willing to take my chances," she said.

Thelma cleared her throat and bent her scrawny neck to look at a series of notes in her hand. It was obvious that she'd been coached.

"Mr. Anslow, the members of the union feel that

in allowing the Blasa Fever testing to go on at the hospital, you've put them in a position to catch a disease that can cripple or kill them. They want it stopped."

"Just a minute," Val interrupted. "Since I'm in charge of that program, I'd like to challenge part of that statement. The members haven't been put in a position to catch Blasa Fever, because contrary to what the newspapers imply, it isn't caught by just breathing it in."

"Then how is it caught?" Cottrell asked.

"Well, we're not sure, but we suspect . . ."

Tom Nordsen waved his hand in a scoffing motion. "It was the same thing with the Legionnaire's disease. They were not sure either. But people kept dying."

"That isn't fair," Brian protested.

"I wouldn't talk about fair if I were you," Cottrell snapped. "How do you think the employees feel, working in a place where they may be carrying a disease home to their wives or husbands or kids? A lot of choice you gave them when you decided to breed a pack of germs next door." He hooked his thumbs in his belt, hitched his khaki jumpsuit higher and spoke to Valerie. "If your father was here, he'd have something to say about this, I'll tell you. There was never a day went by that Alex Traynor didn't look out for his employees."

Brian's face suffused with blood. Pryor had been right, he thought. They'd never believe the program had been Alex's idea.

Valerie held out her hands in a silent plea. "Look, have a little patience, and within a week or two, the volunteers may stabilize enough to be moved to an outside hospital without damaging the program." She paused, then spoke into the silence. "You must realize how many people are counting on this antibiotic. Surely they have a right to be considered too.''

Thelma referred to her notes again. She was an automaton with a single purpose. ''I'm sorry, Dr. Traynor. It's the decision of the union that the Blasa Fever testing must be stopped.''

''And if it isn't?'' Brian prompted.

''Then we strike.''

Brian's voice was harsh. ''You'll have a fight on your hands if you do. There are enough non-union employees at Traynor . . .''

''Guess again, Mr. Anslow,'' Cottrell shot back. ''Thanks to you and that Blasa Fever testing, we've got a ninety percent membership and we're negotiating now to tie in with the Teamster's Union. You allow this to go to strike and we'll see to it that no goods come into Traynor or leave it until this thing is settled. You won't last very long that way, I guarantee.''

Brian's hands balled into fists at his side. ''I don't like threats, Cottrell.''

Thelma's fingers fluttered between them disconcertingly. ''Gentlemen, please. We've said all that needed to be said. I suggest we leave now.''

They filed out as silently as they had come in. At the door, Cottrell glanced over his shoulder and struck a final blow. ''Three days,'' he said to Brian. ''That's all you've got.''

Brian leaned against the desk, his jaw so rigidly set that his neck muscles were corded like rope. He thought back to 1968 when Traynor had been threatened by strike because of an outrageous compensation and sick leave package demanded by Cottrell. Alex had taken precautions then. He had started the factory working overtime to build inventory so that current orders could continue to be filled if the plant was partially functioning.

Aware that shipping personnel might not be able to cross Cottrell's picket lines, he had moved that merchandise to a warehouse outside the plant at a location known only to himself and a few others. He had ordered the managers in the various departments to identify their employees who were not in the union, and who could perform jobs other than those they held. In case the strikers intended to block entrance to the plant, he quietly arranged for key people in each department to live in, so that communication could be maintained. To accommodate those people, he alerted a trailer truck loaded with necessary supplies to be ready to move onto Traynor property at a moment's notice.

In the end, Cottrell had backed down, perhaps because of employee pressure, perhaps because he knew Alex was prepared for a seige. The difference between then and now, Brian realized, was that Alex had been able to anticipate. There wasn't very much that could be accomplished in three days.

Valerie came to his side and touched his arm. "Are you going to call the program off?"

"No."

"Then what will you do?"

His expression was bleak. "I don't know."

At four thirty that afternoon, Arthur Perrault informed Brian Anslow that under the right of review, the Board was calling an emergency meeting on Friday at three o'clock in the small conference room.

At four thirty-five, Paul Haversham drafted a letter to Anshul-Bulden assuring them that the sale of Traynor Laboratories was practically guaranteed.

Chapter 20

In the Semmelweiss shrine, as Eva thought of her lover's bedroom, the February daylight darkened early to herald the twilight. Amid the rumpled sheets smelling of sex, Eva lay in satisfied languor, her eyes half-open, her lips tipped in a lazy smile, her feet under the blanket curled beneath Kirby's. She stirred and glanced at the clock, then slowly disengaged herself from Kirby's restraining arms and reached for her bra and panties. They were on the floor where he had flung them two hours ago in his haste to get her into the bed.

Kirby sat up and clasped her about the waist. His hair was a dark tangle of curls, his sinewy body still moist from their last encounter. "Don't go yet," he murmured huskily. His eyes were fixed adoringly on hers; the coarse skin of his hands she had found so exciting at first now chafed her tender flesh.

There was a petulance in his voice that grated on her nerves. She avoided his searching lips and kissed him quickly on the cheek. "You know I have to be back for dinner. Now let me up."

He shrugged into a maroon Sulka robe she had bought for him, tied it loosely and watched her dress. Other women he'd been with had always gone into another room to put their clothes on. Not Eva. She was as unself-conscious about her nakedness as the newborns he'd delivered this past month on the maternity floor.

Eva was a paragon among women, he thought. She dressed with the same spareness of motion with which she did everything else . . . except make love. In Eva he had found the Marie that *"grandpère"* Semmelweiss had idolized. She was body and soul mate to him. But lately he had felt her retreating from him. She denied it but he knew it was true. And the more he clung, the further she slipped away. It was affecting his sleep, his work. . . . If he lost Eva, he lost everything.

Wrapped in despair, he realized how lonely the room would be without her. Lately he had taken to leaving the bed unmade for days after she left, so the imprint of her body would remain undisturbed. Sometimes at night when he lay on the rumpled sheets, sleepless for want of her, the fragrance of her perfume floated up to him and he would reach to touch the empty space beside him, sure that she would be there. A sense of hopelessness filled him. He leaped from the bed and took her in his arms.

"Eva, leave him and come to live with me. I can't bear it here without you." He could tell from her expression that he'd made a mistake, but desperation drove him on. "I love you, Eva. But not for a hide and seek affair. I want to marry you. Have you with me always. I know I can't offer you much, but you'd never feel the loneliness you do with Brian. I swear it to you." He held her hands in his, raised each to his mouth and kissed it reverently in turn. "Say you'll think about it."

She gazed at his bent head. She should have been flattered. Instead, she felt repelled. The one thing she couldn't stand was a fawning male.

In retrospect, he had capitulated rather easily, she thought. But the promise he had shown of growing as a lover had never come to fruition. His body was magnificent—broad and smooth skinned with the muscular suppleness of a gladiator from a bygone era. But he lacked the sensitivity to know when she needed a master and when a slave. In that respect, her other lovers had outstripped him. And Brian had been superb.

"I'll think about it," she said, belting her cashmere dress.

She remembered her last lover, Grazzi. He had been the son of an Italian count, heir to the vast vineyards that produced the exquisite Bernardi wines. Debonair, sophisticated, unpredictable, he was the antithesis of Kirby Semmel. Initially he had no interest in her. His passion was race cars, his hobby, young girls. She had followed him from the Grand Prix in Monte Carlo to the Speedway in Indianapolis, mastering the intricacies of racetrack parlance and tactics as she went.

Grazzi had raced like a maniac, courting violence and death, but never her. Until on a rain-slicked stretch, on a small Italian speedway outside Milan, he had tried to outmaneuver a Maserati and crashed headlong into it. The driver of the Maserati had died, but Grazzi had miraculously survived with only a broken arm and head injuries.

In a rented *pensione* that overlooked the calm turquoise waters of Lago Del Garde, she had nursed him back to health and seduced him into her bed. It was then she understood why he preferred untutored young girls. Sexually overindulged since he was a young boy, Grazzi was a burnt-out candle with the staying power of a seventy-year-old.

The "grand passion" was in its second month and

already on the wane, when Grazzi's father suffered a heart attack. The Bernardi heir was recalled to Bologna to oversee the vineyards and marry the fiancée to whom he'd been engaged since childhood. By mutual consent, the affair was never revived.

Kirby's voice intruded on her memories.

"When will I see you again?"

What a pity she hadn't consummated the sale of the Semmelweiss Indictment yet, she thought. If she had, she could end this farce right now. Of course, she could mail the check to him with a note, but that would be crude. No. She would have to see him one more time.

"What about Friday?" she asked.

"Fine."

"I'll bring the check with me then."

"Don't make it sound so final."

She patted his cheek. "You *are* a child."

She would miss him in a way. For just a little while she had enjoyed playing the simplistic young girl role where all that was demanded of her was that she was a sounding board for a young man's dreams and frustrations. The reward had been his love, callow but unstinting, and the dubious pleasure of being worshipped as if she was a porcelain doll.

From the multitude of photos on the paint-chipped walls, Semmelweiss' beady eyes glared accusingly at her. For just a second she allowed herself to think of what Kirby would feel when they parted. An uncomfortable knot of remorse formed inside her that gave birth to a spurt of generosity. Instead of the twenty-five thousand she had promised him for the Indictment, she would make it thirty. That should ease the separation for him.

At the door, he took her in his arms. "What time on Friday?"

"Two o'clock." She held up her face to be kissed. "Don't mess my lipstick," she said.

That evening Dennie Redmond trudged up the steps of Angie's building as he had for the past three nights. He lived in a state of terror now, waiting for the axe to fall, powerless by his nature to do anything about it. More than once when he'd passed Brian Anslow in the hallway, he'd been tempted to blurt the whole thing out and throw himself on Anslow's mercy. But he thought of the revenge Bordini would wreak on his mother and the impulse had died unspoken.

He used his key at the apartment door. He no longer had to wonder whether Bordini and Finch would be there. It had become as inevitable to him as the impending theft of the morphine.

They were waiting for him inside, sitting on the opened bed that Angie hadn't bothered to make since morning. In the past few days she had become so jittery, she had ceased to do anything but watch television on the small Hitachi set he'd bought for her birthday.

She stood near the row of plants under the windowsill now, her long black hair cascading around her olive-skinned face. She wore a black sweater and skirt, and fidgeted with a wrought silver cross resting above the mound of her right breast. To Dennie it spoke of her terror more eloquently than words. He knew Angie was Catholic, but she had told him that she had buried her religion along with her mother when she was fourteen.

She looked up as he approached Bordini with dragging footsteps. Her eyes were dull, resigned, a hint of dread in their depths.

Bordini's gaze narrowed in his sardonic face. "I

think maybe you have good news for us tonight, eh, Dennie?"

His intuition never ceased to surprise Dennie. Or was it intuition? He marveled at how relaxed Bordini seemed. He was leaning against the bed, elbows braced behind him, long legs stretched out on the frayed carpet beneath. His fawn colored denims were of a brushed cotton and matched the turtlenecked sweater that hugged his neck. Next to him, Finch sat cross-legged in tee shirt and faded jeans. His face was sharp with tension.

"The morphine came in late this afternoon," Dennie said. "It's in a ten kilometer drum and was put into the vault for quarantined material."

Bordini's swarthy face spread with pleasure. "Then it hasn't gone to the sampling room yet?"

Dennie shook his head. "Tomorrow, I think. After that it'll be transferred to the other vault."

"And when is the Trinicitate going to be made?" Finch asked.

"Friday afternoon. It'll take till then to clean the machines for the new run."

Bordini patted the bed beside him. "Take your coat off and sit down, Dennie."

Dennie hung his overcoat in the hall closet. The sight of himself in the door mirror startled him. His gray suit, snug when bought, was a size too big for him now. His eyes, pouched and strained from sleeplessness, were reddened at the lid line, and the indentations at the side of his mouth had become deep crevices.

He returned to the bed, perched gingerly on the mattress, then drew back as Finch edged closer to him. He could well believe that Finch had spent time in an insane asylum. There was a violence and unpredictability about him that made Dennie quake.

Bordini sat up and gestured with his hands. "Okay. We go for the morphine this Friday. Now here's the way I've got it mapped out. With a closed circuit TV covering every step that morphine makes from the minute it leaves the vault, it figures we've got to make our move after the stuff gets to the manufacturing floor."

"But who's going to get it out of the vault?" Dennie asked.

"You are," Bordini said.

Dennie paled. "I can't. I mean there's no way . . ."

Bordini gestured for silence. "Shut up and listen. At exactly ten after twelve on Friday, Traynor goes out for lunch, right?"

Dennie nodded.

"At twelve thirty, his secretary follows, and you take over the office for a full hour before any of them come back."

He paused and Dennie nodded again. He tapped Dennie's arm lightly. "Now here's what you do. Right after the secretary leaves, you call this personnel guy who holds the other key to yours. What's his name?"

"Burt Findley."

"You tell this Findley that Traynor left orders for the morphine to be brought up to manufacturing for the Trinicitate run and you ask him to meet you down at the vault. Then you call the vault and tell them you're on the way."

"I can't do that," Dennie whispered.

"Why not?" Bordini asked.

"Because there are papers to be made out. A release form that requires my boss's signature."

Finch shrugged. "Forge 'em, dummy."

Dennie said nothing. The enormity of what they were asking was numbing his capacity to think. He had to get out of this. He *had* to!

"All right," Bordini continued. "Now after you get the morphine out of the vault, this Findley takes off and one of the machine operators you've called meets you and takes the stuff up to manufacturing. All the time this TV camera is on you, right?" He didn't wait for Dennie's nod. "Okay. Now when you get to the manufacturing floor, you tell this machine operator that Traynor wants to see the morphine in his office before he releases it for the run. Think of an excuse. He'll buy it."

"Even if he did, he'd stay with me until that morphine was accounted for," Dennie said. "That's the rule."

"No problem. Put the stuff in Traynor's safe. You know the combination. You told me so."

Dennie's voice rose. "Mr. Bordini, this will never work. There are too many things that can go wrong..."

"Nothing will go wrong. Less than an hour and you'll walk out scot free and worth a quarter of a million bucks. Think of what it can buy, Dennie. A place for you and Angie. Insurance for your mother to live her life out in style. She's a nice old lady. Gray-haired with those big flowered dresses she wears. Finch saw her only the other day when she took the garbage out."

"Finch saw my mother?" Dennie whispered.

"Sure. He's keeping an eye on her for you. That Bronx is an unsafe place to live."

His voice grew terse. "Let's get back to business, Dennie. When that machine operator leaves Traynor's office, you take that morphine out of the safe and wrap it like you do the packages for your army friend."

."I'd never get it out of Traynor. The guards at the exits examine any packages leaving the premises."

"You're not going to take it out of Traynor. You're going to bring it to the lab outside the hospital. Now the trick to the whole thing is timing. You make sure that you reach that lab no later than one thirty. And when you get to that guard outside the lab, hand him the package like you always do."

"And then what?"

"Walk out and meet us here. It's as easy as that."

Chapter 21

Friday was one of those cold clear days that skiers pray for but rarely get. The snow from the last fall was packed hard on the ground, and the sun magnified its glare until the whole world seemed bathed in the brilliant white light of a photographer's flashbulb.

At twelve fifteen, Eva Anslow took the Traynor Museum checkbook from the middle drawer of her desk in the office and made out a check to Kirby Semmel for thirty thousand dollars. Not until she had signed it and torn it from the book did she realize that it wasn't worth the paper it was written on. To be valid, the Traynor Museum checks had to be countersigned by the president of Traynor Laboratories.

When her father was alive, he had signed a large batch in advance, but she had used the last of those yesterday. With a muttered "damn," she realized that she would either have to postpone her appointment with Kirby Semmel for another day, or drive out to Traynor Labs for Brian's signature before keeping it. She chose what for her was the lesser of the two evils. She picked up the phone and told Brian she was coming to his office.

At twelve twenty on the same day, David Traynor pulled his Mercedes into the driveway of his Georgian home, slammed the car door and jabbed the bell with his finger. He was filled with determination. He'd made up his mind to reveal to Brian that there'd been a second morphine substitution, and this time he wasn't going to let Claire talk him out of it.

As the weeks had gone by and neither he nor Dennie Redmond had been able to turn up any clues, he'd become convinced that a clever thief was operating in his department and that the incoming morphine was in danger. Twice when the Drug Enforcement inspectors had been at Traynor for their surprise checkup, he had been on the verge of telling them, yet he'd held back for fear of revealing his former addiction and forfeiting his chance at the presidency. But the lie had preyed on his mind.

David knew that the presidency was within his grasp. The Board meeting this afternoon would make it conclusive. But somehow it didn't seem to matter as much as it had. The important thing now was that he unburden himself, because he couldn't live this way anymore.

He thought of his father. He had never been able to measure up to his father's standards and Alex had had too much integrity to lower them enough to meet his son halfway. A sense of shame filled him. His father would never have condoned the self-serving weakness that had allowed the duplicity to go on for even this long. But it was over now. Before he left, he had asked his secretary to set up an appointment with Brian immediately after lunch. He would tell him then.

With an expression of annoyance, he reached for his keys. Where the hell was the maid anyway? Probably in the kitchen, stoned out of her mind. Essie's drinking had gotten out of hand and Claire intended to fire her as soon as she could line up a replacement.

The door opened before he could use the key. Essie

stood there, dustrag in hand, cap askew. She made room for him to enter then closed the door behind him.

"Aft'noon, Mr. Traynor. You a little early."

He blinked twice. It wasn't Essie's business to time him. "Could be. Where's Mrs. Traynor?"

"Upstairs." She started toward the kitchen, then halted. "Your secretary called."

"What did she want?"

She shook her head. "Somethin' about an appointment with Mr. Anslow." Her bloodshot eyes regarded him dully before she lumbered off.

He glanced at his watch. With luck he could catch his secretary before she left. He picked up the phone and realized Claire was on. He was about to switch to the other line when a new voice entered the conversation. Startled, he recognized Paul Haversham.

"Claire, I'd like to comply with your request, but it's impossible right now."

David covered the mouthpiece with his palm and listened.

"Why is it so impossible? I've kept David in line for you. If what you say is true, he should be named president within a few days and you can go ahead with your plans. All I'm asking is a ten thousand dollar advance so I can get started with mine."

Haversham hesitated. "Look, I'm not sure I can manage it. But if I do, it has to be with the clear understanding that there'll be no further advances until everything is finalized."

"Of course."

"All right then. I'll be in touch as soon as I can."

The click of the phone echoed in David's ear.

Seconds later, Claire came tripping down the staircase, long auburn hair flying behind her. She couldn't wait to see Chris's face when she told him about the ten thousand dollars. He had accused her yesterday of fabricating the whole thing. Her fingertips slid sensuously along the polished mahogany of the bannister. She loved beautiful things. Gleaming woods and cut crystal and filmy underthings like the gauzy gray negligee she wore now for David's benefit. She sighed. Thank God she could stop playing that game soon. She'd had it to the point of nausea.

"Essie," she called. "When Mr. Traynor comes in, tell him . . ."

She stopped, aghast. David was still holding the phone, blinking rapidly, his skin a pasty white.

"Tell him what?" he said. He slid the phone onto its cradle, closed the space between them and crowded her against the wall. Not since Vietnam had he felt this exploding uncontrollable rage. He had been manipulated by her now as he had been by his father then. One had spouted patriotism, the other love, but the results had been the same. He'd been emasculated, crippled, his sense of self ground into the dust. His hands clenched at his sides. He wanted to hurt her, punch her. . . . He drew his fist back.

She covered her face with her hands and cringed against a curio cabinet. "David, no! Let me explain."

"Explain what? That you're no better than a whore? That you spread your legs for me so you could control me for some scheme you and Haversham cooked up between you?"

Cornered, Claire's mind worked at triphammer speed. If nothing else, she was a realist. Through one careless mistake, Chris and the fifty thousand dollars had just gone down the drain. If she didn't think of something quickly, her marriage would follow. And right now, she couldn't afford that.

She took her hands from her face. Her looks were her greatest asset with David. In the splash of light that streaked downward from the alcove window, her green eyes were luminous, her unpainted lips quivered like those of a wounded doe.

"It was Haversham's scheme, not mine," she cried. "He made me do it."

He shook her. "How?"

"He knew I needed money. I was desperate for it."

"Why?"

This was the tricky part. David would never accept her being with another man. It would have to be a weakness of hers that was believable yet forgivable.

Tears filled her eyes. She lowered her lids and her voice dropped to a whisper. "It was before you and I got close again. I was lonely. I gambled. I lost fifty thousand dollars at the track."

He stared at her, aghast.

The tears ran down her cheeks unheeded. "Haversham found out about it. He offered to clear the debt. All he wanted was for me to make sure you didn't blow your chances of becoming president. I didn't see any harm in it at first. So when you came to me with the Clary Robling story, I told you not to tell Brian. I thought of it as protecting you against yourself. Until I found out Haversham's real reason for wanting you to be president."

He questioned her with his eyes.

"He wants to sell Traynor, David. He's had an offer from a German company, with a percentage for him that'll make him rich. He's been lying to you about your ability all along. He figures you won't be able to handle the company and you'll be glad to be rid of it in a little while."

He blinked twice. His mouth hardened to a thin line. A sense of triumph swept her. All the fury he had leveled at her was being shifted to Haversham. She could see it in his face. He whirled and headed for the door.

"Where are you going?"

He slammed the door without answering, but she knew. She picked up the phone and dialed Haversham's private office number. It rang four times before his secretary answered.

"Thelma, where's Mr. Haversham?"

"He's out to lunch now, Mrs. Traynor."

"Can you reach him and have him call me?"

"Is it important?"

"Very."

"I'll try."

All that morning, Dennie Redmond had prayed for intervention. Some outside force to make the theft impossible. A power failure, a storm to tie the roads up, another D.E.A. visit . . . When nothing materialized, he still kept hoping. Perhaps David Traynor would send him on an errand or decide to stay in for lunch, or call for the morphine prematurely.

The Fates were against him. Everything went as usual. Except that at twelve o'clock Bordini phoned to assure him that his mother was fine. A mutual friend of theirs was keeping a watchful eye on her.

At twelve ten, David Traynor left for lunch. At twelve thirty, his secretary followed and Dennie was left in charge of the office. He went to the locker room and brought back the shopping bag and comic books he'd prepared. Then with shaking fingers he picked up the phone and told Mildred Benson to put him through to Burt Findley in Personnel.

As Vice President of Personnel, Findley carried the weight of the two thousand employees at Traynor as if it were his personal load. He had never learned to be objective, and his constant aggravation over every puny problem had made him irascible and short-tempered.

His booming voice cut through Dennie's explanation before he could finish.

"Look, Redmond. I'm on my lunch hour. I'm also under doctor's orders not to be rushed, because I've got an ulcer inside me the size of a grapefruit. If your boss wanted me to get the morphine from the vault with you, why couldn't he have arranged it earlier?"

Dennie wiped the phone with his handkerchief. It was so slippery with perspiration he was having trouble holding it. "I can't say, Mr. Findley. I only know he wanted it brought up so he could get the operators started on the Trinicitate before the Review Board meets this afternoon."

It was a subtle reminder to Findley that Dennie's boss was soon to be the president of Traynor Labs, and it brought him up short. "All right," he said grudgingly. "I'll meet you down there in fifteen minutes."

Dennie glanced at the clock. That would be a quarter to one. His deadline to get to the lab with the morphine was one thirty. It was going to be close, but he didn't dare say anything. With a murmured, "See you then," he hung up the phone and hurriedly took the vault release form from David's top drawer. He typed it in triplicate, made three errors which he didn't bother to correct, and painstakingly traced David's signature at the bottom from a letter he'd filched for that purpose. Next he called the supervisor in charge of the Trinicitate run, explained that David Traynor was moving the schedule up for the run, and arranged for a processing operator to meet him at the vault to bring the morphine back to manufacturing.

Despite the fact that it was lunchtime, the warehouse level was a beehive of activity. The elevator opened near the loading dock, where trucks were lined up side by side, waiting to take on finished goods or deliver raw materials.

At the moment, a shipment of dust in tightly sealed bags was being dollied in. It would be used to make allergenic extracts to be sent to allergists for patch tests.

Originally the dust had been obtained from old mattresses that were bought and crushed, but with the advent of foam rubber mattresses and air conditioning, good sources had begun to dry up and the pharmaceutical houses were forced to turn elsewhere. The dust coming into the dock now was a by-product of the cotton ginning process and had been shipped up from Mississippi.

"Set 'er down easy," the dock supervisor yelled to the operator of a crane-like lift whose job it was to stack the goods on four-inch-thick wood pallets and place them one atop the other, making sure that they cleared the twenty-five-foot height of the warehouse ceiling.

Dennie wove his way between stationary cartons and moving dollies, mumbling hellos and answering greetings, wishing he could fade into the white cement block walls that surrounded him.

To the rear of the floor were the two huge vaults made of one-foot-thick concrete with steel double doors, each with separate but interdependent locks. A uniformed guard patrolled the area, and a closed circuit TV camera attached to a huge pillar scaling the height of the warehouse was plainly visible.

Burt Findley arrived at the vault five minutes late, still wiping the crumbs from his mouth with a paper napkin. A corpulent man until a few months ago, he had lost forty pounds at his doctor's insistence and the loose jowls hung from his face like a bulldog's. He wore a checked suit sizes too big for him and greeted

Dennie with an uplifted hand and a concerned eye.

"Redmond, are you sick or something? You look as if you're going to pass out."

"No, no," Dennie hastily reassured. "I'm just in a hurry to get back."

"You keep that up and you'll land in the same fix I'm in. Where are the forms?"

Dennie produced the forged documents. Each team of keyholders was made up of a senior and a junior officer. As senior, Findley handed the papers to the uniformed guard. Dennie's heart beat so loudly, he was sure the personnel man could hear it. For a moment he hoped the guard would recognize the forgery and put an end to this madness before any damage could be done, but the guard merely gave the papers a cursory glance then handed them back for both their signatures.

Dennie fumbled in his wallet for the vault key and waited for Findley to produce his. Findley, he knew, had taken his key from the company safe near the data processing office on the third floor. To minimize the possibility of collusion, only one key carrier out of a pair was allowed to carry a key on his person.

Under the guard's supervision, the keys were inserted simultaneously into the separate locks of the doors. A whirring noise sounded, then a loud click and the massive doors swung open.

The vault was lit by overhead spots. The ten kilos of morphine was in a small drum near the front. The drum was made of heavy composition cardboard with metal bands reinforcing top and bottom. In accordance with regulations, the supplier's code number was on it, but content designation had been left blank.

Dennie lifted the drum in his arms and carried it outside.

"You got an operator meeting you?" Findley asked as the guard closed the doors behind them.

Dennie cocked his head toward the elevators in the front. "Morgan Effram. I see him coming now."

"Good. Then I can go back and finish my sandwich." He shook his head in concern. "You ought to get checked out by a doctor, Redmond. You really don't look good at all." He trudged off with the waddle engendered by his former obesity.

Dennie glanced at his watch. *Ten after one.* Damn Burt Findley. He'd never make it to the lab by one thirty. His shoulders began to ache. The drum weighed twenty-two pounds but it felt like double that. His throat was dry, his breathing shallow. The processing operator coming toward him was strolling at a leisurely pace. He wanted to scream at him to hurry. Instead he waited. And waited.

"Alex's boy change his mind again?" Morgan Effram asked, taking the drum from Dennie. He held it as if it were a feather.

Effram was a strapping six feet two with iron gray hair and a deeply wrinkled face. It was his job to oversee the granulation and processing of the morphine prior to blending it in the big vats. Effram was scheduled for retirement in June. He was also a talker. In the time it took to get from the warehouse level up to the manufacturing floor, he kept a running commentary going that required only an occasional grunt from Dennie.

"Alex didn't do us a good turn by cashing in his chips," Effram grumbled. "Anslow couldn't have the sense of a flea if he allowed this Fever testing that could get us all killed or worse, and now we're going to have to put up with Alex's boy. Everyone thinks that's great because he's a Traynor, but I tell you, he's still wet behind the ears even if he is almost thirty-five. Lately he's been snoopin' around, asking fool questions, checking the lockers when no one's looking. You mark my words . . ."

He glanced at Dennie sharply. "Aren't we going the wrong way?"

Dennie kept his eyes straight ahead. "Mr. Traynor wants the drum taken to his office."

"Why?"

"I don't know. Something about checking the code number or the supplier."

Effram came to a halt. "But that was done in the sampling room yesterday."

"That's what I told him. But he said something has come up since then and he wants to see it before he releases it for the Trinicitate run."

Effram hesitated. Dennie was his superior, but this was highly irregular. Everyone knew that David Traynor left for lunch by twelve fifteen. It would mean leaving the morphine alone with Dennie, which was strictly forbidden.

Globs of sweat stood out on Dennie's forehead. The dial hands on his watch seemed to leap out at him. *One twenty.* He had ten minutes to get that morphine to the laboratory. In desperation he took the offensive.

"Look, Morgan, Traynor was in a bad mood this morning. He almost bit my head off. I wasn't about to question his orders, but if you want to . . ."

Morgan Effram had put in thirty years with the company and he was proud of his unblemished record. He knew that he should check this out with his supervisor before moving ahead. But he'd bought a small retirement home in Florida that was almost paid off, and he needed his next six months' salary to furnish it. Unlike his father, David Traynor had a temper. When riled, he'd been known to fire an employee on the spot and Effram didn't feel like taking any chances.

He hoisted the drum to his shoulder. With only a few months to go, he'd be crazy to stick his neck out. Besides, he'd seen Burt Findley leaving the vault. Findley would never have gone along with this if it wasn't aboveboard.

"You see," he said to Dennie. "That's what I mean about Alex's boy. He doesn't know his ass from his elbow and he's about to become president of the company."

He followed Dennie to David Traynor's office and eased the drum onto the desk.

Against the wall, the floor to ceiling steel safe had been built in along with the bar and had the same walnut facade. Dennie pushed aside the mock brass knob and twirled the combination lock behind it with trembling fingers. Sixty-eight right. Twenty-two left. Forty-nine right. Another turn left. The all important click, and the door swung open. He took the drum from the desk, placed it inside the safe, closed the door, and spun the combination lock.

He rubbed his hands together. "Well, that takes care of that." He walked the operator to the door. "Thanks for coming down, Morgan."

Effram shrugged. "Part of the job. Sorry if I questioned . . . I mean, you can understand . . ."

"Sure. Don't worry about it."

"Thanks."

He waited until Effram disappeared around the corridor then closed the door and hurried to the safe.

The phone rang.

He hesitated.

It rang again.

He picked it up.

"Dennie, where've you been?" Mildred Benson complained. "I've had four calls for Mr. Traynor.

He's out. His secretary is out. You're out. How am I supposed to run a board? On good wishes?"

"Mildred, let me call you back."

"Are you feeling okay, Dennie? You don't sound too good. With this Blasa Fever going around, you ought to . . ."

One twenty-eight. He gripped the phone hard. "Mildred, I've got someone here. I'll call you right back."

"Why didn't you say so?" She hung up.

He turned to the safe. Sixty-eight. Twenty-two. Forty-nine. In seconds he had the drum back in his hands. A deep sigh escaped him. With luck he'd be just a few minutes late.

The door opened behind him. He spun around.

David Traynor strode into the room. He still wore his overcoat. His sandy hair was windblown, his expression one of thwarted anger. "Dennie, do you happen to know where Haversham . . ." He stopped short. "What the hell!" He took in the open safe door, the drum of morphine in Dennie's hands, the shock of guilt on his face. He blinked rapidly. His pink skin suffused to a deep red.

"You son-of-a-bitch," he grated.

In the highly emotional state Dennie was in, if David Traynor had stood his ground, Dennie would probably have confessed everything and thrown himself on his boss's mercy. But David didn't. The weeks of anguished concealment of the Clary Robling incident, the futile search for a culprit, the blow he'd been dealt by Claire, and his inability to vent his anger on Haversham all culminated in the maniacal fury he felt toward this thief in front of him.

Hands balled into fists, he came at Dennie swinging. Dennie congealed. He couldn't think. He just reacted. A second before David reached him, he flung the drum of morphine at him. With the full twenty-two pounds behind it, the metal band of the drum caught David over the left temple. The force of the blow knocked him backward. His head hit the steel edge of the open safe door. Hands outflung, face mirroring shock, he went down with a thud.

Dennie stared at him in disbelief. It had all happened so quickly. He bent over David contritely. The gash at his temple was widening, bleeding, staining the tweed suit. The sight of the blood nauseated Dennie. Threw him into panic. The secretary would be back any minute. He had to get out of there.

He picked up the drum of morphine from where it had rolled near a leg of the desk. He took it to the closet where he had prepared the shopping bag. He wrapped and rubberbanded the drum in the comic books, put it back in the bag and threw an extra few comics over it for camouflage. He glanced at his watch. *One forty-two.*

Jesus!

He lifted the bag and ran from the room.

Chapter 22

At one o'clock in the hospital, Val administered the maintenance dose of the antibiotic and decided the confinement was getting to her. All morning long she'd tried to shake a premonition that something terrible was going to happen, and there was no reason for it. On the contrary, the outlook for the Tetra-2 was as bright as the sun that streaked through the window panes.

As she'd told Brian, in an effort to give him ammunition for the presidential Review Board this afternoon, except for Jefferson Montgomery, every patient in the ward was showing signs of improvement.

In some cases it was slight. Colonel Darwin's fever was down, but the cramping was still evident. The siege of hyperactivity that Tiny Anderson had experienced had caused complications, but they hadn't worsened as they had with Arby. He had lapsed into periods of unconsciousness followed by apathy and was only now returning to his former state of alertness.

Some of the others, like Ansel Golden and Alfie Brockwell, were ambulatory and talkative. Sid Draper could scarcely be held down. His latest antic was soliciting a vote from the volunteers to change the male attendants to female nurses—preferably under the age of twenty-five.

But she wasn't the only one with premonitions, Valerie thought, watching Charley Santos pace the ward restlessly. With the improvement of the volunteers, the guard's vigil had doubled. To Val's annoyance, he now wore his gun and holster on the outside of his hospital gown. In answer to her protest a grim look had crossed his swarthy face, and he'd held his big hands out in a plea for understanding.

"Look, doc, when it happens, it'll happen fast."

"You mean *if* it happens, don't you, Mr. Santos?" she replied scathingly. "It's a good thing you're not involved in a rehabilitation program or it would be a total disaster."

"The man has a complex, doc," Alfie Brockwell had chimed in from his corner of the room. "He thinks he's Scotland Yard and the F.B.I. all rolled into one." He scratched at his motley beard with an index finger and threw Santos a sly look. "Wouldn't surprise me none if he started something here himself just to prove it."

"Button your lip, Brockwell, or I'll button it for you." Santos had retorted.

"That'll be enough," Valerie had asserted. "From both of you."

The exchange had ended there, but the bickering between Santos and the cockney was an ongoing thing. When this was over, Valerie promised herself, she would take a long rest away from the conflicting personalities that were an added drain to energies already overtaxed.

And she would marry Wally.

She hadn't told him yet. It wasn't a purposeful delay. It was just that with the patients' needs tying up either her time or his, the right moment hadn't presented itself.

With luck it would all be over soon, she thought as

she swabbed Ansel Golden's arm with antiseptic. The gripes, the strain, and the uncertainties would be forgotten or forgiven and the only thing that would remain would be the satisfaction of accomplishment and the glow of success.

"Have you given the Food and Drug Administration a preliminary report on the Tetra-2 yet?" Golden asked. Despite his gray crew-cut, he no longer looked like an old man. His blue eyes were clear, his cheeks had filled out, and the jaundice had been replaced with a touch of color.

She smiled at him. "Aren't you being a little premature?"

Her admiration of Golden had increased with her knowledge of him. He was a poor sleeper, and many nights when Wally rested, they talked medicine into the early hours of the morning. For a surgeon, his knowledge of research was surprising, his insights brilliant. But any discussion of re-activating his life continued to be met with the obstinate resistance that stemmed from fear of failure.

"I'm probably rushing it," he admitted. "But I'd like to be here when they credit you with the breakthrough. You deserve it."

"Thanks, Ansel. But I wouldn't worry about it. You're not leaving yet."

"Doc!" The call came from the corner of the room.

She looked around for Wally, then remembered he was in the lab checking on the morning's specimens.

"Doc!"

It was sharper, more piercing now. She turned her head quickly.

Alfie Brockwell stood near the bed like a hulking bear, pajamas flapping loosely at his sides, face taut with panic. He raked his hands through his straggly mane with jerky uncontrolled motions as she hurried to his side. His gray eyes shuttled back and forth, as Arby's had . . . as Anderson's had . . .

"Something's happening to me, doc," he whispered hoarsely.

It couldn't be, she thought. Not at this late date. *It couldn't be!*

He ripped at the neckline of his pajamas, bared his muscular torso. "Too hot in here," he mumbled, licking his lips. "Got to get out." His skin glistened with moisture. His fingers tore aimlessly at the tufts of hair matting his chest.

Val signaled to the attendant. "Get me a syringe of Seconal, stat!" She put a restraining hand on Brockwell's arm. "Hang in there, Mr. Brockwell. We're getting help for you."

From the corner of her eye she saw Ansel Golden alert Charley Santos. A rumble sounded around the room as the patients became aware of what was happening.

Brockwell no longer recognized her. She could see it in his unfocused gaze. "Got to get out," he repeated. He pushed her fingers away, lumbered toward the door leading to the reception dock.

Gun in hand, Santos moved to intercept him. The hospital gown hampered him. His craggy face held a hunter's look, intent, murderous.

He'll kill him, Val thought. "Put the gun away," she cried. "He's sick."

He ignored her.

"That's an order, Mr. Santos!"

He shoved the gun into its holster, uttered a curse. He circled Brockwell, closed in. They grappled, grunting and sweating. The convicts jeered from the sidelines, their liking for Santos forgotten in their need to affirm their brotherhood.

"Take 'im, Brock!"

"Make the pig bleed!"

Tod Preston thrust the hypodermic into Valerie's hand. She ran to where the two men were locked in combat, then ducked as a flailing arm almost knocked her down. She hovered over them, seeking an opening. There was none. Santos threw a punch at Brockwell. It missed. The convict butted his head at the guard's stomach. Santos grunted, exhaled sharply and came back fighting.

She waved the hypodermic in her hand. "Hold him for one second," she cried to Santos.

He nodded, backed Brockwell into a wall, and landed a punch to his jaw. He pinned the convict's shoulder for just an instant. But it was all Valerie needed. She thrust the hypodermic into his arm and plunged downward. Brockwell swiped at it, caught the tip, and dashed it to the floor. Valerie backed off as he threatened to do the same to her.

In a sudden movement, Brockwell bent his knees, ducked low and elbowed a blow to Santos's groin. Santos cried out and doubled over in pain. Crouching, Brockwell crowded him against a wall and locked his arms about the guard. When he straightened up, a triumphant smile was spread across his face and Charley Santos's gun was in the palm of his hand.

He waved it at Val and Santos and spoke in a cold, hard voice.

"March slow-like in front of me. First one moves too quick, I kill." His gray eyes were chips of granite.

She stared at him in bewilderment. "You're not hyperactive. You're not sick at all."

"I never was, doc." He motioned with the gun. "Now move. Not that way. To the lab. And keep your hands where I can see them."

They walked slowly in front of him. The ward held the silence of a battlefield anticipating the first shot.

Ansel Golden stood in front of his bed, anguished helplessness written on his face. Colonel Darwin looked indignant. Sid Draper made a move toward her, then stopped as Brockwell leveled the gun at him.

Jefferson Montgomery rocked on his knees in bed, his fever-glazed eyes bright with hope as the cockney came abreast of him.

"Take me with you, man," he pleaded hoarsely. A chorus among the convicts echoed his sentiments.

Brockwell shook his head. "Sorry, mates. I have to go solo on this one." He prodded Santos with the gun.

"Why the lab?" Santos asked.

Valerie had been wondering the same thing. The quickest way out was through the reception dock to the front door of the hospital. There was a guard stationed outside, but Brockwell had a gun and the element of surprise was on his side.

"Shut your trap," the convict said. "And keep moving."

At the lab door, he ordered Santos to turn the knob and push it in.

Under the fluorescent fixtures, the chalky ceiling and white tiled walls bathed the room in a sterile glow. Wearing a mask and lab coat, Jimmy, the technician, was bent over a microscope, checking the morning's specimens, while Wally used a pipette to mix a cloudy solution over a bunsen burner. On the formica-topped workbench to his right were the virulent Blasa Fever organisms in the process of being cultured to produce the Tetra-2 antibiotic.

Wally looked up. At first he saw only her. "Val, is there anything wrong? You look as if . . ." His fingers tightened around the pipette. "What the hell!"

Brockwell raised the gun. "No noise, Chandler."

He stood with his feet apart and his back wedged

against the open door where he had a view of both the lab and the hospital. From there he could see the door that led into the hallway between the lab and the plant, but the guard stationed outside couldn't spot him through the windowed cutouts. He checked the clock above the empty space that had held the garbage disposal. One thirty. He nodded in satisfaction.

"What do you want?" Wally demanded.

Brockwell's eyes flicked around the lab. "A package came in here a few minutes ago for a soldier named Draper. Where is it?"

Wally shook his head. "There was no package delivered."

Brockwell brought the muzzle of the gun up to center on Valerie's heart.

"Maybe the guard in the hall has it?" Santos suggested quickly.

Wally nodded. "He's right."

"Okay. You tell him to come in here. And no tricks, mind you, or I blow the little lady away."

Wally opened the door and said a few words to the guard. He stepped inside and shook his head at Wally's questions.

"There's been nothing delivered here, Dr. Chandler. I'd know about it if it had. I've been here all morning."

He turned around and his mouth gaped open. He made a half-hearted attempt at his holster. Brockwell's gun swung toward him.

It was the break Santos had been waiting for. With the danger to Valerie eliminated, he made a lunge for the gun, but Brockwell anticipated him. With incredible swiftness for his six feet two bulk, he sidestepped Santos and fired point blank.

A look of surprise crossed Santos's swarthy face.

Blood spurted from his groin. His hands flew outward and he crashed backward inside the open hospital door.

"In the balls, you bloody bastard," Brockwell gloated, keeping an eye on the other guard. "I been wanting to do that for a long time."

"My God!" Valerie murmured. She hurried to bend over Santos, but the convict grabbed her arm in a hurting grip.

"Listen, Florence Nightingale. Nobody moves 'til I say so."

"But he's bleeding."

"Let him bleed." He pushed her against the wall, then held his hand out for the guard's gun. "Take it out of the holster easy-like and bring it here." The guard complied. "Now you pull that bleeding bastard into the ward. I can't stand the sight of him." He motioned to the lab technician. "You help him."

He glanced at the clock. One thirty-five.

"Son-of-a-bitch," he said.

"What do we do now?" Chandler asked.

"We wait," he said.

At one forty-seven Dennie reached the door connecting the plant with the laboratory. He had made it across manufacturing in five minutes. He could have run it in two. All the way from Traynor's office through blending, packaging, and labeling, he had cautioned himself. *Don't hurry. Act natural.* He had waved to people and called greetings while the picture of David Traynor bleeding on the floor of his office rose to torment him. He had feared for his mother and Angie and he had dreaded being caught, but in his naiveté, he had never thought that someone at the plant might get hurt. He clutched the heavy shopping bag to his side. It was too late for hindsight. The important thing now was to deliver the morphine and get out of Traynor fast.

He stepped into the small hallway that led to the lab. The guard was nowhere to be seen. He stood on tiptoe and peered through the cutouts in the lab door. He could see Dr. Chandler. His hands were clenched at his sides. His lean face was grim. Near him, Dr. Traynor looked as if she wanted to cry. A big man with a bushy head of black hair stood facing them both. His back was to the door. They were all unnaturally still.

He knocked gingerly on the door. After a second, Wally Chandler opened it a crack.

"Dr. Chandler, I'm here to——" His words ended in a squeal as the door was flung wide and some-one grabbed him. His arm felt as if it was being wrenched out of its socket as he was dragged into the lab.

The big man shook him as if he was a rag puppet. "You're late, you little shit!" His voice was a deep boom.

"I couldn't help it."

The convict towered over him by at least a foot. There was hair all over him: his head, his beard, his bulging forearms. His eyes were an angry gray, his skin oily. His thick brows plunged downward in a satanic vee. He wrenched the shopping bag from Dennie's frozen grip.

Dennie's eyes darted past Valerie toward the open doorway of the hospital. They widened in horror. A swarthy-faced man in hospital garb lay just beyond it in a pool of blood, hands clutching his groin, mouthing the twenty-third psalm. The lab technician and the hallway security guard were kneeling helplessly over him.

Dennie backed toward the lab door. If he didn't get

out now, he'd never leave this place alive. He knew it. He turned and ran.

Brockwell caught him in two strides. "Where do you think you're going?"

Dennie struggled in his grip. His voice rose shrilly. "Niko promised . . ."

He saw the fist coming at him, but he couldn't avoid it. He threw up his hands, but it was too late. His face exploded with pain. For a moment he couldn't see. He staggered backward, arms flailing for balance. He heard Dr. Traynor call a warning to him, but he was too far gone. He hit the formica-topped workbench head on and with a sweep of his fingers knocked the cone shaped containers to the floor.

The deadly Blasa Fever organisms were freed from their prisons.

In one swift step, Wally Chandler reached the left side of the workbench. Even as Brockwell swung the gun toward him, he pressed the buzzer just beneath the top. A curious creaking sound rebounded from the walls near the doors on either side of the lab.

Brockwell whirled back and forth, unable to comprehend this new turn of events. "What the hell is going on here?"

With a final squealing of rusty hinges, the steel doors, hidden for years behind their oak counterparts, slid tightly shut.

Cut off from the hospital on one side and the manufacturing plant on the other, the lab was as impenetrable as a sealed coffin.

Chapter 23

All Friday morning, Brian tried to ignore the inevitable—the meeting of the Review Board that afternoon to oust him. He had undertaken the presidency of Traynor with two strikes against him, a divided Board and a disgruntled employee faction. Still, his hopes had been high. They weren't anymore. Haversham had needed only the ammunition to unify the employees and the Board against him and the Fever program had supplied it.

Yet, in retrospect, Brian was glad he'd authorized the testing. Until the day he'd had to turn down the lineup of supplicants for the Tetra-2 in Traynor's lobby, he'd operated strictly by the ratio of profit to loss. He'd viewed Alex's bleatings about other dimensions of growth and Valerie's stress on humanitarianism as indulgences that didn't belong in the mainstream of business. But when he'd looked into the faces on that line, his vision of himself as an impersonal moneymaker had seemed callow and unjustified.

He felt differently now. But it was too late to do anything about it. The Blasa Fever program would topple when he did and there was nothing he could do to save it.

At noon he decided against lunch at the company

cafeteria. He drove the Mercedes to Beasley's Diner in Clayville, had a sandwich with Roy Penzinger and kept the conversation fixed on the forthcoming P.A.L. game to be played at Clayville High School.

From time to time he checked his watch. Eva had said she would meet him at Traynor Labs at one thirty to have the museum checks countersigned and he had no desire to rile her by being late. Her temporary "high" of the last few months had evaporated like this morning's fog and she was bitchy as hell to get along with.

Last night she had called him down for not telling her about the forthcoming Review Board meeting. "Not that I give a damn what happens to you," she'd said, "but as Mrs. Brian Anslow, I don't relish being put in the position where Bernice Haversham can drool over me with juicy tidings I'm not even aware of."

It was then he had brought up the divorce. He knew his timing was off. Dealing with Eva now was like walking in a mine field. There was no way to know when she'd blow up. But Val's decision to marry Wally had thrown him into a quandary. If he could convince Eva to relent on her stance concerning Mark, he might get Val to change her mind.

He had suggested a compromise. Mark could spend six months with each of them and have visiting privileges on both sides.

She had leaned against the two-hundred-year-old grandfather clock Alex had bought for them as a wedding gift and lifted her martini glass to him with the enigmatic curl of her lips that set his teeth on edge.

"I'll see you and Val in hell first," she'd said evenly. "My terms stand. If we divorce, Mark goes with me to Europe to live."

He'd shaken his head in disbelief. "What do you

get out of it, Eva? You don't love me. You don't even like me. What makes you hang on this way?''

"Tenacity, darling. It's my strongest asset. Ask the museums who compete with ours for memorabilia. They'll tell you."

He had stalked away then, because the fury inside him was so uncontrollable, he was afraid he'd kill her.

When he returned to the office at one thirty-five, Eva still hadn't arrived. His private line rang ten minutes later and he assumed she was calling to explain. If nothing else, his wife was punctual.

He picked up the phone. It was Lester Pryor.

"Brian, I'm in David's office. I think you'd better get down here right away."

There was something in the tersely controlled voice that forebade Brian from asking any questions.

"I'll be right there."

He took the stairs two at a time. The door to David's office was closed. He pushed it open and drew in his breath sharply.

The steel doors of the safe stood ajar. David lay sprawled beneath them, unconscious, his face waxen, his eyes closed. He bled from a deep gash above his left temple. Lester Pryor's auburn head was bent low as he knelt above him, vainly trying to staunch the bleeding.

Pryor glanced up. The pallor of his skin accentuated the freckles on his cheekbones. "Brian. Thank God you're here."

Brian knelt beside him. "Lester, what the hell happened here?"

"I don't know. I came in a few minutes ago to talk to David about a defective compound that arrived in sampling and found him like this." He nodded toward the white-faced secretary standing near the window. "She came in after I did."

"Did you send for the doctor?"

"He's on his way now."

David groaned, stirred. Brian clutched his hand. It was limp, cold. "David, it's Brian. Can you hear me?"

His eyes fluttered open, rolled back in his head, then steadied. They focused on Brian. His mouth moved but no sounds came out.

Brian squeezed his hand. "Easy, David. You're hurt. The doctor's on his way."

He shook his head. The bleeding accelerated. His chalky lips quivered. "Brian . . . my fault . . ."

"What's your fault? Was something taken from the safe?"

He closed his eyes for a second. Opened them again. "Morphine," he gasped.

"The drum for the Trinicitate?" Pryor guessed.

"Yes . . ."

"Who took it?" Brian asked.

"Dennie . . ."

Brian's voice was incredulous. "Dennie Redmond?"

David's mouth moved again, but the words were too faint to hear. Brian leaned closer. "*Mea culpa* . . ." His eyes closed. He lapsed into unconsciousness.

The door was suddenly pushed open and the company doctor rushed in, bag in hand.

Of Japanese heritage, Dr. Osato was a small dark-haired man in his forties who preferred the steadier pace of industry to the irregular hours of private practice. At sight of David, his sloe eyes widened in his usually impervious face. He muttered something unintelligible, knelt quickly and pushed David's right eyelid upward with his thumb.

Before he could continue, the shriek of an alarm

rent the air in a series of four whoops, ceased, then sounded again.

"What the hell was that?" Brian asked.

The doctor shook his head. "I never heard it before."

"I did," Pryor said. "A long time ago when it was being tested. It's the alarm that kicks off when the steel doors of the lab slam shut. Something's happened in there."

Apprehension flooded Brian. "Let's find out what." He gestured toward David. "Doctor, do what you can for him. I'll get back to you in a little while."

Without waiting for his nod, he sped toward the door. All he could think of was Val . . . the way she had looked the last time he'd seen her . . . the certainty in her voice when he'd feared for her at the outset of the program. "If anything should happen to you . . ." he'd said. "It won't," she'd answered brightly.

With Pryor trailing him by a length, he raced across the manufacturing floor.

Chapter 24

Inside the lab, Brockwell raged like a maddened bull. His wrinkled hospital pajamas bagged about his huge frame. His armpits were ringed with sweat and his face was contorted with rage.

When the steel doors clanged shut, he ran his fingertips along the outer edge of each door like a safecracker seeking an invisible spring. There was none.

He turned around, his gray eyes hardening.

From where he cowered in the corner of the room, Dennie Redmond let out a whimper. He crouched on the metal plate that filled the empty space where the garbage disposal had been. His arms were wrapped around his knees. His cheek was scraped and reddened. One eye was swollen and purpling.

Brockwell strode to where Wally stood with his back against the workbench, one arm flung protectively around Valerie's shoulders. He brought the muzzle of his gun level with Wally's stomach.

"You got those doors closed," he said. "Now you get them open."

"I can't. They work on an electric timer. They're set to open . . ." he glanced at his watch ". . . at eight o'clock tonight."

"How come?"

"Because that's the span of the organism's maximal virulence."

"What the hell is he talking about?" This he directed at Valerie.

Valerie hugged the hospital gown closer about her. The lab was growing cold. "Mr. Brockwell, I don't think you understand what happened here. When Dennie knocked those cultures over, he released hundreds of thousands of raw Blasa Fever organisms. If they were allowed to get out of this lab before six hours were up, it could lead to an epidemic. But by eight o'clock tonight, the bugs will have spent their greatest strength and the danger of transmission will be much less." She faced him squarely, hands jammed into her pockets, feet slightly apart. "You see, Dr. Chandler didn't close those doors to keep you in. He did it to keep the Fever bugs from getting out."

Brockwell was no longer listening. His eyes darted around the room. The lab was divided by a central work counter on top of which the Blasa Fever cultures had stood. Splinters of glass covered the surface now and an innocuous-looking mucous substance bearing myriads of microscopic organisms oozed over the formica, slid along the drawers, and dripped its murderous contents onto the floor.

Against one white tiled wall were workbenches which held microscopes, instruments, slides, small incubators, and petri dishes. Above them were racks of test tubes containing culture media in which swabs were immersed and closed with cotton stoppers. The other wall along which Dennie Redmond sat harbored the supply cabinets and the crematorium.

"No windows," Brockwell muttered. "Where the hell are the vents?"

"There are none," Valerie said. "The lab is controlled for contamination." At Brockwell's angry glance she put it in simpler terms. "Micro filtered air and heat come through those small openings you see in the ceiling. But when the steel doors sealed off the lab just now, those openings closed down also. That's why the lab is getting so cold."

"She's telling the truth," Dennie Redmond said. "There's no way out of here."

"Like hell there ain't." His steely eyes were fixed on the wall telephone near the hospital door. "Who runs things at these Labs?" he asked Wally.

"Brian Anslow. But he can't get you out of here."

"Shut up." He picked up the phone. The busy signal that came through was audible to everyone. He looked at Valerie for an explanation.

"That happens when the switchboard's jammed," she said. "An alarm went off outside when those doors were triggered shut and the plant is probably in an uproar."

He slammed the phone back on the hook and glared vindictively at Wally. "I ought to kill you now," he muttered.

Valerie prayed the lines would stay busy. She knew what Brockwell had in mind. He would threaten Brian with their lives unless those doors were opened. Not knowing that the Fever organisms had escaped, Brian would find a way to open them if he had to dynamite those doors himself. The result would be an epidemic of mind boggling proportions.

What a fool she'd been not to put two and two together. Looking back, she realized there were so many ways she should have been tipped off to the fact that Brockwell was faking. The normal temperatures he'd registered with a disease known for its high fever. The lack of organisms in his stool cultures when the others had been rampant with it. The unusual strength he'd displayed in fighting off Tiny Anderson when the convict had tried to rape her . . . a feat that might have roused her suspicions if she hadn't been so grateful at the time. She realized now that Brockwell hadn't been prompted by the lofty moral fiber she'd credited him with, but had feared that the repercussions of a rape might end the project entirely, or put restrictions on the convicts that would hamper his future plans.

But one thing puzzled her.

The symptoms that Brockwell had displayed were intestinal cramping, apathy, and jaundice. The first two could be simulated. But what about the third?.

Jaundice was a result of bile that was blocked in the liver and absorbed and distributed to all tissue by way of the blood. Some of its causes were acute fever, anemia, the use of sulfur compounds or poisons such as arsenic. But she had detected no signs of these in her examinations.

She glanced at Brockwell. He straddled one of the chairs in front of the workbenches. One muscular arm gripped the chair back. The other holding the gun was perched securely on its edge. His bare feet splayed on the tile floors must have been freezing, yet he showed no sign of cold. His shaggy brows were drawn together. His eyes roamed the room like a caged beast's.

She chafed at her helplessness. It was only a matter of minutes before Brockwell got through to Brian or vice-versa. She had to alert Brian to what had happened. *She had to!*

Chapter 25

Cries of "What's happening?" or "Is it a fire?" followed Brian and Lester Pryor as they wove their way through the separate divisions on the manufacturing floor, until they reached the packaging area, just outside the hall adjoining the lab. In place of the oak door, a three-foot-wide steel slab was wedged solidly into the concrete walls on either side, filling the space from ceiling to floor.

The operator nearest Brian was Gilda Jennings, a thin young woman who'd been with the company less than a year. Her frightened eyes turned to Brian for reassurance.

"When did this happen?" Brian asked her.

"A few minutes ago," she answered. "Just before the alarm went off." Her voice quavered. She fussed with the white cap covering her hair. "Mr. Anslow, what's goin' on here? I have a ten-month-old baby home . . ."

Lester Pryor patted her on the back. "Take it easy. Everything's going to be all right. Just answer a few questions for us. Okay?" She glanced from one to the other uncertainly, then nodded.

"Who was the last one through that door?" Brian asked.

She thought a moment. "It was the security guard. He came to relieve the other one for lunch."

A heavyset blonde operator touched her timidly on the arm. "You're wrong, Gilda. Someone went in after that. It was when you left to get more package inserts. Remember?" Her voice was scarcely audible above the clanking of the machines.

Pryor swung toward her. "Who was it?"

"Dennie Redmond."

Brian and Lester exchanged glances.

"Was he carrying anything?" Brian asked.

The timid operator bit her thumbnail and frowned. Then her saucer eyes brightened. "Come to think of it, he was. A brown shopping bag. It must have been heavy because his shoulder was lopsided and the bag was almost touching the floor."

"Thanks. You've been a big help." He took Pryor aside. "It's beginning to add up, Lester. Dennie knew he could never get that package out of here without having a guard check its contents. He took it to the lab because he's got a contact there who could do the job for him."

"One of our people?"

"I don't know."

"But that still doesn't explain why the alarm went off."

Brian's face held a brooding look. "No, it doesn't."

"Brian, has it occurred to you that those Fever cultures might have been overturned in the lab?"

"I hope to God not."

"If they were and there was seepage into the plant, we could have a case of contagion here that would . . ." He broke off at the sound of running feet. Dora Watkins was racing across the floor in her orthopedic shoes, gray hair disheveled, bosom heaving with her efforts.

"Mr. Anslow," she panted. "You've got to come

back to your office. Everyone's crowding in there trying to get answers. Mildred Benson finally got through to me. That alarm has turned this whole place upside down. The telephone lines are jammed. Word is getting around that David Traynor is hurt and the employees are panicking.''

"I'm on my way.'' He grabbed Pryor's arm. "Lester, get to Joe Barbetta. Tell him that, without making a big show of it, I want him to station double guards at every exit. Until I know what's going on here, nobody gets in or out.''

"Will do.''

He took the stairs back to the third floor with Dora struggling to keep up with him. He tried to concentrate on what had to be done, but his fear for Val got in the way. If he could only know she was safe, he might be able to think straight.

"Dora, is there any way to get a line through to the lab or hospital?''

"Not right now,'' she gasped.

Tension roughened his voice. "Stay on it, will you?''

She nodded. "There's something I forgot to tell you.''

"What's that?''

"Mrs. Anslow arrived just before the alarm went off. She's in your office now, trying to cope.''

When they reached his office, Eva was backed up against the far wall under her father's picture, surrounded by executives and supervisory personnel alike. Her shoulders were drawn back as far as possible, her black hair swirled about them like a waterfall as she shook her head repeatedly at the questions being flung at her.

"I have told you over and over that I just got here,''

she shouted. "I know nothing more than you do."

He had never noticed any resemblance between her voice and Alex's, but he did now.

She spotted him over the heads of Burt Findley and Zack Cottrell and shot him a furious glance. "Here's Mr. Anslow now. You can ask him."

In the babble that followed, he held up his hands for silence. He explained to them that a theft had taken place, but withheld Dennie's name. He told them he didn't know why the alarm had gone off, and ended with, "In a few minutes I'm going to broadcast what I've just told you to all the employees. Right now I want you to go back to your offices and stations and spread the word to keep calm. There's nothing to be gained by panic and the behavior of the rest of the employees will depend on the example you set."

Despite their protests, he blocked any further questions. The noise diminished, then died to an undertone as they filed out. A few glanced back resentfully. He knew what they were thinking. But for several hours, he probably wouldn't have been in a position to order them about like this. To hell with them, he thought. Until that Review Board met, he was still president of Traynor Labs and whether they liked it or not, the decisions were his.

When the last one was gone, Eva faced him angrily.

"You can't brush me off as easily as that. I never felt such a fool in my life. I demand to know what's happened."

"I don't give a damn about your demands," he retorted. Then, abruptly, "David's been hurt."

She drew in her breath. "Badly?"

"I don't know. I left the doctor with him in his office. He was bleeding from a head wound."

She paled. Eva had never been able to contend with illness and the sight of blood terrified her. She had told him at the beginning of their marriage that although she was only three when her mother had died, she had total recall of the fainting spells, the paralysis and the final hemorrhage that had soaked the bedsheets with her mother's blood.

Brian hadn't attached any importance to it until he saw the way it was affecting their son. When he was little, if Mark had a nosebleed or felt ill, he shied from Eva as if he'd committed a crime. It took years to make him understand that the problem was his mother's, not his, and that he was not to feel guilty about seeking help or comfort when he needed it.

Brian felt no compassion for her now. "Don't you think you ought to see how David is?"

She started to say something, thought better of it and left the office.

Dora readied the speaker on his desk. He sat behind it then covered the microphone with his hand.

"Dora, does the speaker system extend to the lab or hospital?"

She thought for a moment. "No, it doesn't."

He nodded, released the mike, and snapped the switch on.

"Ladies and gentlemen, this is Brian Anslow. I know you're all puzzled by the series of alarms you've just heard. I'll clarify it for you as best I can. There's been a large theft of morphine from the vault. We believe that whoever did it took the morphine to the lab to dispose of it somehow. The alarm you heard came from the lab. It followed the closing of a pair of steel doors that sealed the lab off from the plant and the hospital. I don't know what happened in there or why. When I do, I'll tell you. In the meantime, I'd like you to return to work and stay off the phones as much as possible. I'll get back to you as soon as I can."

He switched off. Dora had a hot cup of coffee and a donut waiting.

"Would you believe the coffee cart is up here? Mr. Levy who runs it says his mother always served food at times of stress and he inherited the trait."

She wasn't sure he'd heard. His expression was that of a man keeping a tight rein on panic.

"Dora, has Mildred been able to contact the lab or hospital yet?"

"She still can't get a line through."

"Tell her to keep trying."

"Right."

Minutes after Dora left, Eva returned from David's office. She looked out of breath and Brain suspected she'd been running.

She brushed her hands across her white worsted dress as if there were insects crawling on it. "Ugh! All those people clawing at me, questioning me. I couldn't get three feet without being stopped."

"How's David?"

"Semi-conscious. The doctor has managed to stop the bleeding and he's sent for an ambulance." She raised a perfectly arched brow. "Why are you frowning?"

"Because I meant what I said. No one's getting in or out of here until I find out what's going on."

Her flawless face froze. "You can't be serious. I'm half an hour late for an appointment already."

He slammed a hand on his desk and was gratified to see her jump. "Eva, for God's sake, once in your life try to see beyond yourself. We know that the thief is desperate. He never would have attacked David if he wasn't. Even if you don't give a damn about the people at Traynor, don't you realize that Val could be in that lab with a killer?"

Her face was deliberately impassive.

Her indifference infuriated him. He wanted to shake her until her teeth rattled. "She's your sister. Don't you care?"

Her mouth turned down in an ugly line. "Why should I?" she hissed. "Obviously you do enough for both of us."

The intercom buzzed.

"Lester Pryor is here to see you," Dora announced.

"Send him in."

Eva crossed to the far side of the room, picked up a magazine and riffled through it.

Pryor strode in dragging the timid blonde operator with him. "I've got something to tell you, Brian, but first . . ." He prompted the woman with a touch on the shoulder. "Tell Mr. Anslow what you told me."

"But it may not be important." Her eyes were downcast. She fidgeted with a hairpin she had twisted out of shape.

"Tell him anyway."

She spoke so low, Brian had to lean close to hear her. "It was a few minutes after Mr. Redmond went into the lab. Most of the girls were down in the cafeteria for lunch and we were only a skeleton crew, but I got thirsty."

"Go on," Brian urged impatiently.

She nodded. "Well, I went over to this water cooler that sits right outside the door that leads to the lab hallway . . . the one that's covered over with steel now. I started to take a drink, when all of a sudden I heard a noise. It sounded like it came from inside the lab."

"What kind of a noise?" Brian asked.

"Well, it was sharp. Of course with the clankin' from the machines and all, it was hard to make out, but . . ." Her hands stopped twisting and she faced Brian with sudden bravado. "Mr. Anslow, my husband used to hunt rabbits at his mother's place in Pennsylvania. I.think what I heard was a shot."

Brian tried to control the fear that rose in him. For an instant he said nothing. Then he dismissed her, cautioning her not to say anything to the others when she got back.

"What are you going to do?" Pryor asked after she'd left.

"The only thing I can do right now. Go after more information." He tugged at the scar on his lid. "Lester, there were three guards involved in that Blasa Fever set-up. One was posted between the lab and the plant. The second was inside the ward with Val. And the third was stationed outside the hospital door. Get me that third guard. I want to know if anyone went in or out of that hospital in the last twenty minutes and if he heard . . ."

He came to an abrupt halt. "What's wrong?"

"That's the other thing I had to tell you. Barbetta and I both checked it out. The guard outside the hospital has disappeared."

Chapter 26

In the lab, Val had all to do to control her excitement. She had thought of a way to alert Brian to the deadly danger of the overturned cultures, but it hinged on her ability to lull Brockwell into a false sense of security before the telephone lines became accessible.

The shaggy-haired convict leaned against the wall near the phone, his face taut with anger and frustration. The gun in his hand never wavered from Wally or herself. Dennie sat huddled near a supply cabinet and the room was quiet.

She crossed her fingers and took a step toward him.

His gray eyes warned her.

"Can I ask a question?" she ventured.

For the dozenth time, she wondered if any of the Seconal in the hypodermic had entered Brockwell's system before he dashed it to the floor. At full dosage, it would have put him under in minutes. At half, it should have at least affected his motor system. So far, there had been no reaction at all.

"What kind of question?" he asked.

"I can understand how you faked some of the Blasa Fever symptoms—the cramping and the weakness. But what about the jaundice? How could you ever do that?"

A smirk of triumph crossed his surly features. "You

docs ain't the only ones with tricks up your sleeve. Ever hear of atabrine?''

Atabrine! Of course. The drug used for malaria. It had been noted for its jaundice reaction in World War II.

Her face filled with admiration. "Where did you ever get hold of that?''

She took another step forward.

He shrugged. "One of the trustees in the prison hospital. He owed me.'' He blinked, rubbed his eyes, then shook his head as if to clear it.

Hope surged in Valerie. If the Seconal had taken hold at all, there was a chance. She saw Wally looking at Brockwell oddly. She wished she could tell him about it. Signal him somehow. But she didn't want to take a chance on rousing Brockwell's anger or suspicion. What she intended to do hinged on keeping him unsuspecting.

For a second she let her mind stray to what was happening in the hospital. A picture of Charley Santos rose to haunt her as she had last seen him, bleeding on the floor, tangled in that ludicrous hospital gown he'd always hated. Both hands had cupped his groin and the blood had oozed between his fingers like water through a sieve. "The Lord is my Shepherd . . . I shall not want.'' Anguish filled her. He could be dead by now. And it would be her fault. If only she hadn't made him holster his gun when he went after Brockwell.

She came back to the present as Brockwell took the phone from its cradle.

A broad smile lit his face when Mildred Benson picked up. "Put me through to Brian Anslow,'' he said, then scowled. "Never mind who this is,'' he shouted. "Do what I say.''

In the second it took Mildred to make the connection, Valerie took the final step toward the phone. She was only a few feet away now.

"Anslow?" Brockwell growled.

The voice that assaulted Brian's ears was belligerent, demanding. It conjured up a picture of harshness and violence that made him pray Valerie wasn't there with the owner of it. He still hadn't gotten through to the hospital and there was no way of knowing what had happened.

"This is Brian Anslow," he said, marveling at the composure of his voice. "Who am I talking to?"

"You're talking to Alfie Brockwell."

A bevy of questions crowded Brian's mind. What was the convict doing in the lab? Why had the steel doors closed down? Where were the hospital guards? Was anyone hurt? And always uppermost—*Where was Val?*

With an effort he kept his voice cool. "What can I do for you, Mr. Brockwell?"

"You can open those damned doors, that's what you can do."

"Why were they triggered shut?"

"You're wasting time, Anslow."

"Those doors are electronically controlled, Mr. Brockwell. There's no way . . ."

Brockwell's voice turned ominous. "Lissen, Anslow, and lissen good. I got Dr. Traynor and Dr. Chandler in here, and a punk named Redmond I got no use for. I'll give you half an hour to get those doors open. If they ain't open by then, one of the doctors gets it." A slight movement caught his eye. "Hold on here. What the hell . . ."

He let out a roar as Valerie lunged for the phone. She clutched it for only a second. "Brian," she screamed. "The cultures spilled over. Don't open those . . ."

Brockwell grabbed the phone and hit her on the side of the head with it. She toppled backward. Wally's body cushioned her fall. His arms enfolded her. She closed her eyes against the pain in her head.

From the open mouthpiece she could hear Brian's voice like a broken record. "Val, speak to me. Val, are you okay?" She could only hope he had understood her message.

Brockwell gripped the phone in a crushing hold. His voice was a boom of fury. "Anslow," he shouted. "You got half an hour. Open those doors or I'll blow her away. So help me, I will!"

Chapter 27

In the hospital, the slamming of the steel door leading to the lab was a total enigma to everyone there except Ansel Golden. Valerie had explained the emergency backup system to him one night when he'd questioned her about the possibility of the Fever cultures escaping.

Golden's awareness gave him an edge. Better than anyone there, he knew the calibre of the convicts surrounding him. His allegiance to Freddie Bishop didn't extend to the rest of them. They were killers, rapists, thieves . . . the dregs of society. They were also desperate men with little to lose.

It was beginning to dawn on them that they were unguarded. Charley Santos was bleeding on the floor and the Traynor security cop who had dragged Santos's body from the lab to the hospital with the technician had been relieved of his gun by Brockwell. He had tried to call for reinforcements, but the telephone lines had been busy. Now several of the convicts surrounded him, blocking him from making a move.

Ansel knew the convicts had to be contained in the ward. Not only for the sake of the program, but because they might be carriers of Blasa Fever. Even if the Tetra-2 was a cure, the method of transmission hadn't been established yet.

He could probably stall them, Ansel thought. They

would listen to him long enough for that. But he could never stop them. The only means of persuasion these men understood was force.

Someone had to get to the guard outside the hospital door.

His gaze came to rest on Langsley Darwin standing near his bed a few feet away. The colonel's face was disdainful, his spine ramrod stiff with disapproval. He viewed the wounded guard and the clamor about him as the outgrowth of a disciplinary problem Valerie had refused to recognize.

The man was a jackass, Golden thought. He was also a martinet, with over twenty years of regular army behind him. On the basis of training alone, he was a good choice.

A weakness suddenly washed over Golden, accompanied by a light sweating and slight dizziness. It was a reaction to the Tetra-2 that came at odd times, then disappeared. Holding on to the railing of the bed, he sidled close to the colonel.

"Darwin," he whispered sharply. "Keep looking ahead, but listen to me."

The colonel towered over him by half a foot. At Golden's words his face tightened imperceptibly and he tilted his head downward.

"There's going to be a riot in here unless we get help. Can you back out of the door and reach the guard in front of the hospital?"

Darwin's expression turned scornful. He had long since conceded that Golden was a cut above the other prisoners, though not to the extent that Dr. Traynor seemed to think. However, it took a practiced eye to gauge the possibility of revolt in a situation like this, and Golden simply didn't have the background.

He spoke in an aside. "Golden, you overestimate

this riff-raff. They have neither the stamina nor the courage to . . ."

The surgeon's words were terse. "Darwin, don't be a fool."

A loud roar from Jefferson Montgomery drowned out Darwin's answer. The black raised clenched fists over his head and shook them heavenward as if defying the Gods. His eyes were feverish, his face split in a wide grin that displayed a mouthful of strong even teeth. "What the hell we waitin' for? Man, we ain't never gonna get another chance like this one!"

A rumble of approval filled the room.

"What about the guard outside the hospital?" Tiny Anderson countered. "It ain't worth a belly full of lead."

There were cheers and boos to shout him down. Golden looked around for Darwin, but couldn't see him.

"We don't have to go through the front dock," Montgomery said. He pointed to the floor-to-ceiling windows. "We can make it right through those windows. The guard can't see us from there. By the time he figures it out, we'll be long since gone."

Ansel Golden climbed onto the nearest bed. He stood in its center, a frail man with crew-cut gray hair and a determined expression. He held his hands out pleadingly. "Listen to me, men," he shouted above the tumult. "You all know me . . . the cheapest doc in the pen." There was a spatter of laughter. "I've never steered any of you wrong and I'm not going to now. What Montgomery is suggesting sounds great, except for one thing. You're on an experimental drug for a killer disease. Leave here, and you're all dead men."

"Who you kidding, man?" Montgomery scoffed.

"We dead men anyway. Even if we kick the Fever, what we got to go back to? Lousy food and stinkin' workloads. Guards who take your money in the mornin' and kick your ass at night."

A murmur of assent greeted his words.

"You're speaking for yourself, Montgomery," Golden said. "But you're a lifer. What about the others? You, Thompson. You've only got five years to go, with maybe a parole in the offing before that. And you, Anderson. You told me the other day your lawyer is looking for an appeal. You going to jeopardize that?"

Montgomery began to push past the others. "Shut your mouth, man. You hear me?" His face shone with sweat. His eyes were slits of menace.

The ward was silent, waiting.

Golden stood his ground. "And what if you do make it out of here? How far do you think you'll get? It's twenty degrees out there. You've got no money, no outside help. And look at the way you're dressed. You'd be easy targets in those hospital outfits with every cop in the state after you."

Montgomery reached the foot of the bed and shook the railing in a rage. Golden retreated to its head.

"And do you know what their orders would be?" he shouted at the spellbound convicts. "Shoot to kill! Because you'd be carrying a disease the whole country is scared of . . ."

He choked off as Montgomery pulled him to the floor. He cried out as his head hit the leg of the bed. He felt the boxer's massive hands close about his throat. The dizziness came back as his air passage was squeezed shut. He pulled frantically at Montgomery's fingers. Darkness closed in. His eyes fluttered shut. He felt himself floating . . .

"Let him go, Montgomery," he heard a calloused voice threaten. "Or I shoot your head off."

The steel band around his throat loosened abruptly. The air filtered through to him in a rush. He breathed it into his tortured lungs. Opened his eyes. A young man with a sandy halo of corkscrew curls was smiling at him. He blinked, recognized Sid Draper. Behind him stood the guard who had threatened Montgomery, with a rifle in his hand.

Next to him, giving orders in a staccato voice, was Colonel Darwin, holding an auxiliary revolver the guard had given him. "All right. All of you. Into your beds, right now. First man disobeys me, I pistol whip." His face was animated, his sparse red hair plastered to his freckled scalp. "You all right, Golden?" he called.

"I'm fine," he croaked.

"Then I suggest you have a look at Charley Santos. He's in a bad way. Draper," he barked, "cover my flank. I want every one of those sons o' bitches in bed. You hear me?"

"Yes sir!" Draper held out a helping hand to Golden and grinned. "He's something else, ain't he?"

Golden climbed to his feet. "He sure is." The admiration in the young soldier's voice astonished him. He hurried to Charley Santos's side. Tod Preston was bending over him, trying to staunch the blood that welled up from his groin.

"Move aside, son," Golden said.

Surprised, the attendant looked up. There was no reason he should have obeyed. The wiry little man in the crumpled oversize pajamas was a convict and a patient. Yet there was something in the authoritative voice and pale blue eyes that stopped the protest forming on his lips. He silently complied.

Golden knelt beside Santos. He was in intense pain, but struggling to stay conscious. His eyes were sunken in his head. His broken nose jutted like a beak in his ashen face. He recognized Golden as he knelt beside him. His bloodsoaked fingers plucked at the convict's sleeve.

"Doc," he whispered. "I heard what you done with the men. Thanks. Tell the lady doc . . . she's right. Not all animals." His features contracted fiercely. "Listen, Golden," he gasped. "When it's over . . . ask the warden . . . call my wife. Tell her . . . use the insurance money like we planned . . ."

"Tell her yourself," Golden said. "You're not dead yet."

"Who . . . you . . . kiddin'?" His eyes fluttered shut.

Golden's mind was clicking like a computer. Preston had cut away the lower half of the hospital gown and slit the right trouser leg up to the hip. It exposed a gaping wound in the upper right thigh near the groin, from which blood was oozing steadily. Without going in, there was no way to tell how much damage had been done, but the leg was becoming swollen and discolored and Santos was showing signs of shock.

He had to control the bleeding, Golden thought, then replace what had been lost. He glanced up at the attendant standing by.

"Do you have a blood bank here?"

"No, we don't. Are you a doctor?"

"I . . . yes, I am. What about a plasma expander?"

"We have Dextran."

"Good. Hook up an I.V. Then get me a blood pressure cuff and a heavy sterile gauze pad with some saline solution."

"Yes, doctor." He raced for the supply room.

Golden sighed. It had been a long time since he'd

been called "doctor" with just that mixture of reverence and relief. He glanced about him. Darwin had the ward under control. The men were back in bed. Jefferson Montgomery was handcuffed to the bedrail with the guard keeping a watchful eye on him. Jimmy, the lab technician, was tending to the patients as best he could.

A moan escaped Santos. Golden felt for his pulse. It was rapid, weak, thready. His hands were cold and moist. He was sweating copiously. His eyes, open now, were shiny and glazed.

Preston returned with the supplies. Golden checked the guard's blood pressure. It was barely obtainable, forty over zero. He tapped the I.V., probed for Santos's vein, and found it on the first try. He nodded in satisfaction as the Dextran began its steady drip . . . drip . . . He soaked the gauze pad in the saline, placed it just above the wound and used his fingertips to apply pressure. The bleeding lessened, then stopped.

Colonel Darwin's drawl resounded above him. "Is he going to make it?" It was the emotionless inquiry of the commander in the battlefield.

The casual tone repelled Golden. He had always hated war. He remembered why now. "I don't know." He beckoned to Preston. "Come here, son. Put your fingers where mine are. Like that. Okay?"

The attendant nodded.

Golden rose to confront the army man. "Darwin . . ."

He drew upward to his full height. "Colonel Darwin, if you please." He was a ludicrous figure in his shapeless hospital garb.

Golden's lips twitched. He wondered if the man took his medals off long enough to shower. But give the devil his due. He had performed well under fire. "Colonel Darwin, Santos has to be operated on."

"Well, what do you suggest?"

"I suggest we get a proper doctor in here as fast as possible."

Darwin nodded. "Draper," he called to his second-in-command. "You told me you worked here before you joined up. Who's the C.O. at Traynor Laboratories?"

"Brian Anslow. Used to be head of marketing."

The colonel picked up the phone. The lines were busy. He waited a few seconds, then tried again. This time he got Mildred Benson.

"This is Colonel Langsley Darwin," he said. "I'd like to speak with Brian Anslow." His florid face creased in annoyance. "What do you mean, what kind of colonel? A colonel in the United States Army." He muttered something about thick-headed operators and waited.

Brian's strident voice cut through seconds later. "Darwin, this is Brian Anslow. I've been trying to get through to you."

"*Colonel* Darwin, if you please."

The man's an ass, Brian thought. "Colonel, what's happening there?"

"Well, we've had a near riot here." Distorted by his broad accent the words sounded like *neah rahit heah*. "But we brought in the reserve artillery . . ."

"You mean the guard outside the hospital?" Brian surmised.

". . . and everything's under control. Trouble is, we've got a casualty. One of the guards was shot by a convict named Brockwell."

That explained the shot the packaging operator had heard, Brian thought. "I've just spoken to Brockwell," he said. "I know he's got Dr. Traynor and Dr. Chandler in the lab with him."

"Then you realize we need a medic here."

"What about the attendant? Can he handle it?"

"I don't think so."

Brian was silent for a moment. He was trying to remember something Valerie had told him. Then it came to him.

"Colonel Darwin, some time ago Dr. Traynor spoke to me about one of the convicts there being a doctor. A former surgeon, as a matter of fact. I can't remember his name . . ."

"Golden—Ansel Golden."

"That's it. Is he there?"

"He is."

"Would you put him on, please?"

Disgruntled at having the play taken out of his hands, Darwin reluctantly handed the phone over to Golden.

"Mr. Anslow. This is Ansel Golden."

"Dr. Golden, I'm trying to handle a lot of things at one time, so I'll tell you what's happened as simply as I can."

He went on to explain about the drug theft, the spilling over of the Blasa Fever cultures, and the significance of the steel door sliding shut in the lab. He deliberately omitted Brockwell's threat to Valerie and ended by saying, "I'm sorry, but no one goes in or out of Traynor Labs until the danger of epidemic has passed, and that includes the hospital."

"Mr. Anslow, I appreciate the position you're in, but I don't think you understand. There's a man here with a bullet in his groin."

"How bad is he?"

"He's in shock and edging into coma. My guess is that if a surgeon doesn't go in soon, he'll die."

"Can you do it?"

The question took Golden unaware. "Mr. Anslow, you can't possibly realize what you're asking. Even if I was capable, this is not a hospital that's equipped for surgery. There'd be a minimum of instruments, no anesthesiologist, for that matter, probably no anesthesia." He held up his right hand. His fingers were trembling as if palsied. He spoke slowly. "Besides, it's impossible. I haven't touched a scalpel in fifteen years. One slip of the knife . . ." His voice trailed off.

". . . and he dies. Is that what you were going to say, doctor? And what if you don't operate?"

There was silence.

"Can you do it?" Brian repeated.

Golden's voice sounded as if it was coming from a long distance. "I'll try," he said.

Chapter 28

Brian hung up the phone and stared at the clock. He had another fifteen minutes to come up with some answer for Brockwell. If he didn't . . . His mind shied from the consequences.

If only he could think! The knowledge that Valerie was in that lab with Brockwell had chilled his brain and the convict's ultimatum had numbed it completely. All he could concentrate on was that Valerie was hurt. Or bleeding. Or worse. He had heard the commotion in the lab after she'd pulled the phone away from Brockwell and surmised that she had paid for the revelation about the spilled cultures. But how dearly?

He glanced at Eva. She was curled up on the couch in the far corner of the room, reading *Harper's Bazaar*. Vindictive bitch! He couldn't believe that her studied unconcern for her sister was real. Yet she hadn't said a single word to him since Brockwell's ultimatum. She stood now, stretched, reached for her shoulder bag, and left the room.

He crossed to the window and looked out. In accordance with his instructions to security, a cordon of police surrounded the main building and the hospital. Pockets of employees returning from lunch were gathered outside the fence in growing apprehension, but none had been allowed to enter Traynor. How long can you keep a lid on a time bomb before it blows up in your face? Brian wondered.

He spotted Roy Penzinger standing near his radio car, talking into the telephone. It comforted him to see Roy's broad bulk silhouetted against the metal of the black and white, his cropped yellow-gray hair glinting gold in the sunlight.

He had called the Chief immediately after Brockwell had hung up, and told him of the overturned cultures and Brockwell's ultimatum. He had tried to keep the emotion from his voice, but it had seeped through.

"What do I do, Roy?" he'd asked. "If I open those steel doors now, I release the Fever bug in its most virulent form."

"It would mean an epidemic, Brian."

"I can't let her die, Roy."

"I know."

Brian had suspected for some time that Roy had guessed about his feelings for Valerie. By the way the Chief said the last two words, he was certain of it now.

"What do I do?" he repeated.

"Stall Brockwell. Don't ask me how. I don't know yet. But if we can get the immediate pressure off, we might come up with some answer to this mess."

That had been fifteen minutes ago and neither he nor Penzinger had been able to think of anything feasible since then.

He felt a nudge on his arm and turned from the window. Dora shoved a mug of coffee and a donut toward him.

"If nothing else, we won't go hungry." Behind her mini spectacles, her small black eyes were filled with empathy. She had done a Herculean job of blocking phone calls and keeping people out of his office.

"You know," she said, "I'm surprised those steel

doors in the lab worked at all. The wiring is old and the whole system is out of date."

"When did you find that out?"

"When we did the re-wiring of the plant in 1970. Maintenance debated whether to bother with the steel doors then decided to let it go. The electrician in charge told me they were making a mistake. The wiring could short-circuit any minute, and the timer was obsolete. The new ones he was installing elsewhere had a gadget on the outside to counteract the process in case someone triggered the doors shut by mistake."

He leaned forward suddenly and kissed her.

Her seamed face flushed pink. "What was that for?"

"For giving me an idea." He strode toward his desk.

"How?"

"Never mind that now. Where's Lester Pryor?"

"Right here!" Pryor's skeleton frame appeared in the doorway. He looked as if he'd been running. His auburn hair brushed the top of the doorframe and his breathing was ragged.

"The employees are getting edgy, Brian. They can understand the police surrounding the plant because of the theft, but they can't understand why nobody's being allowed in or out."

"You can fool some of the people some of the time . . ." Brian muttered. He shook his head as Pryor's eyes questioned him. "How's David?"

"Fair. The bleeding has stopped, but he keeps lapsing into unconsciousness." Under Brian's intense scrutiny, he checked his clothing to see that everything was in order. "You see something I don't?" he asked.

"How good are you at playacting, Lester?"

He cocked an eyebrow. "My wife says too good."

"It's important."

His face sobered. "Tell me what you want me to do."

Ten minutes later, Brian called Alfie Brockwell.

"Mr. Brockwell, this is Brian Anslow."

"You're cutting it real close, ain't you, Anslow," the convict said. "How come I don't hear anything happening at those doors?"

"I think I've got that problem solved, but we need a little more time."

The convict's voice turned ugly. "You got no more time, Anslow. Five more minutes and the lady doc has had it."

Brian took a deep breath. At least he knew now that Val was alive. He spoke in measured tones. "And what will that get you, Brockwell? You'll still be bottled up in that lab with no way to get out."

There was a pause. Then, "What do you need the time for?" His voice was heavy with suspicion.

"It took a while, but I located the company that put the electric timer on those doors. The man there says there's a way to open them and he's willing to come out now if I okay it."

"Who you trying to con?"

"Talk to him yourself if you like." He didn't wait for Brockwell's reply. He clicked the phone up and down until Mildred Benson picked up. "Mildred, I was just talking with a Mr. Baron of the Baron Electrical Company in Manhattan. Can you get him back for me?"

"I think so."

Brian frowned. Mildred was overdoing. Her tone had the cloying sweetness of honey. He heard the numbers being dialed. The phone rang twice as rehearsed then Dora picked up in an office a few doors away.

"Baron Electrical," she said crisply.

"Mr. Baron, please," Mildred said.

"One moment, please."

Lester Pryor got on. "Abe Baron here. What can I do for you?"

"Mr. Baron, this is Brian Anslow again. I want you to repeat what you told me about the electric timer on the steel doors. I've got the man listening who can give the okay on it."

The bogus Baron showed his annoyance. "Listen, Mr. Anslow, I'm not in the business of making like a parrot all day long. I got a living to make. But okay, I like you, so I'll tell it to you once more. The timer on those doors can be activated to reverse the time span to zero. It's altogether a five-minute job."

"And those doors will open right up?" Brockwell asked.

"Immediately."

"If it's so easy, why can't you explain to someone here how to do it?" Brockwell asked.

"I didn't say it was easy," Pryor stated. "I said it was quick. The timer is out of date. It's older than I am and only a few people would know how to operate it. Look, I got other jobs to go to. You want me or you don't?"

"How long would it take you to get here?"

"Well, with the traffic and everything, maybe one hour, maybe three quarters."

They waited for what seemed an eternity.

"Okay," Brockwell finally said. He hung up.

Brian closed his eyes and slumped forward in his seat. His face was covered with sweat and his shirt was plastered to his back. He didn't realize the phone was still in his hand until Pryor came in and took it away from him.

"We did it," he said. "We bought another hour."

Brian nodded, but he showed no elation.

Pryor frowned. Brian Anslow was twice the breadth of him, but he seemed to have shrunk in size. In all the years Pryor had known him, he'd never seen fear in his face, but it was written there now.

"What if we don't have an answer by then?" Brian asked.

"We will," Pryor said with more certainty than he felt. It was strange, his reassuring Brian. The one facet of Brian's personality he had always admired was his ability to cope.

Chapter 29

In the laboratory, with the vents closed down, the temperature had dropped to near freezing. Valerie lay shivering on the floor, huddled against Wally for warmth. The side of her head ached with a dull nagging pain where Brockwell had hit her with the phone, but her anxiety was so great she scarcely felt it.

Twenty minutes had passed since Brockwell had given Brian the ultimatum to "open those doors or I'll blow her away." There had been nothing since then. No signs of activity at the door (thank God), no further contact from Brian.

Brockwell stood near the phone. His black hair was an unruly mop. His thick brows were drawn forward in a scowl. He combed his beard with nervous fingers and periodically swiped at the globs of sweat beading his forehead with his pajama sleeve.

If the Seconal was taking effect, it was doing so slowly. He had yawned several times and blinked rapidly once, as if fighting to stay awake, but that had been a while ago.

A low moan sounded from the corner. Dennie Redmond sat on a steel plate between two supply cabinets, as far from Brockwell as possible. His face was swollen and discolored. One eye was closed to a slit. His arms were wrapped around his knees and his slight frame was racked with shivering.

Val felt sorry for him. What he had done was criminal, yet Dennie was only a pawn. That had become clear when he had roused himself from his stupor and crept close to her after she'd been hurt.

She had been lying on the floor close to the crematorium with her head pillowed on Wally's folded lab coat. Her eyes were closed. Wally had moistened a wet towel and was applying it to the throbbing lump over her ear.

Dennie had reached out a tentative hand to touch her arm.

"Dr. Traynor, are you okay?" he whispered.

She opened her eyes.

Wally brushed his hand away. "What do you want, Dennie?" he said bitterly. "A whitewash for what you've done? Can't you see she's hurt? Leave her alone now." His sensitive face was creased in harsh lines, the set of his jaw rigid and unforgiving.

"I couldn't help it," Dennie pleaded. "They told me they'd kill my mother if I didn't do it."

"Who's they?" Valerie had asked.

Brockwell's face had suddenly appeared above them and the answer had died unspoken. Dennie had crept back to the steel plate in the corner where he'd crouched since like a disfigured Buddha. But in the last few minutes, he had been eyeing Brockwell covertly, fear warring with desperation on his lacerated features.

His weak chin set in sudden determination now. He untangled himself from his jackknifed position and moved closer to the convict.

Brockwell straightened and took a firmer grip on his gun.

"What d'ya want?"

"I . . . I want to make a phone call."

His steely eyes widened, then a short laugh burst from him. "To who?"

"To Niko."

Brockwell took a menacing step toward him. "And what'll you tell him, you little son-of-a-bitch? That you screwed up and got here late and got us into this fix?"

Dennie's puffed lip quivered, but he stood his ground.

"You don't understand. If I don't show up, they'll think I reneged and they'll kill my mother. I want them to know I kept my part of the bargain."

"Your mother can fry in hell for all I care," Brockwell said. "Niko's played square with me up to now. I ain't making any calls the cops can trace to him. When I get out of here . . ."

"I wouldn't count on that," Wally said evenly.

Valerie felt a rush of pride in him. Despite Brockwell's threats, Wally had refused to knuckle under.

"You don't think Anslow will open those doors, do you?" Brockwell asked.

Wally walked to the sink and let the cold water run on the towel. "No, I don't." He wrung out the compress. "I think he heard Dr. Traynor and he won"t open those doors under any circumstances."

Valerie prayed he was right on both counts. She didn't want to die, but the thought of Brian releasing those cultures outside this room was horrendous to her. She knew Brian's strengths as well as his weaknesses. He could be coldly calculating in his risk-taking, but not when it came to her. If it were anyone else being threatened, he might take the chance that Brockwell was bluffing. But would he have the strength to do that with *her* life at stake?

Brockwell grinned at Wally. "You wouldn't want to make book on it, would you, doc?"

Wally bent over her without answering. The compress felt good against her temple. She smiled up at him. "Thanks."

"For what?"

"For this. And for being what you are."

The seconds ticked by unmercifully after that. Wally tried to talk to her again, but Brockwell forbade it. He stroked her forehead instead, his sensitive face working as the hands of the clock moved relentlessly on. She wanted to comfort him, to tell him that it was all right, but even if Brockwell had allowed it, she wouldn't have known what to say.

How odd that *she* should want to comfort *him,* she thought. But she had no fear of dying. She had encountered death too much in her work not to have come to terms with it. Rather she felt a sense of waste, of unfinished business. She glanced at the steel door leading to the hospital and wondered what was happening in there. It occurred to her that with Charley Santos wounded, the prisoners had been left unguarded except for the guard stationed outside the front door. If they had managed to escape, not only was the Blasa Fever program scotched, but they posed a threat of transmission to the outside world.

She raised her head and pain knifed through it. Her eyes strayed toward the clock. Two forty. She took a deep breath. A few more minutes and it would be all over.

The ring of the telephone shattered the silence.

Brockwell picked up. His scowl deepened. "You got no more time, Anslow," she heard him say. "Five more minutes and the lady doc has had it."

Don't beg, Valerie silently urged Brian. *And don't blame yourself. There was no other way.*

She strained to hear more, but couldn't until Brockwell turned toward Wally with a triumphant smile.

"And those doors will open right up?" he said into the mouthpiece.

Valerie closed her eyes and turned her face to the wall. She couldn't believe what she'd heard. Brian had sold out. He had bartered her life in exchange for placing a nation at risk of epidemic. Tears stung her lids. Her reprieve was bitter as wormwood.

Wally stroked her hair. His expression was a mixture of relief and chagrin. "Don't be too hard on him," he said. "I might have done the same thing."

"No, you wouldn't." Her voice was wooden.

Brian was concerned with what touched Brian, she thought bitterly. Humanity was another word for "people out there," and Brian had never been magnanimous except when forced into it. She knew he would never have okayed the Blasa Fever testing if Alex hadn't verbally contracted for it with the Food and Drug Administration before he died.

Yet, she had seen a glimmer of change in him. It had come after he'd had to turn away the relatives of the Blasa Fever victims in Traynor's lobby. "I never felt so powerful, or so powerless," he'd told her. "I wanted to reassure them the way I do Mark when he gets sick. And when I couldn't, I wanted to run from them as far as I could." His face had held the kind of compassion she'd waited ten years to see.

Confusion filled her. If he'd meant what he'd said then, he could never open those doors now. The pain in her head grew sharper.

She felt Wally's hand on her shoulder.

"What's the matter with him?" he whispered.

She followed his gaze. Brockwell was rubbing his eyes. He staggered to a chair, slumped into it and shook his head to clear it. His feet were bare. His rumpled pajamas had slid downward to cover them.

"Seconal," she said elatedly.

He waved the gun at them. "Shut up!" His voice was deep but it lacked conviction. Despite the cold, his face was slicked with sweat.

Valerie waited. His lids were closing, his leonine head began to droop.

"You injected him?" Wally's whisper was incredulous.

"Half an hour ago, but I don't know how much I got into him."

Brockwell straightened up in his chair. He swung his head toward them suspiciously, then his eyes drooped again.

She felt Wally tense beside her. "I'm going after him," he murmured.

She nodded, then held up a hand for caution. She didn't want him to rush it. Wally would have one try. If he failed, it could cost him his life.

Brock's lids closed over his eyes. His chin slowly descended to his chest. His breathing became sonorous, rhythmic. His massive bulk overflowed the chair, the thighs unflexed, the legs bowed open, the feet splayed on the icy concrete floor. Only his grip on the gun never wavered. It was pointed at Wally's heart.

Crouching low, Wally crept toward him on hands and knees. The distance between them was ten feet. He made it across four, then congealed as Brockwell's breathing became irregular. The convict shifted position while Wally prayed.

If Brockwell were to open his eyes now . . .

Wally's legs began to cramp. Behind him, he could sense Val's apprehension as if it were a living thing. Brockwell swallowed. His lips twitched. His breathing deepened once again. Wally exhaled on a ragged breath. Once again he began the tedious crawl. Six feet to go. Five . . . four . . .

Dennie Redmond began to snivel. Wedged against a supply cabinet, he sat with his body contorted against the cold. His head was pillowed between his knees and his arms were banded about his legs. His back was a knot of pain, his discolored face stiff and hurting.

All he could think of was Finch and his mother. The consequences of what he'd done, the possibility of death and the harm that could come to Angie, all paled beside that. His resentment of his mother, her stranglehold on his life, her infantile demands, faded beside his need to purge his guilt. He wanted to apologize, to grovel, to beg her forgiveness as he had when he was little. If he could have traded his life for hers right now, he would have.

He rubbed his eyes with the back of his palms and cried out as the salt of his tears stung the torn flesh of his face. He lifted his head fearfully. Brockwell had threatened to purple his other eye if another sound came out of him.

Dennie's jaw dropped open. Something was moving out there. He raised himself further. He had trouble focusing with his one eye, then it suddenly came clear. Brockwell was sleeping on a chair and Dr. Chandler was crawling toward him. Dennie's breath caught in his throat as hope came alive in him. Chandler was almost there!

Brockwell's head suddenly rolled backward. His lids began to unpaste. Dennie panicked.

"Look out!" he cried to Wally.

Brockwell reared backward with a roar. The chair toppled to the floor. Brockwell somersaulted and landed on his feet in a semi-squatting position, the gun held in his hand like an extension of his arm.

"Try that again and I'll kill you," he snarled. He gestured menacingly with the gun and Wally retreated back to Val. He strode to the sink, splashed cold water into his face, and glanced at Dennie with approval.

"That's one I owe you," he said.

Chapter 30

In his office, Brian dealt with yet another crisis.

Ten minutes had passed since Brockwell had granted the bogus Abe Baron a one-hour stay, and Lester Pryor faced him across the desk.

"Brian, we have to consider the possibility that those Fever cultures had time to get into the plant before the steel doors closed down."

He nodded. "I've been thinking of that."

"Did Val and Wally ever establish how the Fever was transmitted?"

"No."

"Then it could mean that every employee here is not only a potential victim of the Fever, but a possible carrier as well." Pryor's freckles stood out in sharp relief against his pale skin.

Brian nodded, his expression grim. He buzzed through to his secretary. "Dora, get hold of Joe Barbetta and Burt Findley. Tell them to come up here right away."

"Will do. Mr. Anslow, I think you should know that someone tipped CBS about the morphine theft. They called a little while ago. I tried to steer them off it, but I don't think they believed me."

"Damn, that's all we need now!"

Minutes later, Dora announced the two men. Joe Barbetta strode in ahead of the personnel chief. His bulbous nose was accentuated by the flush on his leathery face. Even under stress, his white hair was carefully placed and his uniform was bandbox neat. He nodded to Pryor, but directed his words at Brian.

"Mr. Anslow, I've got double guards stationed at every door like you said. But some of the employees are coming up with questions that the guards can't answer. What's this all about?"

"That's what you're here to find out." He hunched forward in his seat as Burt Findley eased his bulk into a wing chair. Speaking quickly but concisely, he filled the two men in on what had taken place. The implications were as clear as they were ominous.

Barbetta's years on the force stood him in good stead. His expression remained impassive. But the personnel man looked stupefied. His sagging face accentuated the jowls that drooped onto his starched white collar. His voice was hushed when he spoke.

"Are you going to open those steel doors?"

Brian didn't answer. His mind was a tangle of thoughts. Even if his emotions weren't involved, where did his responsibility lie? In saving Val and Wally? In protecting his employees from contamination? Or in securing the outside world against epidemic? As it stood now, it was impossible to do all three.

"I don't know what I'm going to do." He glanced at his watch. *Three o'clock.* He felt a tightness in his chest. He had until three forty-five. "There isn't much time," he muttered.

"There's less than you think," Findley said. "The way those employees feel about the Fever now, if even a hint of what you just told me leaks to them, they'll bust out of here like those exit doors were made of papier mâché."

"How long do you think we can keep it from

them?'' Barbetta asked. ''When they realize that no one is being allowed in or out of the plant, they'll figure it out for themselves. And believe me, my guards won't be able to hold them after that.''

''We can't let them out of here,'' Pryor said. ''It could mean an epidemic.''

''Then what *do* we do?'' Barbetta demanded.

''We tell them,'' Brian said quietly.

Forgetting protocol, Findley heaved himself out of the chair. ''You're crazy, man! You'll have a riot on your hands.''

''I don't agree.''

Barbetta shook his head dolefully. ''I didn't cotton much to Alex Traynor, but he would never have tried anything like this.''

''Alex took care of his employees,'' Brian retorted. ''But he treated them like children. He listened to their problems and wiped their noses and helped them prepare for old age. I think they're capable of more than that.''

Pryor was tight-lipped. ''They don't trust you, Brian. It's a big risk.''

''I'll have to take it.'' He turned to Burt Findley. ''How many employees are in the plant right now?''

Findley pursed his mouth thoughtfully. ''Let's see . . . it happened on a lunch hour. I'd say about twelve hundred, give or take a few.''

''Would they fit into the cafeteria?''

''Packed like sardines, they would.''

Brian's voice was terse. ''Pack 'em,'' he said.

The move to the cafeteria took place in the next ten minutes. Each department head led his group to the rear of the second floor, starting with the packaging line in manufacturing closest to the steel doors. Emotions ran high among the employees and what should have been an orderly departure became an unruly exodus.

"There's something screwy going on here," Gilda Jennings told a cohort. "If someone tried to steal some morphine, why aren't the police *inside* the building where they belong?"

"I think they're afraid," the timid blonde operator offered.

"Afraid of what?" a technician chimed in. "That's what I'd like to know. This Anslow gets us on the speaker and hooks us with a line that everything's going to be okay and we swallow it whole. Since when could we count on what he says?"

They marched into the cafeteria shouting and calling to each other. The first to enter took the chairs surrounding the tables. The rest stood fidgeting between them. As their numbers swelled, the noise became deafening. They lined the service center and the pay lanes. They pressed up against the dispensing machines for cold drinks and candy, and swamped the relish buffet and the tray stand.

From where he stood on a dais Barbetta had rigged for him from two metal milk crates, Brian watched them pour in. He could feel their hostility as if it was a live wire crackling between them. In his haste, he had forgotten his jacket in the office. His face was haggard, his shirtsleeves were rolled up, and his blue paisley tie hung at half mast. He could sense their disapproval. The contrast to Alex's spit n' polish decorum was never more vivid and never less appreciated.

He cleared his throat and the noise lessened a fraction. His nerve endings were raw. From his vantage point, he picked out a few familiar faces. Haversham's secretary, Thelma, was seated almost in front of him. Tom Nordsen's blond head popped up among a contingent from shipping. Lester Pryor and Burt Findley were stationed at the entrance and exit doors, guiding traffic and trying to keep order.

He held up his hands for silence and waited until they quieted down.

"Ladies and gentlemen . . . When I spoke to you over the loudspeaker a while ago, I told you that there had been a theft of a large amount of morphine from the plant, and that the alarm you heard followed the closing of a pair of steel doors in the lab. I had hoped that those steel doors were triggered shut to keep the thieves from escaping. I know better now."

A low rumble began in the crowd.

He cleared his throat again. "Those doors were triggered shut because cultures of the Blasa Fever bug were somehow set free in the fight that took place in there."

"Did those bugs get into the plant?" a deep voice asked.

Brian spotted Zack Cottrell, the former union president, in the rear of the crowd. His short stocky body was wedged behind a chair. His bowed legs were hidden from sight.

"At this point, I don't know. Chances are they didn't, but I can't be . . ."

Haversham's secretary sprang to her feet. "What if they did?" she demanded above the swelling roar of the crowd.

There was no way he could avoid it. "Then you are at risk of Blasa Fever."

A scream sounded in the audience. "I'm getting out of here," one woman cried.

Brian raised his hands again. "Listen to me . . . please."

His words were drowned in the clamor as hysteria swept the crowd. What had been a frightened bunch of people turned into a faceless, mindless mass bent on only one objective—getting to those cafeteria doors. Chairs were overturned, people were pushed and jostled as they trampled each other in the mad surge forward. "Help me!" one pregnant woman screamed, clutching at her stomach. Tom Nordsen elbowed his way toward her, his thatch of blond hair bobbing up and down like a buoy in a squall. He put his arms around her and used his stocky body as a shield as she collapsed against him.

Zack Cottrell was the first to reach the doors. As prearranged, Findley and Pryor were no longer there.

"They're locked!" Cottrell bellowed. He jumped onto the nearest table and shook a threatening fist at Brian. "Anslow, open those doors or we'll smash them down."

Brian held up his hands in supplication. "Listen to me," he repeated. "You don't have to smash those doors down. I'll open them for you myself. But first you've got to hear me out."

"We've heard enough," Cottrell cried. "Alex Traynor would turn over in his grave if he saw what you've brought this company to."

A roar of agreement swept the crowd.

"Give the man a chance," Tom Nordsen called from the middle of the floor.

"You should be the last one to ask that," Thelma said.

"That is *why* I ask it," Nordsen retorted. He jumped onto the nearest chair, rolled up the sleeve of his checked wool shirt and bared his arm for all to see. Under the ceiling spotlight, the tattooed numbers stood out harsh and ugly. "We are not Nazis in a concentration camp here," he shouted. "A man has a right to explain before you condemn him."

Brian threw him a grateful glance.

Led by one of their own, the crowd began to quiet. Brian waited until his voice could be heard. With an effort he kept it at a natural pitch. "Those steel doors in the laboratory were rigged for just this kind of emergency. I hope in a little while to be able to tell you that they closed before those bugs had a chance to get out. But if they didn't, as I said before, you are at risk of Blasa Fever. You are also a potential carrier of the disease. But only for six hours. That's the maximal potency of the raw cultures."

"I want to get out of here," a woman whimpered. "You have no right to stop me."

Brian tracked down the voice. It was the timid blonde operator from the packaging line. "Where would you go, Ethel?" he asked gently.

"Home!"

"You can't go home." Tom Nordsen spoke from where he stood. His face was filled with the suffering he had borne. "You give it to your family if you do."

"If you leave Traynor Labs now, you take the chance of setting off an epidemic that could sweep the nation," Brian continued "But Ethel has a point. I have no right to stop you. After you hear me out, if you still want to go, you can. The choice is yours."

"If you hadn't allowed the Blasa Fever testing in the first place, we never would have gotten into this fix," Cottrell shouted.

"That may be true," Brian said. "But that testing enables me to give you the kind of news now that I wish I could have given to Tom Nordsen when he came to me a while ago. It isn't official yet, but the results on the Tetra-2 antibiotic look very good."

Morgan Effram spoke up from where he was crammed against the service line. "Does that mean if we get it we can be cured?"

"I can't say for sure. But I can tell you that there

are nineteen men in that hospital under treatment, and every one of them is showing signs of improvement. The Government is aware of it too. This morning the Food and Drug Administration gave orders to bend every effort to stabilize the drug and mass produce it even while the testing is being finalized. Wouldn't surprise me if we've come up with an antibiotic to lick Blasa Fever."

Morgan Effram raked a hand through his graying hair. "Well, if we've got it licked, then why are we kicking up such a fuss? Seems to me we've got better things to do." His wrinkled face broke into a puckish grin as he turned to Brian. "Listen, Mr. Anslow. You brought us to this cafeteria. Either show us some movies, serve us lunch, or let us go back to work."

A laugh went up from the crowd and Brian stepped down from the makeshift podium. He glanced at the clock over the service counter. *Three thirty.* He had fifteen minutes to think of a way to save Val. The crowd parted for him as he raced toward the exit door.

Chapter 31

In her Soho apartment, Angie sat glued to the Hitachi set watching "Guiding Light." She wore a red polyester pants suit with a drawstring blouse. Her fingers tore at the bow, undid it, then pulled on the strings. A light sweat beaded her face. She could no longer follow the plot. She scarcely heard what the characters were saying. Fear had made her mind a blank.

Dennie was almost an hour late and there was no way of knowing what had happened to him. But it wasn't fear for Dennie that was paralyzing her. It was more immediate than that. She needed a fix. And if she asked Niko for it, he'd find out what she'd done.

Breathing through his mouth as he always did when he was in a temper, her brother paced the small stretch of floor that the room afforded. From time to time he checked his watch and cursed.

"I tell you we ought to get out of here," Finch said. He sat at the scarred kitchen table with a bottle of Johnnie Walker and a shot glass in front of him. He'd been drinking steadily for the last hour. The Scotch had made him morose, edgy.

He slammed a fist on the table. "We're like sittin' ducks here. What the hell are we waitin' for? If that son-of-a-bitch gets caught, he'll spill his guts, mother or no mother."

"I'm not running out on Brockwell. Besides, it

doesn't make sense," Bordini said. "If they got Dennie, the cops would have been here by now." He shook his head. "No. It's something else. I can't peg it, but it's something else."

"What's the difference what it is? You act like you wanna get caught." He baited Bordini with bravado derived from the bottle in front of him. "What's the matter, Niko? Didn't you get enough of that rockpile we were in?"

With a swift movement, Bordini swept the shot glass from the table. It spilled its contents on the frayed carpet and rolled behind a table leg. He bent over the smaller man and raised a warning finger. "Watch your mouth, Finch. That stuff is making you stupid. Sure I got enough of that rockpile. But that morphine is worth two million bucks. Think of it, Finch. Two million. We're not walking away from that kind of money without giving it a chance."

Angie doubled over the edge of the bed. Her black hair swirled to cover her face. She crossed her arms beneath her full breasts and moaned.

Niko straightened up and glanced at his sister. "What's the matter with you?"

Her body trembled. She shook her head and signaled for him to leave her alone.

He looked at her with contempt. "If you need a fix, why don't you say so?"

Her trembling accelerated.

He went to the closet and felt in his overcoat pocket. His sensuous face creased in a frown. He checked the other pockets then shook his head, puzzled. "That's funny. I could have sworn I had . . ."

He turned his head toward Finch. Finch shrugged. "Don't look at me. Ask the princess, there. I saw her go to the closet an hour ago."

Bordini's eyes swung toward Angie in disbelief.

She sprang from the bed and backed toward the bathroom. She had never been good at dissembling. Her huge eyes filled with dread.

He caught her at the bathroom door. His fingers clutched a handful of hair, jerked her head backward until it hit the door with a thud. He ignored her wince of pain and put his face close to hers. "Do you know what you've done?" he said savagely. "You took the last of the stuff. The rest is stashed at the hideaway in Delaware."

"I need a fix," she moaned.

"No way. You get none 'til we get there."

Finch waved his hands for silence. "Pipe down, you two. Something's coming over the TV." He turned the Hitachi up.

"Guiding Light" had been replaced by a blank screen bearing the words "Special Report." Seconds later a newscaster appeared.

"We interrupt this broadcast to bring you a special report. The Blasa Fever testing program at Traynor Laboratories in Clayville, Long Island, which was so recently in the news, has borne strange fruit. At one o'clock this afternoon, a two-million-dollar morphine theft was attempted at Traynor with only partial success. Through a quirk of fate, the thieves are now trapped with the stolen morphine in a steel-encased laboratory adjoining the hospital. Complicating the efforts of the police, who have formed a ring around the plant, is the fact that raw cultures of the Blasa Fever bug have been overturned in the laboratory and any attempts to apprehend the thieves could result in the escape of these cultures. However, the police emphasize that there is no need for public concern. For an up-to-date report on this highly explosive situation, we take you now to our on-the-scene reporter, Milt Resnik, in Clayville, Long Island."

Within seconds the screen faded to Traynor Laboratories and the camera dollied in on a curly-haired blond reporter in a blue mackinaw. His ears were red from the cold and puffs of frost issued from his mouth as he talked into the mike.

"The large building you see in front of us is the main building of Traynor Laboratories. The smaller one attached to it is the hospital. Aside from the TV truck and crew outside the fence, some of the people milling about are relatives of those who are inside. Others are Traynor employees who returned from lunch in Clayville, only to find the doors to the plant closed to them. Inside the fence, along with me and the police who are surrounding the plant, are several public health officials and a spokesman for Traynor Laboratories, Mr. Paul Haversham."

He held up his hand. "Wait a minute now, I think I see the Chief of Police passing on my right. If I could get him to . . ."

He grabbed Roy Penzinger's arm and pulled him into camera view. "Chief Penzinger, I wonder if you would be good enough to clarify a few things that have been puzzling the rest of us. It'll take only a minute . . ."

Penzinger scowled, then grudgingly consented. Naturally shy, he had an abhorrence of public exposure, even to having his picture taken for the P.A.L. bulletin. He avoided the TV camera staring at him like a big eye, and concentrated on the reporter asking the questions.

"Chief Penzinger, as I understand it, the laboratory is sealed off from the plant and the hospital by a pair of steel doors that were triggered shut when the cultures spilled over. And those doors are controlled by an electric timer that will allow them to open at eight o'clock tonight."

"That's true."

"Can you tell us why the employees in Traynor Laboratories are not being allowed to leave the plant?"

Penzinger tugged at the top button of his uniform, remembered he was on television and smoothed it closed. "No, I'm afraid I can't."

"But you do agree that there appears to be a stalemate. The thieves and the employees can't get out, but neither can the police get in."

Penzinger looked uncomfortable. "I suppose you could say that."

In Angie's apartment, Finch flung a muscular arm in front of the TV. "D'ya need more than that? They got 'em caught in there like fish in a barrel. And when they open that barrel, if we're still around, we go down with 'em." He glared at Bordini, who had inserted a cigarette into his white porcelain holder and was calmly lighting it. "You puttin' on an act or somethin'? How come you ain't worried?"

Bordini exhaled thoughtfully. "Because I know Brock. I know the way he thinks. We were cellmates at Rockland for five years before he was transferred to Arbor State. Brock isn't going to sit in that steel trap for six hours and wait for the cops to come and get him. He'll find a way." He gestured toward the TV. "Wait a minute. There's more."

Paul Haversham had taken the microphone. He made a handsome figure in a black suit and dotted silk tie, his overcoat open, the collar turned up. His silvered hair and piercing gray eyes lent solidity to the earnestness of his speech.

"As the only officer of Traynor Laboratories available for comment, let me assure you that just as the company has put the interest of the public in the forefront for the past eighty years, so it will do so today. I give you my solemn word that whatever contamination has occurred within the lab at Traynor will be contained there until all danger of transmission is past. Chief Penzinger and I are in constant touch, mapping strategy together to . . ."

The microphone was abruptly pulled away from him by the news commentator.

"My apologies to Mr. Haversham, but reliable information has just reached this reporter that puts an entirely different cast on the situation taking place here at Traynor. The thieves are holding two doctors hostage in that laboratory with them whom they've threatened to kill unless those steel doors are opened shortly. To accede to their demands would place the nation in jeopardy of epidemic. To deny their terms would mean the death of two doctors who have fought valiantly to stamp out this disease. I, for one, wouldn't want to be the person making that decision."

Inside the apartment, Bordini leaned back in satisfaction. "I told you Brock would find a way," he said.

Chapter 32

In the hospital, Ansel Golden knelt beside Charley Santos. He had felt braver standing up to the boxer, Montgomery, a while ago, than he did right now. The knot in his stomach was reminiscent of his resident days at Bradley Medical when he had approached the O.R. with a haunted face and unsteady hands, grateful when he could assist rather than solo because he hadn't yet learned to cope with being responsible for a human life.

Santos's leg had swollen to twice its size and the bleeding had started again. Golden slapped his face lightly and tried to elicit some response from him.

"Come on, Charley, talk to me!"

Santos's head lolled back on his neck, his eyes rolled upward and the whites became visible. He was slipping into coma. If he was going to operate, it had to be *now,* Golden thought.

He looked around him at the bareness of the ward and his heart sank. The convicts were confined to their beds, their needs catered to by the attendant or the lab technician. Langsley Darwin was in his element. Backed up by the armed guard and the auxiliary revolver he waved about like a flag, the colonel policed the ward as if it were a military barracks. That the prisoners cursed him audibly or under their breaths didn't seem to bother him at all.

Golden tried to concentrate on what he would need. The lack of facilities was appalling and his mind was a blank. If he could only roll the clock back fifteen years. A picture of the gleaming O.R. at Bradley Medical where he'd been Chief of Surgery came back to him with its finely honed instruments, emergency equipment, obsequious nurses, and brilliant lighting. He wanted to laugh at the contrast . . . or cry.

"Is he dead?" Tod Preston asked in a hushed voice above him.

If he was, there'd be no need for this exercise in self-torture, Golden thought. His callousness shamed him and brought a measure of clarity with it.

"No, he's not," he said shortly. "Look, we're going to have to operate." He ignored the sudden blanching of the attendant's face. Preston was stocky and slow-moving, but Golden had noted that he took orders well. "You and . . . He pointed to the lab technician talking to Sid Draper nearby.

"Jimmy," the attendant supplied.

Hearing his name, Jimmy hurried over. He bore a striking resemblance to his sister, Thelma. Tall and thin, with a stoop to his shoulders and a sallow complexion, he looked to be about twenty-eight. His face was sharp and pointed, with a high forehead accentuated by fly-away hair that had already receded halfway up his scalp.

"Did I hear someone say operate?" he quavered.

Golden nodded and straightened up. The dizziness that was a side effect of the Tetra-2 washed over him again. The halt leading the blind, he thought as his two "helpers" stared at him with frightened faces. Aware that it would only complicate the situation if they realized his weakness, he dug his nails into his palms and waited a second before he spoke to Preston.

"You and Jimmy are going to have to assist me,"

he said. "You're also going to have to tell me the most likely place to perform it."

"There's a table in the kitchen," Jimmy said.

"It'll have to do. Now what about a scalpel, clamps, sutures, nylon thread . . ." He ticked them off on his fingers, taking heart as the attendant kept nodding. "And a retractor," he added as an afterthought.

"We've got them all."

"Good. Jimmy, I want you to drape that table with whatever sheets and toweling you can find to absorb the blood. Then get as much light into that room as possible and center it on the table. Got that?" He nodded, but didn't move. "What's the matter?"

"I've never seen an operation," he blurted. He had bulging, myopic eyes. They shuttled back and forth now, as if seeking a way out.

Golden patted his bony back. "That's all right, Jimmy. There'll be a lot of 'firsts' here today." He turned to the attendant. "Do we have any anesthetic on hand? Ether, chloroform, anything?"

"No, there's nothing."

"Well, then, I guess we'll have to do without it." He suddenly remembered one of the ancient surgical mentors at Bradley Medical insisting that any surgeon worth his salt ought to be able to perform without all the fancy equipment that the modern young doctors considered so essential. "Ansel," he used to say, "if you can't do an operation with a rock and the top of a tin can, you're no surgeon."

He was about to find that out, Golden thought grimly. He signaled to Sid Draper. "Do a favor, Draper, will you. Get a stretcher and help us carry this man inside."

"Yes, sir!"

The young soldier had the resiliency of a coiled spring. There was no sign of his recent illness. This was the closest he'd come to seeing "action" and his eyes glowed with excitement as he ran for the stretcher from the supply room.

The kitchen was small, but with the chairs removed, manageable. The table was a metal drop leaf, which opened to three feet by six, ample enough to hold Santos's five feet eleven bulk. Fortunately the fixture over the table was a pull down globe. Coupled with the two high intensity reading lamps that Jimmy had found in the resting room, the light was better than Golden had expected. Tod Preston, who had once witnessed an operation, helped Jimmy drape the table in the sheets and towels. A small sterilizer was set up on the stove and the instruments placed in it.

They removed Santos's bloody clothing and washed him. Shifting him from the stretcher onto the table was tricky. He was two hundred thirty pounds of dead weight. It took all three of them to do it and they almost dropped him mid-way because Santos began to come to. Eyes still closed, he moaned and thrashed his head in obvious pain.

"There's a break in cell block two . . ." he suddenly screamed, then backslapped the transfixed technician with an outflung hand before subsiding into moans again as they positioned him on the table.

Golden spoke tersely to Preston. "Get me fifteen milligrams of morphine sulphate, stat!" The syringe was in his hand in minutes. He injected intramuscularly and waited for Santos to quiet. After a while, he checked the guard's pupils. They were pinpointed. His breathing had deepened, slowed . . .

Dressed in sterile attire, Golden and the attendant cleansed the blood from around the wound. Using a saline solution with sterile pads, they painted the skin with Betadine, then surrounded the area with towels to keep it as antiseptic as possible. Only then did they cut the bandages and remove the pressure pack.

Blood spurted from the wound. Golden bent over it. It was gaping, discolored, and beginning to smell. Without the proper hospital equipment, there was no way he could tell where the bullet had lodged, if it had broken any bones along the way, or if it had to come out. To give Santos a chance, all he could try for was a temporary procedure to stop the bleeding and allow the wound to drain. If he could do even that. Right now his hands felt so devoid of strength, he doubted he could close his fingers about a single one of the instruments the attendant was laying out in a row on a sterile towel.

He straightened up and looked at the faces of the two younger men at his side. They were as nervous as he was, but more obvious about showing it. He smiled at them reassuringly.

"Okay, let's go to work. Jimmy, I want you to monitor his blood pressure, his pulse, and his breathing. Keep taking readings and if there's any problem, alert me. Got that?"

The technician nodded.

Golden bent over the leg. "Scalpel," he called to the attendant. The slap of the instrument in his palm grooved a familiar dent. He made a horizontal incision over the inguinal ligament, then signaled to Preston to hold the two edges of the incision apart with the retractor. He cut through the fascia. All he could see was a mass of blood. Panic set in. If he couldn't identify the vessels, how could he stop the bleeding? Maybe if he opened it up more . . .

He extended the incision. Blood welled up like a geyser. Tod Preston looked as if he was about to faint, but his hands held steady on the retractor.

"My God," Jimmy said below them. "He's bleeding to death."

"Give me a reading on his pressure," Golden snapped at him.

"It's hardly there," he said. "Wait, yes it is, but it's faint."

Golden blindly attempted to clamp the vessels. The blood continued to pump. "Suture," he called to Preston.

He tried to tie the vessel off by suturing beneath it. For a moment it held. The bleeding lessened. The attendant breathed a sigh of relief. Then the suture slipped. Golden clamped again. And again. His hands were sweating and he could feel himself growing lightheaded. He must have been mad to attempt this after so long a layoff. Even the greatest of surgeons had bad days, where a patient died on the table for no apparent reason. If he had brought his best efforts to bear, then the guilt that inevitably followed was less crippling. But that wouldn't be the case here. Santos's life hung on his ability to remember, and right now he wouldn't have given a plug nickel for it.

Where the hell was that femoral artery?

On the third try he found it, traced it along its course to the shattered area of the lateral circumflex branch and clamped down. The bleeding slowed, stopped. An enormous sense of elation filled him. Like riding a bicycle. He hadn't lost his touch, only his confidence.

With the bleeding controlled, another unit of Dextran was given intravenously. "His pressure is climbing," Jimmy volunteered. "Ninety over sixty now."

Golden carefully cut the debris and dead muscle from about the wound, then packed the area with saline swabs. He left the wound open to drain, then checked Santos's pulse. It was holding at 110. Santos began to moan. His head swung from side to side and his face contracted in pain.

"I'd like to get another fifteen milligrams of morphine into him," Golden said. Preston nodded and left the table.

Santos's swarthy face tinged with color. His eyes opened, centered on the globe above him, then moved to Golden's face.

"Where am I?"

"On the table in the kitchen. I've just operated on you."

"Jesus!" His voice was scarcely audible. Then, "I've been to the other side, doc."

"What do you think?"

"I like it better here." He gasped. "I hurt, doc."

"We're getting something for you."

"What's happening to Brockwell and the lady doc?"

"They're still inside the lab. The police can't get to them, but they can't get out either."

Santos bit down on his lower lip as the pain mounted. "If I make it, I'm gonna kill that son-of-a-bitch with my bare hands." He closed his eyes as the attendant hurried in with the hypodermic. "If I don't, you do it for me, doc, you hear?"

"I hear." He tested the syringe, swabbed the skin over the muscle, and shot the morphine home.

Chapter 33

In Brian's office, Eva vented her fury in chain smoking, then stubbing and shredding half-smoked Virginia
Slims in a Steubenware ashtray she had given her
father for his fiftieth birthday. She sat in the couch-
filled area used for informal conferences, legs hiked
up under her wool dress, watching the newscast on
TV and seething with resentment.

Brian's reaction to the knowledge that Valerie was
in the lab with Brockwell was making a laughingstock
of her. The emotion in his voice was absolutely raw
when he spoke to that backwoods Chief of Police,
Penzinger, who had once had the audacity to invite
them to a Clayville policemen's ball. She had inter-
cepted Dora Watkins's glance when Brian hung up
and a shock had gone through her. Eva had known
her father's secretary since she was a little girl. At
times, when she visited her father, she had seen admiration, impatience, sometimes dislike for her in
those logical, bird-like eyes. But never pity, until now.
It galled her and she promised herself that when this
was all over, Brian would pay.

Right now, he looked a good deal older than his
thirty-eight years, she thought with perverse satisfaction. He was talking to the epidemiologist at the Center for Disease Control in Atlanta, trying to map out
a contingency plan for the employees if the Fever bug

had indeed spread to the plant. His eyes were red-rimmed, the groove from his nose to his mouth was deeply indented and the scar above his lid had assumed a purple cast from being rubbed so much. Not that it bothered him. Brian had never been one to care about appearances, even when he wasn't under stress.

Oddly enough, the thought of being exposed to Blasa Fever didn't faze her. Although she hated being around sick people, Eva scarcely remembered being ill a day in her life. It was as if her rejection of the whole syndrome of illness had given her an immunity afforded few other people. It bore out the conjecture of a number of psychiatrists she had read about who said that illness had a mental rather than a physical base, or at least that emotional weakness paved the way for most ailments.

She stretched her shapely legs in front of her now and ran her hands through her silken black hair. For perhaps the tenth time, she wondered what had happened to Kirby Semmel. She was one of the few to get a phone line immediately after the alarm went off in the plant. She had called to tell Kirby that something had gone wrong at Traynor, she didn't know what, but she might be delayed longer than she had expected.

Unfortunately, she had still been on the phone when all those people had come swarming into Brian's office demanding an explanation. Instead of telling Kirby she would call him back, she had made the mistake of asking him to hold on. The hysteria in her voice must have communicated itself to him as she found herself surrounded by that unreasonable shouting horde she couldn't control. She heard him call her name twice as she retreated to the wall. When she finally picked up the phone after Brian arrived, the wire was dead.

Later, she was able to get a call through again, but Kirby was no longer there.

She sighed in exasperation. Kirby Semmel was nipping at her heels like a puppy. He had called four times in the last two days, declaring his love for her and begging that she slip out of her office to see him for an hour as she had at the beginning. She couldn't understand his behavior. Short of telling him outright, she had made it perfectly obvious that her interest had waned, yet there was no pride in him.

He left her no way of ending it gracefully, she decided. The next time she saw him, she would cut the cord sharply, so there would be no puling aftermath—but not before she had the Semmelweiss Indictment in her hands.

She ground her cigarette into the ashtray and focused on the scene being telecast outside Traynor. One of the women behind the fence had managed to insinuate herself between a bunch of reporters. She sneaked past the guard at the gate, ran to Roy Penzinger and pleaded inaudibly for something.

She looked like a character out of a Tolstoy novel. Short and frail, her thin body was weighted down by a heavy checked coat and a wool scarf knotted around her neck. Her face was almost hidden by a print challis kerchief and she wore flat furred boots to ward off the biting cold.

What a queer little woman, Eva mused.

Outside, Roy Penzinger echoed her thoughts as he grasped the woman's clutching fingers and tried to pull them from his coat. He signaled to his deputy, Nate Goren, then countermanded it when the woman said, "Mr. Penzinger, don't you know me? We go to the same church together. St. Catherine's on the corner." Her voice was heavily accented.

He pushed the kerchief away from her worn face and stared in disbelief. "Mrs. Nordsen! What are you doing here?"

"It's Tom. My husband. He's in there." She looked sixty but Penzinger knew she was at least ten years younger. The last time he'd seen so much suffering in a pair of eyes was when his collie had been run over by a truck.

"He'll be all right, Greta. Believe me."

"No. You don't understand. I have a right. My Wendy is dying from this Blasa Fever." Her face was distraught, her expression beseeching. "If Tom goes, there is no one."

"Nothing's going to happen to Tom."

"You promise?" she whispered. In the old country, a policeman's word had been synonymous with a priest's.

"I promise." Some of the fear went out of her eyes. He pulled her fingers from his lapels and handed her over to Nate Goren. "Now go along with the deputy and take care of your little girl. I'll send Tom home to you as soon as I can."

He waited until she was out of sight, then barked to the sergeant at the gate, "Dougherty, you let anyone else in here who isn't authorized and I'll have your badge. Understand?"

The sergeant nodded glumly.

Penzinger glanced about him. Thanks to the television coverage, the crowds were getting heavier and the hysteria was mounting. So was his sense of inadequacy. The one-hour reprieve Brian had maneuvered with Brockwell had given them a much needed breather, but it was no solution. When the convict found out about the ruse he would be twice as vindictive and there was no way in hell Penzinger could stop him. He pounded his gloved hands together to keep the circulation going. The day was colder than a bitch out of heat.

Nate Goren returned. "I left Mrs. Nordsen outside the fence. She's calmer, but she refuses to go home."

Penzinger nodded. "Good enough."

It was the first time the Chief had seen Nate Goren "come alive." Usually, he did the work given to him like a mechanical robot. Goren had been assigned to him two years ago. Although in his early twenties, his round face and smooth skin made him look like a teenager. He was conscious of it enough to grow a mustache to make him appear older. It was a wispy thing with straggly ends and not much shape.

The deputy pulled a small book from his pocket. "You know, Chief, I think your hunch about an outside tie was right."

"Meaning what?"

"Well, I've checked with some of the employees behind the fence who know Dennie Redmond. The way they describe him—shy, upright, a mama's boy . . ." He shook his head in puzzlement. "There's nothing to remotely connect him with a three-time loser like Brockwell. Yet there has to be a connection."

Penzinger glanced at him with approval. The boy was going to make a good cop if he ever got rid of the chip he was carrying. Goren reminded Penzinger of a maverick steer he'd once come across in the Midwest that wouldn't run with the pack. But Penzinger knew the cause of his rebelliousness. Goren viewed Clayville as a "hick town." He was resentful at being "stuck out in the boondocks" and itched to get into the city were the action was. Because of this and because of the promise he showed, Penzinger had come down harder on him than any other fledgling under his wing.

Goren flicked at his mustache. "That reminds me. When you were being interviewed by that TV reporter, a Mildred Benson called. Wants you to call back."

Penzinger grinned. Mildred had been calling every fifteen minutes with bits of information filtering through to her from various departments in the plant. Most had been insignificant, but the Chief had learned a long time ago that if you sift through enough pebbles, you're bound to come up with a nugget of gold.

He picked up the telephone in his car and patched through to her. "Mildred, you wanted me?"

"What took you so long? I got a piece of information I'm sitting on here like a hot stove."

"I'm waiting."

"Don't rush me. One of the labeling operators has been going out with the security guard that's stationed between the lab and the plant. Well, a few nights ago, he mentions to her that one of the Blasa Fever volunteers worked at Traynor Labs before he went into the army. He also tells her that Dennie Redmond has been bringing this soldier 'care packages' every couple of days to keep his spirits up."

"Mildred, did he mention the name of the man receiving the packages?"

"No, he didn't. You want me to ask the labeling operator?"

"No. Put me through to the hospital."

The phone rang twice in the hospital before it was answered.

"Colonel Darwin here," a Southern accented voice said.

Penzinger felt his lips twitching. The man sounded like he had a broom up his ass. "Colonel, this is the Chief of Police. Do you have a soldier who's been receiving packages from a Dennie Redmond of Traynor Laboratories?"

"Yes, I have. He's acting second-in-command here."

"Could I talk to him, please."

There was a pause and some murmured conversation, then Sid Draper got on the wire.

"This is Sid Draper."

"Mr. Draper, are you a friend of Dennie Redmond's?"

"We worked together at Traynor before I went into the army." The voice was cautious.

"And did Dennie meet Brockwell through you?"

There was silence. Then, "I didn't know Dennie knew Brock."

Penzinger's patience snapped. "Listen, Draper. I don't know what kind of protection game you're playing, but I have very little time, so I'll lay it on the line. Your friend, Redmond, is in trouble. He stole a drum of morphine and delivered it to Brockwell in the laboratory. He hid it in some of the packages he usually brings to you."

"He'd never do that!" Draper burst out. "Dennie's one of the most honest . . ."

"I know. I heard that from Brian Anslow. That's what makes me think he was forced into it by someone else. And my guess is you know who that someone is."

There was silence again.

The Chief spoke in a low voice. "Draper, Alfie Brockwell has your friend and two doctors in that lab with him. He's threatened to kill them. I don't know what's going to happen, but you may be the only chance of getting Dennie out of there alive."

Draper sighed. "All right. Brockwell kept the door

between the hospital and the lab open while he held a gun on Santos. I didn't see Dennie come into the lab, but just before those steel doors closed, I heard him yell, 'Niko promised . . .'"

"Who's Niko?"

"He's the brother of a disco dancer I introduced Dennie to. She mentioned him a couple of times when I was there."

Penzinger signaled to Nate Goren for a pad and paper. "Where does this disco dancer live?" he asked.

When he hung up, the deputy was waiting for him. "Let me go, Chief."

He looked at Goren dubiously. "It could be a hornet's nest."

"I can handle it."

Penzinger debated. By rights he should choose someone more seasoned, or turn it over to a precinct in Soho. He stared into the deputy's pleading brown eyes and changed his mind. Goren reminded him of himself when he'd been younger: anxious to jump in even if the water was over his head. He'd send Dougherty with him, he thought. The sergeant had a solid track record.

"Can I go?" the deputy pressed.

"On one condition."

"What's that?"

He pointed to the mustache drooping over his lip. "That you shave that thing off when you get back."

Chapter 34

In his office, Brian wore a path between his desk and the door. He felt as if a steel band were closing about his skull. Five minutes. That's all he had left. And he could think of nothing to save Val.

Pictures of her rose to torment him. The stubborn look on her face when she told him she was leaving for Africa. The shock of recognition between them when she returned. The way her hazel eyes crinkled with unexpected laughter; the sudden stillness of her body before he made love to her.

He thought of her in his arms that night at the apartment in Hicksville. He had meant to leave in an hour, but he had stayed until morning. Their lovemaking had been beautiful, richer than what they had experienced at Bethesda because they expected less of each other. There was no struggle for supremacy, no demands made, no promises elicited. Try as she would to deny it, the perfect melding had been a pact in itself, an acknowledgment of sharing that no marriage certificate could make any more binding.

If Val died, a part of him died with her. Yet the cost of saving her was too much to ask of any man.

He crossed to the window and looked out. The crowd outside Traynor had multiplied. Despite the cold—it was twenty degrees, with a wind-chill factor of five below—those who could get close stood with their bodies pressed against the fence. Others behind them huddled together stamping their feet and clapping their gloved hands. Beyond them the police had ringed the area off, blocking any exit or entry to Traynor Labs. In the distance a white truck tooted its horn in protest.

Brian turned from the window, then suddenly turned back again. He stared at the white truck, his eyes zeroing in on the logo "Custom Cabinets" printed in large block letters across its side. He remembered the tour of the lab Val had given him before he approved the Blasa Fever testing. She had been adamant about changing the garbage disposal system but had decried the fact that the same space couldn't be utilized for the new crematorium. Several supply cabinets had been removed on another wall to make way for the crematorium and a custom-built cabinet had been ordered to fill the area where the disposal had stood.

He strode to the desk and buzzed through to his secretary.

"Dora, connect me with maintenance."

It took a minute for the maintenance man to get on the line. "Yo," he said in a leisurely tone.

"Ira, this is Brian Anslow."

He snapped to. "Yes, Mr. Anslow."

"A while ago, a garbage disposal unit was taken out of the lab and a supply cabinet was ordered in its place. Did that cabinet come in yet?"

"No, Mr. Anslow. I know for sure because Dr. Chandler called about it two days ago."

"What's covering that space now?"

"A steel plate."

"How is it bolted down?"

"It isn't bolted. You see when the disposal unit was originally installed, it was inset on a concrete lip so that the unit would sit flush with the floor. When we removed the unit we simply substituted the plate. It fits snugly onto the lip and the weight of it holds it down."

"Could two men lift that plate?"

"They'd have to be strong and they'd probably wear a truss for the rest of their lives."

"But they could do it."

"Yes."

Brian hung up. He tugged at the scar on his eyelid, while a breathless feeling of excitement tore through him. It was a slim possibility; dependent on so many things, it might never come to fruition. Still it was a *chance* and that was more than he'd had five minutes ago.

He pressed down on the intercom. "Dora, come in here for a minute."

The door opened almost as soon as he released the button. Caught by his tone, she hurried to the desk as fast as her blue-veined legs would carry her. Usually immaculate, her fly-away gray hair and smudged lipstick advertised the state she was in.

"Dora, does the warehouse extend beneath the lab and hospital?"

She smoothed her white blouse over her ample bosom and tucked it into the waistband of her skirt. "I believe it runs beneath the lab but not the hospital."

"Can you check it?"

"If I can find the floor plans. They're pretty old."

She disappeared for a few minutes then returned with a smile of accomplishment and a set of blueprints. Brian spread them across his desk. They were faded and creased, with some of the original inking barely legible. Using his index finger, he traced the warehouse under the manufacturing floor then nodded in satisfaction. The warehouse ended just past the lab.

The hospital had been built later on a separate foundation.

"Dora, locate Lester Pryor for me," he said to the hovering secretary. "I think he went down with Mrs. Anslow to check on David."

"Right." Her footsteps were muffled by the carpet as she hurried away.

Flipping the pages of the blueprint, Brian pulled out a detailed but outdated drawing of the lab. He worked from memory, sketching the changes he recalled, and with a red pencil carefully circled the site where the garbage disposal had stood.

When Lester Pryor strode into the room, Brian was ready for him. He told Pryor he was going to call Brockwell and explained what he wanted him to say.

Pryor's freckled face mirrored his pessimism. "He'll never buy it," he stated flatly.

"He'll have to," Brian said grimly. "It's our only hope."

Mildred made the connection with Brian listening on an extension phone across the room.

"Anslow, what the hell is happening?" Brockwell demanded in his coarse voice. His heavy breathing sounded like a bellows being primed.

Pryor crossed his fingers. "Mr. Brockwell, this isn't Mr. Anslow. It's Abe Baron, the electrician. Sorry I took so long to get here, but I got tied up in traffic on the expressway. Here's the story. I've been working on this timer for ten minutes now and I got to tell you, there's no way. The mechanism is so rusted over it won't respond at all. The only way we're going to get this door open is with an acetylene torch."

Brockwell cursed under his breath. "How long will that take?"

"Twenty minutes, maybe less. It'll make a lot of noise."

"Is Anslow with you?"

"Yes."

"Put him on."

Pryor signaled for Brian to get on the phone.

"This is Brian Anslow."

"Anslow, if you're trying to pull something . . ."

"Brockwell, believe me, I'd like to get those doors open as much as you would. I have no desire to endanger the life of Dr. Traynor or Dr. Chandler—that is if I can take your word for the state they're in."

"Whatd'ya mean?"

"Well, how do I know they're still alive? I heard Dr. Traynor scream. I know she's hurt. She could be dead for all I know."

"She's alive all right."

"If I'm going to give the order to burn that door open, I want proof of it."

"To hell with what you want," Brockwell roared.

The silence that followed was deadly. Not normally religious, Brian prayed. After what seemed an eternity Brockwell spoke again.

"Okay," he said. "I'll put her on."

Across the room, Pryor held his bony fingers up in a victory sign. Brian heard some conversation on the other end of the phone, then Valerie's voice came through shakily.

"Brian?"

A fierce feeling of protectiveness surged through him. She sounded so frail, so defenseless. He would have gone after Brockwell bare-handed if he could have gotten into that lab.

Reason overcame emotion. He spoke quickly. "Val, answer me. Did those cultures seep through to the plant?"

"No."

"You're sure?"

"Yes. Brian, please, you mustn't open those . . ."

The rest was lost as Brockwell pulled the phone away from her.

"Anslow," he said. "Listen good. When those doors open, I'm taking her with me. I want a car waiting in front of the hospital and no cops. Any funny business, she gets it. Understand?" He hung up without waiting for Brian's answer.

Brian buzzed through to Mildred Benson. "Connect me with Roy Penzinger," he said.

The first two to leave Traynor Laboratories were Charley Santos and David Traynor. A murmur rose from the crowd as David was carried out on a stretcher, wrapped in blankets. His head was bandaged. His face was as gray as the slush being trampled beneath the feet of the onlookers.

His sister Eva walked beside him. Elegant and aloof in her leopard coat and crushed leather boots, she ignored the battery of questions aimed at her by reporters and employees alike.

David's eyes fluttered open as the rush of cold air hit his face. His head hurt. He had the sensation of being carried. Images swirled before him like the wavering lens of a camera. Then his vision cleared. He saw that Dr. Osato walked on one side of him, his sister Eva on the other.

Aware that the TV cameras were recording her every move, she bent solicitously over him, careful not to flinch at the blood oozing from beneath the bandages.

"How are you feeling, David?"

"Weak. What happened to me?"

"You were hurt," Dr. Osato said. "Don't you remember?"

He tried. A jumble of impressions formed. Claire

. . . Haversham . . . Dennie Redmond . . . but nothing came clear. He winced as one of the attendants jarred the stretcher. Strange faces swam before him then receded as people leaned down to wish him well. An ambulance came into view with the name Wyandridge Hospital written on it. Someone familiar stood beside it.

Paul Haversham bent toward him in concern. "David, are you all right?"

Memory returned suddenly and with it an insupportable anger. "Judas!" he hissed.

Shock bleached Haversham's face white. "You don't know what you're saying."

Hatred shone from David's eyes. He tried to raise himself on the stretcher but Dr. Osato pressed him back. "Take it easy now. We're going into the ambulance."

He felt himself lifted high then gently set down. Seconds later the doors clanged shut and the motor roared to life.

A cheer went up from the throng as the employees began to file out of the exit doors. They overflowed the inner courtyard and shouted to familiar faces behind the fence. Frantic relatives pushed past the sergeant guarding the gate and threw their arms about their loved ones. There were tears and laughter and smiles of relief. One woman screamed at sight of her husband, then fainted dead away. The noise rose to a crescendo as the crowd swelled, then gradually diminished as they began to disperse toward the parking lot.

A few key personnel were interviewed by the TV commentator for an "on-the-scene" version of what had gone on inside Traynor.

"It was awful," Thelma said, her sallow cheeks drawn, her flat chest heaving. "Cooped up in that cafeteria, fighting to get out, then having to go through the motions of working with this fear inside us, like a lump we couldn't cough up or swallow. We were all pretty scared until we turned on the TV and heard Mr. Haversham say how we were protecting society against the Fever. It made us feel real good. He was an inspiration. He helped us through a bad time.''

Zack Cottrell hid his harelip with the back of his hand as the camera dollied in on him. "As the former union president, I felt it was up to me to give Mr. Anslow whatever help I could to keep the employees calm. It was touch and go there for a while, but we all pulled together and we made it.''

The commentator tried to corner Tom Nordsen, but the Swede broke away. His clear blue eyes searched anxiously through the crowd that poured through the gate in the fence. He didn't really expect Greta to be there. Except for that morning she'd gone to St. Catherine's to pray, she hadn't left their daughter's side. She was a watchdog staving off the angel of death, unwilling to let go even though it would bring peace to the poor little wracked body.

He grieved too. But he sorrowed as much for the loss of his wife as the pain of his daughter. There was a time they could have comforted each other, lent each other the strength to endure. He remembered the concentration camp; the horrors he'd seen, the loneliness of being without her, of not knowing if she was alive or dead. But they had survived that and it had welded them closer together. This was different. Greta had withdrawn from him when Wendy came down with the Fever. Her grief was all encompassing; a private thing to which he had no access.

Then he saw her. She came to him in her checked coat and booted feet, stumbling because there were tears of gratitude rolling unheeded down her worn cheeks. Her eyes were filled with him as they had been years ago and the sweetness of her face told him all he needed to know.

She threw her arms around him and spoke in her native tongue. "I give thanks to God," she said.

Trailing reluctantly behind the others was Mildred Benson. The day had been one she would talk about for a long time. And it wasn't over yet. She looked around for Paul Haversham and spotted him near the TV newscaster. She had an urgent message for him from Claire Traynor. He was to call her immediately.

Like co-captains of a damaged ship, the last to leave were Lester Pryor and Dora Watkins. There was no elation in the act. They stood on the front steps looking back at the lighted windows of the near empty building, aware that the real drama was about to begin. They had been allowed to participate in the rehearsal, but they were to be barred from the main event.

Lester Pryor had taken it particularly hard.

"You'll need help," he'd told Brian.

"Not from you," Brian had said. "You've got seven kids. Besides, you're not strong enough." He'd clapped an arm around the crestfallen man's bony shoulders. "You've done your part, Les," he'd said in an emotion-packed voice. "Get the hell out of here."

Pryor watched now as the exit doors slammed shut and the police moved to guard them. He knew those were Penzinger's orders. But Penzinger himself was nowhere to be seen.

Immediately after David Traynor had been carried to the waiting ambulance, Roy Penzinger had entered the building through a side door. With him were four "volunteers."

"Impressed policemen" was more like it, Penzinger

thought as they raced across the manufacturing floor. They were hand-picked from Clayville's finest, quaking a little at the thought of the Fever, but still game. A stoic himself, it amazed him how men who didn't flinch at the sight of an opponent with a gun in his hand could balk at exposing themselves to a disease like Blasa Fever. It was because they couldn't control the situation, he decided. They didn't want to deal with what they couldn't see. But they were a good bunch. With a little "urging," they had seen the light.

Joe Barbetta waited for them at the steel door that led to the lab. Penzinger didn't like the security man. Barbetta had been on the New York City police force for too many years. He was a man in his prime, angry at being forced to retire, and he saw his present position as a comedown. His nattiness and the swagger he affected were a cover-up for a bruised ego and it rubbed the Chief the wrong way.

At Barbetta's feet were two metal boxes filled with assorted tools and an acetylene torch supplied by maintenance.

"Where's Brian Anslow?" Penzinger asked him.

"He's waiting for us on the floor below."

"Has he heard anything more from Brockwell?"

"No. Nothing." Barbetta turned to the four policemen. "Now, here's what you do . . ."

"If you don't mind, I'll give the orders," Penzinger broke in. His sunburned face was smiling. His eyes were cold.

"Men," he said. "What we got here is a covering action." He pointed to the steel door. "There's a killer in the lab behind that metal door who's been told we're going to burn it open with an acetylene torch. What you gotta do in the next ten minutes is drum up enough noise to make him believe it."

"Who are we covering for?" one of them asked.

"Me," Penzinger replied. "I'll be downstairs with Brian Anslow, trying to get insid that lab through another opening."

Barbetta glanced at his watch. "We're running short of time."

"I'm right with you, bucko," the Chief said.

The man's contempt of him came through like an ill wind, Penzinger thought as he followed the security man to the stairway. Barbetta was one of those New York cops who thought that anything outside the big apple was "kid's stuff." It was unthinkable to him that his jurisdiction at Traynor was being usurped by a Midwesterner with a twang that could be cut with a knife.

There were similarities between the way Joe Barbetta and Nate Goren thought, Penzinger realized. The difference was that his deputy was twenty-three and still learning, while the security man was fifty and thought he knew it all. For a fleeting moment, he wondered how Nate Goren was faring in Soho, then Barbetta pushed open the door to the warehouse and Penzinger blanked out to everything except finding Brian Anslow.

Chapter 35

Angie Borden crouched near her plants under the window of her apartment, wrapped in the green blanket she had dragged from the bed. She shook in spasms, her teeth clicking together like castanets. She was cold, yet there was a fire in her belly. It was a knot of pain so intense that she had bitten her lips through to keep from screaming. That was what Niko wanted, she knew. If she begged . . . if she grovelled at his feet like a whining dog willing to be kicked if it meant being fed, he might be moved to get her a fix. But she wasn't going to do it.

She thought of Dennie and tears of remorse filled her eyes. It was her fault he was involved in this. She had overheard her brother talking. She knew that he and Finch had no intention of sharing the two million with Dennie. No matter how this ended, Dennie couldn't win. If he made it back to the apartment, Niko would kill him. If the police caught him he'd spend years in prison. But at least he'd be alive, she thought fiercely. And she would wait for him. If it took the rest of her life she would wait for him.

She remembered the first time Sid Draper had brought him around to meet her at the Helicopter Club. He had reminded her of a puppy she'd once bought. It was small and puny with a tendency to hide in corners that puzzled her until she found out it was the runt of the litter and used to being stomped on. The only reason she had begun to see Dennie was for the morphine he could bring her. She couldn't recall when that need had changed to love. She knew only that his awkward wanting of her had endeared him to her more than all the "machos" who came sniffing after her at the end of every performance.

Pain knifed through her again. She sucked in her breath, doubled over and waited for it to ease.

Globules of sweat stood out on her forehead. She couldn't hold out much longer. She glared at Niko in helpless rage. He lay sprawled on the couch, gun at his side, arms tucked behind his head, white silk shirt open to the waist. His black trousers fitted his hips with matador precision. His booted legs picked up a muted sheen from the glow of the lamp on the nearby table. They were crossed in a studied nonchalance she knew he didn't feel. Niko was worried and he was trying to keep it from Finch.

With good reason, she thought. Finch was scared. He was also drunk—mean drunk. And the more fearful he became, the less control Niko had over him. Finch sat at the table, hunched over a shot glass of Scotch and a snub-nosed revolver. His pointed face was flushed a reddish hue. He wore a tee shirt and dungarees, and kept flexing his muscle so that the naked girl tattooed on his arm opened her bowed legs to him invitingly.

There was no real reason for Niko to be worried, Angie thought, except maybe that it was taking so long. But judging from the look on his face, she suspected that instinct was telling him something had gone wrong. And Niko went by his gut reaction. Which was probably why he'd been caught so many times, she surmised cynically.

Her stomach churned violently and a moan escaped her. Niko ignored it, but Finch turned on her.

"Shut up!"

"Leave her alone," her brother said. "She's sick."

"Then get her outa here. She makes me nervous."

"It's not smart to send her out there."

"It ain't safe to keep her in here. Look at her. Anything happens, she comes apart."

Niko weighed the alternatives. What Finch had said was true. He couldn't take her with them this way when Brockwell arrived. And he couldn't leave her behind. If she was anyone but his sister, he might think of wasting her. But he could never kill Angie. He had promised his mother on her deathbed he would take care of Angie, and junkie or not, he couldn't bring himself to kill her.

But Brockwell could.

Brockwell was a sadist. At Rockland State, nobody crossed him. Not the cons and not the guards. Brockwell could take a butterfly apart and relish the slow tearing of each wing. Niko remembered the look of enjoyment in his cellmate's eyes as he recounted the way the bank guard he'd shot in Ohio had died writhing on the sidewalk in agony. He'd described the scene scream by scream, until Niko could almost picture "the slimy white of the bloody bastard's insides spilling out over his navy blue uniform."

Brockwell would have no qualms about killing Angie if he saw her this way.

He held out a hand to her and helped her up. "How long would it take you to buy a fix?"

Her black eyes lit with hope. "Coupla minutes. That's all. It's right down the block."

He delved into his pocket and peeled off a roll of bills. "Make it as fast as you can."

She nodded and tucked the money into her bra.

He crossed with her to the door. "Wait a minute," he said. Holding the gun in front of him, he opened the door a crack. The hallway was silent. He peered quickly to the right and left. The stairway leading up to the roof was in shadow. Except for an outdated refrigerator partially blocking the landing to the stairs leading down, the hallway was empty.

"Go!" he said to Angie. She stepped outside and he closed the door behind her.

She made her way down the dimly lit hallway. It reeked of the incense the musician next door burned all the time. For a moment she considered going to the police, then thought better of it. Even if she hadn't wanted to get involved, she was. The cramping in her belly started again. Besides, they'd make her go cold turkey and she could never stand that.

Her footsteps slowed as she reached the old refrigerator near the landing. A peculiar sensation came over her. She felt as if she wasn't alone. She looked back at the apartment, then down at the stairway. Nothing. She shook her head at her own fancies. She was getting as kooky as Niko with his hunches. She hurried past the refrigerator.

Two men stepped from behind it. One was young with spaniel eyes and a drooping mustache. The other was in his early forties with a fleshy face and jowls. They were dressed in civvies, but instinct told her they were policemen.

The mustache pulled out his wallet and flipped it open. "Police," he confirmed. "You Angela Borden?"

She nodded. It was all over for her, she thought. She was surprised at the relief she felt. "I wasn't really a part of it," she said.

The cop with the jowls ignored her, but the mustached one looked sympathetic. He was young and his eyes kept shifting to her breasts. Nausea made her lightheaded. "I need a fix," she said.

A third cop cat-footed down the stairway leading from the roof and joined them. He was older than both the others with a pug nose and a stubborn jaw.

"Anyone up there, Dougherty?" the mustache asked.

He shook his head then jerked a calloused thumb toward Angie. "Who's she?"

"Angela Borden. She just came out of the apartment."

Dougherty whistled silently. "You lucked out. Is Niko inside?" he asked her.

"Yes."

"Anyone else?"

"A crumb named Finch."

"Are they armed?"

"Yes." She touched the sleeve of the mustached one. He seemed the more sensitive of the three. "Please . . . what's happened to Dennie Redmond? I've got to know."

He looked uncomfortable that she'd singled him out. His spaniel eyes had seemed so human. Now, as if a shutter had closed down, the warmth went out of them to be replaced by the impersonal glance of the dutiful civil servant. "I wouldn't know," he said. "Let's talk about that apartment. Besides the door and the fire escape in the front, is there any other way out of there?"

She shrugged. "An old dumbwaiter."

"Where does it lead?"

Her black eyes turned frosty. "I wouldn't know." Her voice was a mockery of his.

Goren turned to the pug-nosed cop. "Take her

downstairs, Dougherty. And check that dumbwaiter out.'' He saw the protest rise to Dougherty's lips, then gradually die. ''Tell the others we're going in. They're to hold where they are until I say otherwise.''

''Right.'' He cupped Angie's elbow and guided her toward the stairs.

He had hated to cut Dougherty out that way, Goren thought, but he didn't have much choice. As Long Island cops, they had no jurisdiction in the city. When he'd called the Narcotics Squad earlier, they'd wanted to handle it themselves. At his insistence, they'd reluctantly consented to his leadership, with the provision that he be backed up by their men.

With guns drawn, he and the partner assigned to him approached Angie's apartment now. Damn Penzinger, he thought. For two years, the Chief had hovered over him like a mother hen—demanding, criticizing, urging caution. Now that he was on his own, he felt like a baby about to take its first steps. The trouble was, he couldn't afford to fall.

They flattened out on opposite walls of the door frame. Goren banged on the door with his gun.

''Police,'' he shouted. ''Open up!''

He heard a muffled curse from behind the door. He jumped back against the wall. Two shots rang out simultaneously. One splintered the door frame inches from Goren's head. He pulled back sharply. The sound of a window being opened came through distinctly.

''They're headed for the fire escape,'' Goren yelled.

His partner used his shoulder to break the door in. It gave easily, the bolts rending from the rotted wood with a screeching noise.

The room was empty, the window wide open. Beneath it, Angie's plants were a disaster. Shards of red clay and black dirt crunched beneath his feet as Goren reached the sill. Gun in hand, he stuck his head out the window in time to see Finch's leg disappear over the roof's edge. Bordini was nowhere to be seen.

"They're up on the roof," he called to his partner. They raced from the room and pounded up the stairway leading to the roof. A shot rang out just as they pushed the metal door open. It was followed by a cry and the thud of a body falling.

His partner's face tensed. "Rudnik was out there as back up," he said.

They stepped onto the roof. The sun was a sinking red ball in the sky. The tarred surface of the roof was slushy where the snow had melted during the day, but bits of frost still clung to the shadowed base of the stone turrets surrounding the building.

The gray building was attached to an old printing plant on one side and an apartment complex on the other. The roof of the printing plant topped the gray building by one floor. A small steel ladder was attached to the side of the printing plant. Both Bordini and Finch were on it, racing to reach the other roof. The body of a uniformed policeman lay sprawled beneath its lowest rung.

His partner pelted for the ladder with Goren a shade behind him. "Halt or we shoot," he called.

Bordini jumped for the printing plant roof, but Finch, lower down, turned and took a shot at the cop.

The policeman stumbled and clutched his thigh. "Sonofabitch!" he gasped. There was more surprise than pain written on his face.

Finch scrambled up the ladder.

Feet planted firmly apart, Goren sighted down the barrel of his gun. Finch tensed his legs to spring. For just an instant, his small muscular body was clearly silhouetted against the sky. Goren squeezed the trigger a second before Finch jumped. The bullet angled into his rib cage and cut through to his heart. Hands outflung, Finch fell from the ladder, landed flat on his back and stared sightlessly at the moving clouds above him.

Goren bent over his partner. The older man waved him aside. "I'm all right. Go after the other one."

Goren took the ladder two rungs at a time. Close to the top he crouched beneath the ledge of the printing plant roof and peered above it.

The printing plant was a corner building. Its asphalt roof was twice the size of the one he'd just left. It was dotted with ventilation shafts and a jutting center staircase structure. The door to the staircase was padlocked. There was no sign of Bordini anywhere.

Using his left hand for balance, Goren leaped over the ledge in a swift motion. Two shots rang out as he dropped to the roof on all fours. One went wide. The other grazed his ear. He scurried behind the closest ventilation shaft. Bordini had to be hiding behind one of the other four. But which one? The clouds shifted and the sun shone again in full force. Goren almost laughed aloud.

The linear shadows cast by the four ventilation shafts were clearly outlined on the asphalt roof. They were exactly alike, except for one. The shadow of the shaft that stood closest to the outside corner of the building had a bulge in it.

Goren began to circle the roof. There were two shafts between himself and Bordini. He raced for the first one and leaped behind it as Bordini fired again.

The bullet chipped the metal rim of the blower near his head. Bordini was getting uncomfortably close. Hoping to get a clear shot at his opponent, Goren edged past the safety of the shaft. Bordini was waiting for him. His next shot blasted the gun out of Goren's hand. It skidded across the asphalt and landed in a pile of slush. Goren cursed under his breath.

Bordini's laugh was high and triumphant. "What are you gonna do now, cop?"

Goren calculated swiftly. Bordini had fired one shot through the apartment door and four up on the roof. That left him with one more. He had to draw Bordini's fire.

He bolted from behind the shaft in a diagonal leap that took him halfway across to Bordini's hiding place. His right foot landed on a piece of slush that gave beneath it. He skidded just as Bordini fired and went headlong into a discarded piece of tarpaulin. The bullet sailed over his head.

Still holding the gun, Bordini turned and ran. Goren tackled him at the far corner of the roof. They grappled close to the edge, panting and gasping with neither one getting a clear advantage until, pulling back in a sudden movement, Bordini flung the gun at Goren in an overhanded throw. It struck him in the forehead. He staggered backward, stunned and blinking, then teetered helplessly on the edge of the roof. He glanced swiftly behind him and spotted a flagpole jutting from the building at an angle.

Still teetering, he hunched his muscles forward to try to regain his balance. In a rush of confidence, Bordini came at him with both arms outstretched. Goren jumped for the flagpole and Bordini plummeted over the roof screaming until he hit the pavement below.

Hand over hand, Goren pulled himself along the flagpole until he touched the edge of the roof. He wondered why he didn't feel more elated. He had bagged his first big prey and all he could think of was that he was glad to be alive. But he wouldn't tell that to Penzinger. He smiled, relishing the future recounting. For Penzinger he would blow it up so it sounded like the Charge of the Light Brigade.

Dougherty's pug-nosed face appeared over the roof's edge. Goren looked up gratefully as the older cop reached out both hands to help him ascend.

Chapter 36

In the warehouse, Brian waited beneath the lab for Penzinger and Barbetta to arrive. The break in the concrete ceiling where the garbage disposal had been was twenty-five feet above him. It loomed as a dark square hole. The steel lid above it sealed off any light that would have made his task easier.

The silence around him was eerie. What had been a bustling, productive operation a short while ago was now a cement block tomb. Cartons of supplies stood on wooden pallets waiting to be stacked one atop the other. The loading lift, never still, idled like a huge steel monster, its jaws apart, its teeth unclenched. A drum of resin compound had been kicked over in the stampede to reach the exit doors. The gritty substance was strewn across the center lane, marring the neatness of the criss-crossed aisles that formed the warehouse traffic pattern.

Brian checked his watch and chafed at the time. Penzinger was taking forever. Brockwell would hold still for only so long, then God knows what he would do. He thought of Val and his throat constricted. If they got out of this . . . No, he corrected himself. *When* they got out of this, he would marry her. He would live with her and back her research, if that was what she wanted. He would grow old with her and he would die with her. But he would never separate from her again. And Mark . . . he would fight for his son as long as there was breath left in his body. But he wouldn't sacrifice his life for him anymore.

He had come to that conclusion even before Eva had taken the decision out of his hands fifteen minutes ago.

She had faced him across the desk after he'd made the announcement to the employees that they were free to leave. She had stood with her feet apart, her hands twisting the tassels of her chain belt like a chatelaine with a set of keys.

"I trust that applies to me too," she'd said. No one looking at her then would have thought her beautiful. Her face was spoiled by the belligerence that made a tight mask of her features.

Hatred welled up in him. It was the first time she'd spoken to him in an hour. "Don't worry. I have no desire to keep you here."

"The feeling is mutual, I assure you."

He was glad there was a desk between them. Had he been closer, he might have been tempted to strike her. "I'm sending you out first with David," he said. "It'll look good for your admiring public that you give a damn . . . at least for your brother."

She walked to the couch, picked up her Gucci bag and slung her leopard coat over her arm. She half-turned toward him. Her slanted eyes gazed at him disdainfully.

"Your disapproval doesn't interest me, but your behavior does. When you're through playing hero, if you're still in one piece, don't bother to come home. Anything you want to say to me after this, you can say to my lawyers."

"What about Mark?"

"He leaves with me for Europe at the end of the week."

She waited for his protest but it didn't come. She wondered what had happened to change him. She had expected him to sit up and beg with a threat of this kind. She hid her disappointment and made a show of putting on her gloves.

"I won't let you take Mark," he said finally.

She laughed shortly. "How are you going to stop me? Prove me an unfit mother? I think you'd have trouble doing that. Besides, after what I've seen here this afternoon, I'd say the shoe is on the other foot." Her glance was contemptuous. "You know, you really had it made. It wasn't your affair with Val I minded so much. It was your damned insistence on advertising it."

Lester Pryor had called from David's office then to say that David was on the stretcher and the ambulance was waiting. She had left without a backward glance.

The sound of racing feet from the direction of the vaults brought him back to the present. Seconds later Penzinger and Barbetta appeared. They arrived simultaneously as if running a neck and neck race that neither had won.

Penzinger clapped him on the back. "Good to see you, bucko," he wheezed.

Brian felt the same way. He tilted an ear upward as a rumble like the sound of distant thunder echoed from the floor above them. "The men must have started blasting at the door."

Barbetta nodded. "They're making enough noise to wake the dead."

"Let's hope Brockwell buys it."

Penzinger glanced at the break in the ceiling and his jaw dropped open. "Holy Mother. How do you expect us to get up there?"

Brian pointed to the loading lift. "With that."

Minutes later, under Brian's direction, Joe Barbetta

sat in the driver's seat of the lift and started the motor. Using the two throttles, one to raise and lower, and one to tilt, he inserted the fork-like prong into a stack of empty wood pallets and deposited them beneath the opening. He repeated the process twice more, lifting the pallets higher each time to sit on top of the ones beneath. When he had constructed a foundation almost twenty feet high, he signaled to the others waiting below.

Brian and the Chief climbed onto the next stack of pallets. They took with them several flashlights, a toolbox, and a rope.

The pallets were four feet square, composed of two by fours covered with wood slats nailed a few inches apart from each other. Bending low, they held tight to the slats of the top pallet as the forked prong thrust inside the lowest pallet on the stack and hoisted them upward. Almost twenty feet up, they jerked to a halt as the motor of the lift died with a sputter. Caught in the rebound, the pallet they were on began to slide from the others beneath it.

Clutching the teetering pallet with both hands, Brian peered over the edge at Joe Barbetta in the driver's seat. Sweating profusely, the security man was attempting to re-start the lift. The motor choked twice, but refused to turn over.

"Trust him to screw up," Penzinger said.

As if in rebuttal, the engine purred, then growled, then roared to life. The pallet they were on steadied down. The stack climbed an additional two feet, moved to the right and with a creaking of wood on wood, slid into position on top of the foundation. Barbetta cut the motor, leaned out of the driver's seat and held his fingers up in a circle of accomplishment.

"What's he want?" Penzinger muttered. "A medal?"

Ignoring the rivalry, Brian took stock of their position. They were approximately four feet beneath the concrete ceiling of the warehouse, which allowed for crouching room only. The ceiling itself was ten inches thick and the concrete had been poured with configurations to reduce its weight and allow for various pipes and fittings.

Using a flashlight, he could see the steel lid that had replaced the garbage disposal on the floor above. It was about two feet square and fitted so tightly into the concrete rim beneath it that it successfully shut out any light that might have come from the lab.

As Brian remembered the layout of the lab, the lid was near a corner, blocked on two ends by supply cabinets. It would have to be lifted outward into the aisle between the supply cabinets and the workbench for a distance great enough to allow a man to squeeze through. Hopefully, the hammering and blasting at that steel door would cover any noise they might make. But that wasn't what troubled Brian.

Only one man could fit through the opening. Brian knew that Penzinger intended to be that man. But even if they succeeded in getting into the lab, there was no way of knowing where Brockwell and Redmond would be at the time. If Brockwell spotted Penzinger, he'd be a dead man a second after his head popped through that hole.

"Roy," he whispered. "You got an extra gun?"

He nodded. "Strapped to my leg."

"Give it to me."

"You crazy?"

"No. Just practical. If you get your head blown off, I'm still going in there."

Penzinger opened his mouth to protest then realized it would be useless. The only other time he'd seen that frenzied look in Brian's eyes was when Mark's canoe had overturned in a sudden squall at Montauk. The tip of the canoe had stunned the boy and Brian had dived in to rescue him.

The Chief reached down, unstrapped the gun and put it into his friend's hand. He didn't have to ask if Brian could use it. They'd whiled away many an hour at his summer house taking pot shots at beer cans. Brian's score had been surprisingly high.

"Thanks," Brian said. He tucked the gun into his belt.

Standing back to back, he and Penzinger raised their hands and laid them flat against the steel lid. They crouched lower for better leverage and, straining every muscle, lifted upward. The lid refused to budge, but the slat beneath Penzinger's foot gave beneath the pressure and buckled with a loud splintering. Welded together as they were, it unbalanced both of them.

"Shit!" Penzinger muttered, trying to right himself.

They tried again. To avoid the same mishap, Brian instructed Penzinger to place his feet directly over the juncture where the slats were nailed to the up-ended two by fours on the pallet. They bent low again, then heaved upward. Within seconds, the strain became unbearable. Perspiration ran down Brian's face. His legs felt like corded steel. His chest was about to burst. A dizziness enveloped him. Another instant and he knew he would pass out.

The lid lifted by a fraction of an inch. With bursting lungs, they held on. Another fraction. Then another.

Brian could no longer see. The sweat was stinging his lids and his eyes felt as if they were going to pop out of his head. The steel lid was above the rim now. They were able to get their fingers through. They began to ease it outward toward the aisle. Slowly. Slowly . . . It made a small scraping noise that worried them, until from inside the lab the clamor at the steel door came through. It sounded like the assembly line at a Ford plant.

They worked gradually, praying that the opening wouldn't be discovered. When it was large enough for Penzinger to squeeze through, he pulled his gun from his holster and hoisted himself halfway up. Beneath him, Brian prepared to follow. Gun in hand, he crouched like a racer ready for the flag to go down. He waited for Penzinger to clear the opening.

Nothing happened.

For what seemed an eternity, Penzinger dangled, his arms above the opening, his legs below. What the hell was going on up there? Brian wondered in anguished suspense. If Penzinger had been discovered, why wasn't there any shooting? And if he hadn't been, then what was the holdup?

A full minute went by. Then Penzinger slowly pulled himself upward and disappeared through the opening. Brian followed immediately. Halfway through, he congealed. He knew now why Penzinger had stopped.

Hidden from Brockwell by the center workbench, as he and Penzinger were, Dennie Redmond sat diagonally opposite him like a battered statue. His face was discolored. One eye was swollen shut. The other stared at Brian in disbelief. He didn't move. He didn't shout. His hands hung limply at his sides and his body shook in uncontrollable spasms.

Was it shock that kept him from crying out? Brian wondered. But even as he watched, Dennie's puffy lips parted in a half-smile. He was *glad* this was happening, Brian realized. It confirmed what he'd felt all along—that Dennie wasn't a willing participant in the morphine theft, but had been forced into it somehow.

It was only after Brian hoisted himself fully through the opening that the intense cold hit him. No wonder Dennie shook. The lab was freezing!

Penzinger had crept to the right side of the workbench. Brian moved left. The noise at the steel door was deafening. The "woosh" of the acetylene torch sounded muffled, but the hammering and drilling that accompanied it were ear-splitting.

Gun in hand, Brian peered cautiously around the edge of the workbench. Brockwell stood a few feet from the steel door leading to the plant. He was in crumpled hospital pajamas and his feet were bare against the cement tiles, but the cold didn't seem to bother him.

Brian suddenly wished he were in better shape. The convict was six feet and well over two hundred pounds, and it was all tough muscle. The gun he held was trained on Val and Wally. They were leaning against the workbench that shielded Brian from view. Wally had an arm around Val and her blonde head was pillowed tiredly against his shoulder. Brian couldn't see her face.

Brockwell's voice sounded above the din. "Now when those doors open, here's the way we do it. You first, Chandler, in case any of those cops get funny. Then the lady doc and myself. Then Redmond . . ." He glanced around the room. "Where the hell is that little . . ."

His gaze came to rest at the lower corner of the workbench. His voice chopped off as his eyes zeroed in on where Penzinger was hiding.

Something had given it away!

There was a rapid exchange of fire. Brian heard Penzinger cry out as Brockwell's bullet caught him in the hand. The gun fell to the tiles and skidded behind the workbench.

The Chief slumped forward, his face contorted with pain. Brockwell lowered his gun until it was level with the back of Penzinger's head.

Brian stepped out from behind the other side of the workbench and took careful aim. "Drop it!"

Brockwell's eyes swung toward Brian. They narrowed cannily, then he shrugged and smiled. "Caught me proper, didn't you? Well, it was a good try while it lasted." He made as if to throw his gun toward Brian, then in a sudden movement reached for Val and spun her tightly into him.

"Brian!" she gasped, clawing at the arm that banded her rib cage in an iron grip.

He watched her struggle in an agony of helplessness. Valerie was tall, but against Brockwell's hugeness, she looked minute. Her lab coat was ripped at the sleeve, the bruise over her ear was a purplish red, and her blonde hair fell in a tangle around her white face. He should have shot the son-of-a-bitch when he had the chance, Brian thought. He cursed the civilized instinct that had stopped him.

Valerie's outcry had told Brockwell who Brian was. His lips curled back, baring strong, even teeth. He put his gun against Valerie's temple and gestured toward the one in Brian's hand.

"Toss it to me, Anslow, or I kill her on the spot." His glance darted downward as a movement caught his eyes. They widened incredulously.

With Penzinger's gun clutched awkwardly in both hands, Dennie Redmond was creeping toward him from behind the workbench. He was breathing heavily. His lacerated face held a mixture of fear and determination.

The fool, Brian thought. The valiant, remorseful fool! Even if he could get a clear shot, he'd probably be too scared to pull the trigger.

Brockwell's eyes gleamed in anticipation. Intent on watching Dennie, his grip on Valerie loosened a fraction. With a sudden jerk, she doubled over and wrenched her body to the right. For just a split second, Brockwell's head was a clear target.

Brian never remembered taking aim. He had the weird feeling that the gun in his palm was a living thing with a vengeance of its own. His hands felt clammy. His throat was dry. He pulled the trigger and prayed.

The bullet caught Brockwell in the left eye. A look of astonishment crossed his features. His hands flew outward, releasing Valerie.

He staggered backward against the door as she ran to Brian's waiting arms. His face was a mess of blood and shattered bone. Shreds of the socket dribbled down his cheek. For a moment he remained upright, the steel door supporting him, then he slid slowly downward, his legs apart, his arms flaccid as a rag doll's. He muttered something, but the clamor at the steel door drowned out his words as the life slowly ebbed from his body.

Chapter 37

Hunched over the wheel of his Audi, Paul Haversham drove to Wyandridge hospital with the speed of desperation.

He had phoned Claire Traynor from the booth in the parking lot. There had been hysteria in her voice when she informed him that David had overheard their conversation that afternoon and knew of their dealings together.

"You got me into this," she cried. "You've got to help me square it. Otherwise, I don't know what's going to happen to me."

He couldn't have cared less. His main concern was to reach David before anyone else did. He had to stop him from unburdening himself before he ruined them both.

He had fought his way out of the traffic snarl caused by police blockades and the mass exodus from the parking lot. But it had taken him almost an hour to pull the Audi onto the highway.

He kicked the accelerator up to sixty-five now and wove his way between the cars. He knew that his influence with the Board had never been greater. He could see to it that their dissatisfaction with Brian didn't change because of today's heroics. Brian had, after all, placed the employees at risk of Blasa Fever and almost caused a company strike. And then there was the surprise of his affair with Valerie Traynor. It could be made to appear to the Board as the reason Brian had endorsed the testing program.

He turned off the highway and sped toward the hospital. There was nothing like a little bloodletting to gain public sympathy. David's being wounded in an effort to stop Dennie Redmond had made him as much today's hero as Brian. There was every chance he would be named president if he kept his mouth shut. Haversham was aware that David blamed him almost as much as David blamed himself for the morphine theft. It didn't faze him. He knew how to control David.

He would explain to David that he had blocked him from revealing the first morphine substitution to Brian because he knew about his former drug addiction. That Asa Rankin had come to him about it, but not before he'd blackmailed Alex.

"Your father paid him," he would tell David. "He did it to protect you. But being the kind of man he was, he couldn't in all good conscience allow you to govern Traynor." Then he would threaten. Subtly, of course. "If *someone* were to reveal what I just told you, David, the Traynor name that Alex took such pride in, unblemished for nearly a century, would be ground into the dust."

David would see the wisdom of remaining silent. He was sure of it. He might be willing to throw away his own future to salve his conscience, but faced with this proof of his father's love, he would never allow Alex to be defamed.

Wyandridge Hospital was a low brick building on the outskirts of Clayville. He pulled the Audi up to the front curb and lurched to a stop.

A blast of cold air hit him as he raced up the front steps. It was during visiting hours but the hospital was well organized and the bustle in the lobby was at a minimum.

"I'm here to see David Traynor," he told the matronly looking nurse at the admissions desk.

She squinted up at him from behind steel-rimmed spectacles and used her pencil as a pointer. "Didn't I just see you on television over at Traynor Labs? You were making a speech about . . ."

"I'm in a hurry, nurse."

She smoothed her cap. "Of course." She pulled a newly typed card from the file. "Let's see . . . Yes. Mr. Traynor is to be allowed one visitor at a time. You can go up as soon as the other gentleman comes down."

"What gentleman?"

"Well, he was tall and balding. White-haired . . . conservative dresser. He mentioned his name but I didn't quite catch it. It sounded like that bottled water they're making such a fuss about. Perrier, or something like that."

"Perrault . . . Arthur Perrault."

She brightened. "Yes. That's it. They must have a great deal to say to one another. He's been up there a long time." She frowned in concern. "Are you all right?" He didn't answer. Her alarm deepened. His shoulders had sagged. His face was the color of putty. His gray eyes held the lifeless look of a beached fish. He turned toward the door. His vigorous stride of a few minutes ago became the halting footsteps of an old man.

Outside he stood with his coat collar turned up against the biting cold. The wind buffeted him, whipping at his hair, his eyes. But he sought no shelter. David was crucifying him in that hospital room. Compared to that the forces of Nature posed no threat.

He had worked it out so carefully. Come so close

. . . There were no contingency plans for failure. He might be able to rebuild, he thought bleakly, knowing his age was against him. But to do so the preservation of his good name was essential, and that would be taken away from him. There was no reason for Perrault to be lenient about implicating him. Word would get around. The pharmaceutical industry was a tight little world.

He leaned heavily against the building for support. His dreams of power were shattered beyond redemption. Financially he was wiped out. His house, his car . . . maybe even his marriage, all down the drain. Desolation swept him. He contemplated suicide, but knew he couldn't do it. He had always scoffed at the bankrupts he read about who stepped out of windows during the crash of '29. He realized now that it took a special kind of courage. One he didn't have.

He walked slowly down to his car. He felt weightless, unmotivated. He had spent half his life at Traynor. It was strange to think there was no reason to return there. He would go home, he thought. It was only a matter of time before Bernice found out. And her contempt would be unbearable.

Chapter 38

At eight o'clock that night, Brian sat alone behind his desk and waited for Val to join him. It was the only promise he'd been able to elicit from her in the few moments he'd seen her after the descent from the lab. His office resembled a battlefront headquarters. It was littered with paper cups, half eaten sandwiches, ashtrays piled high with stubs, empty beer cans, a first-aid kit, discarded memos and a police cap forgotten in the rush to leave.

The aftermath of the rescue had left him badly shaken. He knew that Brockwell had deserved to die, but it didn't help. He was filled with a revulsion that Penzinger assured him would pass, but he wondered.

He had been the last one down from the lab. The passage through the hole in the floor had been painstaking. The opening was narrow and the wood pallets could hold only two at a time, carefully balanced. A ladder had been placed against the stack of pallets to facilitate the descent, but with Penzinger wounded and Redmond in a form of shock, it had taken a full thirty minutes to get everyone down to the warehouse level. Afterward, Barbetta and several policemen had gone back up to remove Brockwell's body.

For the next few hours, until the maximal virulence of the Blasa Fever organisms they had been exposed to was spent, he and Penzinger had manned the phones in his office. They had reassured the Food and Drug Administration, the Center for Disease Control, the news and television media, various health officials, and the public at large that there was no way the raw fever cultures could have escaped Traynor's boundaries.

Penzinger had juggled the phone and a can of Heinekens in his left hand, while his bandaged right one rested in the sling that Valerie had rigged for him in Doctor Osato's clinic on the second floor. The bullet had gone through his palm. Fortunately, it had missed any major blood vessels and would heal cleanly, causing some stiffness at the beginning, but no permanent damage. From time to time, he turned to check on his prisoner.

Dennie Redmond sat on the couch in the corner, holding an ice bag to his swollen face. Valerie had cleansed and applied antiseptic to it, bandaging where necessary. Then, after calling Wyandridge Hospital to ascertain that David was all right, she and Wally had returned to the lab to begin culturing for the next dose of Tetra-2 to be administered to the volunteers.

Brian knew it rankled Penzinger that he treated Redmond like a wayward boy instead of a common criminal. The Chief conceded that Redmond had probably been blackmailed into doing what he did, and that his bravery in the lab should be counted in his favor. But that was for the courts to decide. Penzinger had heard from his deputy. Dennie's failure to seek police help earlier had caused the death of two men and the wounding of three others, and Penzinger would be damned if he'd pamper him any more than he would have Brockwell had he lived.

Despite Brian's protests, Dennie's hands had been shackled and the only privilege Penzinger had allowed was the call to his mother to prove to Dennie that she was alive.

Brian rose from his desk now and passed a hand over his cheeks. The five o'clock shadow had become a stubble. He contemplated shaving, then decided not to bother. He was tired, but more than that, dispirited. He knew that for Penzinger the rescue in the lab had been the culmination of the day's events. For him, what happened with Val in the next few moments would be equally important.

He walked to the window and stared unseeingly at the darkened courtyard below. He had the awful feeling he'd lost Val. She had fled to his arms in the lab when Brockwell had released her, but later in his office, it was Chandler she had huddled with. They had sat on the couch in the corner, heads close together, Chandler's arm entwined with hers, talking earnestly and at length. The rapport between them had been obvious and Brian's uncertainty had grown with each passing second. What if his decision to leave Eva had come too late?

"Brian?" Her voice was so soft he wasn't sure he'd heard it.

He turned around.

She had changed into a dress and carried a raincoat over her arm. The bruise on her face was shiny from some topical ointment she'd applied. She moved hesitantly. The shock of the day's events had left her comtemplative, uncertain.

She draped her raincoat over a chair. "You look terrible."

"I don't feel much better. I guess I lack the killer instinct." Her face broke into lines of sympathy. He ran a hand through his tousled hair. "I'm sorry. I can't seem to sort my emotions out." The last thing he wanted from her was pity.

She went to the bar and mixed herself a Scotch and soda. Her hand trembled. She gulped the drink and strove for composure.

"How are the volunteers?" he asked.

"Good. Better than I expected. We were overdue on the maintenance dose of the Tetra-2, but there doesn't seem to be any obvious regression." She took a sip of her drink. "Wally and I have decided to move the men to another hospital."

"Why?"

"Because of today's publicity. And because of the calls we've been getting in the last few hours. The newspapers have picked up on your disclosure in the cafeteria and there's a good chance they'll prematurely announce the success of Tetra-2."

Brian slammed his hand against the sill. "Damn!"

"Don't blame yourself. There wasn't much else you could do." She seemed better now. The color had come into her cheeks and her hazel eyes were losing the strained empty look she'd come in with.

"Have you chosen the hospital yet?"

"No. But it shouldn't be a problem. The program is much more palatable now that the risk looks less formidable."

That meant he would be seeing even less of her, he thought in sudden anguish. He turned from the window and lit a cigarette. "How's the guard that the convict doctor operated on?"

"Santos is doing great. And there's a bonus that comes with that story. Ansel Golden has decided to seek an appeal. He wants to get back into practice as soon as he can."

The anger left his face. "I'm glad, Val. I know how much you wanted it for him."

She hesitated. "Have you spoken to David?"

He shook his head. "I reached his doctor and I

know he's in pretty good shape, but I haven't been able to get through to him. Have you?''

She nodded. "I just had a long talk with him." She wrestled with an inner problem for a minute, then burst out with, "Oh hell, David just gave it over to Arthur Perrault anyway. I don't see that it makes much difference who it comes from."

"What are you talking about?"

She told him then. About David's former drug addiction, his withholding of the information about the morphine substitution, and the part that Claire and Paul Haversham had played in blocking him from telling Brian.

He was quiet a long time after she finished. Then he ground the cigarette into an ashtray and spoke reflectively. "When David was lying on the floor in his office before the doctor came, he kept repeating the words *mea culpa*. I thought he felt guilty because he hadn't been able to stop Dennie from taking the morphine. I understand better now."

"He's very sorry, Brian. And very sad. I think he realizes now that Claire never really loved him. He's talking of leaving her."

The ring of the phone startled them both. Brian picked up on his private line.

Arthur Perrault's usually ponderous voice bounded with enthusiasm. "Brian, before I even begin, I want you to know how much the Board appreciates what you've done."

"Thank you, Arthur."

"I would have called earlier, but I spent a good deal of time in the hospital talking to David."

"Valerie just told me about that. She's here with me now."

He showed no surprise. "Then you must know that Haversham is finished. I called his home a little while ago. His wife told me that he packed a bag and left. He didn't say where he could be reached, but he did mention that a letter of resignation would be in the mail for me."

Brian was silent. Haversham had carved out his own destiny, yet Brian couldn't help feeling sorry for him. It was an ignominious end to what could have been a brilliant career.

"What will happen to David?" he asked.

"I don't know. I'll do everything I can to help him, but the final say doesn't rest with me. I spent the latter part of the day polling the Board and the only unanimous decision they made was to formally reaffirm you as president as soon as possible."

"They may be sorry if they do."

He made a noise deep in his throat. "Brian, I don't think I can take much more today. You'd better explain."

"If I can. It goes back to when Alex was alive and tried to convince us that it was Traynor's duty to use a substantial share of its profits to better humanity. Like the rest of you, I went along with it, but I didn't buy it. Then something happened to change me."

"Like what?"

"I really don't want to go into it, Arthur, but the outcome was that the word 'humanity,' which had always meant cash outflow when Alex harped on it, translated itself into people for me." He stopped, because Val had come very close to him. Her tilted eyes were shining, luminous.

"Don't get me wrong," he went on. "I'm not trying to preach to you like a convert with a new religion. I don't expect the Board to go along with what I've come to believe any more than Alex did. But it's only fair to tell you that if I continue as president of Traynor Labs, I intend to keep Alex's policy of open-hand-edness in effect as long as I can."

Perrault sighed. "You'll have a fight on your hands if you do. The Board won't take from you what they took from Alex."

"I know that."

Unexpectedly, he chuckled. "And I was worried about the meetings getting dull. I'll tell them what you said, Brian, but I don't think it'll make a difference in their decision. I'll be in touch." He hung up.

Brian turned to face Val. Tears trembled on her lashes and there was a catch in her voice when she spoke. "Alex would have been very proud."

He took her in his arms and kissed her with infinite tenderness. "I love you." His arms tightened as he felt her response. "You can't marry Wally," he said fiercely.

She nodded unhappily. "That's what I told him in your office this afternoon."

If only he'd known, Brian thought. It could have spared him hours of anguish. "Val, I'm going to di-vorce Eva."

She sighed. "We've been down this path before. You'd lose Mark."

"If I have to."

She glanced at him quickly. The impending hurt was there, but with it a new kind of acceptance.

"Eva's been behaving very erratically in the last two months. It's possible that with a little delving I might come up with something I can use as leverage against her."

"And if you can't?"

"Then so be it."

A lot of things had come clear to him today, Brian realized, For the first time since he could remember, he thought of his father without malice. All these years he had seen himself as the victim and his father the heavy. But there were all kinds of victims, he acknowledged now. Perhaps his father had realized, as he finally had, that the only thing he could salvage was himself. That if he clung to the marriage in the name of fatherhood, the bickering and lies could take their toll on his son in worse ways than divorce.

Valerie leaned contentedly within the circle of his arms. "It won't be easy, Brian. Neither one of us is good at compromise."

"Then we'll fight a lot." He grinned. "But we'll make up a lot too." His rugged face took on the intent, passionate look that had always preceded their lovemaking.

"Why don't we go home," he said.